A STOLEN HEART

The Miraveld Chronicles:

A Thieving Curse (book 1—recommended starting place)
The Dragon Prince's Heart (book 1.5; available for free in Selina's newsletter or available for purchase in ebook and paperback)
A Lonely Dance (book 2)
A Fated Quest (book 3—Gareth and Anika's book; recommended to read before *A Stolen Heart*)

Related to The Miraveld Chronicles:

The Crownless Prince (set ~200 years prior to the Chronicles; about Marcus Alimer and Adriana Faine, Cassius's several times great-grandparents)

Also available from Selina R. Gonzalez:

The Mercenary and the Mage duology (Fade-to-black adult romantic fantasy sword & sorcery)
Prince of Shadow and Ash
Staff of Nightfall
Companion novellas:
Servant, Mercenary, Brother Vol. I
Servant, Mercenary, Brother Vol. II
Bells of Winter (novelette)
All five books available individually OR collected together in *The Mercenary and the Mage: The Complete Series*

"The Witch of Stone Gnome Mountain" standalone short story available in *Wags, Woofs, and Wonders* anthology or for free to newsletter subscribers: SelinaRGonzalez.com/newsletter

SELINA R. GONZALEZ

Dedicated to the short kings and the tall queens.

*To everyone who has ever felt the world
has no kindness left to spare for them:
There will be brighter days.
May you know you matter and are loved.*

Callista

Art by Tatum Cito

Vallyn

Art by Tatum Cito

Talland
Kilkreth
Aedyllan
Highro
Ackroyd Est

Palace
Ian & Marie's
house
Eynlae

1

$\mathcal{S}$trangers didn't come to the farm.

Callista stopped picking peas and straightened with a wince, her back muscles protesting. She removed her straw hat and wiped sweat from her forehead as she studied the three men cantering down the road. Only local farmers used the grassy thoroughfare, and those were not farmers. The unseasonably hot autumn sun glinted off the men's weapons and dented, mismatched armor.

Marie hummed in the next row as she picked green beans, oblivious to the impending danger. Perhaps the men would continue down the road and leave them in peace...

The horsemen turned onto the path that led to the cottage and vegetable garden.

"Marie." Keeping her eyes on the intruders, Callista flailed about with her right hand until she found the woman's sleeve. "Bandits. Get down and stay out of sight."

Marie straightened her short, round frame with a groan and pushed a lock of gray hair off her ruddy forehead. Her eyes widened, and she cursed under her breath.

"I can handle them." Callista hoped so, anyway. She was no

warrior, like her father and brothers had been. Royce, with his brawn and self-assured smirk, would have made the bandits think twice about fighting him. She didn't need to fight, though. All she needed to do was scare them off. Her magic should do the trick.

She tugged on Marie's sleeve. "Stay back and let me take care of this."

In the two months since Marie and her husband, Ian, had taken her in, Callista had lost most of their arguments about using her magic to help around their farm. Enchanting made her ravenously hungry, which wasn't good for her overall health. Since Ian and Marie were paying Callista with room and board, using magic didn't usually make sense. But even after using magic, Callista would still eat less than those bandits would steal.

More importantly, Callista longed to use her magic to help instead of hurt. If she did enough good, maybe it would make up for all the abhorrent things she'd done. She hadn't told Marie and Ian about her past, and they hadn't asked. But as her eyes met Marie's, some of her desperation to redeem her magic must have bled through.

Marie sighed and sat behind the tangled vines of the peas. "Be careful."

"I will." Callista set down her half-filled basket and placed her hat on top of it, then made her way out of the vegetable garden. Beyond the garden and the chicken coop stretched Ian and Marie's grazing field for their two cows. Ahead and to her right rose a rectangular cottage built of sunbaked brick with a thatched roof and a single chimney in the center.

A modest home, but a vast improvement over desolate castle ruins.

The horsemen slowed.

"Can I help you?" Callista called over the pounding of hooves.

She kept her head high and shoulders back as she entered into the open space beside Ian and Marie's cottage. Her confident presentation had no effect on the bandits. She was tall, yes, but she was unarmed and scrawny. Even after two months of rarely using her magic and doing a lot of manual labor, she hadn't developed much muscle.

Two of the bandits turned to either side, boxing her in with the vegetable garden at her back. The man in front smiled, more of a mocking leer.

"Hello, pretty little thing."

Internally, Callista recoiled, but she kept her expression neutral. "Are you gentlemen lost?"

His grin widened, revealing several missing teeth. "The man of the house around?"

"Do you have business with him?" Callista buried her hands in the folds of her worn skirt to hide the purple light gathering in her palms. She started composing a spell. Fire would do—the energies of the spell whirled in her mind in a flurry of sixteenth notes.

"We have business with this here farm." The leader dismounted and stalked toward her, gripping the short sword belted at his waist. "I could dress it up in a pretty lie, but we're hungry and tired. That accursed new king's guards keep running us out of every town for not having traditional employment." He spat onto the scant space between his boots and the hem of Callista's skirt.

She dug her heels into the dirt, refusing to let him force her into a retreat.

"So let's keep things simple. You're going to cook us a nice meal. Then, while we rest, you're going to pack up all of your valuables and a week's worth of food for each of us." He leaned toward her, the leer back in place. "And if you do all that proper and meek-like, that's all we'll take from you, girl. We don't have to hurt you."

Callista scowled. "I have a counteroffer." She lifted her hands out to her sides. "You leave now, and I don't hurt *you*." Two vortexes of purple-tinged fire crackled to life, hovering over her upturned palms.

The bandits swore. The leader's horse screamed and turned to run. He bolted after it and snagged the end of the reins. His boots scraped through the dirt, and he put all his weight into pulling back against the horse's panicked tugging.

"Enchantress!" one of the other men cried as the third shouted, "Witch!"

The leader steadied his horse and turned around, fury contorting his features. "I don't reckon our new king approves of witchcraft."

A little fear spiked through her, but she ignored the hypothetical danger. The men in front of her were the actual threat.

"This isn't dark magic. Just a fire enchantment." She fed more magic to the flames, until sweat poured down her face from the heat. "But even if it was, who would tell him? You? King Cassius despises bandits and murderers. I share that sentiment, so I recommend you leave before I act on my distaste."

"You don't have the guts," the bandit on her left said. He still sat astride his horse, but he'd pulled his bow off his back and nocked an arrow.

Callista directed a blast of fire at him, so close it singed his hair and snapped the string on his bow. The bandit shrieked and raced away, abandoning his friends.

She returned her attention to the leader, who clutched the reins of his restless horse and watched her with wide eyes.

"I've killed before," she said quietly. She hoped Marie couldn't hear her over the horses' skittering hooves and the crackle of her magical fire. "I promised I wouldn't hurt innocents, but you aren't innocent, are you?" She tilted her head. "Perhaps I should just kill you, so you can't hurt anyone else."

"No, no, we're not going to hurt nobody!" The bandit leapt into his saddle. "Keep your magic and your pathetic farm, you twiggy—" The rest of his insult was lost in the thudding of retreating hooves.

Dust swirled in the bandits' wake. Callista waited until the men were mere dots in the distance before she released her spell. Her hands fell to her sides, and she slumped forward. A violent pang clawed at her stomach. She clutched her arms over her middle as if the pressure would alleviate the gnawing hunger.

Killing the bandits outright would have used less magical energy. They weren't innocent, but after her promise not to use dark magic, killing with her power would have felt like going back on her word. Besides, three dead men would have been difficult to explain to the new guards posted in the nearby town of Brayden.

And despite her brave words, she couldn't afford to attract scrutiny. There were powerful enchanters at the Royal University who had ways of determining whether someone had cast dark curses. Callista had. That made her a witch, and the penalty for witchcraft was death. While Gareth and the Raylor twins had understood the desperation for justice that had driven her to do things she abhorred, that didn't mean anyone else would.

"Thank you, Callista." Marie came up beside her. She carried her own nearly full basket of vegetables in one hand and Callista's in the other. "Let's get these washed up so you can eat something, hm?"

"I'm sorry." Callista took her basket without meeting the older woman's eyes. "That made me hungrier than I expected—"

"And saved us a lot of trouble. As I keep telling you, eat as much as you want, dear!" Marie poked Callista's upper arm. "A strong gust of wind could carry you away."

Callista forced an uncomfortable chuckle. Even though Marie didn't mean anything cruel by her words, they stung all the same.

Spellcasting negatively affected enchanters in varying ways. For Callista, magic consumed nutrients like a wildfire devoured dry grass. It was why her shoulders were bony, why she could count her ribs if she stretched, and why at the Royal University, she'd borne the taunt *skin and bones* more times than she cared to remember. It wasn't even an accurate insult. She still had some curves and was healthy, so long as she ate enough—which, admittedly, was sometimes hard as a peasant. It wasn't her choice to be all hard angles instead of soft edges.

"I always eat until I'm full," Callista assured her. "You're most generous. Besides, with your delicious cooking, it's difficult to stop eating."

"Flatterer." Marie laughed, making her round frame jiggle in a way Callista found endearing. "And bah, shows what's wrong with this kingdom. Be a decent human and people think you're generous." She shook her head and set off toward the cottage.

Callista followed, grinning.

Whatever Marie claimed, she and Ian were far kinder than Callista deserved. She'd been wandering the countryside for weeks doing simple spells in exchange for food when she met the couple. Marie had asked how her magic affected her. No one else ever cared. Then Ian asked where she was from, and when she admitted she had no home, the couple had immediately offered her non-magical work and a place to live. A month had passed before Callista believed their goodwill was genuine.

"Put the basket on the table and then draw some water, would you?" Marie set her own basket on the worn table.

Inside wasn't much cooler than outside even though all six windows were open, with loose-weave burlap covering them to minimize insects. The central, double-sided fireplace held a tidy stack of logs, ready to be lit when they needed to cook or the temperature dropped during the autumn nights. Two faded green curtains hung from a rod that stretched across the width of the house to the right, separating the common areas from Ian and Marie's bedroom.

Callista placed her basket beside Marie's, then grabbed a small bucket. After drawing water from the well near the house, she helped Marie wash the vegetables, snacking as they went. When they finished, she turned to Marie.

"Mind if I freshen up?"

"Go right ahead, dear."

Callista fetched more water. The black-and-white farm cat watched her from the shade of the house. As ever, when Callista called to the adorable cat, it turned and padded away with its tail held high. She sighed, her childhood dream of owning a cuddly little pet unfulfilled. Someday she would convince the solitary creature to let her stroke it.

Carefully, she lugged the water inside. Marie smiled as Callista made her way to the ladder in the corner. She climbed up, through the hole in the ceiling, to her bedroom.

"Bedroom" was an overstatement. She couldn't stand upright anywhere in the cramped attic without hitting her head on the dusty thatch. Ian had provided her with a straw-stuffed mattress that rested on the floor and a small chest for her meager clothing. Various odds and ends cluttered the corners: old toys that had belonged to Ian and Marie's grandchildren and broken farming tools Ian refused to let Callista mend, because he honestly was going to get to them soon.

Callista had found herself in a humble, honest life. One she dared to think could be good, even if it wasn't the life she'd have chosen. Once, she'd dreamed of using her magic to help people, always having plenty of food, and earning enough money to support her family far away from the awful palace…

But her family was gone, and her future as an in-demand enchantress was lost to her transgressions.

The front door squeaked open and clacked shut, the sound echoing faintly. "My sweet meadowlark!" Ian called.

"What are you up to, coming back from market early?" Marie hollered. "You'd best have an empty cart out there!"

"I could have a full cart and you'd forgive me after one kiss," Ian said.

"Then I shan't let you kiss me—"

Ian made an exaggerated kissing sound as he undoubtedly did just that.

"Fae take you, you're absolutely right." More kissing sounds followed, and Callista chuckled. But then a sharp pain jabbed through her, the echo of her own parents giggling as they embarrassed their children with displays of affection.

She had a place to live, had food to eat, and wasn't expected to drive herself to near starvation to earn it. She was free of promises and the exhausting need for vengeance. Even though sometimes she struggled to forgive herself, Gareth, Anika, and Leo's pardon also meant she was mostly free of guilt.

If only she could be free of the suffocating weight of her grief.

She'd ended the Faine line, but it hadn't brought her parents and two older brothers back. Nothing she had done would give her another opportunity to hear her parents shamelessly flirting. She couldn't bring Jacob back to give him another chance to summon the courage to court the washerwoman that made him tongue-tied. She'd never have to remind Royce he'd lose his job and be thrown in prison if he actually beat up any of the nobles at the university who bullied her. Missing them was an aching hole in her heart that even justice couldn't fill.

Her fingers itched for a flute, a way to process her emotions without words, without magic. The flute her father had given her was gone, traded for gold leaf for a birdcage. Another cost of keeping the promise she'd made to her dying brother.

Callista changed into a new shirt and then put on her sleeveless overdress, ignoring the muffled conversation downstairs.

For the last few weeks, she'd been almost peaceful. The feeling was fragile, a delicate happiness that she feared would shatter at any moment like everything in her life always did, but she tried to hold on to it.

"Callista," Ian called from the base of the ladder, "are you decent?"

"Almost!" She finished lacing the side of her dress, then sat down to pull on her shoes. "All right, I'll be down in a moment."

But, as expected, the ladder creaked, and a head of gray hair with hints of brown poked up through the hole in the corner.

"Patient as ever, I see," Callista said with a chuckle.

Ian's smile creased his suntanned skin. "I'm awfully excited. Or anxious. Both? I have news that'll either be amazing or mean I need to beat a man."

"All…right? News related to what?"

"To you."

Halfway to her feet, Callista froze. What good news could possibly relate to her? She could think of plenty of horrible things, but if it was something like "Gareth changed his mind and has come to kill you," Ian's words wouldn't make sense. Unless Gareth had lied about his purpose, but he was too straight-forward for that.

"Hurry up!" Ian scrambled down the ladder faster than seemed right for his age. Callista followed at a slower pace, apprehension souring her stomach.

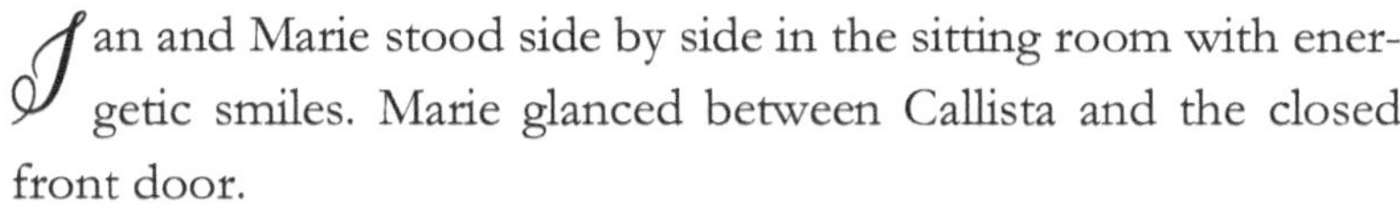

2

*I*an and Marie stood side by side in the sitting room with energetic smiles. Marie glanced between Callista and the closed front door.

"We've never wanted to pry," Marie said, "and you've never mentioned them, so we let it be. But do you have any family?"

Callista's throat tightened. "Not anymore."

The couple looked at each other, their smiles fading into worry.

Ian cleared his throat. "A young man in town was looking for you."

Callista's legs tensed, ready to propel her out of the house.

"He's unusually tall, thin, has dark-brown hair, and well, he sort of looks like you. He says he's your brother." Ian's expression pinched. "If he lied, I'll beat him to a pulp!"

That seemed unlikely, as Ian wasn't much taller than his diminutive wife—although due to all the farmwork, he was strong.

"He's here." Ian nodded toward the front of the house. "I made him wait outside, in case he was lyin'. He's not armed or nothing. Claims his name is Royce."

A torrent of memories washed through Callista. Royce getting in trouble for hitting Jacob after their brother accidentally knocked her over when she was five. The way Royce had lifted her off her feet with his crushing hug when she told the family she was going to attend the Royal University. Holding each other and sobbing after Father and Jacob died in an act of arson aimed at the king. So much sorrow and joy, celebration and suffering. Seeing Royce again would be more than she'd ever dared to wish for. Her heart squeezed, as if, encouraged by the last couple of months, it dared to hope in miracles.

But she'd left Royce bleeding out in Highrook Palace. He'd made her promise to enact the prophecy that would end the Faines, then told her to run. She'd abandoned him to die alone, and then she'd done everything in her power to make King Silas pay for causing the deaths of her father, her mother, Jacob, and finally Royce.

So who was outside, claiming to be him?

There was nothing else for it. She had to confront whoever this was. Might as well do it head-on.

Reaching for her magic, Callista arranged a sleeping spell, legato and slow. Every enchanter experienced their magic differently. Callista always had difficulty explaining how she understood hers. "Like music, plucking the notes for the melody and harmonies from the magic inside me and the energies of the world, then blending them and forming the cadence and tempo…but there isn't actually music. I don't hear anything. It feels like playing music or mentally composing, but the notes are magical energy that I sense" rarely made sense to people. Even among her professors at the Enchanters College at the Royal University of Aedyllan, only a few had seemed to understand.

"Holler if you need help," Ian said.

"Thank you."

It warmed Callista's heart that Ian even offered, but she wouldn't give this imposter a chance to fight. She would render him unconscious and then decide what to do with him. The door creaked as she pulled it open. She squinted against the bright sunlight at the tall, gaunt man standing near Ian's horse and cart.

The man's head was bowed, his attention focused on his hands as he turned a battered straw hat round and round. He glanced up, and Callista's feet stilled on the threshold.

He was pale and no longer well muscled from guard training. His ragged, dark-brown hair was longer, and his posture sagged. But there was no mistaking his features, his gray-green eyes, and the dimple in his chin.

She let her magic fade away and took a hesitant step forward, trying to find her voice.

"Hi, Calli," he said with a quaver.

"Royce!" Callista raced forward and slammed into her brother. She gripped his loose tunic and clutched him close. Sobs wracked her body, and she pressed her face against his bony shoulder. His tears fell on her neck as he embraced her just as fiercely.

Her brother was alive.

She wasn't alone.

If his arms around her hadn't held her up, she might have collapsed to her knees.

Finally, her tears slowed, and her shuddering lungs breathed more steadily. She drew back and dried her face on her sleeve. Royce rubbed his own cheeks with the heel of his hand.

"Royce…how?" Her lower lip trembled. "You were dying…"

He nodded, a bit of pain reflected in the depths of his eyes. "I was. I'll explain, but maybe somewhere private?" He scuffed a boot against the dirt. The footwear was in surprisingly good condition. Actually, all his clothes were, even if they were too big.

"Calli…" Royce peeked at her, then dropped his gaze to the fraying hat in his hands. "Would you come back with me to the inn? We can tell each other everything there."

Callista glanced toward the house. The front door was closed, and Ian and Marie were nowhere in sight. She didn't want them to overhear the things she'd done, but inns also had many ears. She wasn't even certain she wanted Royce to know everything she'd done.

"We can find a shady spot—"

"I'll buy you dinner and we can eat in my private room. No one will hear us." His smile held a little of his older-brother teasing. "You never turn down food."

That was true, and it was approaching noon.

"All right, you win. Ian can give us a ride." She eyed the cart, still containing fresh produce. "He has to go back to the market, anyway."

Royce's smile was tired but genuine. "He did say I'd best not be lying, because his wife was going to give him a tongue lashing for returning before selling everything. He was too excited to find out if I was telling the truth to wait until the market closed."

Callista laughed, and it was the freest she'd felt in a long, long time.

They didn't talk on the short ride into the village of Brayden. There wasn't much they were comfortable sharing in front of Ian.

The Happy Heifer was Brayden's only inn and tavern, located on the edge of town. Ian dropped them off and said he'd stop by when the market closed to see if she needed a ride home. Royce bought bread rolls and steaming bowls of stew, and they took the food up to his room.

After shutting the door and securing the bolt, they sat on the stools at a tiny dining table.

"Nice room." Callista tried to keep her disbelief out of her voice, but this was a room for wealthy merchants or lesser nobles who didn't want to share space with other guests. She glanced at a door in the back corner. "Is it connected to another?" Perhaps it wasn't truly private.

"No, washroom." Royce eased his precariously full bowl onto the table and then tore into a soft golden roll.

She stirred her spoon through the watery stew, searching for words. "I'm sorry, Royce. I shouldn't have left you—"

"No. I'm glad you ran, like I begged you to. Because of that, you're alive, and the Faines aren't." His jaw tightened. "And I'm still alive because you assumed I was dead. They planned to use me as leverage if they caught you, and they thought I might know where you'd hide. As long as you evaded them, they couldn't execute me. They'd have had to admit someone had broken into their vault and escaped with the Fae Blessing and Curse. I reckon that's why they didn't put up wanted posters for you, either. Didn't want to risk anyone knowing the prophecy wasn't secret anymore."

They thought I might know where you'd hide. Callista took a deep breath and asked the question she dreaded. "Did they torture you?"

The flinch that Royce didn't quite conceal was all the answer she needed. If the Faines weren't already dead, she'd do all the terrible things she'd done again to see them punished.

"I admittedly didn't last long." He used his spoon to break apart a large chunk of eggplant in his stew.

"If I'd known—"

"No. If you'd come for me, you would have jeopardized the

real goal." Royce rubbed the back of his neck. "Eventually they forgot about me."

"Then did King Cassius set you free? And…give you a generous amount of coin?"

"Yes." He tore a chunk off his bread roll and dunked it in the stew. "I told him the truth about why I was imprisoned, and he asked me to thank you when I found you." He gave her a weak smile. "So thank you, from our new king."

Her wood spoon scraped around the sides of her bowl. Sure, Cassius Alimer would still be a duke if it weren't for her. But was someone who was grateful that she had caused an entire family to be wiped out and sparked a civil war truly a good man? Ah, well. A problem for someone else. She was done meddling in the fates of kingdoms.

"Now," Royce said, "tell me everything that happened after you escaped the palace."

"Well… First, I read the scroll." She closed her eyes and recited the words. She'd read them often enough.

"Mortimer Faine and his descendants shall prosper and flourish and rule the kingdom of Aedyllan. None shall prevail against their line or their rule so long as this prophecy goes unfulfilled. But beware, oh man, for nothing lasts forever, and such great magic demands a steep price. Beware, for should your line no longer be of noble heart—

A time will come when a fox will speak and seek to offer aid,

A stranger will risk his life to save a girl in chains,

A girl traded for a unicorn, a unicorn for a fiery bird,

And a foreign hero's life will end to save a crying maid.

Then at last shall death and ruin have the final word,

And on the throne of Aedyllan shall never again sit a Faine."

Callista opened her eyes. Royce was watching her, his

expression strained.

"I didn't know it'd be so twisted. You…killed someone?" By his expression, he understood her pain. She'd never wanted to hurt anyone. Her application essay for the Enchanters College had been about using her magic to help people.

"Yes," she whispered. "But it's all right. He recovered."

Royce blinked. Shook his head. Blinked again. "Sorry?"

"A unicorn resurrected him."

"A…all right." Her brother's bewildered expression made her laugh, which eased some of her tension.

Between bites of stew, she recounted the whole story as succinctly as possible. How she'd filched resources from the Enchanters College before taking up residence in the ruins of a castle. Capturing the Raylor twins, stealing the firebird to lure in an Eynlaean knight, and orchestrating the rest of the events. Threatening the twins' lives to force Gareth to surrender, then killing him—how she still wished she'd seen another way, and how grateful she was to have choices again. Her subsequent flight and capture by the trio she'd so wronged…and their mercy after she gave her word to stop using dark magic and never hurt innocents again. Finally, she told him about meeting Ian and Marie.

Callista set her hand on top of Royce's. "Now that you're here and have some coin, we could build our own life. If we can't find our own home before winter, I'm sure Ian and Marie…"

She trailed off. Her brother's shoulders curled in as his chin drifted toward his chest. He wouldn't meet her eyes.

"Royce? What's wrong?"

"I'm sorry," he whispered hoarsely. "Maybe—"

"Sorry? Why, for making me promise? Royce, nothing was—"

"No," Royce said so quietly she had to lean closer to hear. He pulled his hand out from under hers. "I lied—"

With a bang, the door to the washroom opened. Callista jumped to her feet. Purple light swirled around her fingers as she prepared to cast at the four men bursting into the room. But she didn't attack. She had no idea who these people were, and her promise to Gareth was fresh in her mind.

"Who—"

"Royce, Royce, Royce," one of the men said, shaking his head. He was young, around Callista's own twenty-two years, with hay-blond hair. "Were you considering betraying me?"

Trembling, Royce shrank down. He squeezed his eyes shut as if bracing himself.

With a growl, Callista moved to attack, but she'd hesitated too long. A brawny man with a thick neck and ugly grimace barreled toward her. She flung a burst of magic at him, a wall of minor chords, which knocked him back a step. Two of the others darted around the side. Throwing her magical energy into a glissando, she hit one of the men in the arm with a sharp bolt that drew blood, but the other reached Royce.

The squirrely-looking man pressed a curved dagger to her brother's throat. The brute drew a short sword and stepped closer.

She shouldn't have wasted time asking questions.

"Why don't you put that magic away and let's have a chat, shall we?" the first man said, his tone bored. "Or Harvey can practice his carving skills on Royce."

The squirrely man grinned, showing chipped teeth. Royce hissed in a breath and squeezed his eyes shut as the knife pressed against his skin. The brute pointed his short sword at Callista, while the man with the bleeding arm drew a long knife and laid the flat of the blade against Royce's shoulder.

"Who are you?" she demanded.

"Before I get to that, perhaps your brother should tell you the truth." The blond crossed his arms and leaned against the wall.

Helplessly, Callista turned to Royce. When he opened his eyes, they were full of despair. "Please don't make me," he whispered.

"Now, Royce," the blond said, "I thought we were done with this. I say roll over, and you roll over, like a good dog."

Royce grimaced and fixed his gaze on the floor. Callista's blood simmered, and she cast a glare at the blond. She wanted nothing more than to put a magic bolt through the vile brigand's heart. But Harvey still had his knife at her brother's throat, and the brute with his sword stood between her and the leader.

"It's true the king had me tortured for information," Royce said, his words lifeless. "He did want me kept alive in case they found you, but he was paranoid about anyone noticing me in Highrook's dungeons. He entrusted me to Baron Shafer with no explanation, so the baron interrogated me himself."

"Oh, Royce…" She wished she could go to him but didn't dare move.

"After the Faines fell, Shafer knew you'd succeeded. You probably heard he tried to win the throne for himself. After he… failed"—Royce cast a nervous glance toward the spokesman—"he got the idea that you could help him."

His expression crumpled further. "I'm sorry, Calli. They tortured me until I agreed to help them find and catch you. I—I was so tired of the pain. And then they threatened to burn down Ian and Marie's home if I didn't bring you here and get you to explain how you ended the Faines' Blessing."

Callista clenched her fists while she assessed her chances of defeating all four men before any further harm befell Royce. She had just eaten, so she had plenty of energy, but would she be fast enough?

"I can see you're having reckless thoughts about fighting," the leader said with a dry chuckle. "I thought we were going to have a civilized conversation?"

"If we're going to have a *civilized* conversation, tell your men to get their blades away from my brother!"

"Hm, no. In answer to your earlier query, I'm Blaise Shafer, son and heir of Baron Roland Shafer, future king of Aedyllan. I'm here to offer you a deal." He pushed off the wall and stalked toward her. "You see, witch, I need someone capable of casting powerful curses and committing murder. Ironically, I didn't realize until just now that you'd already done both." His smirk was cold as ice.

"If you were eavesdropping," she said, struggling to keep her voice steady, "then you also know I swore to never do either again."

"Boring." Blaise swaggered up to her and threw an arm across her shoulders. "Aren't you at least curious what we want you to do?"

"I won't hurt anyone," she said haltingly.

"I'm disappointed." The nobleman shook his head and gave an exaggerated sigh. "The alternative is that we kill your brother in front of you—and we'll make sure he's dead this time—and then see that you're tried for casting curses, kidnapping, and murder."

They had no proof but her own testimony for those accusations, but that didn't matter. She couldn't let them kill Royce.

"George," Blaise called.

A pained gasp burst from Royce, and she jerked her head in his direction. He quivered on his stool as blood soaked his cut sleeve. The second knifeman tilted his blade back and forth so that the sunlight from the window glinted on its blood-stained edge.

"I think your brother has suffered enough, don't you?" Blaise asked close by Callista's ear, his breath hot on her skin.

The last unbroken part of Callista's heart cracked. Still, she hadn't spent weeks hiding her true feelings and intentions from Anika Raylor to fall apart in front of this condescending villain. She smoothed her face into an emotionless mask.

"What do you want me to do?"

A self-satisfied hum from Blaise brought gooseflesh to her arms. "I need you, my new pet witch, to cast a couple of curses, impersonate a noblewoman, and then…" His lips brushed against her ear as he whispered, "Kill the king."

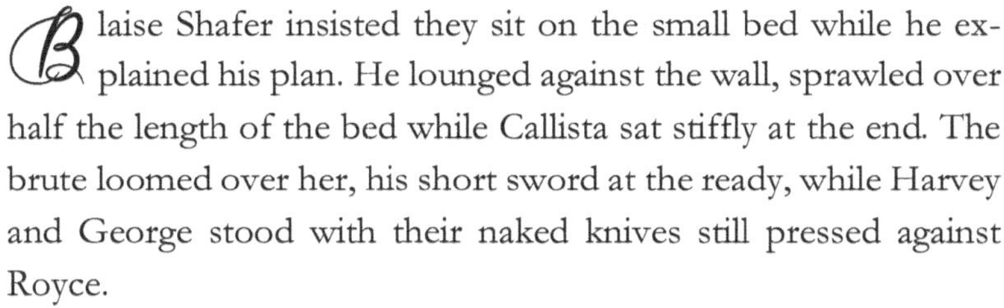

3

*B*laise Shafer insisted they sit on the small bed while he explained his plan. He lounged against the wall, sprawled over half the length of the bed while Callista sat stiffly at the end. The brute loomed over her, his short sword at the ready, while Harvey and George stood with their naked knives still pressed against Royce.

Her brother stared at the floor, apparently oblivious to the blood seeping from his upper arm. Did his face look paler and more sunken now, or had she been so relieved to have him back she hadn't truly noticed? The moment she had a chance, she would make Blaise and his father pay for harming her brother.

"The good news," Blaise said, "is this should be easy. Your brother told us that you're an enchantress of great power, but he swore you would never dabble in dark magic." His grin was as cutting as the blades threatening Royce. "Seems he was wrong. After transfiguring a man into a fox, this should be easy."

"Just explain," Callista said through gritted teeth.

"Tomorrow, Lady Tatiana Ackroyd will set out from her dear father's estate to journey to the royal palace, where Cassius Alimer intends to court her. Rumor says the marriage is decided, so perhaps he foolishly believes the courtship will give him time to wear down my father and others who don't approve. It's revolting that he would even consider the daughter of his easily suppressed rival."

So much information that didn't affect her part in this, but she held her tongue and waited for him to get to the point.

"It's an insult that he's king at all." Blaise scoffed. "He still has Faine blood in his veins! All that trouble you went to in order to ensure that the throne was rid of the Faines, and yet one still wears the crown."

Normally, she'd be tempted to concur, but she resented having any point of agreement with this snake. "Faine blood through the female side and two hundred years diluted. He's of Alimer house. More importantly, everyone says he never supported Silas and his sons and their injustice, cruelty, and debauchery."

Blaise ignored her. "Our plan is to have you cast a curse that will switch your appearance with Lady Tatiana's, and a curse to keep her from telling anyone. Then you will enter the palace in her stead, seduce the king, and kill him on the wedding night. At that point, you can switch back with Tatiana. She and her father will take the fall, Cassius will be dealt with, and you'll be free to go live in some hovel with your brother."

The blood in Callista's veins crystallized. No, no, no. This was exactly the kind of harm she had promised she would never cause again. So many people would be hurt, directly and indirectly, most of them innocent. If these were the measures Baron Shafer was willing to stoop to for power, he would make a horrific king.

"Why me?" Callista asked, grasping for some way to convince Blaise to abandon this madness. "No curse can give me the graces of a lady raised among the nobility. I won't possess her mannerisms, personality, or memories. I won't recognize anyone she knows. *You* would be better suited—"

"Me? Be a woman and let her run around in my body?" Blaise's upper lip curled. "Don't be ridiculous. And never fear. Lord Ackroyd has kept his daughter sheltered at home, and her few friends are low-ranking nobles or peasants who won't be at Highrook. Ackroyd is one of three lords Alimer has placed in charge of reinstituting highway patrols and strengthening neglected border defense. He'll be traveling to fulfill his duties, and his son will remain at home to run his estate. Neither of them will be at Highrook. I assure you my father deemed this the best possible approach."

"What if the curse fails?" she pressed, her hands going clammy. "It's almost unheard of for a witch to curse themselves, and many believe it is dangerous—"

"*Calli.*" The mocking way Blaise said her nickname twisted her stomach. "Do I need to remind you what your lack of cooperation and success would mean for your beloved brother? Do you really want to doom the only family you have left?"

Against her will, her gaze was drawn back to Royce. Tears gleamed on his cheeks.

"I don't even know an appearance-switching curse!" Perhaps she could figure it out, but she had no interest in doing so.

Blaise gave her an indulgent smile. "Finally, a logical argument. Still a futile one." He reached under the bed and lifted a bag, from which he withdrew a thin book with a worn suede cover. He flipped open the book and laid it on her lap. "I understand casting curses is complicated due to the individualistic nature of magic, but for a star pupil at the Enchanters College, this should be easy."

Faded ink sprawled across the yellowed pages in an uneven hand, detailing instructions for casting "a curse for switching places." The author—likely some long-deceased witch's journal— had done an admirable job of describing the process in general terms of magical theory.

The witch's magical expertise aside, Callista did not like this curse.

Beware—when the spellcaster is one of the persons involved, this spell can behave in unexpected ways. Not recommended unless dire. Have a specific and achievable method of curse-breaking in mind before casting to make the curse as stable as possible.

That last bit was common sense. Curses bent magic in a way that was at odds with the natural order. Ordinary spells had natural limits, such as actions they couldn't force or lengths of time they couldn't exceed, but curses violated those boundaries. If a witch didn't specify how a curse could be broken, magic itself would supply a way—or multiple ways. Nature wanted to return to its proper course.

"The curse-breaking," Blaise said, "is to be the king's death."

Her fingers curled around the edges of the book as her vision blurred. She couldn't do this. Cassius Alimer hadn't done anything to deserve death.

"Do as I command, and you and your brother will be safe." Blaise laced his fingers together and placed his hands behind his head. "Royce won't suffer anymore. Once Cassius is dead and Tatiana is blamed, you'll be given a plot of land and three hundred gold. You and Royce can live the rest of your lives in peace. Refuse, disobey, or double-cross us, and Royce will die a slow, torturous death. There will be a lot of screaming involved. And you, of course, will be executed for your many, many crimes."

"I could kill you right now," she said in a low voice.

Blaise laughed. "You could. Perhaps you could even take down Jamie before he puts that sword through you, but could you do that *and* stop Harvey and George from attacking Royce? Do you believe you can vanquish all four of us and still have the time and magic left to heal him?"

Callista stared him down, willing him not to see the truth.

Blaise smiled and took the witch's journal. "Do we have an understanding?"

This was a nightmare. How could she have believed her life would continue in the peace she'd found at the farm? How could the joy of Royce's miraculous return have so quickly turned to ash?

She should have known better. The world was not kind to her. Despair settled like chains around her heart, dragging her beneath waves of guilt. Once again, she was robbed of choices.

"You…you don't have to—" Royce cut off with a scream.

She blinked away her tears as she lurched to her feet. George had stabbed his dagger into Royce's thigh and was subtly twisting it.

"Stop!" Callista flung her hands up, purple magic sparking around her fingers, but Harvey darted behind Royce and pushed his knife more firmly against her brother's jugular. A small movement would result in a mortal wound. Even if she took down their captors, she would reach Royce in time to watch him die in her arms a second time.

"Agree, and George will remove his knife and you can heal your brother," Blaise said.

George tweaked the dagger. Royce screamed through clenched teeth.

"I'll do it!" Callista shrieked, tears blurring her vision. "I'll help you! I swear it; just *stop*! Fae take you, stop!"

George withdrew his dagger, and crimson pooled on Royce's leg. She tripped forward and fell to her knees.

"Hold on, Royce; hold on." She composed a healing spell of intertwining harmonies and directed the purple magic into his thigh. Carefully, she fused his flesh back together, thanking anything and everything good in Miraveld that she'd majored in healing arts at the university. Once his leg was healed, she closed the minor cut on his arm.

But her magic sensed more over his entire body. Faded bruises, welts, healing abrasions, and so many scars. She wanted to rage or weep over how Royce had suffered, but neither of those would help right now. Her brother visibly relaxed despite the dagger at his throat as she healed his many hurts.

"I'm sorry," she murmured as she withdrew her magic. "I failed you—"

"No, you didn't. You got justice for Mam and Dad and Jacob." Royce took one of her hands between his own. "I'm sorry I was too much of a coward to tell you the truth back at the farm."

If he had, she could have taken Blaise and his men by surprise instead of the other way around. But when she met his eyes and saw the fear and emptiness there, she couldn't be angry. She knew what it was like to feel helpless.

"I kept my last promise to you," Callista said. "And I'll keep this one. I'll free you. No matter what it takes."

Footsteps thudded against the floor, and then Blaise was standing at her back. "An impressive show of healing magic, witch. Even after your meal, you must be running low."

Royce cringed. She squeezed his hand to let him know she didn't blame him for telling his captor how her magic affected her.

And Blaise was right. Her stomach was empty, and her arms were heavy and lethargic while her head felt too light.

Hands seized her arms, and then rough fibers scraped against her skin as Blaise bound her wrists behind her back. "You'll get food and drink before you meet Tatiana Ackroyd, but not until Royce is gone. He'll be returned to his cell and kept there until you've fulfilled your end of the deal."

Callista twisted to glower up at their captor. "He'll be treated well. Given more food. And he won't be harmed again."

"Of course." Blaise tapped his forefinger against the tip of her nose. "So long as you cooperate." He looked to his goons. "Have Nevin and Frank escort him home."

Her hope that some of the guards would leave and she'd have only Blaise to contend with was dashed. She had no way out of this. Not if she wanted to protect Royce.

As soon as Royce was gone, Blaise held up the book. "Do you need to study this further?"

Callista scowled at the floor. "No. I understood."

"Good. And you will make the curse-breaking Cassius Alimer's death?"

"As you wish."

"Very good. You learn quickly, pet."

Her teeth ached from clenching her jaw. Could she find a way to foil the Shafers' plan without endangering Royce? No immediate alternative presented itself. She would have to cast the curse, although her reluctance to do so might make it more unstable. But she wouldn't use the curse-breaking her captor demanded. Or at least that wouldn't be the only one.

The deaths of Roland and Blaise Shafer would be another.

And true love's kiss to either her or Tatiana, because some theories believed a loving family member's kiss might suffice. It was a risk. On the one hand, it might not work. On the other, if Tatiana got to her father or brother and the curse broke before Callista rescued Royce, she and her brother would be doomed. But she couldn't live with herself if she didn't cast the curse with her own quiet defiance.

"How am I supposed to get close enough to Tatiana to accomplish this?"

"Tatiana is to be accompanied by her trusted handmaid. That

maid is mysteriously falling ill as we speak. Our...man on the inside"—Blaise smiled as if this were a private joke—"will see to it that you take her place. Ackroyd's guards will leave her at Highrook, so keep interaction with them to a minimum, and no one will notice any shift in demeanor."

Abruptly, Blaise leaned forward, his gaze more focused than previously. "There is one person, though, I believe you should be vigilant around. Someone intelligent, tricksy, and capable of great violence. He's as loyal to Alimer as a faithful dog. Not only is he Alimer's lead general, he's in charge of the palace's security. If you want to succeed—if you want Royce to live—do your best to avoid Vallyn Drake."

4

The guardsmen all straightened when General Vallyn Drake walked past. The moment they saw him, if they were lazing against a wall, they snapped to attention. If they were standing at attention already, they threw their shoulders back and tried to look taller.

It was exhausting.

By the time Vallyn reached King Cassius Alimer's office—on the other side of the labyrinthine royal palace from the training yard—he was gritting his teeth. The guardsman at the door went stiff at his approach, his throat bobbing as Vallyn yanked open the door and stalked inside.

He slammed the heavy oak door harder than necessary before throwing himself into a plush red velvet armchair in front of the huge desk. On the other side, Cassius looked up from stacks of paperwork, the black coils of his short hair bouncing around his face. Amusement twitched the corners of his lips.

"Three months in this oversized monstrosity of a palace, and they haven't stopped," Vallyn said peevishly. He didn't need to clarify. He'd complained several times to his friend and, more recently, king.

"Are the all-black ensemble and billowing cloak supposed to make you less intimidating?"

"The cloak is supposed to keep me warm. This castle is drafty and it's drizzling. I don't see what the color of my tunic has to do with anything."

By the twinkle in Cassius's brown eyes, he was finding it difficult not to laugh. "Perhaps if you didn't storm around scowling—"

"They're the reason I'm scowling! Them and you."

"They're trying to impress you," Cassius said. He leaned back in his plush wingback chair, which looked suspiciously like a throne. Light from the lamp on the table added to the warm undertone of his brown skin. "Most generals and heads of palace defense would be thrilled to have such exuberant respect."

"It's fear," Vallyn muttered. "For whatever blasted reason."

Cassius lifted one eyebrow. "You haven't observed yourself fight, old friend. Do you know, there is speculation that you took the rear of Shafer's forces so completely by surprise because you're secretly an enchanter?"

"Wonderful." That was uncomfortably close to the truth, and Vallyn would prefer the truth stay hidden. He fought the urge to check that his shaggy brown hair still hid the slightly pointed tips of his ears. It was a self-conscious habit that Cassius often teased him about, and it was just the two of them in the study. But the guards' irritating awe of him and speculation about supernatural powers wasn't why he was here.

"Speaking of Shafer—"

Cassius groaned. "We've been over this."

"I'm still against letting his son take up residence as part of the court. I don't care if it's a conciliatory gesture because he's 'putting his son at your mercy.' The younger Shafer will also have more opportunity to cause trouble. It's suspicious. Especially with his arrival coinciding with Lady Tatiana's arrival at the beginning of next week."

"This marriage business is more trouble than it's worth," the king muttered.

Vallyn smirked. "You haven't even met her yet. And she's just here so you can get to know each other and decide if you *want* to get married."

"Yes, but the lords are all breathing down my neck. If one more lord tells me of the 'pressing need to produce an heir at once,' as if that is a simple undertaking with guaranteed results, I'm going to have you throw him in prison." Cassius scowled. "Perhaps I should have you imprison Baron Coplin. He again dared to raise the possibility of seeking an alliance with Talland. Princess Meelah is sixteen! She's twelve years my junior! It's ridiculous!"

"Unfortunately," Vallyn said dryly, "tossing Coplin in the dungeon for a suggestion would make you a dictator."

"Easy for you to say," his friend grumbled. "No one is discussing your private future marital activities over formal dinners. No one is suggesting their daughters and nieces and cousins that you've never met as potential brides every time you come across them in the halls. You don't want to trade places, do you? You can deal with the nobles and things like confirming treasury reports to ensure the crown isn't being cheated by the builders, and I can march about scowling at innocent guardsmen."

Vallyn grimaced. "No, thank you. You wanted the crown, not me, and I already have enough financial headaches dealing with contracts for the guards in Highrook and across Aedyllan. Although, if we switch, maybe you'll finally understand the security nightmare that is the king living in a palace that is under reconstruction—"

"I'm not arguing about this again." Cassius shook his head, and the weary look in his eyes prompted Vallyn to stop complaining.

When the fae prophecy given to Mortimer Faine two centuries prior had, somehow, been activated to switch from a blessing that protected the Faines to a curse that ended the entire Faine line, an earthquake had shaken Highrook. Parts had collapsed or shifted, killing the royal family, as well as a few innocent servants and guards. After Cassius was crowned, Vallyn had tried to convince him to rule from Alimer Castle until the repairs were finished, or at least until the breach in the outer wall was filled, but the new king had felt it was important to reclaim the royal palace.

At least after three months, the construction was nearing completion. Two of the five sites were finished, one should be done within a few days, and the last two were supposed to be completed within a fortnight. Vallyn couldn't wait. One less thing for him to be anxious about.

"Can we at least agree to restrict Blaise Shafer to one wing of the palace?"

"Not without causing me more headaches." Cassius smiled wryly. "I already have to wear this heavy thing." He flicked his hand toward a gold crown glittering with gemstones and half-buried under scattered papers. "You don't want to give me more headaches, do you?"

A familiar sense of warning in the back of his mind tipped Vallyn off that Cassius was done discussing this. He was doubtless moments away from ordering Vallyn to accept that Baron Shafer's son would have as much freedom of movement within the castle as the rest of the court. The sensation was a simultaneously useful and irritating side effect of childhood vows of fealty Vallyn had accidentally magically bound them to keep.

Just one in a litany of reasons Vallyn preferred to hide what he was. The magical binding didn't bother either of them most of the time. Still, it was a constant reminder of how dangerous and difficult to control his fae half could be.

At least the binding magical bargain wasn't visible, unlike his pointed ears. The other physical traits he'd inherited from his father were unusual in Aedyllan but inconsequential, much like the bronze skin and thick coily hair Cassius had inherited from his grandmother and father. No one cared about Vallyn's light skin with its golden undertones or his heavy-lidded eyes set deep into an angular face beneath thick black eyebrows. Pointy fae ears, on the other hand…not so trivial.

With a sigh, Vallyn pushed out of the armchair. "I have a meeting with my captains to get to and guard rotations to adjust once the servants finish furnishing a suite in the southwest wing for Lady Tatiana. Dipper says it should be ready in time for her arrival."

Cassius glanced up. "Perfect. Best idea you've had recently, putting her so close to my quarters."

"And I thought you weren't keen on this marriage prospect," Vallyn teased.

Cassius made a face. "I won't know until I spend time with her, and being closer will make that more expedient. That's all."

"Sure." He headed out the door.

"And Vallyn," Cassius called.

He paused with his hand on the door handle.

"The poor man's name is Steward Morgan, not 'Dipper.'"

Vallyn snorted. "And when he stops bobbing like a dipper bird every time he finishes a sentence, I'll call him that." Without waiting for a reply, he stalked back out into the hall, ignoring the guard, who looked like he had an iron rod for a spine.

5

Within the hour, a new man came to the inn room and informed Blaise things were prepared. Blaise wrapped a light cloak around Callista to hide her bound wrists, and then he and his five lackeys escorted her outside, where another man waited with saddled horses.

Fresh sorrow pressed against Callista as she realized she'd never see Ian and Marie again. They'd never know what had happened or why she'd left. Would they think her ungrateful, leaving without a word? Would they be worried about her? She hoped Ian wouldn't blame himself for bringing Royce to her. It was good the market was further into town, because she didn't know what she could possibly tell Ian if Blaise would even let her speak to him, but she looked for him all the same. He didn't appear.

Why was everything good in her life eventually taken away?

The brute lifted Callista onto the back of a strong horse behind the squirrely Harvey, then tied a rope around their middles so she wouldn't fall off. They rode quickly, but Blaise didn't push the horses beyond what they could handle, and he stopped several times. When they halted for the night, Blaise rubbed down his own horse. He murmured sweetly to it while feeding it oats from his palm. If only he cared half as much about people as he did his animal.

Callista, meanwhile, had been tied to a tree away from the warmth of the campfire with her hands still bound behind her back. Her stomach rumbled and clenched painfully while her captors roasted and ate some kind of red meat. She'd lost all hope of being given even a scrap when Blaise approached her.

"Hungry, pet?"

Surprised, she looked up, squinting against the light of the fire flickering around his outline.

He waved a small piece of meat. "Yes or no?"

With her stomach squeezing like it was trying to eat itself, she wasn't too proud to beg. "Yes, please."

"Oh, a *please*." Blaise crouched. "What good manners my pet has."

Callista swallowed her anger and stared at the meat pinched between his fingers.

"Suppose I'll have to feed you, since you're a bit tied up." He snickered and moved his hand toward her.

Her face burned, but she leaned forward—

Blaise shoved the food into his own mouth. "Mmm."

Heat pricking her skin, Callista turned away, but she heard him lick each of his fingers with exaggerated smacking.

"Tasty. Sorry, witch. I want to sleep soundly, and that means no food for you." With a cruel laugh, he returned to the fire.

Callista slept terribly, shivering in the chill of the autumn night. She was denied breakfast while everyone else ate before dawn. Even Blaise's horse was treated to more oats. Gareth and the Raylor twins had been far kinder captors, and they would have been within their rights to be callous.

But people like Gareth and Leo and Anika, or like Ian and Marie, were scarce. Something about this world of suffering caused the proliferation of Silas Faines and Blaise Shafers. Or maybe Callista's rotten luck ensured the worst of humanity would always find her and those she loved.

They remounted and rode for a few hours. By the time they stopped, Callista felt sick from hunger. Mercifully, one of the men freed her wrists, and Blaise brought her a handful of dried meat.

"By now your brother should be approaching my father's castle," he said. "If they don't hear word from me that all is going to plan, Royce will be torturously killed. Think on that before you decide how to use your magic, pet. Understood?"

Only after she nodded did he hand over the meat. She devoured it, ignoring Blaise's disgusted expression.

They stood at the edge of the forest. A field dotted with hay bales stretched between them and a manor half covered in red ivy. In the distance, a figure solidified into a gray-haired man hurrying toward them.

"Right on time." Blaise crossed his arms and watched the man's approach. "The steward of Ackroyd Castle will assign you as Tatiana's new maid."

Callista's jaw fell open. "How did you get someone loyal to you instituted as *steward*?"

"Oh, he's not loyal to us. He doesn't know who I am or why he's smuggling a stranger into Tatiana's service. In fact he wants no part of it." Blaise's lips curved. "However, he also desperately wants his sweet little granddaughter returned unharmed."

Clenching her fists, Callista struggled to keep her thoughts inside her head. Blaise was a viper, and he should be hanged, not crowned.

Blaise pulled the hood of his cloak up so it half covered his face. "I assume your brother is incentive enough, but you seem like the sentimental type who worries about strangers. If you want the steward's granddaughter to ever toddle back into the arms of her parents and grandfather, you won't speak a word about this plot, me, or my father.

"Cast the curse in the carriage today. This evening your convoy will stop to move a fallen tree. Lean out the window and touch two fingers to your lips to signal that you have successfully cast the curse. After you arrive at Highrook, press for the wedding as soon as possible. Following the ceremony, when you've retired to the king's rooms, kill him and switch back with Tatiana. Only then will you and your brother be released. Agreed?"

"Agreed," Callista ground out.

"I'm glad we have an understanding."

The out-of-breath steward reached them. Sweat beaded on his wrinkled forehead despite the chill in the air. He glanced between Blaise and Callista. "This is the young woman?"

Blaise nodded.

"And…" The man's chin quivered. "Emmy. Is Emmy—"

"So long as this woman leaves with Lady Tatiana and has fit into her new place by the end of the day, your granddaughter will be returned to you tonight."

"Unharmed," the steward said, although it sounded more like a plea than a demand.

"Of course!" Blaise smiled like someone giving a gift. "If you both do your part."

The steward pursed his lips. "Come along, girl." He turned without waiting, his steps so rushed Callista had to hurry despite her longer legs. "What's your name?"

She opened her mouth, hesitated. "Julia."

"Right then. I'm Steward Anders. We'll get you cleaned up and changed into something more appropriate as quickly as possible. Lady Tatiana should have already departed. Luckily for you, she insisted on tarrying in case her maid recovers." He flinched.

What had been done to the poor girl? When would she recover—or would she at all? Fresh anger toward the Shafers warmed Callista's skin.

Could she tell Tatiana the truth and have her lean out the carriage window and thereby at least save Emmy? Perhaps, but it was too big of a perhaps. Numerous things could go wrong. Callista wouldn't risk condemning her brother to a slow, torturous death. She'd made him a promise.

Preventing the heartless Shafers from claiming the throne would be a problem for the future. Today's problem was cursing Tatiana Ackroyd.

Anders ushered Callista inside the manor, through barren corridors and up narrow stairwells. "I hadn't anticipated you being so tall and scrawny. The dress won't suit you, but it will have to do." He opened the door to a small room and waved her inside. "Wash and dress with haste. I'll be back." Without waiting for a reply, he shut the door.

Sighing, Callista rushed through a bath in a cramped tub filled with cold water. A simple brown dress had been laid out for her. It was loose and too short, ending a little above her ankles, but it was made of soft, comfortable linen. She struggled to get a hairbrush through her wet hair, but once she'd gotten through the tangles, she stepped outside.

Anders was pacing in the hallway, wringing his hands. "Finally! Lord Ackroyd wishes for Lady Tatiana to depart at once. You're ready?"

She nodded, and Anders sped through the manor, leading her

into wider halls with sparse but elegant furnishings. They stopped at a door, and he knocked with agitated impatience.

A muffled voice called for them to enter.

"My apologies for the delay. She had to bathe." Anders dropped into an apologetic bow. "This is Julia."

Callista gave her best curtsy. For being out of practice, she thought she did well. Despite having the most peasant students, the Enchanters College was by far the smallest college at the Royal University, so it didn't have separate buildings. She'd bumped into nobles so often that she'd had to learn to curtsy properly to give them one less thing to mock her for.

"Julia is new to the staff here, but she shows great dedication and excellent manners. I believe she'll serve you best as your new lady's maid."

Callista smiled to cover her discomfort at his flagrant lies.

"Only until Katherine recovers," Tatiana said, a note of defiance in her musical voice. "Not that I doubt you'll be most admirable in your work," she hurried to add. "Katherine has been with me for many years, and I'll miss her."

Callista inclined her head. "No offense taken, my lady."

Relief showed in Tatiana's nod.

She was only a few inches shorter than Callista and appeared to be a couple years younger. Blonde hair cascaded down her back. Her round face with soft, full cheeks had a becoming hint of a blush. Gray-blue eyes held a warmth that spoke of a comfortable life. Her figure was likewise soft, with the gentle curves the men at the university claimed to like. Perhaps worse than men calling Callista bony was when they decided to inform her that they preferred "something to hold on to" when she hadn't desired their attention in the first place.

"Are you certain you're comfortable accompanying me to the

palace, Julia?" Tatiana asked. The stiffness in the set of her shoulders and the way she appeared to be chewing the inside of her cheek suggested she was nervous about going herself. "Will your family mind your absence?"

The sincerity in Tatiana's expression pricked at Callista's conscience. It would be so much easier to curse Tatiana if she were self-absorbed.

"I have no family, my lady." She gulped. "It is my honor to serve you, here or at the royal palace."

"I'm so sorry for your loss," Tatiana said, her genuine empathy reminding Callista that Tatiana had also lost her mother. "Thank you for accepting this position. My father is worried about us being caught on the roads after dark before we reach the inn, so I'm afraid we must leave now."

"Of course, my lady." Callista gave a small curtsy and stepped out of the doorway.

Anders cast a relieved look at Callista. "Everything is ready for your departure. Would you like me to escort you?"

Tatiana laughed, an airy, pleasant sound. "That won't be necessary, Anders. Thank you for all your assistance. Let's go, Julia."

Callista followed her new mistress, this time descending wider, better-lit stairwells. A man with graying blond hair paced in the foyer, and he rushed to Tatiana, barely sparing Callista a glance. The younger blond man who trailed after him had to be Tatiana's brother.

"Now, remember—don't let any of them bully you," Lord Ackroyd said, clasping Tatiana's shoulders. "Write to me if you have any concerns or if His Majesty treats you without due respect and honor. Remember, if he asks for your hand, you are not required to accept."

"I know, Father." With a dimpled smile, Tatiana patted Lord

Ackroyd's stubble-covered cheek. "I'll be fine. If by some strange circumstance I'm not, you'll hear about it."

She wouldn't be fine, but not because of any threat posed by the court or the king. Callista barely remained standing still instead of fidgeting.

"Send word to me as well," the brother grumbled. "With Father running all over Aedyllan at General Drake's whims, it's difficult to say how quickly a message would find him. I'll come get you if I have to storm Highrook."

Tatiana embraced her brother. "Always so dramatic, Devon."

"I mean it." Devon released his sister. "But for all my blustering, I've never heard of Cassius Alimer being dishonorable."

"She wouldn't be going otherwise," Lord Ackroyd said. "Speaking of going, though, we've delayed long enough." He pulled her into a tight embrace. "I love you, Tatiana."

"I love you too, Father."

Callista looked away, emotion strangling her as she thought of her own father and her brother Jacob—and how she hadn't had the chance to hug them goodbye.

After another moment, Tatiana chuckled. "I thought you wanted me to leave quickly?"

Lord Ackroyd released her and stepped back. "Wanting you to be on your way and wanting to delay your absence appear to be at odds. Go on." He looked over at Callista. "I trust you'll take good care of my little girl, young woman."

Callista used a curtsy as an excuse to lower her gaze as she lied through her teeth. "Of course, your lordship."

They bustled outside, where three mounted knights waited around a carriage with trunks tied to the roof and its windows open. As she climbed inside, Callista was relieved to see two plush upholstered benches.

Lord Ackroyd helped his daughter get in, murmuring again that she should take care of herself and that he loved her. Devon called after her to remember that she was worthy of courting a king.

The door closed with a loud click, and the carriage lurched forward.

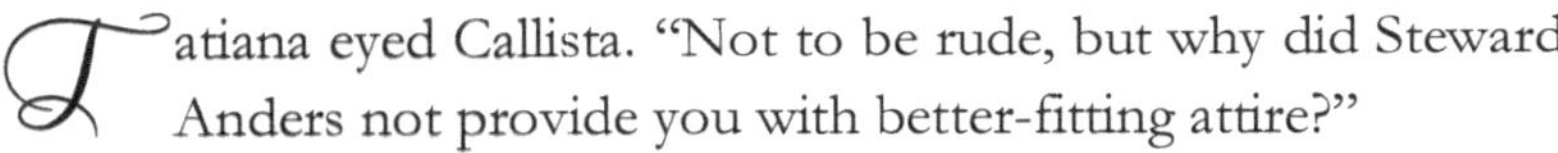

6

Tatiana eyed Callista. "Not to be rude, but why did Steward Anders not provide you with better-fitting attire?"

Callista smoothed her fingers over the dress. "I'm sorry for my appearance, my lady—"

"Oh, I'm not angry! I'm merely curious, and disappointed if our servants aren't being properly provided for."

Fae take this thoughtful noblewoman. She couldn't have been the judgmental and superior type who nearly deserved to be cursed, because of course not.

"I joined your father's estate recently," Callista said, making up the lie as she went. "I had a couple of better-fitted dresses, but both were dingy for a lady's maid at the royal palace."

Tatiana nodded. "Don't fret. I'll send for a seamstress after we're settled into Highrook. In the meantime, I packed some casual gowns. You may borrow them. They'll still be a touch short, but closer than any of Katherine's dresses that might be in with my things. I apologize for not being able to properly outfit you in advance."

Callista couldn't help a smile, even as her stomach twisted. "There's nothing to apologize for, my lady. You're most kind."

"Well, this is going to be a long day of travel." Tatiana wrinkled her nose. "I'm not looking forward to it, so I think I'll nap." She closed the shutters on the right, and Callista did the same on the left. "Thank you. Feel free to sleep as well; I don't mind."

Tatiana curled onto her side, her legs hanging off the edge of the bench since they wouldn't fit. She tucked her arm beneath her head and closed her eyes.

The carriage rumbled and rattled onward. Muted dots of sunlight from gaps in the shutters jittered on the walls. Callista watched as Tatiana's breath deepened and slowed. The small meal Blaise had given her gurgled in her stomach.

Naturally when she met someone to add to the short list of *living good people in Miraveld*, it was someone she was being forced to curse. This was far worse than anything she'd done before. She hadn't known anything about Leo when she cursed him. Anika and Gareth had both hated her from the moment they laid eyes on her, so it was easier to lock away her pity when she had to hurt them. But Tatiana was sweet and thoughtful and trusting.

"My lady?" Callista asked. "Are you asleep?"

No response. Tatiana's expression was serene, her entire body lax with slumber.

Callista closed her eyes, and the image of a bloodied Royce pushed into her mind.

"I'm sorry, Lady Tatiana," Callista murmured. "If I can find a way out of this for both of us, I promise I will take it."

There was nothing for it now. Callista donned the cold, unfeeling armor she'd worn while making the fae prophecy come true. Then she released her magic. Violet light danced over her and Tatiana, swirling in the dark carriage, far too pretty for its malevolent intent. Following the theory of the spell and the push and pull of magical energy, she composed a silent song that combined two interlocking motifs. The curse pulled Tatiana's appearance over Callista like a glove and slid her own appearance over Tatiana.

The magic suffusing her body felt oily and wrong, tempting her to stop, but she couldn't have even if she'd wanted to. A half-finished curse was a disaster waiting to happen. As her victim's appearance shifted, she stifled her reluctance and ignored her rising self-loathing. Then she magically bound Tatiana's vocal cords and hands so she would be unable to tell anyone what had happened or who she truly was.

Callista's magic faded. Hunger chewed at her, and the rocking of the carriage was making her dizzy. The midday meal was still hours away. If she wanted food, she would have to ask, but she wished to interact with the knights as little as possible. Besides, she still needed to exchange clothes with Tatiana. Better to wait, even if she'd be famished by the time they ate.

Tatiana awoke with a groan, and Callista braced herself.

"Oh, I feel strange…" Tatiana's voice came out lower than before—as Callista's voice. She cleared her throat and sat up. "How long was I asleep…?"

Her words trailed off as she stared across the carriage. She rubbed her eyes. Blinked. Then she threw open the shutters of the nearest window, flooding the carriage with sunlight and the rumble of the wheels.

"You…you…"

"I'm you," Callista said, surprised by the sensation of Tatiana's softer, higher voice coming out of her mouth. "I was tired of being the maid." She forced a cruel smile. "I decided I'd rather be the lady. The future queen."

Tatiana gaped at her, then raised her shaking hands to examine longer, more spindly fingers and calloused palms. She lifted a long strand of dark hair and then felt her face as her mouth trembled.

Callista refused to let the ice around her heart break and rejected the urge to cower under the raw hurt and fear in Tatiana's gaze.

"I… Help!" Tatiana lunged toward the carriage door, but Callista shoved her back.

"Don't be ridiculous. There's nothing you can tell them. You'll slow us down for no reason." Callista pulled the shutters closed again.

Tatiana's eyes flashed. "I can tell them—" She made a choking sound and grabbed her throat. "You're not—" She coughed. "I'm—no! You—" Her breath wheezed as she gagged.

"You can't tell anyone the truth. Not aloud or in writing. Don't cause a scene or do something stupid like attack a powerful witch, and you can live."

Trembling, Tatiana curled in on herself. Observing her made Callista feel like she'd been cast from her own body. She watched herself shrink before a terrifying future and a hopeless expression overtake her own face. Turning aside from Tatiana's achingly familiar emotions, Callista focused on her soft new hands with shorter fingers.

"I'll find a way to stop you," Tatiana whispered. "I won't do anything stupid, but it's only so I stay alive."

That brought a small smile to Callista's lips. The noblewoman did have a spine. "Undress. We need to switch clothing."

Tatiana lifted her chin. "What if I refuse?"

Callista tilted her head, turned her hand over on her lap, and conjured a tiny lavender flame over her palm. She waited in silence, letting Tatiana's mind run wild.

A tear leaked down Tatiana's cheek. Her shoulders caved as she turned her back to Callista. "You'll have to undo the laces on the back. I can't reach them."

Switching clothing in the carriage was tricky, but they managed.

Tatiana tugged roughly on the lacing as she did up the back of Callista's luxurious new gown, then sat back down and crossed her arms.

"Fae take you and never return you, you wretched creature." The imprecation was more vehement than Callista would have guessed sweet Tatiana was capable of.

"Don't count on it," was all she said in reply.

They arrived at Highrook Palace around midafternoon the next day. Tatiana had been sullen, but she'd dutifully—if with frequent glares and an occasional challenging note whenever she said *my lady*—played the part of a lady's maid. Callista had ignored the cursed noblewoman as much as possible.

As one of the drivers helped Callista descend from the carriage in the spacious courtyard, she looked up at the looming bulk of the sprawling gray stone castle with a sense of bitterness. This was where her parents and brothers had labored and given their all for King Silas Faine, to be rewarded with death and no recognition.

She'd been inside three times. The first time, she'd been young and had surprised her mother at work. Her visit had ended with a tearful scolding, and only when Callista was older and knew more of the wickedness in the Faine court had she understood why. Then during her first year at the Royal University, her class had been invited to a royal banquet. To her relief, the princes had been absent. The last time, she'd stolen the Fae Blessing and Curse of Mortimer Faine, and Royce had died so she could escape.

Or so she had believed for two years.

Thinking of Royce, tortured first by Silas Faine and then by the Shafers and now alone in a dark cell, Callista straightened. She could do this. She could play the part of Lady Tatiana Ackroyd until she found a way to save her brother without killing the new king. Unless Cassius Alimer proved as crooked as his predecessor, in which case she might do as the Shafers wanted but kill Baron Shafer and his son later.

Bright music drew her attention down from the gray sky and soaring battlements to the expansive double doors, bordered by a wide and ornately carved frame. A row of trumpeters lined both sides of the path leading up to the entrance, and several nobles stood nearby, watching her with curiosity. The doors swung open, and a man strode out into the muted sunlight. The gem-encrusted crown on his head proclaimed him as King Cassius.

The monarch's vestments, from a black velvet doublet over a fitted crimson shirt to a sleek pair of black trousers, were tailored to accentuate his broad shoulders, trim waist, and above-average height. By his confident, powerful stride, he didn't spend all his time lounging about or working at a desk. But it was his face that captured Callista's attention.

A kind, easy smile graced his expression. Beneath his glittering crown, coils of black hair framed his light-bronze face. His dark eyes crinkled slightly, and they held hers, not roving over his potential bride's body.

Callista dropped into a low curtsy and bowed her head, glad that propriety allowed her to break their gaze. If King Cassius kept looking at her with such openness and as if she were his equal, not a bartering chip in the games of politics, she was going to find it difficult to deceive him.

"Your Majesty," she murmured.

A hand appeared before her face, calloused in the same patterns her father's and brothers' hands had been from weapons training. "Welcome, Lady Tatiana. It is a pleasure to meet you."

"It is my honor, Your Majesty." She slipped her hand into his—momentarily surprised by her shorter fingers. She did not enjoy wearing someone else's body. "Thank you for welcoming me in person."

"How could I not?" King Cassius grinned and guided her hand into the crook of his arm. He was markedly taller than her—or at least than Tatiana. "You must be tired from your journey. Come. I'll show you the basics of the castle and then escort you to your rooms so you may rest."

He was going to give her a tour himself? Callista couldn't imagine any of the Faines doing something as mundane as showing a guest to their rooms. Granted, Lady Tatiana wasn't a mere guest but potentially his future queen. Still, being led through the palace on the king's arm was somewhat overwhelming.

"Thank you, Your Majesty. That is exceedingly kind of you."

"Not at all! I wish to ensure you are safely settled in."

As they walked, King Cassius also filled her in on some upcoming events. Tomorrow, they would have morning tea in the gardens, where she would also meet General Vallyn Drake. She smiled and pretended she wasn't nervous. In four days, he would host a modest ball. Officially, it was simply his first party as king, since a ball in Tatiana's honor might suggest that Cassius and Tatiana were formally engaged. Unofficially, however, it was to introduce her to the court. And in a little over a fortnight there would be a feast and a parade for the Maple Moon Festival—a holiday held on the tenth full moon of the year to celebrate the end of the harvest.

Highrook Palace was as huge as she recalled. King Cassius pointed out the hallway that led to the great hall where they had their meals and one that led to the palace gardens. They navigated so many halls and staircases that Callista was certain she would never find her way on her own. At least there were guards everywhere, so if she ever got lost, she wouldn't have to wander far before she found a guardsman to ask for help.

After the king pointed out a hall that led to the royal wing, he turned them down the next corridor.

"Your quarters are down here," he said. "As you can see, you'll be close to my own rooms." His brown cheeks took on a slightly ruddier hue. "But not improperly so! I merely mean we can see each other fairly easily and we'll have opportunities to walk together to meals, which should help in getting to know one another."

She smiled. So even kings could be boyishly awkward—never mind that his endearing nervousness was for Tatiana, not for her. "A wise and appreciated consideration, Your Majesty. I had feared your royal duties would make spending time together difficult."

King Cassius winced. "Unfortunately, that may prove to be true, which factored in to my decision to place you here."

Ahead of them, an unobtrusive door opened, and a pair of burly male servants emerged carrying one of Tatiana's trunks.

"Ah." He motioned toward them. "Your things should all be inside soon, if they aren't already." They followed the servants but stopped outside the door while the servants continued inside.

"Here we are, then." The king motioned to the door as he released her arm. "Yours is the door with the phoenix, but don't worry if you open the wrong one. Currently you're the sole guest in this wing."

Callista blinked. "Oh."

King Cassius's eyes widened, and he reached up with his left hand to wrap a few coils of hair around his finger before abruptly returning his hand to his side. She couldn't help a smile. Jacob had absently tugged on his long hair when he was nervous. Sorrow pushed at her throat, but she willed her heart to be stone.

"It's not for any improper reason," he said hurriedly. "I'm so sorry; please don't think me a cad or worry that I'm trying to isolate you. You're free to go where you like. It was my general's idea, actually—security concerns. Not you!" He flushed. "But, um, er—"

"I am aware that not every guest in Highrook is pleased with our courtship," Callista said, coming to his rescue. "It's easier to know if someone might be targeting me if they have no reason to be in the wing where I am staying."

Visible relief eased the king's shoulders. "Precisely. Thank you for understanding."

"Thank you and your general for being concerned for my safety, Your Majesty. Is there anyone in particular you're concerned about?"

The king hesitated. "You're probably aware Baron Shafer is the most vocal against my choice. His son arrived at Highrook this morning. I don't expect him to cause trouble, but if he bothers you, please inform me."

Blaise was here? Of course he was. He'd want to monitor her himself. How was she supposed to defy Blaise right under his nose? The walls pressed in around her, turning Highrook Palace into a cage.

"Your knights will be given rooms for the night and granted any supplies they require before departing tomorrow," Cassius continued, "but know that General Drake has complete trust in the palace guards. Besides those stationed throughout the palace, there are frequent patrols, so you'll be safe. You'll have full access to the palace staff. Oh—speaking of which, do you require a lady's maid?"

"Actually..." Callista weighed her options. She didn't want to spend more time in close quarters with her victim, and someone who was familiar with Highrook would be helpful.

"This is terribly embarrassing." She tucked a stand of distractingly blonde hair behind her ear. "My usual lady's maid fell ill, so this new girl was brought in, but I'm afraid she's incapable in the role and a bit…recalcitrant. I don't think it's her fault; she simply hasn't been a servant long. If I send her home, I fear my father's steward will release her for displeasing me. I don't want to leave her without work or shelter. I'm horribly sorry to ask this of you, Your Majesty, but might I request a new lady's maid from the palace servants during my stay and a place for my servant among the castle's staff? Preferably…somewhere we won't have awkward encounters with each other? I already feel guilty enough, even though I don't know why she dislikes me so. I assure you I'd never dream of mistreating a servant."

"Mm, I see…" He nodded slowly. "I will ask my steward to see to it—and warn him to place her somewhere away from the guests."

Callista didn't have to fake her grimace. "Probably wise, Your Majesty. Thank you for your understanding. I met her only yesterday, and I tried to make her comfortable, but…she does not seem to wish to work as my personal maid. I'm relieved to give her the opportunity to try something else and avoid her snappishness at the same time."

Cassius waved a hand. "Unfortunately, I have seen jealousy turn to baseless resentment among servants and nobles many times. But never fear. I'm happy to assist." He gifted her with that warm smile again. "I'm afraid I have other matters to address now, but I'm pleased you've arrived safely. It was a pleasure to meet you, Lady Tatiana."

"The pleasure was all mine, Your Majesty." She curtsied, wondering how quickly she was going to tire of the endless obeisance. "I look forward to speaking with you again soon."

"And I with you." King Cassius strode away.

Callista turned to the phoenix-painted door and immediately stepped out of the way of a couple of servants. They bowed and murmured "my lady" as they passed. Before the door shut behind them, she caught a glimpse of the back of a tall, thin form with dark hair—Tatiana was already inside. Squaring her shoulders to resist the urge to crumple, Callista entered her new suite.

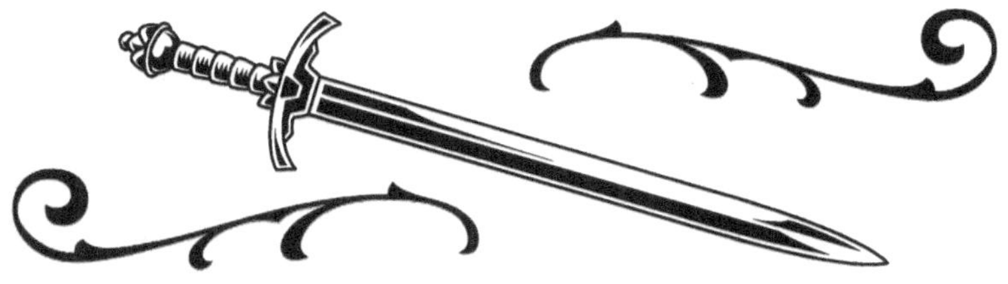

7

Accursed construction work.

Vallyn hurried through the endless halls toward the eastern guest wing. He'd meant to be ominously awaiting his prey, but no. The construction debris had blocked a hall, forcing Vallyn to take the long way around, and he'd already been running behind schedule. Keeping up with his duties when his tired eyes didn't want to focus was proving difficult.

He'd hardly slept the last few nights thanks to nightmares about wars and assassins and saboteurs. When he woke with his heart in his throat, every dark shape looked suspect, as if the intruders in his dreams lurked in the corners of his bedchamber. The worst part was a nagging fear that the nightmares were a side effect of the fae magic he didn't fully understand. All full-blooded fae could create glamours, magically altering the appearance of something or someone that already existed. Fae of the Court of Light had the power to create complex illusions, which were uncomfortably close to hallucinations.

His father had never mentioned their magic affecting dreams—although Vallyn hadn't given Arolyin a chance to explain more than the basics. He regretted that more than he'd ever admit, but not enough to call for his father. No, his worry that his magic was messing with his mind was another symptom of the same fear causing the nightmares. That was all they were. Normal, human bad dreams, brought on by stress.

Vallyn had promised he would protect Cassius. Now that his friend was king, that responsibility weighed on him. It didn't help that Cassius had allowed a wolf into the pen.

At last Vallyn reached the correct hallway and found a door with a white heron painted on a field of vivid green. After taking a moment to compose himself and check that the pointed tips of his ears were hidden under his hair, he banged on the door. Then he stepped back and crossed his arms.

A thin man answered the door with a nervous energy to his movements that reminded Vallyn of a chipmunk. "Can I help you, sir?"

"I wish to speak to Sir Blaise Shafer."

The man ducked a half bow and glanced into the room. "May I ask who is calling?"

"General Vallyn Drake, and I won't be denied."

"Oh." The servant quailed back. "Yes, sir. General. My lord? Just a moment—"

"I'm here, Harvey," a deeper voice said lazily. "Return to unpacking."

As the servant scurried away with a suspiciously sharp glance back at Vallyn, the wolf stalked forward. Blaise Shafer crossed his arms and leaned against the doorframe. He was taller than Vallyn and exaggeratedly tilted his head down to meet Vallyn's gaze. But despite Blaise's slight tan and strong build, which spoke to time spent training outdoors, Vallyn was the more muscular of the two.

The baron's son flicked his gaze up and down Vallyn. "To what do I owe this honor, General?"

"I feel it is my duty," Vallyn said, letting his scowl deepen, "to inform you that the palace is secure. The guards are well-trained and keep frequent patrols. You have access to this wing and the neighboring east guest wing, the great rooms during public gatherings, and the gardens, courtyards, and stables. Your servants have access to this wing and the servants' areas, so long as they do not disrupt the palace servants or wander into other wings. Trespassing can result in sentences from confinement in one's quarters up to execution if malevolence is proven. You can rest assured you will be quite safe during your stay."

"Mm. You mean to say I can rest assured you'll catch me if I try anything against His Majesty. And probably that you'd love an excuse to throw me in the dungeon."

"If you wish to speak candidly, yes." Vallyn uncrossed his arms and rested his left hand on the pommel of his sword. "I don't trust you. Your reasons for coming here and your father's suddenly conciliatory attitude are suspicious, and I doubt it's a coincidence you arrived on the same day as Lady Tatiana Ackroyd. So let me tell you plainly, Shafer: cause trouble for any members of the court, step out of line, harm anyone within these walls, so much as attempt to harm my king or his prospective bride, and I will put my sword through your heart without hesitation, without mercy, and without remorse."

Blaise blinked languidly. "My. Quite the speech. Do all members of the court get your unique flavor of hospitality, or am I special?" Interest lit his eyes. "What about Lady Tatiana herself? Will you warn her off causing any trouble? Or will you perhaps chaperone their every meeting?" He snickered.

"Do not think that because I'm paying extra attention to *you*, the rest of the palace security won't be as strong as ever," Vallyn said in a low voice. "This isn't the Faine court. Anything does *not* go."

Blaise tilted his head. "You're right. If it were the Faine court, that blessing would still be in place, and you wouldn't be so worried about your king. I do wonder if somewhere along the line an Alimer heir was illegitimate. Since, you know, Cassius didn't go down with his Faine cousins like he should have."

It took every ounce of Vallyn's self-control not to grab the insufferable knave by the doublet and slam him into the stone wall. "It would seem two-hundred-year-old fae prophecies are more intelligent than you are and can better discern the difference between a corrupt house and a virtuous one. Perhaps I needn't worry about keeping an eye on you. You're either too empty-headed to cause harm or so stupid that when you attempt it, you'll be caught at once."

Blaise tilted his head back and watched Vallyn through slitted eyes. "I'd be careful who I go around insulting if I were you, Drake. Alimer can make you his general and give you a sham lordship, but it doesn't change what you are. The son of a disgraced wench who was stripped of her title and name and a nobody father who didn't even bother to claim you."

Tension ratcheted down Vallyn's spine. Part of him wanted to argue. That story mixed truth and assumptions, and nobody had the right to insult his late mother. But beside the fact that his father hardly deserved to be defended, he wouldn't give Shafer the satisfaction of seeing him go on the defensive.

"Does it chafe, Shafer?" he asked instead with a mocking tilt of his lips. "Thinking that the circumstances of my birth make me lower than you but knowing that my title and power are greater? Does it burn you up inside knowing that your father knelt in utter defeat at the point of my blade?"

Blaise's eyes bulged. His face flushed crimson.

"Enjoy your stay at Highrook, *Sir* Shafer." Vallyn spun and strode away, his back tall. If his black cloak snapped and billowed smartly behind him, well, that wasn't intentional.

Blaise didn't attempt a response. The door simply clicked shut, giving Vallyn a surge of gratification. The son of Cassius's greatest rival was at least a little rattled.

Yet the tremble that went through Vallyn's fist meant Blaise wasn't the only one affected by their conversation.

It shouldn't matter. Vallyn had earned his knighthood, his rank as captain of Alimer Duchy, and his titles of general and lord. But even though most of the court didn't dare say it to his face, many did judge him for his past. A past he had no control over.

Irrelevant. Cas cared for him like a brother, and the opinion of no one else mattered. Especially not the opinion of a snake like Blaise Shafer.

Those thoughts weren't useful, especially when he had more pressing worries. For example—he cursed as he glimpsed the afternoon sun through a nearby window—he was late to accompany Cassius to welcome Lady Tatiana.

He headed toward Cassius's office. Perhaps he'd be lucky and catch his friend leaving. Instead, as Vallyn turned in to the hall that led to the king's office, he spotted Cassius walking at a leisurely pace ahead of him.

"Cas." He sped up as Cassius glanced over his shoulder, and within moments, he was walking at his friend's side. "Did I miss Tatiana's arrival?"

"You did. Is everything all right?"

"Sorry." Vallyn sighed. "Unfortunately, matters of palace security come first. Endless paperwork, wolves to warn that the sheep are well guarded…"

"*Val,*" Cassius groaned. "What exactly did you do and to whom?"

"Relax. I merely exchanged a few polite words with Blaise Shafer."

Cassius's lips pressed into a line as he gave Vallyn a flat look.

"Fine, maybe not all were polite. I explained which parts of the palace he's welcome in, apprised him of the consequences of ignoring that, and strongly advised that he behave himself. I might have mentioned his father kneeling at my feet after the final battle of Althre Fields, but he insulted my mother first."

Cas lifted an eyebrow.

"I swear I didn't touch him. Or even draw a weapon."

"At least there's that," Cassius grumbled as he pushed open the door to his office.

Vallyn claimed one of the two chairs on the near side of the desk while Cassius made his way to his own chair. Papers and books littered the desk's surface, as usual.

"What was your first impression of your potential future wife?"

Cassius set his crown on the desk, then leaned back in his chair and laced his fingers together behind his head. "She's pretty. On the taller side of average, intelligent eyes, a sweet voice, luscious blonde hair, a round, full-cheeked face, and an appealing figure."

"Already eyeing her figure, are you?" Vallyn chuckled, and Cassius reddened.

"No! I mean…well, can you blame me? She has nice curves… ugh." Cassius wrinkled his nose. "I told myself I wasn't going to care about that. Such things don't last and ultimately are far from the most important."

"Indeed. Then what of her personality and character?"

"I talked to her for all of twenty minutes, Val. I don't know." Cassius fiddled with the dark curls on the left side of his head. They were already looser than those on the other side, but telling the king to stop fidgeting felt wrong. "Although…"

Cassius explained how Tatiana had requested a replacement lady's maid.

"Interesting. But this works out well," Vallyn said. "We can instruct this maid to watch for any suspicious behavior."

Cassius dropped his hands to the arms of his chair. "Now you're even suspecting my prospective bride?"

"We did intimidate Lord Ackroyd into supporting you—"

"You're paranoid."

Vallyn winced. He'd told himself the same thing when he'd gotten up in the middle of the night to confront a dark shape: a cloak thrown over a chair he'd moved out of place. Still, his job was to be cautious.

"It isn't paranoia when people actually hate you. Better to be suspicious than wrong."

His friend eyed him. "Is that why you have dark circles under your eyes?"

"Great, thank you," Vallyn mumbled. He rubbed his eyes. At least Cas hadn't noticed they were also bloodshot from lack of sleep.

"My friend, you're doing an excellent job, and I am perfectly capable of taking care of myself. Why don't you get some rest?"

"That anxious to return to whatever this is?" Vallyn nodded toward the desk.

"Honestly, no." Cassius wrinkled his nose at the paper-strewn desk. "The more I strive to put the kingdom in order, the more I realize what a disaster my predecessors made of things. I don't think Silas was even trying."

Vallyn frowned, remembering Blaise's comments about the Faines' Fae Blessing and Curse. "He didn't think he needed to. Blessing and all."

Cassius slumped back in his chair. "If I could magically travel through time, I'd talk to my many-greats-grandfather Mortimer about caution when asking boons from fae. Or advise him to politely decline." Immediately his eyes widened. "No offense—"

"No, I agree. I've experienced the importance of being careful with fae magic myself."

"Mm, true. Given our situation, I suppose I can't be too harsh on Mortimer…although, unlike my ancestor, *I* had no idea those oaths would be magically binding, and they only affect us, not the entire kingdom. I think I get a pass."

Vallyn tsked and shook his head. "Our oaths only affect us? I'm hurt. Here I thought my service secured that crown for you, which affects the entire kingdom." He motioned toward the bit of gold with a smirk.

"Now I'm hurt." Cassius pressed a hand to his heart. "*I* thought you agreed to be my general because you believe in me."

"Ahhh, yes, of course! Also that." Vallyn chuckled. He stood and flicked a bejeweled point of the crown. "I think I chose my liege and closest friend pretty well."

"Flatterer."

"I'll leave you to…all this, then."

"And get some rest?" Cassius sent him a pointed look.

In response, Vallyn inclined his head, then left the study. He'd never been able to sleep during the day unless he was ill.

As he walked through the halls, his mind was filled with thoughts of threats and fae deals and the consequences of fae magic.

Cassius had inherited his father's ducal estate far too young after the tragic death of his father. At the time, Vallyn and Cas already thought of each other as brothers. Vallyn's mother had passed less than a year prior, so Vallyn had understood Cassius's pain.

Then Cassius had confided that he was terrified to take his father's place. How was a fourteen-year-old boy supposed to publicly accept the oaths of all the lords, knights, and common men who owed fealty to Alimer Duchy? Vallyn had been only eleven himself, but he'd declared he would be the first to swear fealty. After Cassius found the book with the oaths, they held their own private ceremony.

Cassius swore that Vallyn would be his subject under his protection, provision, and jurisdiction. In return, Vallyn swore to serve, obey, and protect Cassius. They added their own promise to always be there for each other. In a moment of childish impetuousness, they clasped each other's forearms and declared they would keep those oaths and be brothers until death.

Unfortunately, Vallyn hadn't known then that fae magic loved deals and oaths. His magic had gleefully ripped free, encircling their hands in lines of silver.

That was the only time Vallyn had called for his father from the fae realm. Alone and terrified, he'd waited two days for his father to arrive. He'd never forget the way the blood had drained from his father's face when he recounted the oaths.

"Fae promises are demanding and dangerous," his father explained. "Responsible fae word their bargains and oaths carefully."

"What happens if fae break their word?" Vallyn asked, his lower lip quivering.

Arolyin hesitated. "It depends on the wording of the bargain. The binding might merely alert the wronged party and help them locate the oath-breaker. Fae who break serious vows might lose access to their magic. But oaths that invoke death…"

His father looked away. "Your magic is weaker than mine. But if either of you breaks your vows, there is a chance the magic could kill the oath-breaker."

"Can I undo it? If we both say we didn't mean it—"

"No, son." Arolyin sighed. "You both must keep your oaths, which means you can never change your mind and come live with me." More anguish darkened his father's expression than had when his mother, Deanna, died. "The only way you'll be free of your promise is if Cassius Alimer dies."

When Vallyn relayed the information to Cassius, he left out the part where a wildness had sparked in his father's eyes. To be safe, Vallyn had made his father promise not to kill Cassius.

Over the years, fear of the accidental binding had faded. But sometimes when Vallyn considered ignoring one of Cassius's orders, his magic reared up in the back of his mind like a threatened snake.

Vallyn didn't care to find out what would happen if the snake ever struck.

Since they would have kept their oaths anyway, the binding rarely bothered Vallyn. What bothered him was how easily it had happened. It was a constant reminder why he had to keep a close rein on his magic, and it had driven him to practice his magic in secret until he could control and use it.

At least if someone did try to assassinate Cassius, Vallyn had both his warrior skill and his magic to protect his brother. And he would do whatever it took to protect Cassius.

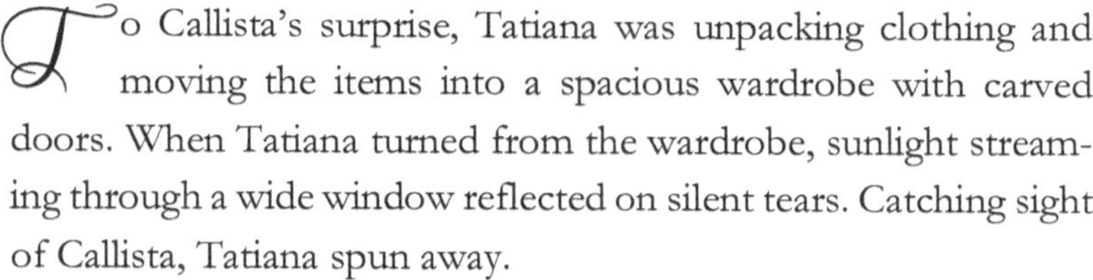

8

o Callista's surprise, Tatiana was unpacking clothing and moving the items into a spacious wardrobe with carved doors. When Tatiana turned from the wardrobe, sunlight streaming through a wide window reflected on silent tears. Catching sight of Callista, Tatiana spun away.

"What are you doing?" Callista asked, keeping her tone neutral.

"I'm a servant," Tatiana said crisply. "I'm serving."

It was still unsettling to see someone else wearing her appearance and hear her voice from another's mouth. Worse was hearing someone else's voice every time she spoke.

Callista tilted her head, her shockingly blonde hair sliding over her shoulder. "You're trying to make sure I keep you around so you can determine a way to undo this curse."

Tatiana's momentary pause confirmed the theory.

"I'm afraid even if I kept you as my servant, that would not help you break the curse." Callista crossed to the plush four-poster bed and sat on the edge. Soft fabric distracted her, and she rubbed the luxurious blanket. "I've arranged for you to be employed elsewhere in the palace."

Slowly, Tatiana turned toward her, a chemise clutched in her hands. "You…aren't going to toss me out into the streets?"

Callista ran her uncalloused fingers over the spiraling curved ridges carved into one of the bedposts. "I took your identity specifically because it was convenient, and I wished to live in Highrook. I don't bear any personal malice against you. I have been homeless, penniless, and alone. I have no desire to inflict that upon you. Behave yourself, stay quiet and out of the way, and don't attempt to reveal me, and you may live in peace."

After a long moment of silence, Tatiana murmured, "Shall I take that as a threat?"

Callista shrugged and fixed her attention on a painting adorning the wood-paneled wall across from the bed. The unicorn lying peacefully in a paddock was a pale, scrawny thing compared to the one she had met. "Take it however you like."

She hated this. When she had played the role of cold-hearted villain previously, she'd been able to cling to her purpose. She'd seen no other recourse, no other path to justice for her family and everyone else in Aedyllan. The Faines had needed to be stopped.

However, the young woman before her had done nothing to deserve this suffering, and this time Callista's wicked deeds were in pursuit of a goal she did not believe in. Now that she'd met King Cassius Alimer, she recoiled at the idea of harming him.

But then she thought of Royce. Of the wounds and scars he already bore, the hollow look in his eyes, and his screams as Blaise's lackey had taken pleasure in inflicting pain on him. Didn't his suffering matter? After two years of grieving her family, of nightmares about Royce bleeding out, she couldn't lose him again or let him be hurt anymore.

It would shatter her beyond repair.

A single, traitorous tear escaped down her cheek.

"What right do you have to cry?" Far less vehemence filled Tatiana's words than Callista deserved.

Callista flicked away the tear and stood. "You don't have to keep unpacking those."

Without waiting for a response, she strode back into the sitting room and crossed to the window. The faint reflection of a girl with round cheeks and blonde hair made her flinch. She focused on the landscape past the glass. Her suite on the third floor looked out over an orchard within the palace walls. Autumn had touched the trees, turning the leaves red and yellow. The towering walls rose and fell with the shape of the mountain and blocked much of the view beyond the palace, but green foothills were visible in the distance.

Try as hard she might, though, Callista couldn't remain focused on the pleasant view. She wanted a few minutes to herself, where she didn't have to pretend she wasn't dying inside.

Someone knocked, and she spun toward the door, impatient for the new maidservant. "You may enter." She hoped that was what a real noblewoman would say.

Unfortunately, it was one of Tatiana's guards, under the watchful eye of a palace guard, who wanted to ensure she was settled in. Likely he would take that report back to Lord Ackroyd, so Callista made her reassurances that she would be fine as convincing as possible. Tatiana hovered in the door to the bedroom, watching with a resigned frown.

The guards left, and Tatiana huffed an anguished laugh. "It pains me more to know my father is going to think I'm safe and happy."

"You'll be employed by the palace. You'll be safe."

Callista hoped so, anyway. Servants hadn't been safe under Silas Faine's rule, but King Cassius seemed different. Of course, if

Callista killed the king, they would both revert to their own appearances, and Tatiana would take the blame. Her stomach twisted.

This was all so very wrong.

Moments later, there was another knock. This time, a man with squinty eyes and a receding hairline above his incredibly pale face entered, followed by a woman in her forties.

The man bobbed a bow. "I'm Steward Morgan. This is Serena." He motioned to the woman. "She will be your personal maid while you reside here, if that is acceptable to you."

Anyone would be more acceptable than the lady she had wronged.

"My lady." Serena curtsied. A few gray strands snuck through her sandy-brown hair, and her hands were lightly folded over the skirt of her green wool dress. She was of average height and build, with bright, intelligent eyes and a carefully neutral expression.

"Welcome, Serena." Callista smiled. "I appreciate your help and hope it's not a terrible inconvenience to you to be asked to change positions so suddenly."

Serena's countenance softened. "Not at all, my lady."

Steward Morgan turned slightly. "Is this the servant you wish to be rid of?"

Callista's cheeks heated. "This is Julia, and we proved to be a poor match, so yes, I requested she be given a position in some other part of the palace."

Tatiana's jaw tightened.

The steward hummed. "I see. Unfortunately, we recently finished hiring a full staff. But we'll find something since His Majesty requested it." He bowed to Callista, another awkward bobbing motion. "Should you need anything that Serena cannot provide, please do not hesitate to send her to ask me." Yet another bow. He looked at Tatiana and motioned with his head toward the door.

"Come along, then."

Tatiana gulped, then seemed to gather herself and followed. Callista opened her mouth to wish the young woman well, but it would sound insincere to Tatiana, and guilt stayed her tongue.

The door closed, and Callista and her new maidservant stood in silence. What in Miraveld would an *actual* noblewoman do now? Give some kind of command? Ask the woman about herself? All she wanted to do was close herself in a dark room, but would that seem odd?

"I apologize," Callista said. "I didn't mean to keep you standing here. I'm afraid I'm fatigued from my journey and not quite myself." Thank the stars Tatiana hadn't been here to hear that remark. "But it is a pleasure to meet you, and I do hope we will get along well."

Serena finally smiled. "I think we will. In fact, I suspect this will be an easier and more agreeable position than chambermaid. Do you require any assistance? Perhaps with unpacking? I can help in any way necessary before I move my things into the maid's room in this suite."

"Oh." Callista considered. "Actually…might you help me undress? I'd like to take a nap, and this gown has rather a lot of laces. Julia started unpacking my things, but the rest can wait until you're settled in and I've had a chance to rest."

Serena curtsied. "Of course, my lady."

Callista had never had a personal maid before, although Tatiana had helped her lace up the dress at the inn that morning—after watching Callista struggle and then saying with disgust that she was *not* going to allow her body to arrive at Highrook looking like a dog had dressed her. It was embarrassing to be assisted with something as simple as changing clothing, but with all the complicated back laces on Tatiana's garments, she would have to get used to it. After Callista changed into a nightgown and closed the curtains, she made for the plush four-poster bed and its excessive number of embroidered pillows.

"Would you like me to wake you in time to go to supper in the great hall?" Serena inquired. "Or would you prefer I arrange for food to be brought here?"

Callista stilled. "Is that an option?"

Serena nodded.

"Oh, you're the best!" Callista grinned at the older woman before dumping excess pillows on the floor. "Something brought in here would be wonderful. Whatever is quick and easiest to bring all the way here is fine. Thank you!"

"My pleasure, my lady." Serena's smile looked genuine as she slipped out of the room and closed the heavy door with a soft click.

The moment the maid was gone, Callista climbed into bed and curled onto her side, pushing her foreign blonde hair out of sight. Dim sunlight still filtered around the edges of the thick brocade curtains, but alone in the dark, she could fall apart. For the first time since Royce had appeared like some kind of blessed miracle and everything had turned into a nightmare, there was no one she had to perform for.

No brother from whom she had to hide the truth that she was cracked and fragile inside. No mocking kidnapper threatening her brother and reveling in any hint of fear. No innocent young lady whom she had to pretend to not care about hurting. No king, nobles, or servants to convince that she was Lady Tatiana Ackroyd.

It was a good thing Gareth and the Raylor twins had refused her offer to use a binding spell, or either Callista or Royce or both would already be dead. Guilt still weighed on her. She had broken her vow scant months after making it.

But it was to save her brother and against her will. That counted for something.

Didn't it?

Maybe it didn't. All she knew was she was so tired of being alone, of everything she loved being ripped away from her.

Callista buried her face in her pillow to muffle her sobs, then let herself cry. For every shattered dream, for every injustice, for every impossible decision demanded of her.

When her tears were spent, as she drifted to sleep, Callista made one more promise.

"I don't know how yet. But I'll save you and find a way for us to be free together, Royce. I swear it. And this vow, I will not break."

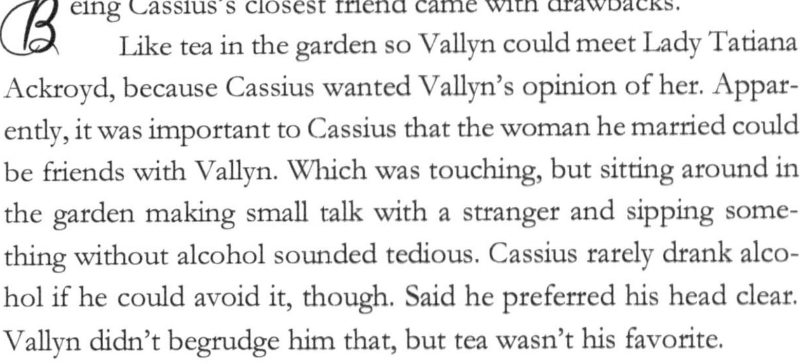

9

*B*eing Cassius's closest friend came with drawbacks.

Like tea in the garden so Vallyn could meet Lady Tatiana Ackroyd, because Cassius wanted Vallyn's opinion of her. Apparently, it was important to Cassius that the woman he married could be friends with Vallyn. Which was touching, but sitting around in the garden making small talk with a stranger and sipping something without alcohol sounded tedious. Cassius rarely drank alcohol if he could avoid it, though. Said he preferred his head clear. Vallyn didn't begrudge him that, but tea wasn't his favorite.

At least he'd talked Cassius out of inviting some other unwed ladies of the court. Vallyn was *not* going to let Cas set him up with some stranger. Particularly when the entire point of this meeting was to get to know Cassius's potential bride. One objective at a time was a wiser strategy.

He checked in with the guards stationed around the gardens. He'd arranged to have all the entrances into the autumn section of the gardens blocked so their tea wouldn't be interrupted by nosy nobles or anyone looking to cause discord.

The gardens were as expansive as the rest of the palace and had four sections, designed so the plants in each would be at the peak of their beauty in a different season. He thought it would have made more sense to mix the various seasonal plants together throughout the entire garden instead of having entire sections that were drab when out of season, but he was neither a horticulturist nor a royal.

Satisfied with the security, he strolled along the white stone paths to a pergola in the autumn section. The open wood structure had spaced slats for a roof, but the red-leafed vines that consumed the pergola were so thick that the roof nevertheless provided some shelter to the marble table and wood chairs inside it. The protection would have been nice if it were raining, but instead the leaves cast a chilly shadow and obstructed the view of the vivid blue sky.

Within moments of his arrival, servants appeared carrying covered silver platters. He stayed out of their way, watching with disinterest as they arranged teapots and teacups, miniature pots of honey, and plates full of tiny pastries and cakes. A servant set cushions on the chairs, and another placed blankets in the corner for easy retrieval if needed.

The servants departed, leaving Vallyn alone with the vibrant trees, the fragrant autumnal flowers, and the chirping of a few crickets hidden somewhere amid the shrubbery. He rubbed his eyes, the lull in activity reminding him he needed to find a way to get a decent night's sleep.

The soft tap of footsteps drew his attention, and he dropped his hand from his eyes.

A woman followed one of the winding paths of white cobblestones. He didn't recognize her, but he knew one thing—this tall, angular young woman was not meant to be here. Her elegant crimson dress indicated she was a noble, but not one he recognized. How in Miraveld had this lady gotten past the guards?

"Halt!" Vallyn gripped the hilt of his sword as he strode

toward her. "Who are you?"

She took half a step backward and blinked. "I'm Lady Tatiana Ackroyd—"

Vallyn barked a startled laugh. "I think you'll find lying to me is a bad idea."

This young woman, while moderately attractive, couldn't be the woman Cassius had described. Everything about her—her dark hair, thin face, and build that was so slight as to be almost gangly—was so wrong for Lady Tatiana that her claim was laughable.

The woman paled, but her stoic expression gave nothing away. "I beg your pardon?"

"Impersonating a noble is an offense, punishable by fine, imprisonment, or death." Vallyn swept his gaze over her. He didn't see any weapons. Carefully, he let a little of his fae magic reach out to sense her and jolted. An enchantress. An unusually powerful one. "Who are you, and what have you done with Lady Tatiana?"

Her entire body went rigidly still, as if turning to stone. She lifted her chin, and her eyes flashed with indignation. "How dare you? Who are *you* to accuse me? I am the daughter of a lord of the court, here as a personal guest of His Majesty the King so that he might court me. I've given you my name, yet you've shown me no such courtesy."

"I'm General Vallyn Drake, confidant of the king and head of the royal guard and armies." He took a menacing step closer, until she was within his reach. "I can kill you this moment if you don't tell me who you are."

A tick along her lower jaw hinted that he'd intimidated her. She was taller than him by a few inches, and she used every bit of her height to look imperiously down her nose at him. "This is how King Cassius's general behaves? Threatening execution without evidence?"

If she weren't a lying infiltrator, he'd be impressed with her ability to stand her ground.

"Evidence? I have not met Lady Tatiana, but I know you're not her. To start…" He held up a strand of her dark hair. "Your hair is not blonde."

The imposter's lips parted, her countenance caught somewhere between shock, confusion, and fear. "My hair *is* blonde, though?"

Before Vallyn could make any sense of such a blatantly false claim, Cassius's voice interrupted him.

"Vallyn, what *are* you doing?" His friend hurried over to his side.

Vallyn dropped the woman's hair but did not back out of her space.

"Lady Tatiana," Cassius said, "I hope my general wasn't bothering you?"

Lady…that couldn't be right. Vallyn looked between his friend and the young woman. "Are you two pranking me?"

The enchantress's momentary surprise shuffled behind a cold mask. Cassius turned toward Vallyn, his bulging eyes clearly asking *what is your problem?*

"Ca—Your Majesty, this woman looks nothing like you described yesterday."

"Erm…yes. She does."

"*This* woman? This woman is blonde, with a round face and full apple cheeks and a curvy figure?"

Blushing, Cassius grabbed Vallyn's arm painfully tight. "I'm so sorry, Lady Tatiana. I fear my friend may have come down with a fever. Please excuse us for a moment."

The woman curtsied, but Cassius was already dragging Vallyn away from her, past the pergola and toward the evergreens in the winter gardens beyond it.

"What is *wrong* with you?" he hissed. "I know you are…passionate in your duties, but I have my hands full enough without worrying about smoothing things over with Tatiana after you…whatever that was. Why were you in her face and touching her hair and glowering at her? This is bizarre behavior even for you."

They reached a semicircular alcove cut into a tall hedge with a bird bath in the center. Cassius marched inside and spun on Vallyn, anger radiating from his narrowed eyes and clenched jaw. "Explain yourself."

"*Me?* That woman is unusually tall and skinny and has *black hair*, Cassius!"

Cassius studied Vallyn, his displeasure morphing into concern. "Are you feeling all right, old friend? How's your magic doing?"

"I'm fine." He scowled. "And this prank isn't funny."

"Not a prank," Cassius said soothingly. "I believe that's what you saw."

Vallyn stared at his friend. "You…think I'm seeing things?"

"Well, one of us is."

"You're telling me you saw a blonde?"

"Yes, and so did everyone who saw her yesterday, as well as the guards *you* put around the garden. She's blonde, like her father and brother. You're the only one seeing something else, Vallyn."

That couldn't be true. For a wild moment, Vallyn considered running back to the pergola to reassure himself that he had seen what he remembered seeing.

"I could sense her magic," Vallyn said. "Perhaps she's using it to disguise herself—"

"You told me you can't see through fae glamours."

"She's not fae, I'm nearly certain. It's not a glamour. She's human, but she has an unusual amount of magical energy."

Cassius's frown deepened. "Can you sense a spell or curse?"

"Well…no. So far as I know, my magic doesn't give me that ability—"

"But it gives you the ability to see through spells?"

Vallyn faltered. "I—I don't know. All I know is I see a different girl than you described. I don't know why or how or what it means. But you can't expect me to trust some woman pretending to be someone else."

With a sigh, Cassius rubbed his temples. "Val… You've been under a lot of stress, much of it self-inflicted—"

"I'm not hallucinating threats! That woman is hiding something."

Cassius watched him with pursed lips. Finally, he sighed. "There are three likely explanations. One, you're right; she's an imposter and only you can see the truth. Two, you're half right, and that is Lady Tatiana, but for some reason she has enchanted her own appearance or been cursed, and while her appearance is a lie, it is not for treacherous purposes, and she is *not* an imposter. Or three, somehow—sleep deprivation, fever, paranoia, or your fae magic misbehaving—"

"But my magic has never deceived *me* before! I'm certainly not ill, and I don't think I'm *that* tired or paranoid, Cas."

"But you could be seeing something that isn't there," Cassius persisted. "If the first option is true, it would be irresponsible for me to be alone with her. But if it's the second or third, I can't alienate her and her father with wild accusations."

Begrudgingly, Vallyn nodded his agreement. What if something *was* wrong with him? What if his magic was playing tricks on him because he so often ignored and suppressed it? Was that possible?

He couldn't outright dismiss the idea. Once, when he was six, he'd conspired with Cassius to steal a pie from the castle kitchen by replacing it with an illusion, but he'd been a hungry child with no control over his magic. He'd conjured a mirage pie four times the size of the original and made the cook faint. The cook had sustained injuries, and Vallyn had been terrified someone would discover his secret. Then when he was eight, he'd made his entire bed invisible in the throes of a nightmare. His mother's scream had awoken him, and she'd shrieked again when his bed reappeared with him on it. As much as his instincts protested otherwise, his magic betraying him wasn't outside the realm of possibility.

"Vallyn." Cassius took a deep breath, and when he met Vallyn's eyes, there was something lurking there that made Vallyn's gut clench.

"Contact him. He knows more about your fae magic than you do. He might know whether what you're seeing is real."

Vallyn was shaking his head before Cassius finished speaking. "I haven't seen him in six years."

"Maybe that's part of the problem."

"I'm not seeing things." Vallyn worked his jaw. Even he heard the uncertainty in his own voice.

Cassius held his gaze without saying anything. His soft frown said that he understood and wouldn't insist, but that he also thought Vallyn was being foolish.

"I'll contact my father." He stared at the white pebbles beneath his boots.

"Good," Cassius said. "For now, apologize. Let's get through tea like civilized people, and you can keep an eye on her." He clasped Vallyn's shoulder. "But try to get more sleep, my friend. And some relaxation. You're concerningly agitated."

"Next you're going to tell me to get a wife," Vallyn muttered.

The side of Cassius's mouth pulled up. "If a woman would help you unwind, that would be marvelous. Do you want to interview some ladies like you did the guards?"

Vallyn rolled his eyes. "All right. I promise to act like every-thing is fine at tea if you promise not to set me up with a stranger."

"Deal."

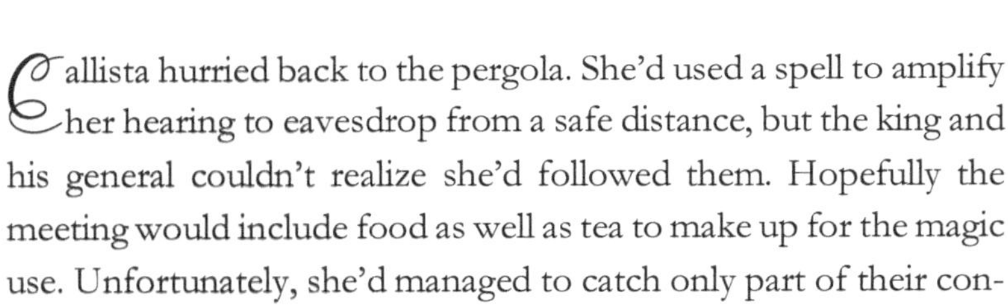

$\mathcal{C}$allista hurried back to the pergola. She'd used a spell to amplify her hearing to eavesdrop from a safe distance, but the king and his general couldn't realize she'd followed them. Hopefully the meeting would include food as well as tea to make up for the magic use. Unfortunately, she'd managed to catch only part of their conversation, and what she'd heard had also turned her stomach.

Somehow, by a cruel twist of fate in a string of bad luck, General Vallyn Drake could see her. The *real* her. It sounded like King Cassius was skeptical, so she was safe from the executioner's block... for now. There was no way that would last if Drake convinced the king of the truth.

And that accounted for half of her worries. *Fae.*

General Vallyn Drake was fae. Or at least he had fae magic, whatever that meant. All she knew was that the Fae Blessing and Curse of Mortimer Faine had been terrible. It had let the Faine kings become complacent and cruel, and the prophecy had required Callista to do horrible things. Then the curse had caused so much death to end the Faine reign. In old stories, fae were far more powerful than any human enchanter, they tended to be vain, and they didn't take kindly to being double-crossed. Some were violent, others were tricksters, and none were to be trusted.

Perhaps Cassius Alimer had more in common with his Faine relatives than she'd hoped. Perhaps Vallyn Drake's fae magic had protected Cassius from the effects of the curse. What had she walked into? She'd never wanted anything to do with fae, and now a man with fae magic had focused his attention on her.

Callista stood near the pergola, steadying her breath and forcing her face into a careful mask of manufactured serenity. For now, she had to get through this meeting with a king and a powerful general who suspected she was a fraud.

How would the real Tatiana handle being falsely accused by a man who was seeing things or lying? She didn't have time to decide, as the two men were nearly to her.

"Lady Tatiana." King Cassius smiled. In the bright sunlight, his crown was almost blinding. "Please forgive us for so rudely leaving you alone." He looked expectantly at his general.

Drake offered her a stiff bow. "I apologize for my rudeness and for offending you, Lady Tatiana." He said the name with a hint of sourness, like he resented being forced to call her by a name he didn't believe belonged to her.

Callista looked from Drake to the king and delicately cleared her throat. "I'd appreciate an explanation, if you don't mind. I didn't come here to be accosted and falsely accused, and…" She made a show of shifting and glancing about. "I'm unsure I'm entirely comfortable with him, erm…glaring at me. Perhaps we could have this tea alone?"

"Why?" Drake snapped, his dark eyes assessing her, then sliding past her to the table. "Idiot," he said beneath his breath and strode past her. "We left her unsupervised with the food."

Her mouth fell open as she spun around to stare at his back. "I'm sorry—are you accusing me of attempting to poison the king? How would that make sense? I eat with the king for the first time, when I haven't even been here a full day, and he falls dead while I'm fine, and I'm going to…what? Blame the kitchen staff? Not only do you think I'm an imposter and an assassin, you think I'm a particularly dull one!"

The general, holding one silver platter lid aloft, went still. Callista mentally chastised her loose tongue. What was she thinking, yelling at the king's trusted general, who already disliked her? Pretending to be a lady must have given her extra courage. Or everything else she'd been through had worn down her patience.

King Cassius laughed uncomfortably. "My sincerest apologies, Lady Tatiana." He swept in front of her and caught her hand, then pressed a soft, quick kiss to her fingers. "I think, perhaps, we should reschedule. My friend is out of sorts, a bit feverish, and possibly hallucinating. I beg your pardon for abandoning you again, but I must take him to the physician."

Stepping away from her, the king motioned to the table. "Feel free to enjoy the refreshments. I'll arrange another meeting, and I swear on my honor it will be better than this one. Is that acceptable?"

He looked mortified and unsure of what to do as he leaned toward Drake, one hand reaching for his friend even as his pleading gaze locked with hers.

"Of course, Your Majesty." Callista curtsied, and relief eased Cassius's expression. "It is forgiven. Please, see to your friend—I do hope he is all right."

"Thank you." Cassius grabbed a fistful of Drake's cloak and dragged him away.

As soon as their rushed footsteps faded, she collapsed onto one of the chairs. She poured herself some tea, then perused the adorable miniature snacks. There were buttery shortbread fingers that melted in her mouth, bite-sized tarts packed with sweet and tangy flavor, crackers topped with creamy cheese, and more. She tried at least one of everything, listening to a bird whistling somewhere as the vibrant red leaves of the vines covering the pergola glowed in the sunlight. For a few blissful minutes as she enjoyed the beautiful garden and delicious food in peace, she forgot about her wretched situation.

But as she walked back to the palace, her thoughts turned gloomy.

The general—the king's confidant and the one person Blaise had warned her about—knew her secret, at least in part. Was it her own fault? After all, she'd been reluctant while casting the curse, a small, deep part of her hoping it wouldn't work.

Blaise couldn't find out. If he learned that her ruse had been discovered already, he might have Royce killed. Not to mention that General Drake's suspicions had ruined her tea with the king. If Blaise realized how badly the courtship was going, he might hurt Royce anyway.

She would just have to convince General Drake to trust her until she found a way to save Royce.

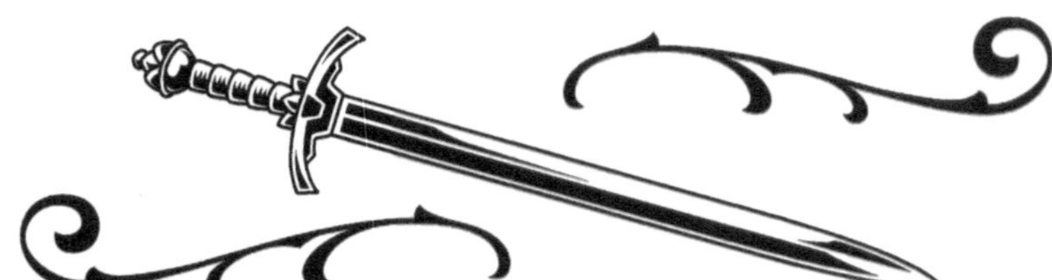

11

Vallyn didn't speak as he let Cassius hurry him inside the palace.

The young woman had been right. Poisoning the food or tea wouldn't have made sense, and she wasn't an idiot. She'd spoken too confidently, and her green eyes were too intelligent for that.

Could he truly be wrong? Was he seeing things? And if he was…what did that mean? His father had warned him once that half fae were rare, and they tended to move to the fae realm, where they became fully fae. What if his half-fae status or how often he buried his fae side was making his magic unstable? Could he be casting a subconscious illusion? Or perhaps it was an odd way his magic was reacting to the magic he'd sensed in the young woman?

As much as it galled Vallyn, he did need to talk to his father. Arolyin would have answers.

And he clearly needed sleep, as accusing the woman of being a poisoner had been stupid. If she was Lady Tatiana, she might never forgive such an offense. If she was a fraud, he had ruined any chance of catching her off guard.

Once inside the palace, Cassius stopped and released his firm grip. "I don't know what to do, Val. Do I order you to my office to harangue you? Do I take you straight to Wilmina to see if she can discover what's ailing you? Should I order you to go to your room, sleep, and contact your father?" He rubbed his forehead, bumping his crown. "I've always trusted you. More than I trust anyone. But—"

"I know!" Vallyn hung his head. "I didn't think it through."

"I'm beginning to wonder if overseeing palace security isn't the right fit for you."

Vallyn jerked his head up, a stab going through his heart as surely as if Cassius had slid a knife between his ribs. "What?" His voice came out strained and hoarse. "You don't mean that. Surely you can't mean that."

"What am I supposed to think? You're stressed, I suspect you're barely sleeping, I overheard servants gossiping about you snapping at the guards and being on edge, you're threatening my guests—"

"I barely threatened Blaise—"

"—and now you've accused my potential bride of being an assassin!"

"Even if I'm seeing things, she's still hiding that she's an enchantress!"

Cassius straightened his crown. "I want to believe you. I do. But when I arrived today, you were holding a strand of her hair and crowding her—would have been leaning over her if she were slightly shorter. Hardly how you'd treat a random man that had wandered in and whom you suspected of being a secret enchanter."

Leaning over and *slightly shorter* distracted Vallyn. The woman he'd seen had been *taller* than him by a good three to four inches. How did that even work? But then his mind caught up to the rest of what Cassius had said.

"Wait. You don't seriously think I fabricated this entire thing to cover up that I was flirting with your potential bride…do you?"

Cassius hesitated, and then his shoulders fell. "No, you're right. That's as ridiculous as thinking she poisoned the food. I'm growing too accustomed to the lords' games and everyone having a hidden motive."

"Clearly, if you're faster to accuse *me* of having a hidden motive than you are to suspect Tatiana, a complete stranger!" Vallyn drew in a deep breath through his nose. "Although I suppose I'm also so used to suspecting everyone that I went too far in accusing her. Still, *I* would never suspect *you*."

Cassius flushed. "I'm sorry. But you know it's not that I don't trust *you*, right?"

"You mean you don't trust my fae side."

"Vallyn, *you* don't even trust your fae side."

They stared at each other until Vallyn's shoulders crumpled. "Maybe you're right and I just need to sleep." He rubbed his palm against the leather-wrapped pommel of his sword. "Still, I can't in good conscience ignore this. Can I at least assign a guard to her?"

Cassius's expression hardened. "No."

"We can tell her it's for her own protection—"

"If we were going to assign her a guard for her own protection, we would have done so yesterday. After your display just now, a guard would be insulting. She might be so offended she leaves. I would be without a prospective bride and be humiliated in front of the court. I'm not risking driving her away over circumstantial evidence. I'm sorry, Vallyn. No guard unless she requests one herself."

Vallyn ground his teeth as he felt the command become a magical compulsion. As if he needed reasons to remember why he didn't trust his fae magic. Still, Cassius had a point. Vallyn had grossly mishandled this. He'd either revealed his knowledge to an imposter too soon or alienated Cassius's future wife.

Well done, Vallyn.

He inclined his head. "As you command, Your Majesty."

"Oh, stop with the 'Your Majesty.'" Cassius groaned. "Both of us could have handled that better. How about you visit Wilmina now? She'll have something to help you sleep, and—"

Now it was Vallyn's turn to groan. "Don't tell me to talk to her again." Wilmina had been the physician at Alimer Castle ever since Vallyn could remember. When Cassius asked her to move to the palace, she'd informed her new king he couldn't convince her to stop working for him if he tried.

Cassius held up his hands. "I'm just saying, she lives up to that proverb about gray hair and wisdom. And if she can keep a king's secrets, she can surely keep yours."

Vallyn was unconvinced Cas had any secrets, but it was true he'd never known the old physician to be anything less than trustworthy. That didn't mean he loved the idea of telling an acquaintance his deepest fears.

"Let me know when you hear from Arolyin," Cassius added. "Actually, if he comes, perhaps we can arrange for him to see Lady Tatiana."

"A good idea. And…I'll talk to Wilmina," Vallyn added grudgingly.

"Good." Cassius clapped his shoulder. "And maybe take a nap. If you're going to be in charge of Highrook's security, you need to take care of yourself, or Miraveld knows how you'll be able to take care of anyone else."

A fair argument, although Vallyn didn't want to admit that. "And you? Going to take care of yourself?"

"I'm going to order myself a hot bath and attempt to soak away the knots in my shoulders. Maybe you should try that."

"I might." Vallyn bowed his head. "Thank you, Cas. And I apologize for my behavior and for causing you more problems."

"Forgiven. Now get going." He nodded down the hall. "Physician."

"I'm going; I'm going." Vallyn rolled his eyes, drawing a snort from his king.

On his way to the healing room, Vallyn asked a servant to send someone to prepare a hot bath for him in his chamber. When he knocked on the physician's door, a voice immediately called for him to enter.

The smell of dried herbs made his nose twitch. Sunlight and fresh air filtered in through a window with open panes. The healing room was the size of an entire suite, although one side was full of empty cots. The other side, where Vallyn stood, held several tables with an assortment of jars, herbs, and healing instruments strewn over all but one, and a couple of chairs. Wilmina, a woman with wide hips and gray hair pulled back in a bun, swatted a fly with a rolled-up piece of leather, then turned to him.

"Ah, General Drake." She curtsied, although not low—probably more due to age than lack of decorum. Her narrowed eyes assessed every inch of him as her head tilted. "Stress and sleeplessness?"

He flinched. "Erm…"

"You're clearly uninjured, and rather than having a sense of urgency, as you do when someone else is injured, you seem like you don't want to be here." She flapped a hand at him. "You don't look flushed, sweaty, shaky, or otherwise ill, which leaves an ailment of the mind, and the dark circles under your red eyes suggest you aren't sleeping, at least not well."

With that pronouncement, Wilmina bustled over to one of the tables shoved against a wood-paneled wall. "Valerian should help." She pulled out a mortar and pestle and some dried root. "Now. While I grind this, take a seat, and tell me what troubles you."

Shock robbed Vallyn of any answer. He'd never cared about rank and station, and Wilmina had always been friendly, but he was a lord and a general now. He'd never confided in her before. Why in Aedyllan would she expect him to suddenly divulge his secrets?

"I'll wait here…" Her disapproving glare silenced him.

"You." She pointed the pestle at him, then at one of the chairs. "Sit."

Vallyn sat. "I don't know what Cas—His Majesty told you, but I don't need to talk."

"His Majesty?" Wilmina paused to glance at him. "He hasn't said anything. I can see just by looking at you that you need to talk, even if you don't realize it. Now. What is it that keeps you awake, young man? I promise it will not leave this room, nor will I judge you for whatever it may be. But sometimes, the best way to cut loose an invisible burden is to talk about it."

That seemed unlikely. He more often worked through stress with long training sessions. Granted, although those training sessions had made him a skilled knight, they hadn't solved the problems. Sometimes it put them into better perspective, but fixed? No.

Sighing, Vallyn leaned back while the physician returned to her grinding. He would stick to obvious facts that weren't personal, just to appease her and Cas.

"I'm in charge of Highrook's security, and although I was captain of the guard at Alimer Castle…this is different. I don't know whose smiles are fake, who is angry or desperate enough to attempt harm, and I don't know all of these guards and servants like I knew everyone at Alimer Castle. Keeping a king alive and safe is complicated, and he keeps inviting foxes into the henhouse! But he doesn't *see*; he doesn't understand all the dangers."

Wilmina nodded, still grinding the root.

"I'm not criticizing him, exactly," Vallyn hurried to add. "Cassius has always been gracious, and I respect and admire that, but what if it gets him killed, and I'm not good enough to stop it? The stakes are so much higher, and I'm not perfect. I've already made mistakes today—not ones that endangered Cassius, but ones that made his life harder and made him question my capability. What if he's right that I'm not a good fit for this position? I could make other mistakes, not be perceptive enough or fast enough, and my best friend could die. The entire kingdom could suffer because he trusted me."

Abruptly realizing how much more he'd said than he'd meant to, he clamped his mouth shut.

Wilmina turned so she could look at him while continuing the rhythmic motion of the pestle. "That is a lot of pressure. You take your duties seriously and care deeply about your friend. That is admirable. Is there something you could be doing that you are not?"

Vallyn hesitated. "I feel like there is something, but I don't know what."

"Do you have lots of time you are squandering?" She gave him a pointed look. "*Squandering.* Rest and some recreation are important and do not count."

If anything, he wasn't resting enough, but he had a feeling telling her that would earn him a scolding. "I suppose not."

"Is there an aspect of your duty you have neglected? A course of action you know you should take that you have been avoiding?"

"Well, no."

"Do you have a gift for prophecy, that you could know things before they occur?"

That drew a short laugh from him. "No." His magical abilities did not extend that far.

She nodded. "Then what more could you do, General Drake? You have done all you can, and that is all that is required of you. You are correct: you are not perfect. No one is, but that admittedly can be a difficult goal to stop aiming for. Still, if that is your goal, you will never be satisfied with yourself, and you will always carry guilt that you should have done more, even if it was impossible. You need to trust yourself—and more importantly, trust others."

"I do trust others," he protested, but a voice whispered he was lying even as he said it. "Mostly."

"You said you feared not being wise enough or fast enough." Wilmina's steady gaze held his as she paused in her grinding. "Do you think that protecting the king falls to you alone?"

"I suppose I do. We have—" He stopped himself, shocked he'd almost divulged his greatest secret. "I made a promise to protect and serve Cassius that I intend to keep."

She nodded thoughtfully. "Does this promise require you to do everything yourself? Does it, for example, preclude you from trusting the guards?"

"Well…no—"

"Sometimes, we have to release the things we cannot control." Wilmina held up the mortar full of powder. "I can give this to you. I can tell you how to best use it. I cannot force you to listen. I can't even force it to work. It should help your muscles relax and help you sleep, but it can affect different people to different degrees. If it does not help as much as hoped, was it because I was lax in my duties? Because I did not try hard enough to help you?"

Vallyn squirmed, as much as he could allow himself to as a

full-grown man and general. "For you, no, but for me—"

"Oh, please. Don't use a harsher standard on yourself than you do on others. Not only will it make you miserable, but eventually you'll hate yourself so much you'll resent everyone else for not suffering under the same burden of impossible expectations. You'll start using that standard on others even if you don't mean to. One day you'll look at yourself and realize you don't remember when you became cruel."

Her words arrested his tongue, leaving him stunned.

Wilmina transferred the powder into a leather pouch. "Next time you are drowning in your own unrealistic expectations, take a few deep breaths. Think of what you'd tell your friend if he told you he felt the way you do. If the king told you he fears failure and that he'll never be good enough, how might you respond? Perhaps you won't be able to extend that same compassion toward yourself right away, but over time, you might."

She offered the pouch to him, and he took it silently, her advice echoing in his mind.

"Stir a teaspoon into warm tea until the powder is dissolved and drink it before bed. Honey in the tea can aid sleep as well. If you can get some tea with lavender or chamomile or both, I'd recommend that."

Not Vallyn's favorite, but he'd attempt it if it had a chance of helping.

"Do *not* use liquor. You may fall asleep, but it will not grant you a restorative sleep, and you are likely to wake during the night. If your mind is racing and you cannot sleep, take calming breaths. A slow, deep breath in, and a long, steady breath out, repeated several times, while you focus on your breath instead of your thoughts. And find something that brings you joy instead of stress. No one can work all the time." Wilmina smiled in an almost doting way. "You will be all right, young man."

"Thank you." He stood, and beside her squat frame, he almost felt tall. Such a small package to hold so much wisdom and candor. "For the valerian, and for listening and the advice."

Wilmina nodded. "Of course. It's both my vocation and my joy. What are you going to do now?"

"Now? Take a bath."

She chuckled. "Excellent. Oh!" She spun away and seized a bundle of small, dried purple flowers on long green stems. "Put the lavender in your bath water. It should help you relax."

"Thank you."

"You're very welcome." She patted her apron. "I have tinctures to finish. Come by any time if you need anything, even just to talk, General Drake."

He inclined his head, but Wilmina was already rushing off, so he left quietly.

As Vallyn made his way to his room, he passed guards standing at their posts or making their rounds. As ever, they stiffened when they saw him approaching, but this time, he noticed other things. The way they saw him coming long before he reached them. The way their gazes swept their surroundings, even as they straightened their posture and squared their shoulders. The way they met his gaze and returned his small nod.

He'd been thorough in interviewing the guards and researching their backgrounds, and in observing and aiding their ongoing training. He'd meticulously planned the guards' posts and patrol routes.

Even though part of him insisted he needed to be available at a moment's notice, he did trust them. If someone hurt Cassius, it would not be for lack of preparedness or vigilance. That brought him some comfort, even though a niggling at the back of his mind whispered it wasn't enough.

When he reached his room, servants were on their way out. One bowed and informed him his bath was ready, with a small cauldron of water over the fire so he could further heat the water as it cooled. Vallyn thanked the man and slipped inside, locking the door behind himself.

The hot water soothed his taut muscles, and the scent of the lavender eased more of his tension. Vallyn took slow breaths the way Wilmina had instructed him. To his surprise, it helped. His thoughts stopped racing, and more tension eased out of his back and shoulders.

After his bath, he dug a dark-red gemstone the size of a robin's egg out of his dresser. Arolyin had given him the enchanted stone when he was young. His father kept a matching one carved from the same rock. The last and only time Vallyn had used it was the accidental binding fiasco. Hopefully Arolyin wouldn't panic.

After a moment's hesitation, he sent a pulse of silvery magic into the cool surface of the stone. In response, the stone glowed red. Somewhere in the fae realm its twin would also glow.

It might take days for his father to travel between realms. Would the stone reveal Vallyn's location? If Arolyin went to Alimer Castle instead of Highrook that would further delay his arrival. No point in sitting around.

Perhaps he should check on things in the palace or go to the training yard…no. No work. He could walk in the gardens. That was a leisure activity, right? Maybe he'd take a little detour by the kitchen to get a snack first…and pass by the northeast wing where Shafer was staying on the way. Totally coincidentally, of course.

12

Callista was lost.

When she'd left the gardens, she'd considered asking a guard for directions, but the route Serena had taken when she led Callista to the gardens this morning hadn't seemed that complicated. Besides, the guards all looked so stone-faced and serious. After seeing how intimidating General Drake could be, she didn't blame them for looking so stern.

Furthermore, even though Cassius had changed the royal colors to the Alimer blue and gold from Faine black and silver, every time she looked at a palace guard, she thought of Royce and Jacob and her father. Once, any of those guards might have been her father or brother.

Then King Silas Faine had wrongfully seized a man's lands and home, and in retaliation, the man had burned down the inn where the king was staying. Silas Faine had escaped the inferno, protected by the fae Blessing. Her father and Jacob hadn't. The king hadn't cared, so Callista had enacted the prophecy to end the Blessing, and Silas Faine had died.

The thought of talking to any of the guards brought a lump to her throat, so she didn't.

But although Callista had picked the entrance that she thought was correct, had gone up the same stairs she was certain she remembered coming down, and had taken a hallway that looked familiar, after at least twenty minutes of walking and turning in to identical halls, there was no denying it. She had to be in the wrong wing entirely, or she would have found her suite by now.

As none of the guards had stopped her, she hadn't wandered into an area she wasn't allowed to be in. She could just imagine trying to explain that to General Drake after he already suspected her. The problem was, she'd gotten so turned around she didn't know which direction she was walking anymore. There was nothing for it but to go back to the last guard she'd passed and ask for help, no matter how awkward it would be or how badly it would make her heart ache.

Trudging back the way she'd come, she found a guardsman with a coarse gray beard and thickly corded neck. He eyed her as she approached, but then his hard expression eased into a smile.

"You're lost, aren't you, my lady?"

She breathed a relieved chuckle. "That obvious?"

"Seemed a bit early for you to be heading to lunch, but there's nothing wrong with that. But then you came back so quickly, and lookin' rather like a child who didn't want to tell her mam she broke something."

Callista raised her eyebrows. "I looked that embarrassed?"

The guard shrugged one shoulder, the straps of his pauldron giving a soft groan. "I've ten grandchildren and an experienced eye. Where are you meant to be, then, my lady?"

She cleared her throat. "My quarters are in the southwest wing, I believe?"

The guard's eyes widened. "Oh! Lady Ackroyd! You've got the wrong floor entirely, I'm afraid. Happens easily if you enter from the gardens. It's the mountain, see, makes everything uneven. Some entrances from the gardens are a floor higher than others. You didn't go up enough floors—and begging your pardon, my lady, but you were headin' the wrong direction. You'll want to go back that way down this hallway, make a left, take the stairs at the end of that hall up one floor, then take a right. Follow that hall to the end and take a right. You'll pass three turns to other halls. Take the fourth hall to your right, and your quarters should be down that hallway. Begging your pardon, my lady, but I'm afraid I can't wander so far from my post except for an emergency, otherwise I'd escort you myself."

"That's all right. I understand entirely." She barely stopped herself from blabbing that her father and brothers had been guardsmen, but thankfully her mind caught up to her tongue. "Thank you for your aid, Sir…?"

"Oh, no title. Just Titus Wright, my lady." He bowed. "My pleasure. Good luck with the maze that's Highrook Palace."

Callista laughed. "Thank you, Titus." She would praise the guardsman to the king if she got the opportunity.

She went back down the hall, took a left, and found wide, carpet-lined stairs that led up on her right and down on her left. As she started up the stairs, voices echoed down, bouncing off the painting-adorned walls. A woman said something, and someone snickered.

"Oh, I strongly disagree," a familiar, smug male voice said. "Making Ackroyd's daughter queen would be ridiculously foolish. It's shortsighted, and she's hardly fit for the court."

Callista internally cursed. She didn't want to see Blaise anyway, but given Blaise and his companion's topic of conversation, an encounter would be particularly uncomfortable. She fled back down the stairs, hesitating briefly before racing down another level. For good measure, she descended another flight and found that the stairs ended there, so she took off at a brisk pace down the corridor.

This hallway was austere. The floor was uncovered stone, as were the walls, lacking the wood paneling elsewhere in the palace. Plain candlesticks shoved into iron rings cast flickering circles of weak light across the hall. Unornamented doors were set into the walls, and narrow, shadowy corridors branched off. A faint clatter echoed from an open door further down the hall, accompanied by loud voices. Relieved, Callista slowed. It was implausible that Blaise would descend to a servants' floor. She could stall down here for a few minutes.

A shriek came from down the corridor, followed by a loud clang.

"What is that?" a woman screamed.

"Where did it go?" another female voice demanded. "I'll wring its neck!"

A small form burst from the open door and into the hall, flee-ing the orange glow of firelight in the room. The dark blob raced at a surprising pace away from the incoherent shouting. It took a moment for Callista to identify it: a wet lesser gryphon fledgling. The creature held its dripping wings awkwardly out to its sides, and its taloned front feet and feline back paws scrabbled over the stone floor. Focused on escape, it made directly toward Callista. She bent down to catch it. There was no way she was letting that woman hurt the poor thing. Unfortunately, the fledgling skidded to a stop out of her reach and turned around.

"Oh no you don't," she murmured and stretched out her hand. With an enchantment composed of powerful, harmonizing chords, a shimmering barrier of purple blocked the hall. The crit-ter scrambled to turn away from the sudden obstruction, and Callista let the magic fall and darted forward. She grasped the middle of the drenched fledgling, gently pinning its wings to its sides.

"Gotcha."

It was so tiny and fragile, its ribs sticking out against its dark, slicked-down fur. She scooped the fledgling into her arms and cradled it against her chest as she stood. It wiggled, its talons and claws catching on her dress, and nipped at her fingers with its pale beak.

"Shhh, you're safe." Callista adjusted her hold to minimize the creature's movement. "There, there." She stroked her thumb down the white feathers at the back of its wet head, beneath its furry cat ears.

A red-faced woman ran into the hall, her head snapping back and forth. "Where'd that little—" She cut off with a startled gasp, and then her eyes narrowed at the tiny gryphon in Callista's arms. Her mouth opened and closed.

"Thank you for finding my pet." Callista smiled serenely. "I'm terribly sorry if the little dear caused you any trouble. He likes to run off." Or she. Whichever the fledgling was.

"Yours?" the woman stammered. "You're keeping that vermin as a *pet*?" A couple more women stuck their heads out the door, peering at her with confusion.

Callista worked to keep her pleasant expression in place. "Oh, please don't call him that. If he's caused any damage, I'll repay you. I'm Lady Ackroyd. Please accept my apologies."

Somehow, the first woman's face took on an even deeper shade of red. "Your ladyship! No, no problem! My apologies." She curtsied roughly, then bustled back into the room, the other servants rushing out of her way.

The lesser gryphon fledgling stopped struggling. While Callista continued to stroke her thumb down its feathers, it peered up at her and gave a little *keek-keek.*

"Yes, you're going to be all right." Callista eased her hold, and this time, the fledgling didn't try to escape. Instead, it tucked its head against her chest, pressing in close as it shivered. "Oh, you poor thing."

She headed back, her focus on the creature soaking her sleeves. "Let's get you dry and warmed up, little one. And figure out whether you're a he or a she. Either way, don't worry. I'll keep you safe from the mean ladies."

She looked up from the gryphon, a little spring in her step as she approached the stairs. Her own pet! Not a cat, but close enough. Then all of her levity fell away, and she froze in place.

A man lurked at the edge of the steps, tucked against the wall in the shadows. She gulped and took a step back as the man pushed off the wall, the sword at his hip swaying.

Vallyn Drake stepped into a pool of candlelight, his expression unreadable.

Callista clutched the fledgling closer as if it offered some comfort. Had Drake seen her cast that spell? Was it foolish to hope he'd come down afterward or hadn't noticed? She forced her shoulders straight, refusing to act guilty.

"I can't imagine you have the gift of foresight and thus came down here specifically to rescue a hapless baby lesser gryphon"—the general's lips twitched, almost as if he wanted to smile—"so what, pray tell, were you doing down here, Lady Tatiana?"

Callista scratched the soft feathers beneath the fledgling's beak as she said, "I got lost. A guard…"

She jerked her head up, realizing this was her opportunity. Drake was in charge of the guards.

"One of your guardsmen was most kind. He explained where I'd gone wrong and gave me directions. He was also apologetic that he couldn't escort me himself because he needed to stay at his assigned post. His name was Titus Wright. He does his duty admirably and comports himself well, General."

Drake's eyebrows furrowed above his narrow eyes. "Oh... good. I'm pleased to hear it. Although, if he gave such competent directions, once again: Why are you here?"

Her gaze drifted down again. "I wished to avoid someone."

He watched her, clearly waiting for her to elaborate.

"I was going up the stairs but overheard someone coming down discussing me. I decided I'd rather not join that conversation."

"Not complimentary, I take it?"

As if he cared. He already hated her. She just shook her head.

Drake's heavy sigh sounded almost sympathetic. "The court can be a cruel place, my lady. At least I understand now why you were racing down the stairs like something was on your heels."

Callista peered at him. Had he also borne the court's derision, or was he mocking her for not having the spine to face her opponents? Based on his scowl, perhaps it was both.

"You don't know who it was?" he asked. "I like to keep a close eye on anyone openly criticizing His Majesty."

She didn't know if the real Tatiana would recognize Blaise's voice, so it seemed safer to pretend she didn't know. "It was a woman and a man, but I didn't stay around to learn more."

"I can't blame you." Perhaps not judging her, then. Drake shifted from foot to foot before squaring his shoulders, looking very much like a guardsman himself.

It was a shame he was her enemy and a fae. His deep-set eyes were a dark, rich brown, and his defined cheekbones were striking. Even with a cloak partly hiding his physique, he was clearly strong. His tousled dark hair provided an odd counterpoint to his otherwise stiff demeanor. He wore all black, and he looked good doing it. The stories that said fae were beautiful didn't lie.

"I owe you an apology," Drake said suddenly. "For earlier this morning. I was delirious from lack of sleep and…" He worked his jaw, his eyes darting over her. "I saw things that weren't there."

Callista had the distinct feeling he was lying through his teeth and still saw her, not Lady Tatiana. "You've slept since this morning and are miraculously cured of making baseless accusations, then?"

Drake's throat bobbed. "I've caused you grave offense." He bowed, surprisingly deeply. "Please forgive me, Lady Tatiana. At the least, do not blame King Cassius. He's a good man, who was most displeased with me for ruining this morning's tea. Please give him a second chance?"

The look he gave her was beseeching, almost desperate, betraying a surprising amount of naked emotion compared to the cold-faced man who had approached her with such menace in the gardens. If Highrook's guards took their duty to defend the king half as seriously as their general did, Cassius was well guarded indeed. No wonder Blaise Shafer thought it would take betrayal by the queen to kill the king.

"His Majesty has been kind to me," Callista said carefully. "I will withhold my judgment of him until we have had more time to get to know each other."

Drake nodded, clearly relieved. "May I escort you to your quarters, Lady Tatiana? I mean you no harm," he added, so her distress must have shown on her face despite how she'd tried to hide it. "I know how to get to your rooms. I can also guarantee you protection from any members of the court who may be displeased with your presence."

Callista recalled the king's admission that her placement in a solitary wing away from the rest of the court had been the general's suggestion. "You believe I'm in that much danger?"

"Physically, no. But members of the nobility often wield sharp words with greater skill than they do any weapon."

The way he said that, how he understood her impulse to run rather than face the nobles gossiping about her…

"Are you not a noble?" Would Tatiana have already known that? Oh well, no taking back the question now.

Drake stiffened and straightened his sword belt. "I was knighted and now have a lordship, but my parents held no titles."

The fledgling squirmed in Callista's arms, and she struggled to keep it from leaping away.

"Are you going to keep it?"

"Of course." Callista bristled. "I'm not going to cast it aside now that I've claimed it. No one deserves that." She whispered to the animal, "Don't worry. I'm your family now, little one."

Something softened in Drake's expression. "I'm glad to hear it. Will you trust me to escort you to your suite, my lady?"

"Are you offering because you don't trust me to wander through the castle alone?"

He reddened. "I was trying to be polite."

Callista would rather avoid Drake, but she could see no way of saying so that wouldn't further arouse the general's suspicions. "All right. Thank you, General Drake."

13

$\mathcal{L}$ady Tatiana was becoming a greater mystery by the moment. Vallyn kept sneaking glances at her as they walked up the stairs and turned down a hallway. He respected that she was astute enough not to have taken his offer to escort her at face value. Even more, he respected her courage in having called him out for his behavior. She'd shown some cowardice in fleeing the other nobles, but she was new to the court. Besides, he did his own share of hiding, usually in more subtle ways than running down stairwells. Her rescue of the fledgling and her declaration that she wouldn't abandon the creature were the actions of a caring soul.

What unsettled Vallyn was the barrier of purple magic Tatiana had cast across the hallway. She had magic and she knew how to wield it. The barrier had caused the gryphon to change course, which meant the magic truly existed; he couldn't have hallucinated it. Yet he'd never heard that Lady Tatiana was an enchantress, and she hadn't mentioned it.

True, Vallyn kept his own magic secret, but that was different. Human enchanters were uncommon, but not feared or hated.

And, of course, Tatiana was still dark-haired, unusually tall, and thin with a sharp beauty. Something was wrong with her appearance or his perception, and both possibilities unsettled him.

They left the stairwell and passed a stationed guard, and he made eye contact with the guardsman and nodded. The man slightly inclined his head, a silent declaration that all was well. But then a thought occurred to Vallyn.

"Just a moment, Lady Tatiana."

He approached the guard. The man tried to stand even taller, sticking out his chest in a ridiculous manner. A brief conversation confirmed his nagging suspicion. Blaise Shafer had recently descended those stairs—accompanied by Lord and Lady Holbrook, which was unsettling. He'd thought Lord Holbrook was loyal to Cassius. Vallyn thanked the guard and returned to Tatiana's side.

They continued in silence, Vallyn stewing over Blaise's actions. He nodded at another guard, then snuck a glance at Tatiana.

She had asked a guardsman for his name and specifically commended him. Most nobility viewed the guards as if they were décor unless there was need of their swords. Either she was humble and thoughtful, or she was an imposter and the guard was part of her scheme. Perhaps she wanted Master Wright to be given more responsibilities so he could help her more.

The idea that one of his carefully selected guardsmen might be false prickled along his arms. He had so recently told Wilmina that he trusted the guards. Perhaps that was his answer. He couldn't let his paranoia and confusion affect his command.

He needed to stop overthinking. Besides, walking in sullen silence probably wasn't helping Lady Tatiana's impression of him. He searched for an appropriate topic of conversation and snagged on the sleeping critter in her arms.

"Have you had a pet before?"

"No." Tatiana cast a gentle smile down at the gryphon. Damp fur and feathers stuck against its sides. "I wanted a cat when I was little, but we never got one."

"What will you name it?"

She stroked her forefinger between the gryphon's rounded, furry ears. "I don't know. Perhaps I will try names until one fits. Naming a living thing seems like it should be thoughtful, you know?"

"Cassius would agree with you. We found an orange tabby kitten when we were boys and had quite the argument over naming it." He smiled at the memory. "I wanted to call him Blade for his sharp teeth and claws. Cassius thought that was terrible and declared you shouldn't name a cat after a weapon."

"What did you end up calling him?"

"Whiskers," he said with a melodramatic sigh. "Terribly unimaginative."

Tatiana chuckled, and he realized it was the first time he'd heard her laugh. "I'm torn between agreeing with you that Whiskers is boring and agreeing with His Majesty that Blade is an awfully violent name for a poor, fluffy cat."

Vallyn's mouth twitched. "You've clearly never witnessed a cat with his mouth full of bloody feathers."

"Ugh, speaking of which, what do gryphons eat? I am *not* feeding it live birds and mice." She groaned. "And how do you housetrain a lesser gryphon?"

They fell into discussing ideas for the feeding, care, and training of feral gryphon fledglings. Vallyn thought it couldn't be much different from a cat or bird, as it was kind of both. He found himself volunteering to have someone bring her a tray of fine gravel for housetraining.

"Your maid can clean and change out the gravel as needed—"

"Oh, no." Tatiana shook her head. "I took responsibility for the gryphon, so that means all of it should be my responsibility."

He almost tripped over his own boots as he stared up at her. Thankfully her focus was on the fledgling. Sure, Lord Ackroyd was a lesser noble and had some unusual ideas about leveling the differences between different ranks of nobility, but he employed a full retinue of servants. Such an odious task wasn't something most people would happily commit to if they had an alternative. Even Vallyn would rather let a servant deal with such a task.

Once again, he was faced with a thread that could easily weave into two opposing tapestries. Either Lady Tatiana was a compassionate and humble individual, or she was someone else. Perhaps she wasn't a noble at all, which would explain why she wasn't bothered by menial labor. Perhaps that was also why she had thought to praise a common-born guardsman.

Although, if she was a peasant who had stolen Lady Tatiana's appearance, at least she wasn't abusing her newfound status. He'd witnessed people elevated to a higher position or granted more wealth become haughty more than once.

"Well." Tatiana's voice pulled him from his thoughts. "Here we are." She drew to a stop and motioned with her elbow to a door painted with a phoenix. "Thank you for helping me find my way back, General Drake."

"Why did you commend Titus Wright?" The question burst out of him.

Tatiana's eyebrows knit. "Because he helped me and you're his commanding officer?"

"But why do you care?"

Her shoulders set into a rigid line. "Guards are so often taken for granted, and their lives are in danger every time they report for duty. Even if there's no trouble, it's exhausting work. Standing still but keeping their minds focused, watching for any sign of trouble, remembering who went where and when, knowing if they slip, other people might be hurt. They train hard so they'll be ready if a fight comes. And yet, the court overlooks them. It's demoralizing knowing those they swore to protect don't spare them a moment's thought."

Tatiana ducked her head. "Or, er…I imagine it would be. A little appreciation, even for small efforts, goes a long way to help anyone's motivation and sense of pride in their work."

Vallyn nodded slowly. She sounded more sincere than many members of the court, but that didn't mean she was a good person.

"How would you have me reward him, then?"

A muscle ticked near her temple. "Are you mocking me?"

"No?" What had he done wrong now?

"I said he deserved thanks. I'm not an idiot child who thinks a guard deserves a medal for smiling and answering a question. I thought it would mean more coming from his general." Scarlet crept into her cheeks. She turned sharply and reached for the doorknob. "Never mind. I thought you were different."

Different? Vallyn caught her arm. "What—"

"Let go!" Tatiana yanked her arm from his grasp. The lesser gryphon fledgling stirred, and she made soothing shushing noises at it.

Vallyn held up his hands in a placating gesture. "Forgive me, my lady. I shouldn't have grabbed you." Internally, he cursed himself for yet another mistake. "What did you mean, 'different'?"

Her mouth puckered, and she inched back a step. The moment stretched on, and Vallyn worried she wouldn't answer him. All she'd have to do was enter her room, and propriety would demand he leave without learning what she'd meant.

At last, the fight drained out of her. "You spoke to that guard with respect, not brusque command. You made eye contact with every guardsman we passed. Not in a threatening way, but more like an acknowledgment that they're doing their duty. They straighten when you're coming because you motivate them to excellence."

Vallyn couldn't help a snort. "They fear my reputation from the war and the training fields. That's all." He wished she were right, that there was more respect and loyalty than fear. It seemed unlikely.

Her eyes searched his. "If it were all fear, I'd see more resentment and less pride on their faces." She lifted a shoulder. "If you want to motivate through fear, that's your choice. That's how the Faines did it, but I hoped for better from our new king and his general. You have more power over the guards' loyalty and thus the king's safety than you might realize."

Tatiana bobbed a curtsy and turned toward her door as if her words hadn't just slapped him in the face. It was as if she knew Wilmina had told him to trust his men, and so she'd told him a secret that would help ensure his men trusted him in return.

Someone who was plotting against the king certainly wouldn't be so worried about the palace guards and their loyalty.

"Lady Tatiana?"

She paused halfway through her door.

"Thank you. I value the guards, but I'll make sure they know that."

Her smile seemed more pleased than his words warranted, and it made him oddly jumpy. He nodded to the fledgling.

"Best of luck training your new—ahem, sorry, your *already owned* pet." Vallyn winked, and Tatiana laughed. A small, brief laugh, but it was honest and made her eyes crinkle in an endearing way. "Um, until next time, then, Lady Tatiana."

He bowed and hurried away.

What was wrong with him? Endearing? In the best-case

scenario, Tatiana was courting his best friend! And in the worst, she was a fraud with sinister motives. There was a good chance he would either watch her marry Cassius or oversee her execution.

He'd hope for the former. Although it seemed Cassius's conversation skills might need some work. Twenty minutes of showing her around Highrook Palace, and all Cas could say about her was that she was affable? Ten minutes in her presence, and despite her secrets Vallyn found her compelling and was tempted to like her.

Like her as a friend, of course. If she did marry Cassius, she'd practically be his sister-in-law, and he should like his sister-in-law. But liking some enchantress assassin would be decidedly *not* good.

He'd just have to hope she was as genuinely kindhearted as she appeared.

14

Callista closed her door and leaned back against it, letting out a breath. That had been too close.

General Drake had been suspiciously nice. Probably a plot to trick her into complacency so he could discover her secrets, and the worst part was, it had nearly worked. For a few minutes, she'd forgotten he would more likely kill her than smile at her if he knew the truth. A shame, because he had such a nice smile…

She pushed away from the door, absently scratching the back of her pet's neck. Such thoughts were not only ridiculous but dangerous.

A door creaked, and Serena emerged from her small room. Callista quickly hid her surprise. Getting used to having a lady's maid would take time.

"How did…" The older woman's smile faded to confusion. "Is that a lesser gryphon fledgling? My lady," she added with a quick curtsy.

"It is." Callista lifted the creature, and it chirruped and swung its legs. "I saved him—or her—from an angry laundress. Which makes the little fluffball my responsibility…" She winced. "If you don't mind? Do animals or lesser gryphons specifically bother you?"

"Not at all. Actually, my father was a kennel master, and my brother was obsessed with falcons for a while, so I grew up taking care of animals." Serena strode over and reached out. "May I?"

With a nod, Callista handed over the fledgling. It nipped at Serena's fingers, but she made a soft *tch* noise, and the fledgling pulled its head back to stare at the maid. She maneuvered the gryphon onto its back in her arms and pushed its tail and limbs out of the way.

"Female," she said confidently. "Have you owned a lesser gryphon before?"

Callista's face heated. "No. I'm afraid I don't know much about their care, but I'm a quick learner, and I'll do my best to ensure she isn't a burden for you."

Serena laughed. "Oh, don't worry yourself about that, my lady. If anything, I'll appreciate having something else to do. Being a lady's maid keeps me less busy than being a chambermaid, and I get restless easily. First, we should set up a box with sand or gravel and train her to relieve herself—"

"Oh, yes! General Drake said he'd ask someone to send some gravel in a box for that."

Serena's eyes widened. "That's…very kind of him."

"You seem surprised."

"Well—he's intimidating. The stories of him from the fight for the throne sound like legends about heroes of old. The guards swear up and down that he can disarm any of them in the space of three breaths, and he's always striding about the palace with his sword and a forbidding look on his face."

Interesting. The way Serena talked about Drake's fierce reputation still sounded more like awe and respect than true fear. Certainly it was different from the fear her brothers had experienced serving under Silas Faine. A fear of punishments that didn't fit the infractions, executions without trials, sustaining injuries and being forced to retire without appropriate pensions, and the dreaded duty of turning away petitioners.

"Granted," Serena continued, "I don't see the general often and have never interacted with him, but he doesn't look capable of smiling."

"Oh, he can smile." Callista took the fledgling back. It chittered and tried to pull its wings free. "We should dry her off. And perhaps ensure there's nothing fragile around that she might break."

After a gentle yet thorough toweling down, Callista placed one of the unnecessary pillows from her bed on the deep stone windowsill in the sitting room. The fledgling curled up on the cushion in the sunlight for a nap.

At that moment, servants arrived with a short planter full of gravel and a tall bird perch. The men helped rearrange some furniture to make room, for which Callista profusely thanked them. After the servants left, she and Serena moved anything breakable into cabinets or drawers and covered the upholstery in extra linens.

That complete, Callista wandered over to the window.

The lesser gryphon had tucked its head against its side, but its tail hung over the edge of the pillow. Now dry, it had lighter coloring than she'd thought. The white baby down on its head was already being replaced with gray adult feathers, so eventually, it would be all gray. Gray wings faded to silky gray fur on its back and a fluffy gray tail Callista suspected would become more poofy as it grew.

It looked so innocent and vulnerable sleeping there. So alone and desperate for rest and safety.

A yawning abyss opened in Callista's chest. How was she supposed to take care of a pet? She couldn't protect Royce or even herself. And when she'd done what she'd been sent to do or found another way to break the curse, what would happen to the gryphon? Sneaking out an animal that everyone believed belonged to Lady Tatiana would be difficult. Had she saved the creature only to abandon it later?

A tear escaped. She wiped it away and hoped Serena hadn't noticed.

Her heart was going to ruin her cover and get her and her brother killed. Just like her foolish heart had endangered her mission to activate the fae curse on the Faine line every time she'd hesitated to do the cruel things that the prophecy had required.

She'd made it through that by lying to herself that she didn't have to care so much about strangers. The world had never cared about her or her family. No one else would have gotten justice for her father and mother and Jacob.

After the Faines fell, Callista had let herself care again. Marie and Ian had invited her into their lives, and she'd been relieved to have someone to love again. But who would care if Callista was hanged for her crimes or if the Shafers murdered her brother? If she was executed, Marie and Ian would probably be disgusted that they had let her under their roof. The realization threatened to snap her heart in two.

It was up to her to look after herself and her brother, and if a few innocents were caught in the middle… No one had cared when it was *her* innocent family that suffered, so why should she care? Was that what she wanted, though? To be just like everyone else, who only worried about themselves?

Caring about this lesser gryphon, about Serena, about Tatiana, about anyone other than herself and Royce might doom her and her brother. But when her soul was screaming for someone, any-one, to notice her and care, how could she embrace the same self-serving callousness that she hated? Yet if Callista wanted to survive, she wasn't sure she had a choice.

And the weight of that might crush her before this was over.

Gryphon fledglings were adorable little menaces.

Lesser gryphons were primarily diurnal to Callista's understanding, so why the fledgling had decided the middle of the night was the time to run and fly around the suite knocking over anything it could was beyond comprehension. Serena had been a lifesaver, helping with corralling and cleaning up after her new pet during the night and all morning and through the early afternoon. Callista had finally convinced her maid to go take a nap—actually, she'd finally ordered Serena to go rest, much to Serena's amusement. At least she had agreed.

In one of the gryphon's bouts of chaos, she'd flown into the window and hurt her wing. Thankfully, Callista hadn't detected any broken bones. Likely a sprain. She could heal it easily, but to do that, she needed a couple minutes alone with the animal.

She sat in a chair by the fireplace in the sitting room while the lesser gryphon slept on her lap. When she was so peaceful, it was difficult to believe how chaotic she could be when awake. Several minutes after Serena closed her bedroom door, Callista healed the fledgling's tweaked wing. The purple glow of her magic tinged the white and gray feathers a shimmery lavender. The critter shifted with a sigh and nuzzled deeper into the folds of Callista's sapphire dress. She was going to be covered in gray cat hairs.

The injury had been minor, and the gryphon was small, yet the magic use still made Callista want a snack. The fluffball looked too cozy and peaceful to move, though. She glanced out the window, trying to gauge the time by the position of the late afternoon sun. Supper couldn't be that far off. She could wait until Serena awoke and fetched their food. Maybe she'd just rest her eyes for a moment…

A knocking sound startled Callista. Her movement displeased the fledgling, who released a disgruntled squawk and jumped to the ground. It stuck its cat end up and spread its wings as it stretched. The knocking sounded again.

Callista opened the door and gaped at the king standing in the hall. "Your Majesty." She dropped into a curtsy. "I'm so sorry—did I forget a planned engagement?" She hadn't seen the king since their failed attempt at tea the day prior, and she swore they hadn't made new plans.

King Cassius shook his head with a smile, his short curls bouncing with the movement beneath his crown. "No, not at all. I was able to get away from my other duties early. I hoped you might join me for a walk in the garden and then accompany me to supper in the great hall?"

"Oh." Truthfully, Callista didn't want to do any of that, but she'd have to stop taking her meals in her room sooner or later. "Of course…" She looked down at the gray cat hair speckling the front of her dress. "May I have a moment to freshen up?"

A screech preceded a rustling of wings, and then the fledgling landed on Callista's shoulder. The king stepped back, alarm crossing his face.

Callista stiffened. She hadn't considered that King Cassius might disapprove. Would he make her get rid of her new pet? Or might her choice make him reconsider marrying Lady Tatiana?

The king chuckled, and some of the tightness in her shoulders eased. "Vallyn mentioned you'd saved a lesser gryphon fledgling. It's cute. How are things going?"

The creature interrupted with high-pitched chirps. It lightly gripped her hair in its small beak.

"Tss," Callista hissed. The gryphon released her hair, stared at her, and then screeched again, close to her ear. "Ow." She smiled wryly. "She's energetic and demanding, and apparently needs food before I leave. I'm so sorry to keep you waiting—"

King Cassius laughed. "No, please, don't worry about me. This corridor is an effective hiding place from the demands of the lords since they're not allowed here. I should thank you for giving me an excuse to linger in solitude." His brown eyes twinkled.

She laughed politely. "I'll be back shortly, Your Majesty."

Callista closed the door and turned around to find Serena had emerged from her room. Serena volunteered to take care of the gryphon, so Callista went to her room. She rushed through brushing away the cat hair and combing through her hair. Satisfied she was presentable, she took a deep breath and released it slowly before leaving her suite.

"I apologize for keeping you waiting, Your Majesty."

With a soft smile, the king straightened from where he had been leaning against the wall. "No, I apologize. I should have sent a servant to warn you I was coming." He offered her his arm, and she slipped her hand into the crook of his elbow.

As they ambled through the halls, a memory unsettled her. She hadn't thought about it at the time—she was used to being taller than many men—but as she stood at Cassius's side, several inches shorter than him in Tatiana's body, she realized she'd been taller than Drake when they'd walked through the halls after she rescued the gryphon. Drake was shorter than the king, but she didn't think he should be shorter than Tatiana. Was Drake somehow…counteracting the curse? No, impossible. Surely a guardsman would have noticed. She had to be misremembering. Regardless, Drake was a problem. The sooner Callista could end the curse, the better.

But unless she found another way to rescue Royce or Tatiana fell in love, the only way the curse would break was if she murdered the man at her side. Perhaps she could confess and ask the king for his help to rescue Royce?

Ha. Cassius had a benevolent smile, but that didn't mean he would forgive a would-be assassin. No king would. Even if by some bizarre reversal in her luck he wasn't angry with her deception, Shafer might kill Royce before they could rescue him. It wasn't worth the risk.

Her stomach churned, and she locked those thoughts away, willing herself to go numb.

Getting through this garden stroll and then dinner in front of all the nobles would be difficult enough without the weight of her deal with the Shafers crushing her.

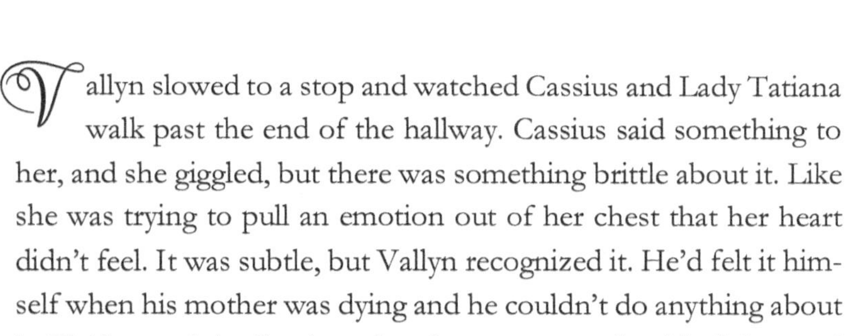

15

allyn slowed to a stop and watched Cassius and Lady Tatiana walk past the end of the hallway. Cassius said something to her, and she giggled, but there was something brittle about it. Like she was trying to pull an emotion out of her chest that her heart didn't feel. It was subtle, but Vallyn recognized it. He'd felt it himself when his mother was dying and he couldn't do anything about it. He'd seen it in Cassius when he was mourning his father and bending under the pressure of being a duke at fourteen.

What was Lady Tatiana Ackroyd grieving? Her mother had been gone for many years, but then, that was a pain that lingered.

Despite Vallyn's misgivings, her sorrow pricked his heart. Cassius's voice faded, and Vallyn shook off the sensation and continued. Sympathetic or not, Vallyn had a duty to discover if Tatiana's secrets posed a threat to his friend and king.

A couple of minutes later, he rapped his knuckles on the door to Tatiana's suite. A servant with gray streaks winding through her braided hair opened the door and gawped at him before dropping into a curtsy.

"My lord general. My lady is not—"

"I'm here to speak to you, actually."

The servant lifted her head. "Me?"

"Might I come in?"

"My lord?" Her gaze darted up and down the hall.

"I simply think we would be more comfortable if we could sit to talk," he said. "I don't plan on sticking my nose anywhere it shouldn't be."

The servant blushed. "Of course. Please, come in—oh no you don't!" She tossed open the door and rushed into the room.

Vallyn followed her, and his confusion abated. The woman grabbed the gray-and-white lesser gryphon fledgling who had been squatting down and whisked the creature over to a long planter full of fine gravel.

"You relieve yourself *here* and here only, miss fluff!"

A disbelieving chuckle escaped him. "Tatiana named her Miss Fluff?"

"Oh, no, her ladyship hasn't named the fledgling yet." She nodded triumphantly as the gryphon put the gravel to use and then turned back to him. "Thank you so much for having the perch and gravel sent. Please, have a seat, my lord."

Vallyn crossed to the armchairs that faced the cold fireplace. Were those bed linens thrown over the furniture? Ah, probably to protect it from the fledgling's antics.

"Whose idea was it to cover the furniture?" he asked as he sat.

The woman smiled. "Mine, although her ladyship insisted on helping." She folded her hands in front of her skirt and stood by the other chair. "How can I help you, my lord?"

"Please, sit. And I'm sorry, your name is…?"

"Serena, my lord." She sat in the other armchair, crossed her ankles, uncrossed them, leaned against the back and straightened again, then angled more toward him.

Why did everyone have to get so fae-cursed nervous around him?

Except Tatiana, who had more reason than most to fear him yet acted far calmer and more controlled around him than did many people who had nothing to hide.

"Serena. It's a pleasure to meet you—" Vallyn cut off as the gryphon fledgling leapt into his lap. The tiny beastie spun around and around, its small, razor-sharp talons and claws pricking through his trousers. Finally, it curled into a ball on his legs.

Serena moved to get out of her chair. "Apologies—"

"No, it's…fine." He waved a hand.

"She was napping on Lady Tatiana's lap in that chair before His Majesty came to escort my lady to supper." Serena chuckled. "She must think that's her spot now."

"Well, who am I to argue with her?" Vallyn grinned. "Back to the purpose of my visit, though, Serena. I wish to know what you think of your new mistress." He sobered his expression. "Nothing you say will make it back to Lady Tatiana, nor will it affect your employment in Highrook."

Serena's lips parted. "Has her ladyship done something to warrant such an interrogation?"

"No." Thank the stars that the rumor that fae couldn't lie was a myth, a misunderstanding of the magic that prevented them from knowingly taking false vows and deterred them from breaking their bargains. "But we would like to know her demeanor in private and how she treats her subordinates."

"Of course. Admittedly, I had some trepidation about this appointment. I'd heard her ladyship had a disagreement with her previous maid, which could have been a bad sign. Now, though, I'd guess her former maid tried to take advantage of Lady Tatiana's kindness. Her ladyship sees to her own needs as much as possible, is thoughtful of my needs, and always seems worried she's troubling me, as if my entire job is not to assist her. For example, I have to argue with her to let me take care of her new pet. And she's so gentle. Miss Fluff can be a menace, but her ladyship refuses to abandon the fledgling, especially now that she's tweaked her wing…"

Serena frowned. "Although her wing has seemed fine since I awoke from my nap… That is, I was not slacking, my lord. Her ladyship insisted that I rest after the gryphon kept waking us."

Interesting. Vallyn stroked the back of his forefinger down the gryphon's spine and let a little of his magic ease into it. It brushed against the remnants of human magic. Tatiana's magic felt like both velvet and steel, gentleness and strength. Humans always suffered a physical consequence for using their magic…yet she had sacrificed hers to heal a tiny lesser gryphon. That hardly spoke of a malicious soul, but even the worst villains had hobbies and something of a heart.

"What else?"

Serena hummed. "Her ladyship is a little melancholy. She always covers it quickly, and it is not my place to ask. I enjoy working for her."

All intriguing, and it fit with the picture of the kind noblewoman. Only her secret magic and the dark-haired woman Vallyn saw didn't fit neatly into the puzzle. Vallyn absently ran his fingertips through the gryphon's soft cat fur. "Can you do something for me?"

Serena eyed him warily.

"Lady Tatiana's former maidservant, Julia, is living with a cowherd and his wife in their little cottage on the first hill to the northeast of the palace. I believe Dip…the steward said she'd been put in charge of a flock of geese. I considered going to speak with her myself, but I suspect she wouldn't be honest with me about what caused the discord between her and Lady Tatiana."

Cassius had actually pointed that out. Vallyn had power the girl might either fear or want to exploit against her mistress, either of which could distort her testimony.

"But you," Vallyn continued, "she might be honest with. Tomorrow His Majesty is spending the morning with Lady Tatiana, which will provide you an opportunity to visit Julia. I'll have a guard escort you. See if you can determine if the maid has any valid complaint against her former mistress."

Serena bowed her head. "As you command, my lord general."

"Now." Vallyn looked down at the lesser gryphon. "I am afraid you're going to have to move." Gently, he scooped up the fledgling. She adjusted her wings and peered at him. He deposited her on the seat of the chair, and she gave a sad, hawklike cry. "Oh, you'll be fine, little one."

Whether Lady Tatiana was authentic or a fake, Vallyn did believe she would take good care of the fledgling. In fact, even though it might mean there was something wrong with him, he found himself hoping Tatiana wasn't a fraud at all.

The next day, Vallyn hurried through the castle corridors. He was meant to be joining Cassius and Tatiana for a second attempt at tea, but he'd felt restless. The breathing exercises and valerian that Wilmina had given him had improved his sleep. He'd found Titus Wright and expressed his approval of his handling of Lady Tatiana's inquiry, and the man had seemed so bolstered by the acknowledgment that Vallyn had resolved to find some reason to directly praise at least one guard every day. Despite how it eased some of his anxiety about palace security, he still felt on edge, so he'd trained before dressing for the meeting. Unfortunately, he'd stayed overlong at the training yard. Now he was late, and Cassius was alone in the garden with Tatiana.

Truthfully, Vallyn was less worried about Tatiana harming Cassius than he had been, but he wouldn't let his guard down. Still, she hadn't been the main source of his agitation today. That honor went to Blaise Shafer.

Guardsmen had reported overhearing Shafer and his friends criticizing Tatiana, often in ways that were veiled insults to the king. To Vallyn's frustration, it wasn't enough grounds to have Shafer confined to his rooms, but he'd still instructed the guards to pay extra attention to Shafer and the nobles he regularly consorted with.

Outside, despite the sun climbing in the gray sky, the autumn day held a chill. He pulled his cloak around his torso. A fine mist hung in the air, tiny droplets landing on his face as red and yellow leaves crunched under his boots.

He slowed as he neared the pavilion and tried to look less like he'd jogged there. A quick brush of his fingers through his shaggy hair confirmed the pointed tips of his ears were hidden. Voices sounded up ahead, then a woman's laughter. He rounded a large bush covered in dark-red leaves, and his brow furrowed.

Cassius had set his crown on the table beside the teapots and platters of treats, and his head was bent down as he wiped at something on his powder-blue doublet with a napkin.

"Oh, no, stop, you'll only rub it around," Tatiana said, good-natured amusement coloring her tone as she pulled Cassius's hand away from his chest. "The laundry staff would prefer you let it be. I solemnly swear to pretend it never happened and I can't see it."

Vallyn approached the table, and Tatiana rose to her feet and curtsied. "General Drake."

"Lady Tatiana." He turned to Cassius. "Your Majesty…" His gaze dropped to the bright-red smudge in the center of Cassius's doublet.

"The pastry had it out for me," Cassius said. "I try to eat it, and it spits out its raspberry filling with calculated aim for my heart."

Vallyn snorted. "Shall I imprison the pastry for this effrontery?"

"Perhaps after we have tea. Come, sit. And tell me why you're late."

"Apologies, Your Majesty, Lady Tatiana." Vallyn bowed, then moved around behind Cassius to the third chair. "I'm afraid I lost track of the time."

Cassius narrowed his eyes. "Doing what?"

"Don't let His Majesty bully you," Tatiana said lightly. "He was late himself."

Cassius's bronze skin reddened. "Tattler. And it isn't my fault the nobles are always accosting me in the halls."

"But you're the king," Tatiana said. "Shouldn't they respect you enough not to bother you when you're simply walking in your own castle?"

"That's my opinion," Vallyn grumbled.

Cassius smiled resignedly. "If they want to see me in a timely fashion, that's their best method. Sometimes I have to ask a guard to hold them back so I can get to my next engagement, but I try to talk to them as long as I can. A king's function is to serve and lead the kingdom. After my predecessor's tendency to rebuff any attempts to approach him with requests or complaints, I am extra careful not to treat my nobles with such disregard."

Tatiana smiled, but then something flickered over her face, a moment of tension or discomfort. Her expression smoothed in an instant. Perhaps he'd imagined it.

"Now that we're all here, allow me to serve the tea, my lords," Tatiana said. Vallyn narrowed his eyes, but she was busy pointing out the teapots. "The servants said this one is a white tea with berries and lemon. This one is black and spiced with strong notes of cinnamon. This one is green tea with ginger. And this one is an herbal blend with peaches and honey. Which would you prefer, Your Majesty?"

Cassius reached for the pale-yellow pot containing the spiced black tea. "Oh, please, there's no need—"

"I insist." Tatiana snatched away the yellow teapot. "Do you prefer one of the teacups?"

With a shrug, Cassius indicated one painted with delicate blue flowers.

Vallyn shouldn't panic. It would still be the height of foolishness for her to poison the king's tea right in front of him. Unless perhaps she planned to use a slow-acting poison, or one that had to build up in his body to take effect.

She did nothing that appeared suspicious as she poured the tea and handed the teacup to Cassius. As she couldn't have known which tea or teacup he would choose, the alternative was that she'd poisoned them all. If her plan was to run away before anyone realized Cassius and Vallyn were dead, she would want them to drink first.

He couldn't accuse her of being a poisoner again without proof. But pressure built in his chest as Cassius moved the teacup toward his lips.

"I didn't poison it." Tatiana tilted up her chin and stared Vallyn down.

He shifted in his seat. "I didn't say you did."

"Yet your expression and the fact that you were lifting your hand to stop him indicate you were about to suggest it. Again."

Vallyn reddened. He hadn't realized his hand was, in fact, hovering above the edge of the table. "I was reaching for the tea, to serve myself."

"Afraid I'll poison you as well, General?"

"Now, let's be civil, please." Cassius took a pointedly long sip of tea. "Vallyn. Which tea did you desire?"

"The ginger." At least that had a slight bite to it. "I can—"

Tatiana took the teapot. "I was taught that to serve a beverage at a shared meal showed respect and goodwill." Her knuckles whitened as she clutched the handle. "While it appears that contrary to your kindness yesterday, you harbor no goodwill toward me, I would still like to extend it to you, General Drake."

Cassius choked on his tea, and Vallyn looked over in alarm, but Cas simply cleared his throat and daintily wiped his mouth, poorly hiding his smirk.

Tatiana certainly had the spine to be a queen. Her precise combination of gracious gentility and sharp reproach was as masterful as any courtier's.

"Very well." Vallyn motioned for her to proceed. "On the condition you allow me to pour your tea, my lady."

Tatiana's eyes widened, but she inclined her head. "I would be honored, my lord."

He suspected she held the teapot higher than necessary, splattering the tea a bit and cooling it, but he kept that to himself. As he kind of deserved it, he was more amused than offended.

"And your choice of tea, Lady Tatiana?"

"Surprise me."

He reached for the same spiced tea Cassius had chosen,

watching her face. Her expression remained calm and neutral. At the last moment, he switched to the white tea with berry. Something flickered in her eyes; surprise, maybe. It didn't seem a negative emotion, though.

Vallyn poured the tea—close to the teacup so as not to splatter her tea—and placed the cup in front of her. She took a sip, and her face and shoulders eased as her eyes drifted closed.

"This one is my favorite." She looked to Vallyn with a slight smile.

"You mean it's the one you would have chosen if you'd felt you didn't have to prove you hadn't poisoned any of them by letting Vallyn pick?" Cassius said with a pointed glare at Vallyn.

A slight blush colored Tatiana's pale cheeks as she took another sip.

Part of his mind rebelled, but Vallyn took a drink. His tea was warm rather than hot, but it was still pleasant. Assuming it didn't kill or weaken him.

"Which of these pastries are your favorites?" Cassius asked. "I can ensure that the kitchens include them in the selection for tomorrow's party."

"That's *tomorrow*?" Vallyn thought back—yes, it was already the third day since Tatiana's arrival. "Of course it's tomorrow. Thank you for mentioning it, or I might have missed it entirely."

Tatiana stilled with her teacup near her lips. "Party?"

"The ball I mentioned," Cassius said. "To unofficially introduce you to the court."

"Oh." Tatiana's face paled. "I forgot as well."

"All of the excitement and lack of sleep from taking care of a lesser gryphon put it right out of your mind, no doubt," Cassius said, his tone lightly teasing. "But your favorites?"

Vallyn sipped his tea to hide a frown. Tatiana's hands fluttered awkwardly over the table as she pointed out the desserts she loved. Why did she look so nervous? Perhaps she was worried about the party because Lord Ackroyd had sheltered her—and there had been the whole Blaise Shafer in the stairwell incident two days ago.

"What are your hobbies, Lady Tatiana?" Cassius asked.

Tatiana adjusted her position on her chair. "I enjoy academic reading. Spending time in nature can be pleasant. I play the flute."

"Truly?" Cassius leaned forward. "I would love to hear you play."

Her gaze fell to her hands around her teacup. When she spoke, her voice was strained. "I'm afraid I've lost my flute, Your Majesty. I haven't played in many months."

"Why didn't you replace it?" Vallyn asked softly.

She tilted her teacup, watching the remaining tea slosh around. "It was a gift from someone I lost, and I haven't had the…time to look for a new one."

"I'm sorry for your loss," Vallyn said at the same time as Cassius said, "I'm sorry to hear that."

Tatiana took a deep breath, then drank her remaining tea. When she lifted her head, her smile was tight. "Thank you. What are your hobbies, Your Majesty?"

Whoever she had lost, that wound was still tender—likely more recent than her mother. Could she have had a lover or friend who'd died? It didn't matter. If Cassius didn't think to buy her a new flute, Vallyn would do it himself. And give it to Cassius to gift to her, of course.

They fell into pleasant, if mundane, conversation. The clouds cleared, and sunlight chased away the mist and highlighted the rich red of the ivy covering the pavilion. Vallyn let Cassius do most of the talking while he nibbled on sweet treats and observed Tatiana. She wasn't as stiffly formal as most courtiers and didn't worry herself with all the complicated little rules of etiquette that Vallyn thought were needlessly confusing and impossible to remember.

There was definitely a sorrow about her, though. Tiny things he recognized from experience. Moments when she was disengaged for the blink of an eye. Laughter that died off quickly and smiles that looked like they took effort.

While whatever weighed on Tatiana stirred Vallyn's sympathies, her hesitations sharpened his suspicions. Minute pauses, like she was struggling to decide what to say. While there could be many reasons, from self-consciousness to fatigue, it could also be that she was trying to think of an appropriate lie, because she wasn't Lady Tatiana at all.

How long would it take for his father to arrive? He needed answers, and he needed them soon.

After tea, Vallyn walked with Cassius back to the king's office.

"A rough start, admittedly, but I think that went well," Cassius declared.

"Certainly better than last time. And without any poisonings, it seems."

"No thanks to you and your paranoia." Cassius bumped his shoulder into Vallyn's. "But I do think this could work, Val. I don't feel a strong connection with her, but she's mesmerizingly pretty and pleasant. Thoughtful and not self-obsessed. And she's not afraid of you." He chuckled. "I can choose to love her. It might not be a passionate marriage, but that's hardly the most important thing. I don't think we're incompatible at least."

Vallyn frowned at his friend. That didn't sound compelling, but his marriage didn't have massive political implications, so perhaps it made sense Cassius was approaching this so…logically. However, Cassius wasn't drawn to Tatiana? Vallyn suspected her of being a fraud and still kept liking and admiring her despite his reservations.

"I hope you're right that I'm paranoid," Vallyn said, "because she's a remarkable young woman. Speaking as an observer, I'd say you get along well."

A passing guard stopped to bow. Vallyn nodded at the man, but Cassius hardly seemed to notice as he continued down the corridor, his left hand straying up to tug at his hair.

"I'd hoped for more than 'you get along well' for my wife. I get along well with my horse." Cassius dropped his hand to his side. "But a king has a responsibility to his kingdom. His heart is hardly a concern."

Vallyn grabbed Cassius's arm and forced him to face him. "The king's heart concerns me. Won't the kingdom suffer if its king and queen don't like each other?"

"I don't doubt we can like each other enough to make it work." Cassius shook his head, and his crown slid a little. He adjusted it and started back down the hall with a muttered, "Why must I wear this thing all the time?"

"Because you're the king, and we don't want anyone to forget it so early in your reign?" Vallyn said dryly as he fell back into step alongside Cassius.

"Being king is so much trouble," Cassius said. "I never had to worry this much about public perception as a duke."

They reached the door to Cassius's office, and Vallyn opened it for him and returned the guard's bow with a nod. "If it's any consolation, I think you're doing an outstanding job."

One side of Cassius's mouth pulled up. "You're biased."

"Nonsense. I always tell you when you're being an idiot."

One of the guards near the door choked on a suppressed gasp, but Cassius laughed.

"When are you free today?" Vallyn asked. "I'm hoping to have a report from Lady Tatiana's new maid."

Cassius groaned. "I'm booked back-to-back until supper and again after. Just come by any time. I'll probably be relieved to use your 'important security information' as an excuse for a brief respite from the clerks and nobles."

"I wish you luck, then."

Vallyn waited until after lunchtime to head to the southwest wing. As he hoped, he caught Serena leaving Tatiana's suite with her empty meal tray. When she saw him, she immediately changed course to meet him toward the end of the hall.

"My lord general," she said and dropped into a curtsy.

"Just General," he said. Technically, Cassius had granted him a lordship, but it was an empty title. His holding was little more than a couple acres of untamed forest. Vallyn didn't mind. The title was for the sake of the court. "Did you speak to Julia?"

Serena nodded. "She is…strange. Angry, almost hurt, but could give no reason for it. She claimed a gut feeling that Lady Tatiana doesn't deserve her title but had no evidence. It appears she gets along all right with the farmer and his wife. After she left to see to her duties, they said she is helpful but not talkative. Forgive my boldness, General, but I suspect Julia is envious of nobles and was belligerent toward Lady Tatiana out of prejudice."

That sounded plausible. Even though Lord Ackroyd had a reputation for wanting to reduce class separation between lesser and greater nobles, so far as Vallyn knew, his ideas didn't extend to the peasantry. Perhaps Julia found that unfair. Whatever the cause, it didn't sound like Julia's dislike of Lady Tatiana was rational.

"Thank you, Serena." Vallyn nodded. "I won't keep you from your duties."

She curtsied and then left by the door leading to the servants' staircase. Vallyn stayed where he was, strumming his fingers against the leather-covered hilt of his sword.

Whatever magic Lady Tatiana Ackroyd possessed, whether she was hiding her true appearance or Vallyn was hallucinating her alluring dark hair and oval face, no credible evidence pointed to her being a fraud or a threat. Did that make him a paranoid cad?

He dragged a hand down the side of his face and started down the hallway. If he was the problem, then he'd have to fix the mess he'd made. Maybe he should give Tatiana a flute himself as a peace offering.

A crash and a scream interrupted his thoughts, and he'd drawn his sword before he even identified the source.

Tatiana's room.

Vallyn's fae magic strained to break out of the mental vault where he kept it locked away. Without slowing to knock, he threw open the door and barreled inside.

Instead of an assailant, he found Tatiana standing in the middle of the room. She stared at him with wide eyes, her mouth hanging open and both hands outstretched toward him. She lowered her hands, and her expression reverted to that pleasantly neutral look she usually wore.

Vallyn didn't like it. He didn't want her to feel the need to don a helm of indifference around him.

"Close the door!" Tatiana rushed toward him.

Bewildered, Vallyn backed up, pushing the door closed behind him, and spotted the cause of her alarm as the door clicked shut.

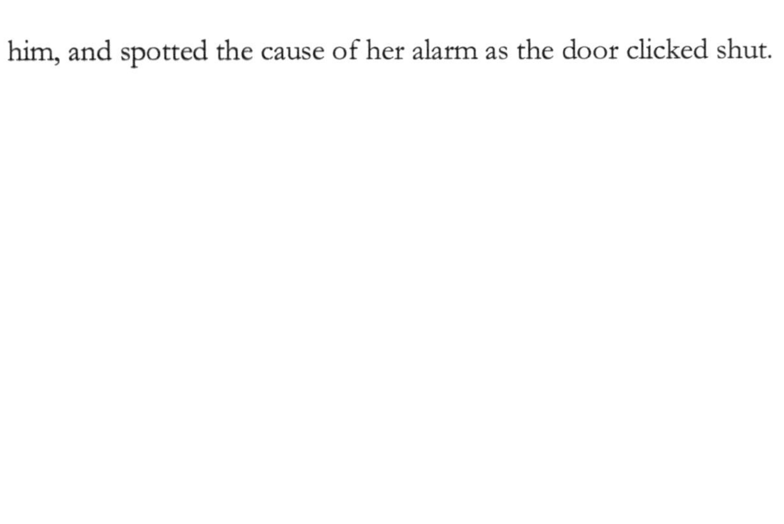

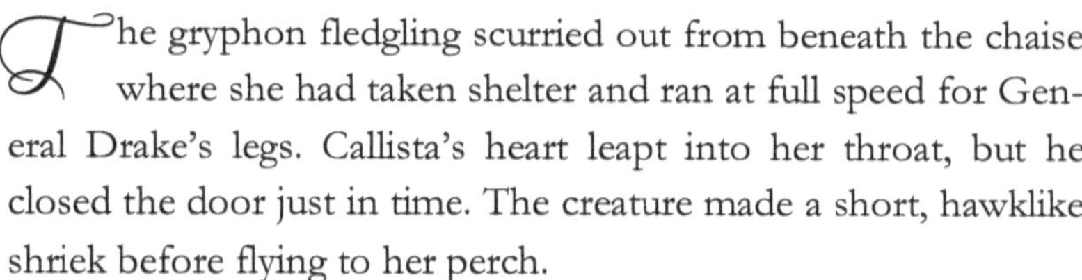

16

he gryphon fledgling scurried out from beneath the chaise where she had taken shelter and ran at full speed for General Drake's legs. Callista's heart leapt into her throat, but he closed the door just in time. The creature made a short, hawklike shriek before flying to her perch.

"Sorry, my lord." Callista lowered her gaze to the carpet. She had failed to control her pet. Worse, she'd brought the general running with her scream, over nothing more than a broken decoration. She weakly motioned toward a white stone pedestal that would be about three feet tall—if it weren't lying on the ground with the top slab broken off. "She crashed into that."

The whisper of metal against leather indicated the general had sheathed his sword. "You're all right, then, my lady?"

She nodded, still not looking at him, and wrapped her arms over her stomach. How she would love to fall through the floor instead of standing before a man who was at once distractingly attractive and the greatest threat to her mission. "I thought the pedestal was going to fall on her. Thank you, though, for rushing to my aid."

"I'm relieved you're both all right."

At that, Callista glanced up. Genuine concern showed in his eyes, and much of his wariness from tea that morning was gone. Maybe he did mean it.

"All right physically. Now I have to deal with the mortification of explaining to His Majesty the destruction I've brought into his guest suite." She hugged herself tighter—the same way she'd often held herself when cold and alone in that desolate castle.

The troublemaker in question chirruped. Her alert cat ears swiveled toward Callista, and her tail swung lazily back and forth.

"You're lucky you're adorable," Callista muttered.

Drake chuckled. "Have you named her yet?"

She shook her head.

"Nothing fit right?" He hummed as he regarded the fledgling. "Seeing her gray coloring, I'd thought perhaps Misty, but that's too…soft for such a chaotic bundle of fur and feathers. She's more storm than mist."

"Truthfully, I've been stalling because I fear I'll have to give her up." Why was she even telling him this? Maybe because she hoped that since he also cared about animals, he'd understand. "I'm growing attached to her, but…I don't know if I can tame her, or even if it would be fair. I hope we can at least last until she'll have a better chance of fending for herself and not ending up half-drowned in the laundry."

Speaking of finding the lesser gryphon reminded Callista that she'd only been on that floor because she'd been in a part of the castle where she didn't belong—rather like the man in front of her. She eyed him, her forehead wrinkling despite her attempt to keep her expression blank. "Why are you in this wing? His Majesty said no one else was staying here."

Drake opened and closed his mouth. "I wasn't trying to catch you doing something nefarious, but nothing I say is going to sound convincing, is it?"

That drew a wry smile from her. "Probably not, especially since you've insinuated you think I could be doing something nefarious."

"Anyone can be nefarious, Lady Tatiana. Those charged with protecting the king during a fraught period of transition do not get the luxury of assuming the best of people."

The words seemed to cost General Drake—his fierce veneer slipped, revealing a heaviness to his voice and weariness to his carriage. Did he stay up every night cataloguing what everyone in the palace had done so he could identify anything suspicious?

"That's an exhausting way to live," Callista murmured. She'd know.

For weeks after she stole the scroll, she'd hardly been able to rest. Every interaction she'd had during the day had run through her mind on repeat, evaluated for any sign of danger. Rustling leaves or snapping twigs had prompted her to hold her breath, convinced the guards had found her. Nightmares replaying her worst moments or predicting her capture and execution had poisoned her sleep.

"That's putting it mildly," Drake muttered. He rubbed his forehead, shoving his shaggy hair up and then letting it flop back down in further disarray. Fatigue filled the general's dark-brown eyes, and it encouraged unwelcome feelings of sympathy.

"Hops tea can help." The words spilled out, and when Drake frowned at her, she wished she hadn't spoken.

"With?"

She fiddled with the long ties of her dress's corded belt. "Sleep. If you're struggling with that. I used to have nightmares brought on by stress. An occasional cup of hops tea before bed helped me."

Drake eased a step closer. "What stress caused your nightmares?"

She huffed and snuck a glance at him, but his expression was sincere. "That's personal."

They stood in silence. The fledgling glided down from her perch and wove between the general's legs before stretching out on top of Callista's feet.

"In my dreams," Drake said softly, "men sneak around Highrook. I spot them but can't make my mouth work, and I run as slow as congealed tree sap. Or I get lost in this ridiculous palace, or the halls keep getting longer no matter how far I run. Sometimes that's when I wake, but other times, I don't wake up until I find Cassius with a knife in his back or a man bending over him with a sword."

He flexed stiff fingers at his sides. His quiet honesty made Callista want to be honest in return, but she couldn't. The nightmares she'd had—or the one she'd had last night—were not Tatiana's dreams. Besides, this was probably a ploy. A calculated use of vulnerability to trick her into revealing her secrets.

Still, it would be cruel to accept his openness and offer nothing in return, so she made up something that was close enough to the truth.

"I'm sorry. I've lost people who mattered to me," Callista admitted. "Those losses haunt my dreams. Other times, I've feared I would lose someone or been unsure of the outcomes of private situations. That feeling of helplessness, that worry for the unknown…it can feel like something has sunk its claws into you and won't let go. But I've found sometimes, all I can do is take my focus off the things I can't control. There's always something I can do, even if it's not related."

Perhaps that explained why she'd been so eager to care for the lesser gryphon. It gave her something she could actually *do*.

She met his eyes and smiled. "At least you have good men under your command. If someone does infiltrate Highrook, you won't be trying to stop them alone."

"Yes…" Drake straightened. "Speaking of which, thank you. You were right—telling my men that their efforts are seen and appreciated does strengthen loyalty, in both directions."

He'd acted on her advice? A pleased blush heated her cheeks. "Good. Well, whatever business you had in this wing, thank you for trying to aid me."

General Drake bowed. "It's my duty. I may be suspicious and will deal decisively with anyone acting on wicked or deceitful intentions, but it's not because I enjoy being the king's blade. I do those things because my aim is to protect the innocent."

Callista fought to keep her fear concealed deep inside. She couldn't allow any real cordial feelings toward Drake. If he learned the truth, he might not give her time to explain before he put his sword through her.

He shifted and looked everywhere but at her. "Sometimes it's difficult to balance being both protector of the innocent and scourge of the guilty when the palace is full of shadows, and sometimes monsters wear the guise of lambs. But though I suspect you have secrets, Lady Tatiana, I'm inclined to believe His Majesty is correct and you're guiltless."

The fingers of his left hand tapped against the pommel of his sword, and she abruptly realized the handle and pommel were both wrapped in leather. He often wore fingerless gloves as well. That would prevent his skin from coming in contact with steel when he wielded it, which had to mean that reports that fae were weak against pure iron were as true as the stories of their beauty. She should determine how to get some iron, just in case.

Drake offered her a tired, lopsided smile. "Can you forgive a paranoid guardsman for taking his duties too seriously?"

That feeling of empathy toward him surged again, and before she'd even considered her words, Callista said, "Forgiven, General."

"Perhaps you can save a dance for me at the party tomorrow night? Assuming Cassius doesn't claim every one, which he'd be a fool not to."

Oh, right. Balls involved dancing. Callista concealed her discomfort behind a smile. "It would be an honor, General."

"Good." Drake slapped his palm against his right thigh. "I should go. Good day, Lady Tatiana." He bolted from the room.

The fledgling rolled off Callista's shoes with a confused-sounding cry.

"I don't understand him either, girl." Callista knelt and stroked her pet's back.

She's more storm than mist.

"Stormy."

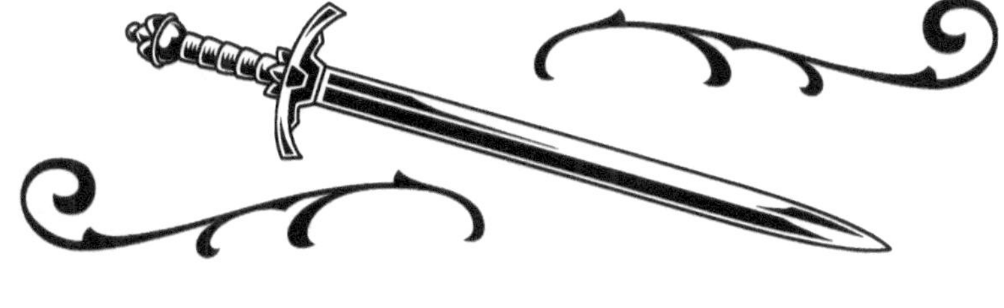

17

allyn turned back and forth in front of the large mirror in his bedchamber. He hated that he cared how he looked. He'd always wanted to look respectable, but he'd felt extra pressure since moving to the royal court. The crisp outfit with not a button out of place was armor against the snide nobles, who seemed to be constantly on the hunt for any sign of weakness or imperfection.

He ran his palms over the thin black doublet, which had been designed to be loose enough to allow him to fight should he need to use the sword belted at his hip. Subtle silver thread traced a pattern of diamond shapes over the doublet, and a row of small silver buttons ran down the front. Matching buttons secured the sleeves of his black shirt around his wrists. Just enough ostentation to fit in with the nobles without being flashy enough to draw attention, although he thought the silver stitching a bit much. In fact, his black trousers were also a bit tighter than he preferred, and he favored longer tunics over doublets.

But it wasn't about what Vallyn liked. It was about reflecting well on his king. Cassius would probably tease him about wearing all black again, but the color matched Vallyn's opinions on court parties.

And if all-black ensembles made him appear a little more threatening despite his being shorter than over half of the noblemen, that was a fortuitous side effect.

Satisfied with his appearance, Vallyn snuffed the candles. He didn't keep a personal manservant. He'd grown up without one and found having someone constantly hovering uncomfortable.

At least his morning visit with Wilmina had been helpful. She'd given him more herbs—including some dried hops flowers—and let him rant about how confused a "potential suspect" made him feel. Wilmina's opinion had been that this person sounded like someone she would like, and she'd seemed to be hinting that she thought Vallyn liked this unnamed woman. She'd recommended being honest that he knew the suspect's secrets.

Unfortunately, Cassius's orders to not risk offending the Ackroyds prevented Vallyn from doing so—quite literally, as the fae binding would not let him confront Tatiana. The odd feeling of magic warning him to obey had added to his frustration. But then Wilmina had made him remove his tunic and rubbed a sweet-smelling salve into his knotted shoulders. He hadn't felt so relaxed in ages.

The halls were mostly empty save for guards with overly stiff posture. As he neared the ballroom, the tension returned to his shoulders in defiance of Wilmina's ministrations. Chattering courtiers bedecked in brightly colored clothing and glittering jewels meandered through the open double doors. Vallyn gritted his teeth as he slowed to a snail's pace to avoid running into anyone or looking rude by weaving around them. Music drifted out of the ballroom, a melody of strings and wind instruments buried under the noise of the guests.

Someone stepped up beside him, and a woman asked, "Will you wear the sword when we dance, General?"

Vallyn raised his eyes to meet Tatiana's as they both came to a stop. For once, he swore he detected genuine amusement in her expression, not feigned levity. Torchlight reflected in her irises, flickers of orange in a sea of green that captivated him. Something odd stirred in his chest—something foolish and approaching traitorous that he stamped down like embers escaped from a fire. *Cassius's intended, you dolt.*

"Sorry, what was the question?"

"Will you wear the sword when we dance?" Tatiana repeated, a little louder.

"I go nowhere without my sword." He swept his gaze down her figure without conscious thought. The ruby of her dress was breathtaking on her, and the flowing design made her look even taller. Yet the gown didn't fit her perfectly—loose around her chest and hips and not touching the floor as the other ladies' gowns did.

Interesting that whatever enchantment changed her appearance didn't fit the clothing to her real body. What did she see when she looked at herself? The tall, dark-haired woman with a sharp-edged beauty? Or the soft, shapely blonde? Realizing he'd been staring for longer than was normal or appropriate, he turned back toward the ballroom.

"Your dress is beautiful," Vallyn said, steering clear of any compliments to features that might not be real.

"It's not ostentatious?" Tatiana ran her fingertips over the skirt. "I worried it was too bold, but Serena assured me it was perfect."

"For your official introduction to the court, it's probably the right amount of ostentation. I'm sure His Majesty won't be able to take his eyes off of you." Assuming the woman Cassius saw looked as good in red.

They entered the ballroom. A quiet gasp escaped Tatiana, and she stopped walking. He looked over and stilled.

Tatiana stood with her head tilted back. Her wide eyes roved the ceiling with delighted awe, and much of the melancholy that he usually sensed in her disappeared. Vallyn tore his attention away from her and directed his gaze to the ceiling with effort.

Even after seeing the grand ballroom a few times, he had to admit it was spectacular.

A soaring vaulted ceiling painted powder blue stretched over the expansive room. Carved swirls painted white created an ethereal pattern, like twisting clouds against the sky. Light reflected off the polished marble floor from gilded sconces on the walls and three chandeliers glittering with teardrop crystals. At the far end of the ballroom, above a dais with a golden throne and crimson cushions, the swirling white molding on the ceiling framed a painting of a rearing silver unicorn, its horn shining with silver leaf.

"Impossibly grand and too beautiful for words," Tatiana murmured. "I thought he was exaggerating."

Vallyn turned back to her. "Your father?"

The wonder drained from her eyes, and something cold and heavy took its place. "Yes." Her chin quivered. "Pardon me, General. I need a refreshment." She scurried across the ballroom, dodging the couples who had already taken to the dance floor.

"Vaaalll." Cassius's voice from the direction of the dais prompted Vallyn to turn. His friend strode over, shaking his head. "What in Miraveld did you say to her this time?"

Vallyn shrugged. "I have no idea. She said she'd thought 'he' was exaggerating the ballroom's grandeur. I asked if she meant her father. She said yes and rushed off."

"Perhaps she misses him. They're quite close, by all accounts." Cassius sighed. "Well, I have more guests to greet. Try to be *friendly* tonight, General."

Vallyn plastered on an overwide smile. "When am I not?"

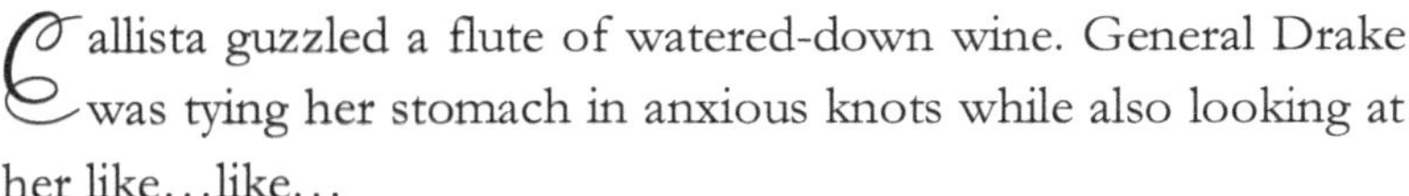

$\mathcal{C}$allista guzzled a flute of watered-down wine. General Drake was tying her stomach in anxious knots while also looking at her like…like…

Like she'd seen young men at the Royal University stare at young women they were attracted to.

No, she had to be misreading him. She was Tatiana, and Tatiana was courting Drake's best friend. She had thought Drake had decided to trust her, but perhaps he was watching for her to make a mistake and reveal her true identity.

Then she nearly had.

First, the ballroom had amazed her, the artistry and beauty moving her toward delight she hadn't felt in a long time. But then it had reminded her of her father and brothers trying to describe it to her, and grief had stabbed at her heart. She couldn't afford to let her churning emotions affect her. When she returned to her chambers, she could fall apart all she wanted, but until then, she had to be Lady Tatiana Ackroyd.

Callista closed her eyes and focused on the music. The musicians were masterful, weaving harmonies that provided a pleasant distraction. The flautist took over the melody, the bright notes soaring, and a pang of envy went through her. Would she draw suspicion if she purchased a flute as Lady Tatiana? She'd already slipped and told Cassius she played—

"Lady Tatiana," a male voice said.

Her lungs tightened, and she opened her eyes to Blaise Shafer's smirking face. "Yes?"

"I'm Sir Blaise Shafer, son of Baron Roland Shafer." He bowed with a flourish of his hand. "It's a pleasure to meet the likely future queen of our beloved kingdom." The flash of his smile felt closer to a predator baring its fangs.

"A pleasure," Callista managed.

"Might I have this dance, my lady?" Blaise held out a white-gloved hand.

Callista eyed the appendage like it was a serpent. Too many people stood nearby for her to question his invitation, and she knew enough about nobles' dance functions to know turning him down would be offensive.

So she pulled on her practiced small smile and curtsied. "You may, Sir Shafer."

Blaise led her into the middle of the ballroom amongst the other couples. Thank fate that he was wearing gloves, as she wasn't, and his skin against hers might have been more than she could bear. He drew her into dancing position.

"What do you want?" she hissed.

"To know how your courtship with King Cassius is progressing, of course."

Callista glanced around. None of the other dancers were close. With the chatter of guests and the cacophony of clinking dishes, tapping footsteps, rustling clothing, and music, it was unlikely anyone would overhear them. But then her gaze caught on General Drake. He stood near a wall, watching them with a dark expression that chilled her blood. If she could cast spells to increase her hearing, what could someone with fae magic manage?

She would continue to play the part of Tatiana Ackroyd. "Better than I imagine you and your father are hoping that it is."

Surprise showed on Blaise's face.

"My father warned me you oppose this courtship and potential marriage." She lifted her chin, wishing she were her usual height and Blaise weren't several inches taller than her. "I won't be bullied, cowed, or manipulated into running away."

"Is that so?" Blaise tugged her against him, his hand tightening around hers to the point of pain. He leaned so close his lips touched her hair as he murmured, "No one will overhear us. So listen here, you infernal little—"

"Pardon me."

General Drake's low voice next to them made Callista jump, and even Blaise startled back a step. They stopped dancing, and Blaise's grasp on her hand and waist eased as he angled toward Drake. "Can I help you, General?"

Drake smiled coldly. "I'd like to cut in, if you don't mind."

"What if I do mind?"

"I don't actually care."

A muscle ticked in Blaise's jaw. "Where are your manners, General?"

"Mine?" Drake's eyes flashed, and Callista wondered if they'd had such battles of will before. "I'd rather not make more of a scene than we already are, but Lady Tatiana looks uncomfortable. If you don't do the chivalrous thing and bow out, well…" He rested the palm of his left hand on the pommel of his sword. "Things might get embarrassing for you."

"I was unaware that the scope of your duties included harassing innocent members of the court." Blaise's hand tightened around hers, and Callista hid her pain with effort. She didn't want this standoff to escalate any further.

"My duties include protecting the king and his prospective bride—and that includes protecting her from suffering through a dance with an untrained wolf pup. She may be too polite to decline, but I rarely get accused of being polite. I won't ask again, Shafer."

"So be it. You can have her if you want her so badly." Blaise shoved Callista toward Drake with such force that she tripped forward and caught herself against the general. At the same moment her palms collided with Drake's chest, he grabbed her arms and steadied her.

Blaise scoffed behind her back. "Although I thought she was for the king. So what is it, Drake? Did His Majesty decide he didn't want her, so his dog took the scraps? Are you less loyal than you pretend to be? Or is the king so pathetic he can't woo a woman himself and is having you do it for him?"

Callista jerked her hands away from Drake's doublet like she'd been burned, but he guided her over to his side with unhurried gentleness. His stony glare never left Blaise.

"Go attempt to put that silver tongue of yours to work sowing discord elsewhere, Shafer. I knew you were an unchivalrous fool, but I didn't think you'd announce it to the entire court so candidly." Drake glanced around them, and Callista finally turned her attention away from the two men she most wished to avoid.

Many of the couples around them had ceased dancing to gawk. A few people shook their heads or whispered to each other, and one woman was looking at Blaise with open distaste.

Blaise took a deep breath that escaped sharply from his nose. "You win this round, Drake." With that, he stomped away.

Drake watched him go, his jaw clenching and…was that a hint

of a golden glow in his eyes? No, she must have imagined it. He turned toward her, and she braced herself for that same fury and suspicion, but his gaze softened to concern. She wanted to bask in his kindness, and she hated herself for it.

"Are you all right, my lady?"

Callista drew a calming breath. *Be Tatiana.* "Yes, thank you. I should have turned him down even though it would have been impolite, but—"

"But how could you know he would dare to be so rude in polite company in full view of the court?"

"Yes." She glanced around, relieved to see that the other couples had returned to dancing.

"Well. As long as we're here anyway…" Drake bowed and held out his hand. "May I have this dance? Just to keep you company and away from anyone else with less than kind intentions until His Majesty is able to dance with you himself."

"I did promise you a dance." Callista painted on a smile. Everything in her wanted to leave, to return to her room and hide from Blaise and Drake and her entire miserable situation.

But her problems two years ago hadn't disappeared when she hid herself in that ruined castle, and her problems now wouldn't solve themselves if she cocooned herself in her cozy bed in the palace, either.

As Drake took her hand and moved into frame, Callista had the disconcerting sensation of being disconnected from her body, somehow both outside of it and overlapping herself. She blinked hard, and when she opened her eyes, she felt fine.

She mentally shrugged off the momentary discomfort and placed her hand atop Drake's shoulder. Gentle pressure on the back of her shoulder guided her forward as they began to dance.

Callista had once overheard a couple of shorter men at the

Royal University complaining they had limited potential partners and gave up attending dances because "women don't want to dance with short men. It doesn't work." She always wondered if they'd actually tried. Drake didn't lead or dance any worse because he was a few inches shorter than her. In fact, he was an excellent dancer, to the point that her own self-consciousness faded—

Wait.

Once again, General Drake was shorter than her. Probably around the same height as the real Tatiana. Did that mean…

She'd grown accustomed to Tatiana's hands, so they no longer seemed strange, but she didn't think her hands had changed back to her own longer fingers. And the strands of hair over her shoulder were blonde. She glanced around, but no one was staring at her. The king caught her looking at him and smiled but continued his conversation with a nobleman, not at all acting like Tatiana had abruptly grown taller.

"Is something wrong?" Drake asked quietly. "You've gone pale and…well, rigid."

Callista whipped her attention back to Drake. As close as they were, his head was angled back the tiniest bit to meet her eyes. He truly saw *her*, not Tatiana. She gulped. "Everything's fine."

This didn't make sense. That spell had been complicated and powerful, harder and more draining than any enchantment she had previously cast. How could it allow one person to see her so differently than everyone else, down to her height? That sensation returned, of being indistinct and both overlapping and pulling apart.

She tripped backward out of his arms. "Sorry, I—I feel light-headed."

Drake's thick eyebrows pinched together. "Here." He guided her off the dance floor to some chairs, his sword bumping against her skirt. "Sit, and I'll bring you some refreshments."

"Oh, no; I'm—" But he lightly pushed her toward a wood chair and then strode away.

With a sigh, Callista sat. The thin cushion slid, and she had to adjust it to get comfortable.

Why did Drake not only see her as herself but somehow cause her to *feel* like herself whenever he interacted with her? Like her own body and height? Yet no one around them had reacted as if she had changed appearance.

Small blessings. She might have been beheaded immediately if she had changed appearance in the middle of the ballroom. Still, something was wrong. Fae take Blaise for not listening to the warning that cursing oneself was a bad idea.

As if Blaise had been summoned, she spotted him standing on the opposite side of the room, glaring at her. His upper lip curled as their eyes met, and then he turned to another man and said something that made his companion laugh and cast her a judgmental look.

Someone in on Shafer's plot? After all, if Baron Shafer wanted the crown, he had to be gathering support behind the scenes. An idea blossomed. If she could determine who was working with the Shafers and bring that information to the king, would that be enough to earn her a pardon for her part in the conspiracy?

Perhaps, but would it be enough to convince the king to rescue Royce *before* confronting the Shafers? That seemed considerably less likely. All of this assumed she would even be able to explain herself to Cassius before Drake decided they couldn't trust a word she said. If Drake would threaten a baron's son in the middle of a ballroom for simply being a knave, what in Miraveld might he do to a peasant witch?

Her mood soured further. Was it even possible to save both

Royce *and* Cassius?

"Lady Tatiana?"

Callista looked at the troublesome general in question. Concern for her was all over his face again, and she hated it. Why couldn't he keep looking at her with distrust bordering on loathing? Why was it so tempting for her to get lost in those intense dark-brown eyes, in the memory of the gentle strength of his hand at her back and the feeling of his muscled shoulder beneath her palm… He was the greatest threat to her mission to save Royce. This handsome and thoughtful version of General Drake existed for the woman he thought was Lady Tatiana. And whether or not she was Tatiana, his kindness was that of friendship.

"Are you all right?"

"Um, yes. Thank you." Callista accepted a goblet and a small plate of pastries from him and focused on the food. There were several mini lemon tarts and some fried dough balls covered in a sweet, sticky glaze. Her favorites.

"I think I correctly remembered the ones you said you like." Drake crossed and uncrossed his arms, started to reach for his hair, and then clenched his fists at his sides.

"You did, thank you," she whispered.

Another problem—if she killed the king, Drake would be hurt, too. The way those two interacted, he would feel Cassius's death as acutely as she still felt the deaths of her family.

But this was no time for such thoughts.

Callista had locked her heart away before; she could do it again. She would smooth her expression into unfeeling stone and convince herself she was made of ice.

"Val, Lady Tatiana." King Cassius's warm voice intruded on her thoughts, and she jerked her head up. The king grinned and slapped Drake's shoulder. "I cannot express how happy I am to see you two getting along."

Callista smiled. "General Drake has been quite kind."

Cassius gave his friend an approving nod, then eyed the drink and food in Callista's hands. "I was going to ask for a dance, but it seems—"

"No, I'm fine." She needed to get close to King Cassius, if only to show Blaise she was making progress so he wouldn't hurt Royce. She placed the goblet and plate on the seat next to her and stood. "I would love to dance with you, Your Majesty."

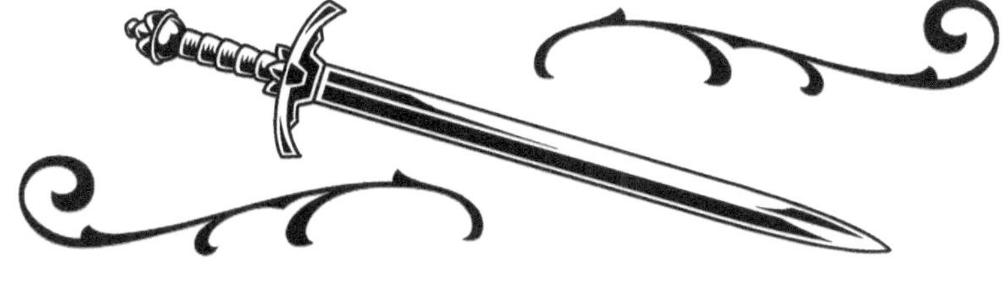

19

allyn watched Cassius and Tatiana take to the dance floor. Whatever had ailed her, she seemed to have recovered. Maybe she just didn't like dancing with him. Perhaps it was a resurfacing of whatever grief had affected her when she spoke of the "he" who'd told her about the ballroom.

He'd never met anyone so perplexing. She was relaxed and stony by turns, warm and then ice cold. At times there was a haunted look in her eyes; other times her expression was completely inscrutable, as if she'd locked every emotion away from any prying observers. Her aching sympathy when she'd told him that constantly evaluating everyone was an exhausting way to live haunted him. She'd said it like she knew the feeling, but how could that be?

And dancing with Tatiana had felt more right than dancing with any partner he'd had before. He liked how she'd felt in his arms, how smoothly she had followed his lead. Since she'd never visited the court before, he hadn't expected her to be such a good dancer. On the other hand, out on the dance floor, she and Cassius looked more awkward and uncertain than he'd hoped for his friend.

Ah, well. They had time to figure that out…

He'd have thought they would at least look in each other's eyes, though.

Vallyn squinted, as if that would change what he was seeing. Cassius wasn't looking at Tatiana's eyes. More like at her nose, which wasn't like Cassius. And Tatiana herself was looking slightly above Cassius's head. Watching them made him dizzy, so he turned away and frowned for a new reason.

A guardsman was making his way around the edge of the ballroom, his attention locked on Vallyn. There couldn't be any good reason for that.

Vallyn met the man halfway. "What's happened?"

The guard bowed. "Forgive the intrusion, General. There's a man at the front gate. He has no papers of identity or anything that would allow him entry. However, he claims he's your father."

Vallyn barreled past the guardsman and partying nobles, ignoring their offended looks. Once out of the ballroom, he broke into a jog, heedless of keeping his attire neat.

He needed his father to see Tatiana at once.

When he reached the front gate, he found his father leaning against the wall and glaring at a guardsman rather like a man would look at a hole in his favorite pair of boots.

"Father."

Arolyin Drake faced Vallyn with a relieved grin. "Son. Good to see you."

Vallyn turned to the guardsman, who was looking a little sheepish. "Thank you. You did your duty well." He waved to his father. "Come inside."

He led the way across the courtyard, his footsteps rushed.

"Something you have to get back to?" Arolyin asked, a hint of amusement in his tone.

Vallyn forced his steps to slow—not that his father was having any difficulty keeping up, as Arolyin was several inches taller. "Apologies. I'm eager to get your opinion on something."

"Ah. But first." His father grabbed his arm and forced him to stop just inside the front doors of the palace. Gone were his smile and any trace of humor. "Perhaps alert me next time you move over a day's ride away. Do you have any idea how panicked I was to get a message from you after all this time, likely indicating you need help, only to arrive at Alimer Castle and realize I couldn't sense you? That you weren't there, and almost no one else was, either? I thought—I thought..."

His fingers tightened on Vallyn's bicep, and his throat bobbed. "I thought you were dead," he whispered. "I thought I was too late."

Vallyn's mouth went dry. "I'm sorry, I..." Words failed him. There was no good way to say he hadn't even thought of updating his father. Nothing could have prepared him for the ragged pain and terror reflected in his father's eyes.

"I know you think I don't care." Arolyin's shoulders slumped. "But I always love you, Vallyn. I always care."

Not enough to stay in Aedyllan after Vallyn's mother died, but they didn't have time for an argument. And his father was still watching him with a pleading expression.

Vallyn shuffled his feet. "You came when I called. I know."

It was hardly what Vallyn would call love. Not what he'd wanted as a child. But Vallyn had also been given the choice to leave his own home and become fae to live with his father, and he'd turned that down. Perhaps he couldn't judge Arolyin for not making a sacrifice he himself hadn't been willing to make.

Arolyin didn't look convinced, but he nodded and released Vallyn's arm. "So...Cassius is the king now and you're his general?"

Vallyn nodded.

Arolyin took a step back and inspected Vallyn and then the wide entry hall. A guardsman stationed further down the corridor was resolutely not looking at them. "Your men certainly respect you." There was a strained quality to his smile. "I'm proud of you, Vallyn."

He didn't need to ask what his father was thinking. In the past, Arolyin had made it clear he'd hoped to see Vallyn earn respect in the Light Court. Vallyn didn't know much about the fae realm, but his father had hinted that he held a title and no small amount of power in his home.

"Thank you," Vallyn said. "Shall we continue?"

Disappointment pinched his father's eyes—dark and narrow and deep-set beneath thick eyebrows, just like Vallyn's. "What do you need help with?"

There was a hint of poorly concealed hurt to his words, but Vallyn elected to ignore it. Perhaps Vallyn had called Arolyin because he needed something, but his father was also visiting only because he'd called.

"It's easiest to show you." Vallyn led the way through the candlelit halls, doing his best to ignore the guardsmen standing at exaggerated attention as they passed. "I don't want to color your perception. I need your unbiased impression."

"All right…"

"I'll explain everything shortly."

"*Everything?* Really?" Arolyin raised an eyebrow.

Vallyn pressed his lips together. "Everything relevant to my question."

Arolyin snickered, but he didn't say anything else as Vallyn led the way through the labyrinthine palace.

Back in the ballroom, Cassius and Lady Tatiana stood together near a table of desserts, talking to a small cluster of nobles as Cassius introduced her to the court. Vallyn dragged his father into an empty, shadowed area.

"Do you see Cassius?" Vallyn asked.

"Yes. The crown suits him. I didn't expect that for some reason."

Because you considered killing him once? Vallyn clenched his teeth until he could lock the old anger away. "The young woman on his arm. What do you see?"

Arolyin tilted his head. For the blink of an eye, his irises glittered gold. "She's cursed."

Vallyn's mouth fell open. "She—what? You can tell?"

"It has altered her appearance."

"Her appearance, yes." In his excitement, Vallyn had to work to keep his voice quiet. "That was what I meant by what you see. What does she look like?"

"Tall, almost as tall as Cassius. Pale. Black hair. Thin—almost concerningly so, if I'm honest. Her dress doesn't fit her particularly well, probably because it fits her cursed appearance."

"I'm not hallucinating," Vallyn murmured. "Cassius—everyone else—sees a blonde with round cheeks who is a few inches shorter than the woman I see."

Arolyin spun toward Vallyn. "Really? I wouldn't have guessed… Oh, the power you could have had…"

"What are you talking about? Why can I see her? Her true appearance? That is what she really looks like, right?"

His father glanced over his shoulder toward Tatiana again. "Yes. The curse transforms her into the blonde."

"Like an illusion or glamour?"

"No." Arolyin met his eyes. "The curse is human in origin, not fae. It changed her, physically. To everyone else, likely even to herself, she looks like a tallish, beautiful, softly curvy blonde."

"Wait. Are you saying you can see that, too?"

"If I concentrate. It's a lie, so it's harder for me to see. With your powers blunted by your human blood, I suppose you can't see the lie at all." Arolyin scratched his clean-shaven chin. "I would have guessed it would be the other way around."

Vallyn gripped his sword to avoid the urge to check that the pointed tips of his ears were hidden. Even though no one was near them and they were both keeping their voices down, his father talking about his secret made him uneasy.

"If it's not an illusion, why can we see through it? I can't even see through glamours."

The corner of Arolyin's mouth pulled up. "Few fae can. You could, though, if you were fully fae."

Vallyn watched Tatiana ease away from Cassius's side to grab something off the dessert table, which she stuffed in her mouth as if hoping no one had noticed.

"But all fae can see through curses like that?" The question spilled out. It was hardly what was most important right now. Tatiana's appearance was a lie, and what mattered was finding out why.

"No." Arolyin's unexpected answer pulled Vallyn's attention away from the cursed woman. "Our family's surname wasn't always Drake."

Vallyn waited for further explanation, but his father just stared at him, as if that answered his question. "So?"

"So, my great-grandfather changed his surname after a dragon blessed him and his line. Our family is dragon-blessed."

That still didn't answer anything. "All right...?"

Arolyin sighed. "Do you not know anything about dragons? They can sense if someone is lying, Vallyn. That gift manifests differently in fae. The dragon's blessing gave our family the ability to detect lies not in words, but in magic. That girl's appearance is not merely cursed, it's meant to deceive. Your Drake blood cuts through the false exterior to show you the truth."

Vallyn gripped his sword. "Are you saying she isn't Tatiana Ackroyd?"

"That I do not know." Arolyin returned to observing Tatiana. "Her appearance is meant to deceive, but who and to what purpose, I can't say. It could be as nefarious as yes, she is impersonating this…"

"Tatiana Ackroyd."

"Right. That woman *might* be someone else entirely. Or it's possible she didn't like her appearance and wanted something she thought others might find more appealing. Perhaps someone else concealed her true appearance to hide her from someone who wished her harm. If she's been this way since childhood, she herself might not know what she truly looks like." Arolyin shrugged. "There could be any number of explanations from protective to innocuous to malevolent, so I would advise caution."

Vallyn recalled the first time he saw her, when she insisted her hair was blonde. "Would my seeing through her curse affect her in any way?"

Arolyin considered. "Possibly. If you touched her or even just got close enough, it's feasible that you seeing the truth might cause the curse to waver. Not enough for anyone else to see through it, but enough that it would affect her perception of herself."

"Which might make her feel lightheaded and confused," Vallyn whispered. "Particularly if she has no idea what she truly looks like."

"It could," his father said. "Has she done anything to make you think the deception has a nefarious purpose?"

Honestly, no, but Vallyn couldn't bring himself to say that.

Something held him back. A niggling deep in his gut, warning him that something was wrong. But lately, he often worried something was wrong. His nightmares had gotten less frequent, but they weren't gone. His reluctance to fully trust Tatiana might be baseless paranoia.

But at least his magic wasn't showing him things that weren't there.

In fact, he alone saw what *was* there.

"It might be a bad idea if she isn't aware she's cursed, but is there a way to break it?"

Arolyin gave him a flat, disappointed look.

"I know there's always a way to break curses," Vallyn hurried to add. "I meant—can you tell what will break her curse?"

"I'm afraid it doesn't work like that. I can't even tell if someone cursed her or if she cursed herself."

"Cursed herself? That's incredibly difficult and dangerous, isn't it?"

"True." Arolyin turned back toward Cassius and Tatiana and crossed his arms. "But that girl is one of the most powerful human mages I've seen in centuries."

Across the ballroom, Cassius took Tatiana's hand and led her onto the dance floor. There might still be an innocent explanation. But if she was a witch who wanted to get close to the king to kill him, who better to disguise herself as than the woman the king was courting?

20

ack on the dance floor, Callista was able to release some of the tension building in her spine.

Cassius watched her closely. "Was something wrong?"

Her gaze snapped over to him. The king's eyes, a rich, inviting brown with veins of honey, held kindness. Far more than she would ever have guessed to see from a royal.

"I'm all right. I just..." A bit of heat crept into her cheeks. "I don't love being the center of attention."

"If it's not impudent, may I ask why?"

The question was so genuine and free of demand that Callista found the answer pouring from her lips before she thought it through. "It always ends with shame and heartache."

Cassius slowed so they were taking smaller steps. "What do you mean?"

Fae-cursed slip of her tongue. How could she answer that as Tatiana?

"When I was younger..." She licked her lips. "I wasn't as pretty. Sometimes people would mock my appearance. Frequently, actually." Or her plain, worn, patched clothing, because that was all she'd been able to afford, or how often she made a misstep of etiquette because she hadn't been raised among the nobility, but that wouldn't be true of Tatiana. Nor would Tatiana likely have ever been mocked for how much she ate.

"I could also be a teacher's favorite. When you're held up in front of others as an example of doing something well, jealousy can make people vicious."

Cassius grimaced. "I have observed something similar, yes."

"Everyone was polite just now, but I wonder what they're thinking. Are they looking for flaws, weaknesses, some misstep to mock me for behind my back? How many of them hate me simply for being here?"

Old wounds ached in her chest, but she locked them away.

"While dancing, I notice them less, and I can pretend their attention isn't all on me."

The king nodded. "If you marry me, they'll always be watching, Tatiana. And they'll often be judging."

"I know," she murmured. "Does it not bother you?"

A wry smile twisted his mouth. "It used to more. When my father died and I became Duke Alimer, there were many who thought I was too young, who were waiting for me to fail. Even those I knew wanted me to succeed were watching so closely. All the attention felt stifling. But I had a choice. I could let the mockers break me—I could even help them by fixating on their opinion—or I could do what I knew was right. One day, I told myself I would let them stare. Let them judge. It would take more than stares and words to stop me from leading my people and seeking justice and honor. Besides, like you said, sometimes it's jealousy, and that has nothing to do with me and everything to do with their own pettiness."

Callista wasn't sure it could be that easy, not for her. When someone's attention lingered on her, a frantic voice whispered that somehow they *knew*. They knew the terrible things she'd done.

"But I understand," Cassius continued. "Vallyn still hates being stared at or giving public speeches or anything of that nature."

She gaped at him. "General Drake? But…he's a general. Doesn't that involve a lot of, well, giving speeches and standing in front of a lot of people?"

To her astonishment, Cassius laughed. "It absolutely does, and I'm not sure he has forgiven me for that aspect of his position." His expression turned thoughtful. "You could ask him how he manages it. His way involves a lot of intimidating scowling, and you were all grace and smiles, so maybe he should take advice from you instead."

Callista chuckled. The song ended, and they bowed and curtsied. As they straightened, she noticed someone standing in the shadows at the side of the ballroom, watching her.

General Drake.

How surprising.

But he wasn't alone, and the man with him watched her, too. The stranger was taller than Drake, but otherwise, they looked incredibly similar. The same light skin with warm undertones, the same handsome square jaw, similar deep-set and heavily lidded eyes, and the same black hair, although the stranger's was longer. The taller man didn't look much older than Drake, and he was…well, if General Drake was handsome, his companion was gorgeous. An older brother? She hadn't heard he had family, but then she hadn't heard he *didn't*, either.

"Who's with General Drake?"

Cassius turned. "Val's father…"

"What?" Callista nearly shouted, her mind spinning. At Cassius's startled look, she cleared her throat. "Sorry…he doesn't look old enough for that."

"Erm, some people age slower, I suppose." He released her and bowed. "Would you excuse me?"

"Of course." She curtsied, but Cassius was already walking toward Drake and…Drake's father.

When she'd eavesdropped on the king and general after that first fateful meeting, Cassius had told Drake he should contact someone about her. Drake had sounded far from happy about it, but Callista's nerves had overpowered her will, and she'd cut off the eavesdropping spell and retreated before she'd heard who exactly Drake was going to contact. If Drake was fae, his father had to be as well.

Sweat slicked Callista's palms. She left the dance floor and found a relatively empty area of the room to stand in where she could see Cassius and both Drakes.

All three men were watching her, and when they realized she was looking at them, they abruptly turned away.

The room tilted, and she leaned back against the wall to steady herself.

Had her deception been uncovered? Should she run? Escaping the palace would be difficult, and as soon as it was discovered she was missing, Blaise would send word to his father. Royce would be killed long before she could reach the Shafers' castle.

If by some miracle Drake and his father hadn't discovered the truth, Callista had another problem. The king was consorting with wicked and cruel fae. Just like Mortimer Faine had over two hundred years ago. The cycle was starting all over again.

And yet…

King Cassius isn't cruel, and neither is General Drake.

The thought persisted, fighting against her instinct to dismiss them all as corrupt.

From the history books she'd read, Mortimer hadn't been

cruel, either, though. A touch power-hungry and merciless, but ultimately fair, and his son was called King Jairus the Wise. Perhaps Mortimer hadn't had bad intentions when he bargained for that blessing from the fae that eventually caused his descendants to become arrogant, selfish, and vicious.

Cassius might be a good man and still doom their kingdom by consorting with fae.

And why had Drake been reluctant to ask his father for help? What if his father was more like the vicious fae of lore than Vallyn Drake himself appeared to be? If that was the case, it was even more disconcerting that Cassius had suggested Drake contact his father.

The three men leaned close, one or another occasionally flicking a glance her way while she pretended to watch the dancers. Callista drew on the energy of her magic and her surroundings and composed what she needed—a complex and percussive spell for eavesdropping through noise. It took her a moment to get it right. She had to treat the voices of the king and the fae as the melody while relegating the music and other conversations to hushed harmonies.

"So we continue as we have," Cassius said. "We proceed as if she is Tatiana and nothing is amiss while also watching for anything strange or suspicious. If she isn't Tatiana, I don't want to alert Lord Ackroyd until we know where the real Tatiana is—or if Ackroyd himself sent a decoy to deceive me. If she is Tatiana, I don't want to offend or frighten her."

"I also don't know how we'd tell her without telling her about me," General Drake said. "I don't want to share that unless necessary."

"Being fae isn't an embarrassing disease," grumbled a stranger, so that had to be Drake's father.

"Do you know the last time I heard fae used as a curse?" General Drake snapped. "This morning."

Suddenly Callista understood why Drake disliked being the center of attention.

"Back to Tatiana," Cassius said. "She might have a reasonable explanation but doesn't trust me enough to share yet. As we grow closer, perhaps she will tell me her secrets herself, at least regarding her magic. She must know she has that, right?"

"As much power as she has," the elder fae said, "she must know what she is."

"She at least knows basic barrier and healing spells," General Drake added.

Callista clenched her skirt. He'd seen her raise that barrier in the basement and hadn't said a word. It seemed they were both good liars. And how did he know she knew how to heal? He must have sensed some lingering trace of her magic in Stormy, but the realization that his magic was that strong frightened her further.

"Ah, yes," Cassius said. "Clearly we should worry about the intentions of the girl who uses her magic to save baby animals. Until I see compelling evidence that she isn't a good person or isn't Tatiana Ackroyd, I'm going to continue to believe both."

"I may not know humans as well as the two of you," Drake's father said, "but you have this in common with my kind: most of the time, the righteous still have their vices and the wicked still have their virtues. She has been here four days. You don't have enough information to know if her kindness is her exception or her rule."

Callista cut off the spell and let the music fill her ears. She inched back until her back pressed against the stone wall, then splayed her hands over the cool rock, using it as an anchor.

Was that what she was? A wicked person with a few virtues?

The thought seared her. That wasn't who she wanted to be. Her promise to Gareth and Leo and Anika made her want to be more. Living with people as genuinely kindhearted as Marie and Ian made her long to be better. Even Serena and Cassius—perhaps even General Drake—made her want to be more than a villain in someone else's story.

Fate and promises had pushed her to commit monstrous acts in order to defeat monsters. After the unicorn Tempest had declared there was still good in her, Callista had dared to believe that those actions hadn't made her irredeemable.

Would Drake and the king agree if they learned the truth?

At least for now, she was safe. But if she made a misstep that proved her guilt, General Drake would burst into her suite again, this time to drag her to the dungeons. Assuming he didn't kill her on the spot. Perhaps he'd keep her alive if he didn't yet know where the real Tatiana was.

Would he care about Royce's life? About the Ackroyds' steward's granddaughter, little Emmy? Would he even listen to her explanation?

Perhaps she should confess now rather than waiting to be caught. Between Cassius and Drake, Cassius was friendlier. Could she demand an audience with the king?

She had nothing to offer—no proof of the Shafers' involvement or their plot, no list of conspirators, nothing but her own word and Royce's imprisonment. And if the king made a move against the Shafers while Royce was still in Baron Shafer's dungeon, would they kill Royce and dispose of his body before the king's knights could rescue him? It was a risk she wasn't yet ready to take, but she worried she might not have a choice. Her other option was to eventually kill Cassius.

Lock it away.

The guilt, the shame, the desperation to save Royce, the longing to find a way to do so without harming anyone. If she didn't lock it all in the darkest, deepest parts of her heart and bury it beneath frozen stone, she would break.

Get through the party. Get through tonight.

After that, she would put more effort into devising a way to save Royce that didn't involve murdering the king or anyone else. And perhaps she'd search for a way to convince Cassius to stop consorting with fae.

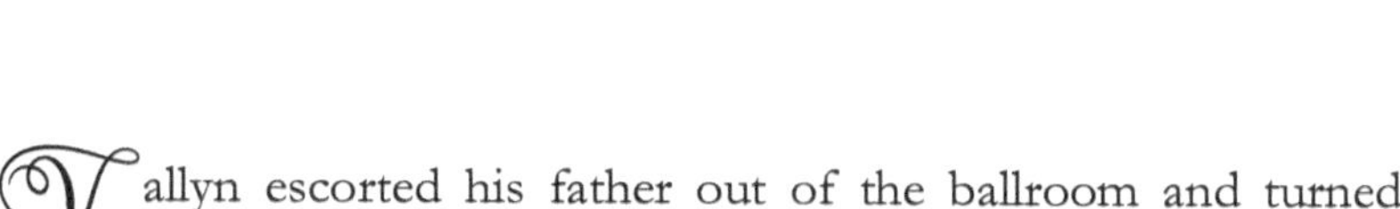

21

allyn escorted his father out of the ballroom and turned stiffly to face him. "Do you require a bed for the night?"

Arolyin's evaluating stare made Vallyn want to flinch back, but he held his ground. He was beginning to think he'd have to repeat the question when his father asked, "So you received your answers, now you wish to be rid of me?"

"You never seemed interested in staying before." Vallyn's anger wavered as regret flashed across Arolyin's face. "Do you need a room for the night or not?"

"You could use more instruction and information about your magic and heritage—"

"Quiet." Vallyn glanced at the closest guardsman, but the man was several paces away and busy scanning the corridor near the entrance to the ballroom. Grinding his teeth, he grabbed his father's sleeve and dragged him along. "There's a vacant room near mine where you can stay for the night *only*. I have too many things to worry about to add you to the list."

"Like whether your magic can make you hallucinate?"

Heat touched the tips of Vallyn's ears. He glanced around, relieved to not see any guards or servants nearby in the shadowy hallway. "It can't; now I know. Moving along."

"How many other misunderstandings might you have about your magic, your nature, yourself, life? There's so much I can teach you. Let me help you."

Vallyn marched onward, every stride longer and faster than the last. He didn't slow to check whether his father followed until he reached the guest suite and threw open the door. Arolyin was right on his heels, and he stopped a scant pace away and folded his arms over his chest.

"Here. I have matters to attend to in the morning, so you can see yourself out."

"You called me," Arolyin said, his even tone and expression giving nothing away.

Vallyn steeled himself. "Thank you for your assistance."

After a prolonged staring match, Arolyin's shoulders fell. "You are so much like your mother."

Fingers curling, Vallyn opened his mouth to say Arolyin didn't have the right to talk about her, but Arolyin continued first.

"Deanna was so proud and stubborn. Independent and sure she was right. It was what drew me to her." He took a deep breath. "It was why I thought she'd be all right while I dealt with a war back home. And I truly believed I'd be back faster."

"Yes, yes, time moves differently between realms. I've heard this before." Vallyn moved to leave, but Arolyin grabbed his arm and tugged him inside the room. Dim moonlight illuminated the plush chairs and low table before the cold fireplace and made the carpet look a faded gray.

Arolyin nudged the door closed with his boot. "Please, give me another chance. I thought I was doing the right thing, respecting your mother's wish to be left alone. Every time I visited you, her mind hadn't changed, so I'd leave again. And then when you said you didn't want to return with me after she…" He swallowed. "I respected your wishes as well. But I was wrong. I shouldn't have given up so easily—"

"Why didn't you ask if I wanted you to stay?" The words burst out of Vallyn and spilled around them, seeping into the cracks in their relationship, unable to ever be taken back.

Arolyin retreated a step, but his grip on Vallyn's arm tightened.

"You were right to respect Mother's wishes. I never blamed her for not wanting you to live with us, but I never understood why you kept flitting back to the fae realm. Why you didn't live in Aedyllan, somewhere I could visit you. Every time months or years went by before you bothered to appear again and have as much of a relationship with your son as a magic tutor might with a student, it hurt." The words tumbled out, as if this dam had been waiting to be unstopped for a long time.

"But after…after she… All I had left was the Alimers and a father I barely knew, and you wanted to take me away from them! I don't understand how a fae becoming human works, but if you could choose to be human for romance, why not for family? I know I'm not her, but why wasn't I enough for you?"

Vallyn tugged his arm free and withdrew another step, as if that would provide protection from the vulnerability of his outburst. At the least, maybe it would hide the moisture clinging to his eyelashes. "I need to go. I shouldn't leave the ball this early, and I need to observe Tatiana."

He shouldered past his father and gripped the door handle.

"Val—"

"Don't." The carved edges of the wood handle dug into his hand as he tightened his grip. "Don't give me excuses or blame me as a child for not asking you to stay, not when I couldn't bear to hear you say I wasn't worth staying for. And definitely don't offer to stay now, because I won't believe you, and it's too late, anyway. Everyone believes my father is a foreign wastrel who abandoned my mother and never claimed me. You don't look old enough to be my father, anyway."

Vallyn shoved out the door and slammed it behind him. He sprinted down the corridor, determined not to give Arolyin the opportunity to speak to him again. He'd said far too much.

His shaking hands clenched at his sides. Safely away from Arolyin's temporary suite, he stopped. Everything in him wanted to return to the party at once, but he could just hear Wilmina chiding him for pushing through instead of taking the time to address his turmoil. Inspecting what he felt was far from appealing, so instead he closed his eyes and breathed until his heart stopped pounding and his hands stopped trembling. Slowly, he uncurled his fingers and opened his eyes.

Back inside the ballroom, he kept to the edges of the party, watching for trouble. Blaise Shafer prowled about the room wielding his silver tongue, sometimes drawing laughter, sometimes prompting scowls. Vallyn wasn't sure if the scowls were directed at Blaise or due to agreement with whatever horse droppings he was peddling. As much fun as it would be to throw the churl in a cell, until he did something more than twist words, Vallyn's hands were tied.

Tatiana danced twice more with Cassius and stood by his side while he talked to nobles. Eventually, she edged away until she stood alone in a corner beside a picked-over dessert table.

Squaring his shoulders, Vallyn made his way to her. She paled slightly when she saw him approaching, but quickly smiled—a polite, forced smile.

"General. Did your father leave so soon? I admit to being a little offended you spent so much time staring at me yet didn't think to introduce us." Her skin pinked, as if perhaps she hadn't meant to be so accusatory.

Vallyn's lips parted. "How'd you know he was my father?"

"His Majesty said so."

Loose-tongued idiot. How was he supposed to explain this while obeying Cassius's command that they treat Tatiana as innocent and do nothing to offend her? "My apologies. He had a long journey. I showed him to some accommodations for the night."

Tatiana nodded slowly, and he had the unsettling suspicion that her green eyes read far more on his face than he'd allowed with his words.

"You certainly got your good looks from him."

"But not his height, I know," Vallyn said before he'd fully processed what she'd said. He pressed on, refusing to overthink her choice of words. "My mother was tiny."

The sorrow that passed over her face indicated she'd caught the past tense, and he braced for her condolences. "Whose personality is yours more like?"

Vallyn faltered, mingled relief and surprise momentarily tangling his thoughts. "My mother's, I hope. Actually, my father did just say I'm as proud, stubborn, independent, and convinced I'm right as she was." He winced. "I think he meant it as a compliment but saying it to you after how I've behaved makes it sound more like an indictment."

Tatiana tilted her head as she studied him, her brow furrowed. She gave a small shake of her head, and Vallyn wished he knew what she was thinking.

"So is your height why you don't like giving speeches or being the focus of attention?"

Vallyn frowned. "What? Oh. Cas mentioned you also don't like being stared at. I didn't realize he'd told you I don't, either."

His friend was up to all manner of secret sharing tonight. Perhaps he'd been so insistent they give Tatiana the benefit of the doubt because he was warming up to her.

"No, not my height. I don't like feeling under scrutiny, vulnerable and unprotected." He grimaced. When would it be acceptable to leave the ball? The majority of the nobles were still dancing and chatting, but the pace was slowing. He needed sleep and a break from the upheaval in his chest that was preventing his mind from controlling his tongue.

"I understand the feeling," Tatiana whispered. She'd turned to observe the dance floor rather than facing him. "Do…you ever wonder if it'd be a relief? If people knew everything you hope they'll never learn about you?"

"Because then I wouldn't have to wonder what they'll do or think?" Vallyn's fingers were in his hair, making sure his ears were covered, before he caught the action and forced his hands back down.

She took a deep, slow breath and opened her mouth. But then a shudder went through her, and her chin trembled. Her gaze was fixed on something across the room, and Vallyn traced her line of sight to Blaise Shafer, who glared at her with vengeful promise in his sneer.

"My lady, has Sir Shafer threatened you?"

Tatiana jolted. "Surely he wouldn't dare." Her throat bobbed. "Pardon me, General. I'm tired, so I'm going to retire."

"I'll accompany you."

Her head snapped toward him. "Why?"

"To ensure you're safe." Vallyn shifted on his feet. "If you'd prefer, I can send another of the guards with you—"

"No, that's all right. They have their own assignments." Her eyebrows rose. "Ah. I'm *your* assignment, is that it, guardsman?"

she asked, a subtle undertone of teasing in her voice.

"I'm off duty," he said with a smile. "This is simply me being chivalrous."

"Well now I feel guilty for ruining your relaxing evening."

Vallyn snorted. "Truthfully, giving me an excuse to leave is doing me a favor. I'm more comfortable on the training fields than here."

"You don't say?" Tatiana looked pointedly at his sword. "All right, General Drake. You may escort me. Let me make my apologies to His Majesty."

She slipped over to Cassius and curtsied low. As she finished speaking, Cas's searching gaze found Vallyn, and he nodded. With a shallower curtsy, Tatiana left the king and made for the doorway. Vallyn wove through the thinning number of dancers and met her at the door.

They walked in silence through the candlelit corridors until they reached her suite.

Tatiana turned to him, and he prepared to bid her good night. "Why is your father here?" she asked in a rush.

No lie materialized in his weary mind, so he settled on a version of the truth. "He has an area of expertise that will help me with a security matter I'm investigating. I asked him to come here so we could discuss the details in greater depth."

Which they were done with, unless Arolyin decided to be stubborn about this "let me teach you" thing.

"Oh," she said. "Did you get your answers?"

Vallyn hesitated as he looked into Tatiana's mysterious green eyes. "Not yet."

Her gaze dropped to the floor and remained there as she curtsied and turned toward her door. "Thank you for escorting me. Good night."

"Good night." He bowed and started to leave, but Tatiana's

quiet voice halted him.

"General? I don't think being like your mother is a bad thing. It sounds like she'd be proud of you."

His mouth dry, Vallyn turned around just in time to see her disappear into her room and close the door behind her with a soft click.

The midmorning sun glared in through the towering windows lining the corridor as Vallyn stomped from his office. A day and another night had passed since the party, and his time had been filled with work. The reports from Lord Ackroyd and the others in charge of capturing bandits and getting guard posts in place were mixed at best. For every letter with good news, there was one with bad news.

Vallyn organized reinforcements and sent supplies and gave advice as he could, but acting from the palace limited him. His place was here, protecting his king and friend. That didn't eliminate the guilt he felt reading casualty reports at his ornate desk in a spacious office and retiring at night to a decadent bed.

Matters of state had kept Cassius busy as well. While Vallyn dealt with the military aspect, Cassius managed his royal duties while facing complaints about property damage caused by both the bandits and the soldiers sent to stop them.

But not today. Today—

A figure pushed out of the shadows ahead of him, and Vallyn stifled a groan. His father approached with his thumbs hooked into his belt. "Val—"

"I'm busy," Vallyn said, angling away and passing Arolyin without stopping.

"I'm leaving."

Vallyn's feet rooted to the carpet. He had rebuffed all of Arolyin's attempts to speak to him since the ball, hoping to make this moment hurt less. It hadn't worked.

"I knew you would sooner or later." He didn't bother turning to face his father.

"I'm leaving because you don't want me here," Arolyin said quietly. "And I understand. I've been a coward. I'm doing what I should have done every time I saw you, since I first laid eyes on you. I'm offering to stay now, if you want me to."

Vallyn's silence was loud even in his own ears, but he'd watched his father walk away too many times, and he'd learned to live without a father. Maybe he was a coward as well, terrified that if he said yes, his father would change his mind—or worse, that he'd stay for now but vanish in a fortnight, a month, a year.

"Very well," Arolyin murmured. "You still have the stone. Call on me if you change your mind, son. Or if you need help. Maybe you don't want me to stay anymore, but if you decide you want more than what we've had…I want that, too. I've wanted it for years. I'm done being too proud and afraid of pushing you further away to admit it. Good luck with the girl."

His father walked past him, his shoulders sloping downward. Vallyn stood as if he'd become part of the architecture, watching Arolyin walk away and around a corner.

He took a deep breath that trembled in his chest. A few more breaths, during which a guard several paces down the hall kept glancing at him with wide eyes, and then he managed to pick up his feet and move down the corridor. He nodded at the guard.

"Guardsman."

The man paled several shades and ducked his head so fast he was likely to break his neck. "General."

Shaking his head, Vallyn continued on. He didn't have time to determine the guard's problem. This time, he was not going to be late. But all the guards he passed were oddly jumpy or started sweating when they saw him approaching. The pair outside Cassius's office shrank back as he neared, their gazes resolutely fixed on the opposite wall.

Vallyn opened the door the moment Cassius called for him to enter and quickly closed it. "We need to postpone. Something is wrong."

Cassius looked up from a ledger, squinted at Vallyn, then leaned back. "Mmm. Is there?"

"I approved all the guards, but some may have been turned, or the guard's been infiltrated somehow." He pointed at the door, his heart pounding harder with every word as his worst fears were realized. "They're nervous. Suspicious. They—"

"Vallyn. My friend." Cassius leaned forward to rest his elbows on the table. He knit his fingers together as his lips twitched against a smile. "First, you're wearing that murderous look again. Is something bothering you? Before the guards."

Vallyn opened his mouth, but before he could get a word out, Cassius tsked.

"Don't lie."

Fighting a losing battle not to glare at his friend, Vallyn tossed up his hands. "Yes! I have a list! This isn't a good time for this trip, Cas. I have too much work and too many things to worry about without you traipsing through the woods—"

"You'll be with me." Cassius lifted a brow, that infuriating smile still playing about his mouth. "Are you saying you can't protect me?"

"It still makes you more vulnerable—"

"Is that what was bothering you, then?"

"No." Vallyn scowled. "My father, who finally left, by the way, so maybe I can let that one go. The reports about the bandits. Sir Shafer's troublemaking. He threatened Lady Tatiana, I'm sure of it, but she won't tell me, so I can't help! I feel trapped in this sprawling mass of stone and unable to do anything about any of it."

Cassius sighed. "Val, you're doing a lot about the bandits. Organizing the soldiers' efforts and keeping them provided for is important. As for Blaise, if he does have ill intent, at the least you can be confident your excellent security has stopped him from trying anything."

Vallyn crossed his arms, stubbornly refusing to give Cassius the satisfaction of knowing he was correct.

"Second, as to why your guards seem nervous…" Cassius choked on a suppressed laugh. "What have you eaten today?"

Vallyn bristled. "I've eaten. You don't need to mother me—"

"I didn't ask *if* you ate. I asked *what*." Again that barely hidden laughter that was about to make Vallyn stab something.

"Fine. Some sausage this morning for breakfast. Had a servant bring me some pastries because I was still hungry. It's still food, so don't tell me sweets won't keep me full—"

"Oh, not that at all. You must have been very focused on your work, and you picked a fine day to wear a light-blue tunic."

"What is that supposed to mean…" Vallyn peered at his shirt, and the words died on his lips. Suspicious dark-red drips and a large splotch of crimson stained the front of his tunic. He reached toward the big spot and stilled at the sight of a bit of red on the edge of his sleeve. "Jam. The pastries were filled with a berry purée."

Cassius burst out laughing, and Vallyn turned a flat, unamused glare on him, which made his friend laugh harder.

"You—you've been storming around the palace…" Cas wheezed. "Striding about like you do, with—with—with that 'cross me and die' scowl of yours…" His shoulders shook. "And what looks like blood splattered on your shirt. Probably making unintentionally aggressive eye contact with every guardsman you passed." He lowered his voice. "And you're next!"

The king collapsed back into his chair, still laughing. Vallyn dragged his hand down the side of his face and groaned. But Cassius's laughter was infectious, and Vallyn smiled despite himself. He gave in to a few chuckles while Cassius pulled himself together.

"And here I thought I was going to be on time today," Vallyn said. He heaved a melodramatic sigh. "It seems I have to return to my room and change."

"We'll meet you at the stables." Cassius waved a hand, still grinning. "Maybe try to look less like wrath incarnate when you walk through the palace."

"I don't do it on purpose," Vallyn muttered. He turned toward the door, then called over his shoulder, "Don't forget her gift."

Cassius opened a desk drawer and withdrew a long, narrow wooden box. "Got it."

Vallyn nodded, then stepped out of the office and stopped to look at the guards. "It's jam." He tiredly motioned to his tunic. "Not blood."

One of the guards chuckled nervously. "Of course, General. I—I knew that. I mean we didn't even notice. General."

Would it break his fae bargain to ask for a demotion? Not that he was seriously considering it, but the idea of fading into obscurity did hold a certain appeal…

All right, fine. Maybe he did need to take a break.

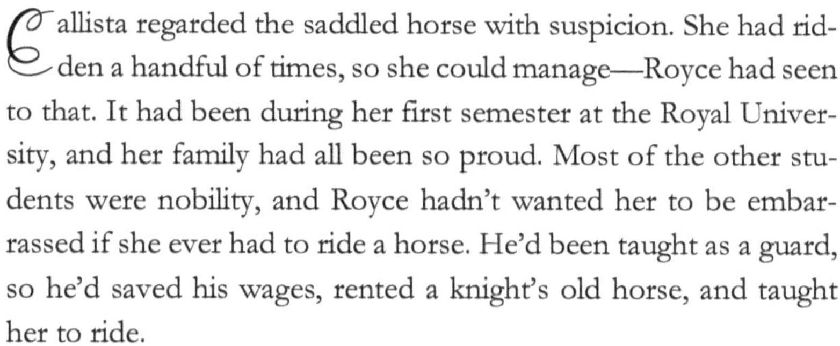

22

Callista regarded the saddled horse with suspicion. She had ridden a handful of times, so she could manage—Royce had seen to that. It had been during her first semester at the Royal University, and her family had all been so proud. Most of the other students were nobility, and Royce hadn't wanted her to be embarrassed if she ever had to ride a horse. He'd been taught as a guard, so he'd saved his wages, rented a knight's old horse, and taught her to ride.

The last few times Callista had been on a horse, though, her hands had been bound. She was hardly an experienced rider. Was Tatiana? Would it confirm General Drake's theory that she wasn't Tatiana if she mishandled the horse?

She took a deep breath. *For Royce.* She could handle horseback riding to keep Royce alive.

The thought made bile push at her throat. She'd spent the day since the party thinking of possible plans to save Royce that didn't involve committing regicide. All of them she'd discarded as unacceptably risky. She didn't even know where Shafer Barony was, so any plan that involved her absconding from Highrook ended in failure. Blaise Shafer possessed enough intelligence to have a plan in place to notify his father if anything happened to him. And as kind as Cassius was, no sane king would wait to arrest the traitors within his own castle until he could send men to rescue some peasant he didn't know.

Not to mention, to fully explain, she'd have to confess everything—and that meant admitting Royce was a castle guard who had betrayed his king. A wicked, now dead king, but would Cassius and Drake see Royce as a traitor not worth saving? She'd made a promise to save her brother. She hoped to keep it without committing murder, but if her nightmares were any indication, there wasn't another way. Last night she'd awoken from a dream where she'd been handed a dagger and told to kill either Cassius or Royce.

Her sole remaining family member, who had already suffered more than he ever deserved, or the king that Aedyllan needed. It seemed inevitable one of them would die, and either way, it would be her doing.

Callista shook her head, as if such thoughts were a fly buzzing around her ears. She needed to focus. This outing was a chance to win King Cassius's trust and get a better feeling for how he would react to the truth.

Assuming Cassius ever turned up.

At least the weather was her favorite. The air was comfortably cool, and the sun shining in the clear blue sky warmed her skin and clothing. She would be content to curl into a ball and nap in a sunbeam like Stormy.

A piebald horse standing nearby snorted and tossed its head, also apparently tired of waiting. Next to Callista, the easy-going chestnut gelding she was to ride nibbled at the edges of some overgrown grass.

The piebald stomped a hoof, its muscular side rippling. Callista chuckled. Undoubtedly General Drake's horse. Naturally, the taller and leaner white steed that had nuzzled at its handler's pockets as if searching for food was King Cassius's.

On the other side of the stable yard, four guardsmen waited by their equines. Three of them kept teasing the fourth about the lady he was sweet on. Yet still no Cassius or Drake.

If she were Tatiana, she'd feel slighted. Callista felt dread.

Was this a trap? The king had been his usual smiling self the couple of times they'd walked together to meals. A few times, though, she'd caught him watching her intently.

Footsteps crunched on gravel, and the guards snapped to attention. Callista turned from her horse. General Drake approached her, his cloak billowing behind him and his usual scowl etched in place as his gaze swept over the stable yard.

"Has His Majesty not arrived?"

"Not yet. I was beginning to fear I'd been forgotten."

"He should have beaten me here." Drake gripped his sword and spun toward the waiting guardsmen. "Escort Lady Tatiana to her suite and guard her. Do not let *anyone* other than me or His Majesty enter her chambers. Protect her with your lives and do not leave her until I give the order, is that clear?"

He didn't even wait for the guards to say "yes, sir" before he ran back the way he had come, but he only made it a few steps before he skidded to a stop.

"Cas?! Where in Miraveld have you been?"

Callista tiptoed forward and peered around Drake and past a bush covered in crimson leaves. Cassius was walking toward them, unhurried and trailed by an older man carrying an armload of books.

The king pointed a long box at Drake. "Please tell me you didn't go into a frenzy because I was late."

"You should have beaten me here!" Drake's hands fisted at

his sides until his knuckles turned white. "What was I supposed to think?"

Cassius winced. "I was waylaid by Baron Shafer."

Blaise's father? The breath seemed knocked out of Callista. Was that a good or a bad thing for Royce? For her? She pressed her hands against her skirts to steady them.

Ahead of her, Drake went rigid. "He's here?"

"Unfortunately." Cassius rubbed his forehead. "With claims that his demesne has been overtaxed for the last ten years. Shafer says if I truly mean to right the wrongs done by the Faines, I should undertake to pay their debts." He waved to the man behind him. "After suffering through his ranting and smug looks, I now have to visit the treasury to compare Shafer's accounts with the crown's."

"Don't you have clerks for that?" Drake asked.

Cassius's nose wrinkled. "I had to promise to oversee it myself to get him out of my office."

"He's bullying you," Drake said with a grunt.

"Yes, but if I refuse, he'll have more fodder for the dissent his son is trying to sow."

"You probably won't even find anything!" Drake threw his hands out to the sides. "It just amuses him to make you bend to his will and waste your time on his whims."

That didn't surprise Callista in the least based on her interactions with Blaise Shafer, but it did make her want to weep. She had nearly broken herself to get men who took twisted enjoyment in abusing their power off the throne.

"I'm aware." The king sighed. "But just because I'm miserable doesn't mean we all have to be. I insist—no, wait. I *order* you both to go without me. No arguments, Val."

Callista blanched. Go into the mountains alone with a fae who found her suspicious? No, thank you.

"What?" Drake exclaimed. "That's…" His fist shook at his side. He took a deep breath and then offered a small bow to the king. "I can't argue with an order."

Cassius's triumphant smile faded. "I was joking, but I do want you both to go. Give me the satisfaction of knowing that even if I'm coughing on dust from old books, you two are having fun. Please?" He leaned to the side to better see Callista. "I sincerely apologize for keeping you waiting and for not accompanying you, Tatiana. I hope the beauty of the falls will make it up to you, and I swear I will make time for another outing soon."

Drat the king and his genuine goodwill.

Callista curtsied. "I'll have a lovely time in your honor, Your Majesty."

"Excellent! If you can convince General Dour here to have a lovely time as well, you'll have my eternal gratitude. And you two can use this opportunity to get to know each other better. If Val trusts and likes you, I'll know I can trust you as my queen as well."

A nervous giggle betrayed her forced smile, but the king didn't seem to notice.

"Good." Cassius waved the box again, then looked at it with a jolt. "Oh! Lady Tatiana." He strode forward, and Callista hurried to meet him partway. "I'd planned to give this to you at the falls. It was such a romantic scene in my head." A bit of red crept into his brown cheeks. "I'll settle for giving it to you now, but perhaps you can wait to open it until you're at the falls. Imagine me surprising you with it there."

She accepted the simple wooden box with a curtsy. "Thank you, Your Majesty."

"You're welcome, Tatiana." Cassius nodded, the movement small to keep his glittering crown in place. "I'll see you both at supper, then." He departed, and his clerk scurried after him.

"Well," Drake said. "I suppose we should depart."

They didn't speak as they rode out of Highrook and into the mountains. Even the guards were quiet, speaking in succinct whispers rather than how they'd bantered while waiting. Serena hadn't been jesting when she'd said most people feared the general.

Callista was grateful for the peace, though. The rocky trail wound through thick forest and occasionally rose steeply before leveling out again. Yellow birch leaves fluttered in the slightest breeze, flashing in the sunlight as if made of gold. Amid the cool evergreens, orange, yellow, and red autumn leaves provided bursts of breathtaking color.

They rounded a bend around a boulder, and the path widened to a long, straight stretch. Maple trees lined the path, their red leaves fluttering to the ground and blanketing the path in crimson. As they rode through mottled patches of sunlight, the horses' hooves stirred up the leaves. Every bend in the trail revealed new beauty.

A contented sigh escaped Callista's lips. Despite the company, this outing was exactly what she needed. It was beautiful in a way that made her believe, even for a fragile moment, that there was still peace and hope in the world.

Then Drake spoke, shattering the moment and reminding her that she was not the sturdy maples or the enduring evergreens. She was the leaves scattered over the ground, crushed beneath the hooves of the horses.

"Is something wrong?"

Almost everything was wrong except for the forest around

them, but she could never begin to explain that, least of all to a fae who reached for his sword at the slightest provocation.

"No." Callista smiled sweetly. "Why do you ask?"

"You sighed."

She almost laughed. "It was a happy sigh. The beauty here…it's like it encourages you to draw a deep breath when you hadn't even realized how shallow your breathing had become."

Vallyn stared at her, then took in the surrounding scenery. For the first time since they left the palace walls, he looked up at the branches, and his slow perusal of their surroundings didn't look like he was searching for threats. "It is beautiful. Invitingly peaceful."

Every time Callista had glimpsed him since they left the castle, he'd worn a frown. Even now that his expression had eased, there was a tension along his jaw and a rigid set to his shoulders.

"It doesn't seem you've accepted that invitation." She directed her horse closer to his—or tried to. The horse always seemed uninterested in following her directions, although she wasn't sure what she was doing wrong. "Why didn't you want to come today?"

"Work," Vallyn grunted. "I'm drowning in it."

"In…nodding at guardsmen?"

His lips thinned as he cast an unamused glare her direction.

"I admit I have no idea what you do all day. Other than scowling." She punctuated this with a chuckle and was rewarded with a huff and an eye roll.

"You and Cas," he muttered. "I have to reply to missives from the guard outposts around Aedyllan and the forces sent out to suppress the bandits. The accounts for the guards' wages for the next quarter need my approval. My captains and lieutenants give me weekly reports, which would have been today, but I had to reschedule at Cas's insistence. More paperwork, more reports;

simply too many things to do to be gallivanting into the woods to eat food that could be eaten just as well at the palace."

"I see why His Majesty insisted you go," Callista said as she wrangled her horse away from the irritable general.

Vallyn groaned. "Not you too. You, Cas, the royal physician, everyone is determined that I rest and make time in my schedule for relaxation."

"No one wants the head of palace security to work himself to death."

"That would be unfortunate," he allowed.

A chill gust created a susurrus of fallen leaves. Blonde strands of hair whipped into Callista's face, and Drake's shorter locks lifted slightly. He transferred his reins to one hand, his free hand flying up to smooth his hair in a movement that bordered on forceful. As if he couldn't stand to have his hair out of place, except that his hair was always shaggy and chaotic.

In some accounts of the fae, they had pointed ears…

With a subtle flick of her fingers that released the tiniest hint of purple sparkles, Callista fashioned another burst of wind, directed at Drake's head. Some of her energy rushed out, making her hungry, but not enough to cause problems. They would eat soon, anyway.

Drake muttered an imprecation under his breath. He rapidly fixed his hair on one side and then the other, but Callista glimpsed the short pointed tip of his ear.

Why didn't he hide them with his magic? Fae supposedly could use their magic to change their appearance, and it seemed like he didn't want anyone to know—

"Did you do that?" Drake directed his horse over to hers.

Callista donned her most confused expression. "Do what?"

"That wind."

The redirection opportunity presented itself so perfectly, it was difficult for Callista to feign offense. "I—I beg your pardon? Have you no manners?"

Drake frowned, then turned crimson. "That—no, that's not what I—I wouldn't say something so indecorous…" He groaned. "Never mind. Forget I said anything, please."

He moved his horse over, affording them more space, and Callista's shoulders eased.

"Are we getting close?" she asked. "I haven't ridden so far in some time."

"Nearly there. We should hear it soon."

Sure enough, by the time they reached the end of the maple colonnade, a distant rumble filtered through the trees. The sound of water grew louder until the forest opened up ahead of them as the trail turned to the right.

Just past the trail, the ground dropped off in a small cliff overlooking a river coursing between rocks in a rush of whitewater. Orange and red leaves framed the moss-covered rock that rose on either side of the river. A short way up the river, a stone bridge stretched over the water, its arch framing the waterfall beyond it.

"Cassius thought you'd like it," Drake said.

Callista gave a little start and realized she'd stopped her horse. "This is breathtaking. It's a shame he couldn't come with us."

Drake's gaze was so intent she wanted to quail beneath it. "Is it?" he asked.

Her eyebrows drew together. "What?"

"Are you truly disappointed he isn't here?"

"Spending time with His Majesty is the entire point—"

"Yes, but do *you*, as just Tatiana, wish he were here, as just Cassius?"

Callista rubbed the thick leather of the reins between her

fingers. "Are you asking if I'm in love with him?"

"Or like him, at least."

She looked back to the waterfall and the shimmer of mist rising from the churning waters. "Cassius is kind and has a smile that makes me feel at ease and cared for. I suspect he's a good man and, more importantly, a good king."

A king she had to find a way to save—from herself.

"Is that enough for you?" Drake asked, oblivious to her inner turmoil.

The struggle of turning her horse to continue along the trail added to her growing discomfort. "Enough for what, exactly?"

"To marry him!"

"Is that even the right question?" Callista mused, half to herself. "People frequently marry for status or wealth or protection. Many shallow things can be reason *enough* to marry. You aren't wondering if I will marry the king—you want to know if I'll love him if I do."

"And?" Drake said.

Callista hesitated. What would Tatiana say? Maybe it didn't matter. If she were discussing her own marriage, what would she say? Honesty would be more convincing than any curated answer.

"King Silas and the Faines were a blight on this kingdom, turning the throne into a cesspool of cruelty and injustice. I admit to being among those who were suspicious of King Cassius as an Alimer with distant ties to the Faines, but unless he is an exquisite actor, he is nothing like them. I respect him—as a man and as a king—and I would respect him as my husband. Do I love him? I believe with time and faithfully choosing to care for him, I would eventually."

"I suppose that's acceptable." Drake side-eyed her. "You didn't mention if you find him attractive."

"He's handsome. I wouldn't say I daydream about him, but I certainly don't find him repulsive."

Drake coughed to cover a laugh. "Not the highest praise, but satisfactory, I suppose. Attraction is the least important, as appearance changes. At the least, you would remain faithful to him, yes? Even if attracted to someone else?"

"Of course." Callista looked at him with genuine affront, the mental separation between herself and the role of Tatiana blurring further. "I keep my promises. If for any reason I felt I could not take the marriage vows with full intention of keeping them until death, I would not take them. Physical attraction can fade or grow, be encouraged or starved. I would not break marriage oaths simply for a handsome face and dark eyes."

He blinked. "I'd be concerned that you're thinking of someone in particular, but I suppose Cassius's eyes could count as dark."

"Of course I'm not." But why *had* she said dark eyes? *General Drake's eyes are dark brown.*

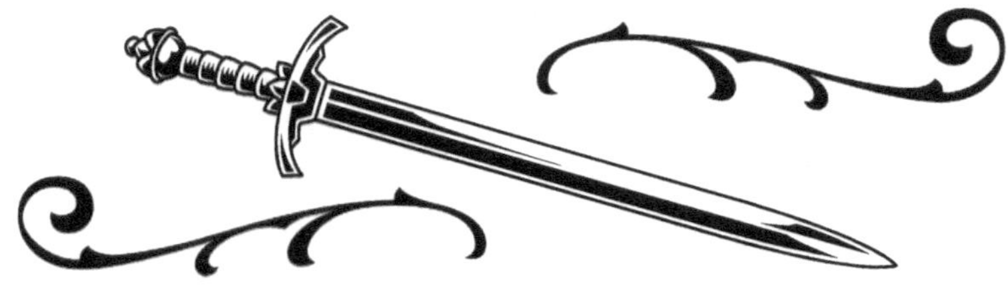

23

My eyes are darker than Cassius's. Vallyn almost blurted the thought out loud but blessedly had the presence of mind to keep it to himself.

Tatiana turned her head away, but not fast enough to hide her blush. "It was a random example."

She…no. There was no chance in Miraveld and the fae realm combined that Tatiana was hinting she found *him* attractive.

Why did that disappoint him? Before he could examine that any closer, she spoke.

"How do you think His Majesty will view and treat me if we wed?"

"With utmost care, respect, and faithfulness," Vallyn said. "I have no doubt that Cassius would never take the marriage vows if he did not intend to keep them as if his life depended on it. And he does find you attractive, if you're curious."

The fake her, anyway. If she knew her appearance was false, would that compliment make her feel worse?

"But," Vallyn hurried to add, "he cares more about character and loyalty."

Still, he couldn't help wondering: If her curse ever broke,

would Cassius find her true appearance as attractive as Vallyn did?

His breath stuck in his lungs. Attractive? No. He couldn't think of her as attractive. She was courting Cassius, more or less.

Nothing is official and they aren't even betrothed.

Vallyn slammed the door on that voice. Even if he were hopelessly in love with Tatiana, if she was already married to Cassius, he would never act on it. Just because they hadn't taken their vows yet didn't mean Vallyn could see her as anything other than a friend and Cassius's future wife.

Unless she was a fraud; then he would see her as an enemy.

But over the last few days, she had done nothing suspicious. Someone who praised Cassius with such sincerity couldn't be plotting to harm him. Right?

They reached the clearing by the side of the bridge. The waterfall was louder here, but still at a comfortable enough distance that they could talk without shouting. Vallyn pulled Riven to a halt.

"This is where we'll eat." He dismounted and went to help Tatiana, who once again seemed to be struggling to guide her horse.

Once the horse stilled, Tatiana accepted his hand and dismounted shakily. He knew Lord Ackroyd had sheltered her, but he'd assumed a young noblewoman would be a better equestrian. Tatiana stumbled as her boots hit the ground, and he gripped her shoulder with his free hand to steady her.

"Thank you, General." She lowered her pine-green eyes to meet his, and something twisted in Vallyn's chest.

"You're welcome." Why was his voice so breathy? She was so close...

As if his mind had abruptly broken free of a thick fog, Vallyn realized they were far too close for any semblance of propriety. He released her and moved back with the speed of someone evading a chimera's serpent tail.

Around them, the guards dismounted and unpacked the food and drink. One laid a blanket over the grass.

Vallyn cleared his throat. "While they ready our meal, perhaps you could open your gift?"

Tatiana blinked rapidly. "My…oh, right. Yes. His Majesty's gift." She withdrew the rectangular box from the strings that had tied it to the back of her saddle.

While she slid open the top, Vallyn held his breath. Last night, he had stolen into town for two reasons. One, to sit in a tavern and drink an ale in a dark corner where no one knew who he was or bothered him. Two, to find a flute.

Tatiana stared at the open box in silence. Her expression appeared to be carved from unfeeling marble again, the only indication of her mood the rigidity of her spine and shoulders. He gradually released his breath, and still she did not move or speak, but the box quivered in her grip. Vallyn's heart sank into the pit of his stomach.

"I'm sorry," he said in a rush. "I was wrong. Don't blame Cassius—it was my stupid idea."

"You suggested that he buy a flute for me?" she asked in a quiet, measured tone.

"I bought it and told him to give it to you." Vallyn pinched the bridge of his nose and closed his eyes. "The trip, the location, the things you actually liked, that was all Cas. I'm the idiot who thought you'd appreciate a new flute." With a sigh, he moved to take the box. "I apologize; I didn't mean to hurt you—"

"No." Tatiana pulled the box against her chest and curled protectively over it. "Why this one?"

Vallyn stilled with his hand outstretched toward her. "I don't know."

"Why?" she repeated quietly.

His hand drifted down to his side. He worked his throat and hoped he wasn't blushing from the mortification he felt. "It's stupid."

"Tell me? Please?"

"I saw it and it reminded me of you. I don't know why."

A complete lie. The black ebony used for the body was reminiscent of her hair, and the mouthpiece was carved from maple, pale like her skin. The end had a ring of iridescent mother-of-pearl that lent it an unusual, almost magical elegance. Its box was lined with green velvet, the color of her eyes. It had caught his eye at once, and it felt so…her.

"Please," he said, "let me get rid of it. I'm sorry I offended you."

Tatiana raised her head. Unshed tears shimmered along her eyelashes. "I'm not offended. It's beautiful. Thank you, General Drake. Truly."

Vallyn opened and closed his mouth, then finally managed to say, "Cas paid for it."

Tatiana laughed and wiped her eyes. "I will thank him as well."

She walked out into the middle of the bridge. Vallyn drifted after her, his feet moving of their own accord. She gently set the box on the waist-high wall of solid stone and withdrew the flute. Placing it to her lips, she closed her eyes and played.

The clear, strong notes soared over the rush of the water. He didn't recognize the song, but the minor key and slow, swaying tempo held him captive. A sorrow that spoke to the deepest, most guarded parts of his heart suffused the rising and falling notes. Somehow, without words, the flute spun a story of loss and despair. His body stood on the bridge, watching Tatiana play, but her song swept his memories back.

Watching his mother slowly fade. Struggling with his maddening powerlessness against her illness. Burying her alone because his father hadn't been there.

Mourning when first Cassius's father and later his mother died, first because of how much it hurt to see Cassius's sorrow and second because Duke and Duchess Alimer had been the closest thing to family other than his parents that Vallyn had ever had.

How he hadn't been able to sleep the night after he'd first taken a life in a fight against bandits at nineteen years old.

Collapsing to his knees in his tent following the first battle to subdue Lord Ackroyd after the fall of the Faines. Removing bloodstained armor with shaking hands, the full horror of every life he had taken crashing down on him. His revulsion with himself after he'd realized how his wild fae side had reveled while he'd struck down fellow Aedyllanians who were following their liege's orders.

When the last note died away, Tatiana lowered the flute and opened her eyes. Sunlight sparkled on a tear rolling down her cheek. Vallyn licked his dry lips and was startled to taste salt. He dragged the back of his hand across his cheek, and it came away damp.

For several heartbeats, they stood in silence.

"Why that song?" Vallyn finally asked.

Tatiana didn't look at him as she said, "It felt right."

There was something deeper there, some secret that Vallyn would have given anything to know. A week ago, it might have been out of a cold desire to catch her in deception, but that wasn't what he felt now.

He wanted to understand her, and he wanted…

What did he want?

She laid the flute back on the velvet and slid the lid closed with a quiet thunk. It was as if the flute had stripped away the mask she usually wore, leaving her vulnerable and tender, but she closed away the depth of her emotion along with the flute.

It dawned on Vallyn then.

He wanted to know her secrets because he wanted to comfort her. Not to use her hurt against her, but to help her. Listening to her play that mournful song as only someone who had suffered much could have played it had awakened something protective in him. Vallyn wanted her trust. He wanted to dry her tears.

Shaking his head, he stuffed those feelings down. Caring about her was well and good, but this was veering dangerously into…something more. Something he could not feed, because he would never betray Cassius.

They spoke little over their meal and the ride back down the mountains. The silence, while not uncomfortable, provided abundant room for Vallyn's confused thoughts to multiply. So he turned his mental attention to the tasks he needed to finish. That was plenty to keep his mind off the woman riding at his side until it started to rain, at which point his irritation at the rain soaking his cloak took over his consciousness. At least his cloak had a hood, otherwise the rain would have slicked his hair down around the pointed tips of his ears.

After they turned their horses over to the stableboys, Vallyn wished Tatiana a good day and headed out into the rain. He stilled as she asked one of the guards to guide her to her room.

"Sometimes I still get disoriented, and I'm much too tired from that ride to wander in the wrong direction." She laughed nervously and clutched the box containing her new flute over her stomach.

Before he even realized what he was doing, Vallyn turned

around and said, "I'm so sorry, Lady Tatiana. I should have offered. Please, allow me to escort you."

"Oh. Thank you." She didn't look at him as she scurried over to walk by his side.

Would they ever not be awkward around each other?

They hadn't gone far into the palace when a servant sheepishly stepped into their path and held out his arms, blocking their way. "Forgive me, General, my lady. I'm afraid I have to ask you to take another route. This hallway is temporarily closed for cleanup."

"Cleanup?" Vallyn peered past the man at other servants wielding brooms, buckets, and rags. "What happened?"

The servant winced. "Lord Blenner ate something rotten in town and not only regurgitated the spoiled food in the hallways—twice—but attempted to do so into the nearest receptacle he saw. Unfortunately, that was a vase, which he dropped, and there are porcelain shards everywhere in addition to the more unpleasant mess."

Vallyn grimaced. He didn't care for Lord Blenner, but at least he was one of the lords fully in support of Cassius. Although support from someone who would now be known for spilling the contents of his stomach all over the carpeted halls wasn't particularly compelling.

"Ah. Thank you." Vallyn turned to Tatiana. "Would you rather go through the gardens or take the long way through the palace?"

She glanced out the windows at the steady rain and sighed. "As much as I want to get to my room quickly, I don't feel like going back out into the rain."

Neither did he, but he wasn't about to admit that. "This way, then."

Since Highrook was built on the uneven side of the mountain, its floors were oddly laid out. Generations of Faines had added to the palace, which had sometimes involved closing a hallway to add a room or resulted in stairways in random places. There were a few ways they could reach Tatiana's suite. He looked up at her as they walked.

"Would I be correct in assuming you'd prefer a route with fewer stairs?"

She frowned at him.

"You mentioned you haven't ridden that much in a while." Vallyn shrugged. "If your legs are sore, perhaps stairs aren't ideal."

Tatiana's lips parted. "Yes, actually. Thank you."

"This way, then." Vallyn turned down another hallway but slowed his usual quick pace so she wouldn't feel rushed.

At the end of the hall, they turned a corner and passed a massive steel-encased door with four locked bolts as long as his forearm. Tatiana stared at it, her eyes wide.

"It leads to the royal vault," Vallyn said.

She nodded, but something flickered in her eyes—fear? Her steps quickened until she was walking ahead of him, and he had to jog to stay next to her.

Did he dare ask why the vault bothered her? No. Prying rarely helped anything.

"We're turning here." Vallyn touched Tatiana's arm to get her attention, as she appeared ready to charge on in the same direction they'd been going.

Tatiana followed, but as they continued down the hallway, her breathing became faster and shallower. Her knuckles whitened around the flute box, and instead of hurrying, now she was slowing, every step dragging more than the last until she stopped.

Vallyn faced her, his concern growing. "Are you all right?"

She didn't answer, her attention fixed on a spot near the wall.

Her chest heaved. Vallyn couldn't see anything, but when he looked back, her lower lip was quavering. She blinked unfocused eyes. Her hands shook until the flute rattled against the side of the box.

"Tatiana?" Gently, he pried the flute box out of her clammy hands. When she didn't respond or even seem to notice, he gripped her shoulder. "Tatiana!"

She whipped her head toward him. Her controlled mask of gentility had vanished, and the color had drained from her face. The anguish in her eyes hammered at Vallyn's heart as she drew in a labored breath.

"What is it? What's wrong?" He forced her to turn away from the wall. "What's going on?"

Tatiana shook her head. "I—I…" He felt her shudder as her gaze darted around the corridor. Somewhere in the distance, a door banged, and she jolted like a startled rabbit. "I can't…"

Cautiously, Vallyn let his magical senses reach out, searching for a threat or something to explain her erratic behavior. Nothing. No lurker, no trace of some magical threat, no weapon or trap— nothing that his magic could find. Yet he sensed her terror.

At a loss for what to do, Vallyn pulled her into an embrace, awkwardly holding the flute box behind her back. "I don't know what's happening, but you're safe."

To his shock, she leaned into him. A tug on his cloak marked her clutching the material as if her life depended on it. Her chest shook with an unsteady breath.

"It's all right," he said softly.

Tatiana tightened her grip on him and slumped, her head falling to rest on his shoulder.

For a moment, Vallyn forgot to breathe. His heart knocked against his ribs with such force she had to feel it. That protective, caring impulse rose again inside him with a roar.

"Whatever is going on, you can tell me," he said softly. "If you're in danger, I'll protect you. If you're afraid of something, let me help you. If there's something you're hiding because you can't trust anyone, trust me. I promise I'll keep you safe. Let me help you."

He stood there, holding her and waiting. Should he tell her the things he did know about her? Would that make her more or less likely to trust him?

But then a male voice echoed against the stone walls. "What in the forsaken fae realm?"

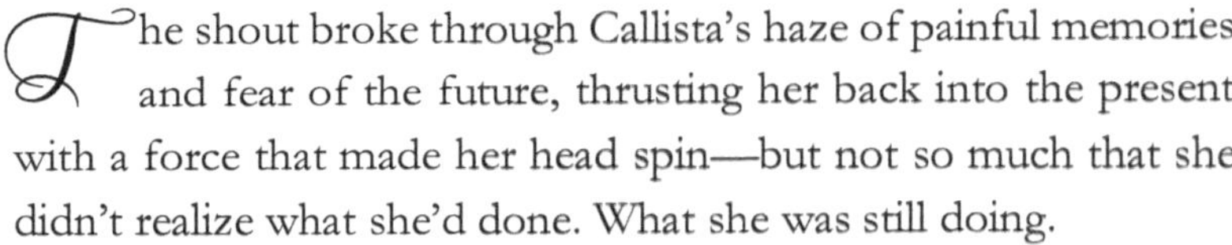

24

The shout broke through Callista's haze of painful memories and fear of the future, thrusting her back into the present with a force that made her head spin—but not so much that she didn't realize what she'd done. What she was still doing.

Maybe she'd spent two years alone with minimal human contact and spent the last week aching for comfort, but to accept it from *General Drake?*

Callista tore away from him, embarrassment heating her cheeks. How could she have let herself get stuck in the memory of the last time she had been in that hallway? Why couldn't she have suppressed the sharp-edged agony until she had reached her own room and could break in private?

But she hadn't expected it, and the memory had been so vivid. She'd smelled Royce's blood and felt it covering her hands, had heard the shouts of the guards as they'd broken past her feeble barrier. She'd been thrown back to that moment when Royce had begged her to promise to make the prophecy and the curse on the Faines come true, and then she had left him to die alone at the hands of guards he had worked with and considered friends.

No. Worse. She'd abandoned him to be captured and healed

so first Silas Faine and then Roland Shafer could break him over and over again in attempts to get to her.

Now Royce was alone again. She would not abandon him to die or suffer this time.

Everything had crashed together, threatening to drown her. Then Drake was comforting her, and she hadn't been held with that kind of tenderness and genuine concern since she was a child. Still, how weak and pathetic and unspeakably stupid—

A harsh laugh cut through her mental self-flagellation. "I knew our new king was weak, but I hadn't guessed he was so little of a man he would let his war dog take the woman he is supposedly wooing."

A shiver cut through Callista. With a gulp, she slowly pivoted to face Blaise Shafer. He stood several paces down the hall with another young nobleman whose name she didn't know.

"What business do you have in this area of the palace, Shafer?" Drake asked in a menacing rumble.

"Deflection, fascinating." Blaise grinned, but his gaze cut over to Callista, and anger shone through for the blink of an eye. "*I* was enjoying a walk and conversation with a friend inside where it is dry. The better question is why you decided to have your dalliance in a public corridor. Surely one of your bedchambers would have been better suited."

His companion snickered.

Callista crossed her arms. "I'd heard you were heartless, Master Shafer, but I hadn't realized you were also brainless. Perhaps you are too vain and malicious to have any true friends, so you don't know how to recognize when someone is simply comforting a friend.

"If you must know, we were discussing my late mother. My grief overcame me, and General Drake, knowing such loss himself, offered me consolation. Something I imagine you have never offered another human nor experienced in your entire miserable life."

Blaise clenched his jaw, and his nostrils flared.

"If that's true," the other nobleman said, "please, allow me to comfort you next." His leering grin drew a disgusted huff from Callista.

"Keep speaking." Drake stepped partly in front of her. "I'll happily wait for either or both of you to say something egregious enough for me to arrest you. If all you have the spine for is veiled insults without a basis in reality, do us all a favor and turn tail like the spoiled pups you are." He turned to Callista, held out the flute box, and offered her his arm. "Shall we continue?"

She took back the precious flute. After a moment's hesitation, she turned her back on Blaise and slipped her hand into the crook of Drake's elbow. He looked over his shoulder.

"Follow us, and I'll take it as an act of aggression toward His Majesty's future bride."

Blaise and his companion did not follow.

Down a hall and partway up a flight of stairs, Callista released Drake's arm and shifted a step away from him. The dizzy, out-of-place feeling she'd been experiencing ever since she'd frozen in panic abated.

"Thank you," she murmured. She still hated herself for leaning on him and feared what he might make of her strange behavior. However, not acknowledging how he had comforted her and come to her defense felt wrong.

"It was nothing." Drake cleared his throat. "Was that truthfully related to your mother?"

"In some way." It was neither accurate nor untrue, as the way the royal family had mistreated their mother had influenced Callista's decision to help Royce steal the Fae Blessing and Curse.

After a few beats of silence, Drake said, "My offer remains. If you decide to trust me, I'll listen, and if you need help, I'll help you. So far as is in my power, I will keep you safe."

She smiled tiredly. "Does this mean I'm no longer suspected of nefarious schemes?"

Regret pinched his countenance. "I am sorry for that, Lady Tatiana. I want to say I have reasons, but that doesn't change that I have treated you poorly."

"Well, this is a large step in making up for it." Callista waved the flute box.

"That's from Cassius," he protested without much conviction.

"I know."

They walked the rest of the way to her room in silence, save for a brief goodbye before he left.

Callista smiled at Serena and said the trip had gone well, then slipped into her room, claiming to be tired and promising to tell Serena about it later. A gray ball leapt from the bed with a chirp, and Stormy flew right at her chest. She caught the fledgling with a laugh and cuddled her, but the embrace reminded her of Drake's. As awkward and terrible as that had been…

It had also felt wonderful. Safe. Warm. She wanted to feel his strong arms holding her again, and she hated herself for wanting that.

Fate had aided Callista in bringing down the Faines, but where there were no blessings or curses involved, the universe seemed aligned against her. Anything good fell to pieces. Anything bad got worse. Even when things had fallen into place for the prophecy, it had left Callista feeling trapped and weary. Drake's kindness was the universe mocking her.

A mistake could put Royce in danger—he might be in danger even now because of what had transpired with General Drake. As much as she wanted to believe Drake's promises, she didn't dare trust him. Fae couldn't be trusted. In her experience, neither could nobles.

If she wanted to save Royce, she couldn't trust Drake.

It was all unfair, yet nothing felt as unfair as the fact that her fragile heart was drawn to a man who would never hold her like that again. He would never betray Cassius, so he would likely avoid any hint of impropriety in the future.

And if Drake ever discovered who and what she truly was, his promises to protect her would vanish like smoke on the wind.

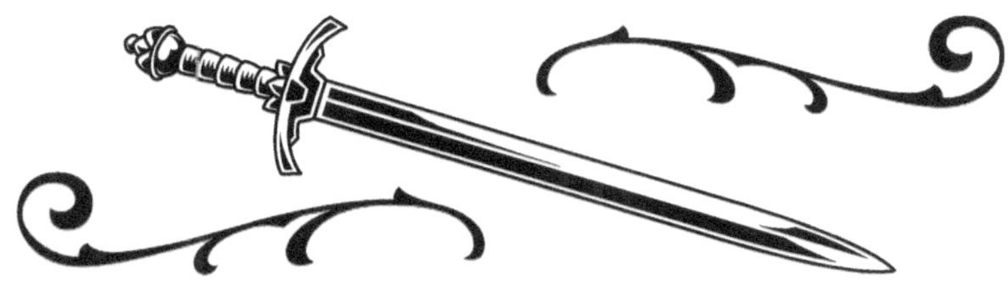

25

*C*assius was in his study, which was both a relief and a disappointment, as Vallyn simultaneously wanted to explain what had happened before it spread through the rumor vine and wished he didn't have to broach the subject at all.

As Vallyn entered, Cassius straightened from where he had been hunching over a ledger on his desk. "Ah, excellent." He made a shooing motion toward the clerk seated opposite him. "A good time for a break. David, go for a walk and do anything else you wish and come back when you're ready."

"Yes, Your Majesty." The clerk bowed and left the room.

Cas leaned back in his chair. "So. How did it go?"

Vallyn collapsed into the chair, scowling when the hilt of his sword dug into his side. He adjusted it and leaned against the back of the chair.

"Oh. What went wrong?"

"Nothing…sort of?" Vallyn focused his attention on the rain-streaked window behind Cassius. "The ride was excellent, the weather perfect until we reached the palace, and you were right, she loved Violet Falls."

"What about the flute?"

"Ah…"

Cassius frowned. "She didn't like it? I thought your idea was brilliant, and the flute you picked was beautiful."

"That…is the problem." Vallyn fiddled with his sword belt. "She froze. Wasn't reacting at all, and I was worried she was offended. I may have blurted that it was all my idea and she shouldn't blame you, but it turns out she *did* love it, and…" He cringed. "Sorry, Cas. I didn't mean to steal your gift. I did tell her that the trip was your plan, though, and that you paid for the flute."

Cassius chuckled and rubbed his forehead. "The flute was your idea, though, so maybe it's fair I didn't take credit. She probably likes you now, which is a good thing."

"She does seem to trust me more…"

Why did things have to be so complicated? And why did everything in him resist telling Cassius about what had happened in the hallway?

"It sounds like a success. So why do you look like a squire about to tell his master that he broke his sword?"

A startled laugh wrenched out of Vallyn. "Something…odd happened as I was walking Tatiana back to her room." He moved his attention back to the gray clouds out the window. "We had to take a detour, and she seemed disturbed by the vault door? Then when we were two hallways from the vault, she stopped and stared at the wall as if she'd seen a ghost."

Cassius strummed his fingers on the wood cover of a closed book. "Peculiar. The royal vault doesn't have any terrifying reputation that I'm aware of."

"Me neither." Vallyn lifted one hand in a confused shrug. "I couldn't sense anything magically, either. But she was falling apart, like she was going to either cry or run away. It was awful, Cas. I didn't know what to do, so…" His face heated. "I hugged her and tried to comfort her.”

Silence stretched out between them, and Vallyn forced himself to look at his friend.

Deep furrows marked Cassius's forehead. “Tried? Did…you not succeed?”

“Um…er…well… No. Or yes? She seemed comforted.”

“Then what's wrong?” Cassius asked. “I admit to being disappointed *I* wasn't there to do the comforting. But if you didn't offend her, I don't see a problem. Unless you gave her a flute and comforted her, so now she's madly in love with you.” His laughter cut off abruptly. “Wait. You don't think you accidentally seduced her…do you?”

Cassius's expression and carefully neutral tone were difficult to read, but Vallyn knew his friend well enough to sense a bit of anxiety and uncertainty—and a smidge of jealousy.

“No.” That single syllable tore through Vallyn's chest. *What is wrong with me?* He pushed aside the tangled feelings he had toward Tatiana and focused on his friend. “The problem is Blaise Shafer.”

Immediately, Cassius's eyelids lowered, and his lips pinched together. “You have an obsession.”

“I have a duty to keep an eye on a suspicious person who openly dislikes you.”

A smug miscreant who was clearly up to something, if only Vallyn could determine what.

All right, perhaps he was a bit obsessed.

“Many people do and will dislike me,” Cassius said, and exhaustion made him look years older. “Did Blaise actually *do* something?”

Vallyn hesitated. “He may have seen me comforting Tatiana, and he may have concluded that I'm seducing Tatiana away from you. She accused him of being so terrible he didn't understand comforting a friend and claimed that she was grieving her mother." He couldn't help a bit of a smile. "She was kind of amazing. I think she will make a good queen, Cas. But Blaise and Sir Morris are still likely to use it to spread rumors in an attempt to undermine you. I think you need to be seen with Tatiana. Acting lover-ly."

"Lover-ly?" Cas huffed a laugh. "That is a good idea, though." He glanced over the papers and ledgers scattered across his desk with a grim expression. "I suppose Baron Shafer will have to wait while I deal with his son."

"Or you can have the clerks take over. That is their job," Vallyn said dryly.

"All right, oh wise advisor." Cassius crossed his arms. "What exactly do you propose I do with Tatiana?"

Some feral, fae part of Vallyn snarled in his chest. He didn't examine why. "How should I know? I haven't courted anyone, either."

"Perhaps a stroll through the gardens and lunch in them, but without closing them off to everyone else," Cas mused. "So people will see us."

"Perhaps just the two of you. Well, with guards nearby, obviously."

Cassius shook his head. "No, that would look like I'm keeping you two apart, which would feed the rumors. You supporting us while we 'look lover-ly,' as you so elegantly phrased it, would be better."

"This is why you do the politics and I do the fighting."

"That sounds like you're insulting my fighting capabilities."

"Well, you have never beat me in a practice duel..." Vallyn grinned.

"Bah, you probably cheat with fae magic."

"I do not and am offended you'd even suggest it." Truthfully, he didn't, but less because it would be unfair and more because he worried he would hurt Cassius. When he fought with his fae magic engaged, he was faster and stronger, but also more ruthless and less affected by bloodshed.

Someone knocked on the door, and a muffled voice shouted, "It's David, Your Majesty."

Cassius called for him to enter. "Well, I fear I must return to this mess. But thank you for alerting me. I'll speak with Tatiana tonight about our idea to combat wayward tongues."

Vallyn nodded and rose. "I have my own work to return to." Work he had forgotten about. How had he forgotten how much he had to do?

His thoughts ricocheted back to the moment Tatiana had slumped forward and lowered her head to his shoulder. No, that couldn't have anything to do with it.

Although he wished he could gloat about it to that young woman who had told him when he was seventeen that no girl wanted to be held by a man who was shorter than her. "It's not romantic or comforting. We want to be able to lay our cheek against his chest or at least the front of his shoulder."

It hadn't seemed to bother Tatiana one bit.

Vallyn stomped down those distracting, useless thoughts. He had work to attend to, and Tatiana was already taken.

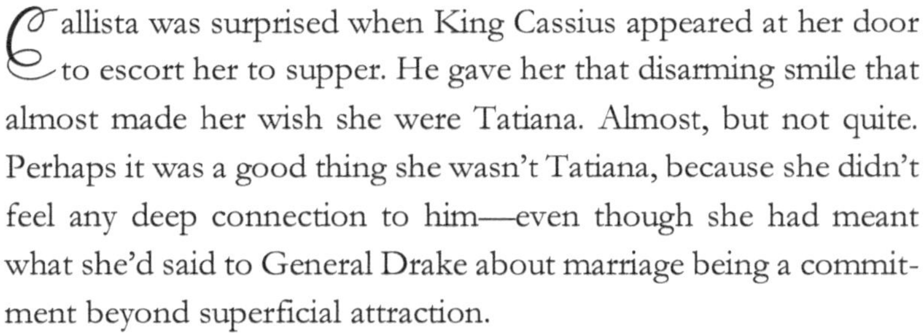

26

allista was surprised when King Cassius appeared at her door to escort her to supper. He gave her that disarming smile that almost made her wish she were Tatiana. Almost, but not quite. Perhaps it was a good thing she wasn't Tatiana, because she didn't feel any deep connection to him—even though she had meant what she'd said to General Drake about marriage being a commitment beyond superficial attraction.

"I thought you'd be busy dealing with Baron Shafer's absurdity," she said as she closed the door before Stormy could escape.

Cassius grimaced. "I realized some things are more important. I don't want to be the kind of husband who neglects his wife. It seems right that I behave during our courtship as I plan to during our marriage."

"Are we officially courting now, Your Majesty?" She slipped her hand into the crook of his elbow, and they started down the hall.

"Is that agreeable to you?"

Well, it was certainly useful for getting closer to the king. Callista smiled. "It is. Thank you, by the way, for the flute and the outing. It was beautiful, and I regret that you weren't there."

The words felt false when they shouldn't. What was wrong

with her?

"I'm glad you enjoyed it. I'll have to think of a better gift, though," he added sheepishly. "Val informed me that he told you the flute was his idea. How is it? Have you played it yet?"

Drake hadn't mentioned that she had played it at the waterfall? Then she wouldn't, either. Playing had been more vulnerable than she'd expected as she'd thought of how much she missed her family. It hadn't helped that the flute her father had purchased for her, while far cheaper, had also had a body of black ebony. Even though Drake didn't know any of that, the moment on the bridge still felt personal.

"I have, yes," she said simply. "It's an excellent instrument."

"Vallyn also told me about…whatever happened after you two passed the door to the royal vault."

Her mouth went dry. It had taken hours to pull herself back together and feel like she could be sweet, innocent Tatiana again. After so much effort to control her emotions, her one failure might be her doom.

"You don't have to explain," Cassius said gently. "Just because we're courting doesn't mean you're comfortable sharing everything with me. I recognize that may take time. But if you ever decide to confide in me, I swear I will listen without judgment. I want you to know you're safe with me—not just your person, but your heart as well."

Fae take him. If Callista hadn't stolen her place, Tatiana would be a lucky woman. Killing Prince Gareth had been difficult when she'd hardly known him. Killing Cassius might be impossible. Yet she still didn't know how to save Royce and the king.

"I hope I didn't overstep," Cassius murmured.

"Oh, no. Thank you. But you're also correct—there are some things I'm not quite ready to share."

Maybe she should. He'd promised to listen without judgment. Gareth and the Raylors had understood and released her. Maybe Cassius would. But explaining would take far more time than they had on their walk to the great hall, and it wasn't something she should do in public, anyway. Not yet. Soon.

When she was certain she could tell him without forfeiting Royce's life.

The king's voice intruded on her thoughts. "There is one other thing. Blaise Shafer."

Callista nearly tripped over her own feet. If he already knew she was a traitor, would he even listen to her explanation?

"I want to clarify that I don't mind that Vallyn comforted you, and I don't blame either of you," Cassius said. "But Roland Shafer and his son are proving to be thorns in my side, and Blaise is likely to attempt to weaponize what he saw, or thinks he saw, against us. I'd like to combat that by spending some time with you tomorrow afternoon in the gardens, with them open to the court, so we can be seen together. Perhaps even…well…put on a bit of a show of being close. Only if you're comfortable with that."

Oh. Right. She blushed, although whether it was from remembering Drake's comforting embrace or considering Cassius's suggestion of acting like a doting couple, she couldn't say.

"I see the wisdom in that, yes. And I'm certainly not opposed to spending time with the man I'm courting."

The pleased, boyish smile Cassius sent her made her heart ache, so she changed the subject. "Can I bring my gryphon?"

"Er…is that wise? Will it behave?"

"Honestly, I'm not entirely sure," Callista admitted. "We've been bonding, and she comes every time I call her now. She's incredibly intelligent. Still admittedly causes some chaos, but you should see the way she mopes about when she gets in trouble. I swear she's trying to make me feel guilty. It usually works, too. I've been wanting to take her outside, anyway. I think she's big enough now she would survive on her own, so if she runs away, I won't be overly worried. As much as I want to keep her, I want her to have a choice in what life she lives."

"Well, I look forward to meeting her," Cassius said as they approached the great hall's side door, which only royalty used. She prepared to leave to enter with everyone else as she usually did, but his hand covered hers, keeping it on his arm. "Tatiana, would you sit by my side tonight?"

Surprise and the fear of being stared at all night left her uncertain how to respond. "That…is quite a declaration, Your Majesty."

"Not one you're ready to make?" His hand slipped off hers, and he lowered his arm. "I'm doing this all wrong, aren't I? I should have *asked* you if I could court you officially. And I probably should propose before I have you sit at my side in front of the court."

"You haven't done anything wrong, Your Majesty. I just want to do this properly. Rushing things will likely encourage speculation as to why." There, that sounded like a plausible reason for her hesitation.

"Oh. Right. Of course." Cassius looked down at his boots only to have to jerk his hand up to stop his crown from sliding down, and he quickly straightened. "Then I'll talk with you again after supper, Tatiana."

Stormy swayed on Callista's shoulder. A pouch with the flute tucked inside it swung from her belt as she walked down to the gardens. She finally felt confident enough in her sense of direction to get there without help from Serena or Cassius.

Thankfully, after raining all night, the weather had cleared. The sky looked like a gray wool blanket, but sunlight broke through here and there. Still, she was glad for Tatiana's warm woolen dress.

Callista found General Drake waiting at the entrance to the gardens. He smiled when he saw the lesser gryphon. "I see she hasn't escaped yet."

Callista scratched Stormy's feathered neck. "We'll see if it lasts." Stormy cawed and jumped up, her wing brushing against Callista's cheek as she flew to Drake's shoulder. Her cat ears twitched, and she rubbed against the side of his head.

"Traitor." Callista chuckled.

Drake petted Stormy's chest. "Those claws of hers are sharp. They don't bother you?"

"Usually they just prick slightly and don't leave any damage."

"Usually?"

She tucked her hair behind her ear. "I might have a couple scratches. She doesn't mean to do it. Do you, Stormy?"

Drake's hand froze with his fingers buried in Stormy's feathers. "Stormy?"

"You were right. She's more storm than mist." Callista felt her face reddening. Why was he staring at her? "I wonder why His Majesty isn't here yet."

Drake opened his mouth, but Cassius's voice interrupted him. "I'm here!" The king jogged over, panting slightly. "I was determined to be on time today, but I'm beginning to understand why events start when the king arrives."

Callista eyed the coils of dark hair framing his face. "No crown today, Your Majesty?"

"Ah…apparently not." Cassius grimaced. "I took it off to wash my face and seem to have forgotten to put it back. I've been advised to wear it constantly to remind people that I am king whether they like it or not, but I'm not sure it's worth keeping you waiting to go back for it."

"It seems to me," Callista said, "people should respect you regardless of whether you're wearing a glorified piece of jewelry."

Drake choked, and Cassius's mouth fell open.

"A—a…" Cassius coughed on a startled laugh. "A glorified piece of jewelry?"

"If the crown itself made you king, being king would be as simple as theft," Callista said, although she was wishing she'd kept her mouth shut. "It's a symbol, yes, but it's also just a particularly sparkly hat."

Drake snorted and then clapped a hand over his mouth, which startled Stormy. The fledgling gave an indignant cry and leapt to the ground, where she proceeded to wind around Callista, brushing against her skirt.

"It seems your gryphon does like you," Cassius noted. "You said her name is Stormy?"

"Yes." It felt improper to admit that she'd gotten the idea from Drake. "Shall we continue into the garden, then?"

"Since it seems I can leave my sparkly hat where it is"— Cassius chuckled—"yes, let's continue."

He offered her his arm, and they started down a white stone path. Drake walked on Cassius's other side, and Stormy settled back onto Callista's shoulders.

"Honestly," Cassius said after a few steps, "it's a relief to be without it. It's heavy and cumbersome, and right now, I'm wondering how much I deserve it…" He cleared his throat. "Forgive me. We're supposed to be enjoying ourselves."

Callista eyed him. His shoulders sagged a little, and his eyes were bloodshot. Perhaps if she showed a willingness to listen and support him, he would grant her the same kindness when she summoned the courage to tell him the truth.

"Is Baron Shafer what's troubling you?"

Cassius shook his head with a heavy sigh. "I had a judgment this morning, and—you don't want to hear this."

She searched for something to say that would encourage him to open up but not pressure him. "If you would rather put it out of your mind, I'm happy to help. But it seems you want to talk about it."

"He does," Drake said. "Cas usually needs to talk after difficult judgments."

Cassius scowled at his friend.

"What? You said you wanted to bond. And as queen, she should know these things." Drake fell back a few steps. "So be honest with her."

Cassius's steps slowed. "As a duke, I found judgments the hardest of my duties, and they're worse now that I'm king. They can involve pointless squabbling between parties when I'm judging disputes. When I'm judging wrongdoing, though, sometimes passing a sentence is complicated. At times nothing seems harsh enough, because no sentence will undo the suffering of the victims. Other times, extenuating circumstances make it difficult to know where the line between justice and mercy should be drawn. Sometimes, what is right and what is wrong is abundantly clear, but it can still be difficult."

No sentence will undo the suffering of the victims was exactly how Callista had felt about the Faines. But seeing to it they would never hurt anyone again had helped.

Then Cassius spoke again, and she regretted ever encouraging him to open up to her.

"I sentenced a witch to death," he said softly. "He abused his magic to cause suffering for his neighbors out of petty rivalry. No one could prove what he was doing until he cursed a pair of oxen to rampage, and a child died. A dean from the Enchanters College aided the investigation, and the man's guilt was clear, his cowardice and cruelty were repugnant, and he knowingly broke several laws regulating magic use with no defense for his actions. He wasn't even remorseful. But he had a wife and two small children, and they were present at the hearing. She begged for him to be spared, but what kind of king would I be if I allowed someone so thoughtlessly wicked to go free?"

Her stomach churned. Would Cassius decide her case had extenuating circumstances that allowed mercy? Or would he see her as another cruel, cowardly witch with clear guilt?

Telling the king the truth no longer seemed reasonable.

Callista willed herself to go numb and be Tatiana—who would have no reason to fear how King Cassius might sentence a witch. "That does sound draining and difficult. I admire your heart for seeing justice done in Aedyllan. There's been rampant disregard for how innocents have been harmed in this kingdom in recent years. It's a relief to know you won't turn your back on those who have been mistreated."

She'd never said something at once so true and so false. Her father and Jacob had been innocent when they died in that fire designed to kill Silas Faine, and no one had cared. Her mother had been innocent when she fell sick, yet the Faines had offered no aid despite the fact that she'd faithfully served them for years, even nursed their children. Her friend who had been assaulted by one of the Faine princes and her friend who had died at the hands of bandits had both been innocent, and no one had done a thing about either.

But Tatiana was one of the innocents. Callista was not. Royce was a thief and traitor to the last king, even though he'd had good reason. After everything Callista had done, would Cassius order her execution and not worry about what happened to Royce?

She couldn't think about this right now, or her distress would become apparent.

"Thank you for listening," Cassius was saying. "These judgments weigh so heavily, and it's helpful to not carry it alone."

Mercifully, a group of three noblewomen emerged from another path in front of them, and their greetings redirected the conversation. Faking pleasantries Callista could handle; it gave her something to focus her attention on instead of the despair building in her heart.

While the noblewomen commented on the weather, Callista shifted closer to the king and leaned against his shoulder.

"I'm terribly sorry, ladies," the king said. "But I promised Tatiana I'd be focused on her. Please excuse us."

Without waiting for a response, he continued further into the gardens. After several steps, he glanced over his shoulder, then said, "I'm unsure whether I should be pleased you're feeling this comfortable with me or impressed at your acting ability."

"You did say to give them a show." She kept as close to him as she could while they walked, even though her taut nerves wanted to flee the garden and Highrook entirely.

Cassius led them through the summer garden, which was mostly dormant apart from some bushes and trees that still had autumn leaves. After the rain, many of those leaves carpeted the ground, but the groundskeepers had swept the paths clear.

"I know this area looks a bit sad," Cassius said, "but there's a lovely spot just ahead, even with most of the greenery fading. Ready?"

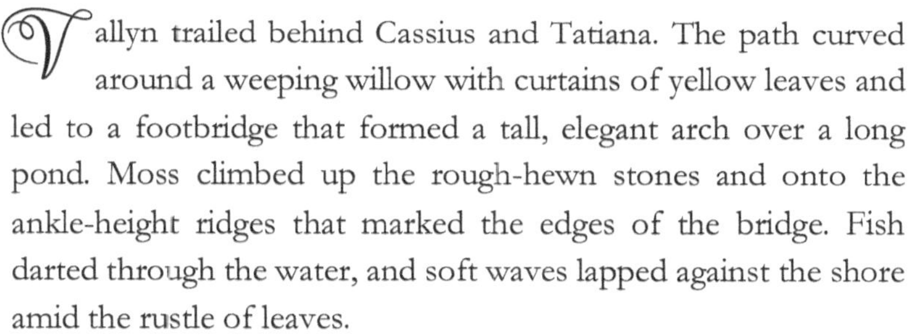

allyn trailed behind Cassius and Tatiana. The path curved around a weeping willow with curtains of yellow leaves and led to a footbridge that formed a tall, elegant arch over a long pond. Moss climbed up the rough-hewn stones and onto the ankle-height ridges that marked the edges of the bridge. Fish darted through the water, and soft waves lapped against the shore amid the rustle of leaves.

Vallyn stopped at the edge of the gravel path to give Cassius and Tatiana some space as they halted at the apex of the bridge. Tatiana whispered something, and Cassius withdrew his arm from hers so he could slide it around her waist and pull her closer. A lump formed in Vallyn's throat.

He was happy for them. After everything Cassius had been through and how difficult these last couple months had been, he wished his friend all happiness.

Yet something deep in his heart recoiled as Cassius's thumb rubbed Tatiana's side.

Whatever this feeling was, Vallyn refused to give it a foothold. He would not envy Cassius's romance. Besides, he had too many worries to consider a relationship of his own.

"Stormy, no!"

Heedless of her mistress's cry, the fledgling dove at the pond. Stormy flew back up, a fish clutched in her front talons.

"Oh—I'm so sorry—"

Cassius laughed. "Don't fret. I don't think the pond will miss one fish. We simply won't tell the groundskeepers."

Stormy landed on the shore beneath the swaying branches of a willow and set about tearing into her catch.

Voices sounded behind Vallyn, and he moved out of the way of a group of courtiers. He gladly let them pass him without a word, but several lingered on the bridge to speak with Cassius.

One lord tried to ask Cassius something, but Cassius held up his free hand. "Please, Baron Davon. Let us have an agreement. I won't bother you with matters of state when you're spending time with your family, and you will allow me some peace to savor my time in my lady's company."

The baron mumbled his apologies and the group moved on, their chatter fading into the distance.

Cassius sighed. "I apologize."

"Whatever for?" Tatiana asked. "If being interrupted is normal for you, I should get used to it. And they weren't rude."

"Most of them scarcely acknowledged you."

"I'll take that over the snide comments."

Vallyn prickled. "What snide comments?"

Tatiana and Cassius looked over at him. "Just…last night at supper, a few of the nobles were loudly whispering about my 'indiscretions.' It was worse than their usual insults about my clothing or my manners or my father."

"The Shafers?" Vallyn demanded, his blood heating.

"Among others."

"Val," Cassius said, warning in his voice. "Still not treason."

It felt like it should be treason.

A piercing cry echoed through the air, and Stormy flew back to the bridge and landed at Tatiana's feet. She frowned down at her pet. "Charming."

Stormy's cat ears swiveled. Bits of blood stained the little gryphon's talons and beak. Perhaps a lesser gryphon wasn't the most royal of pets, but somehow, it suited Tatiana.

She turned back to Cassius. "May I have the honor of playing the flute for you, Your Majesty?"

Vallyn perked up. He'd hoped the flute was in the narrow pouch hanging at her side…even though he was slightly annoyed that she would be playing for Cassius, not him. Which didn't make any sense.

"I would be honored and delighted to listen to you play," Cassius said eagerly.

Footsteps sounded behind Vallyn. He turned, and a burning desire to unleash his magic leapt in his chest.

Baron Roland Shafer's pinched scowl contrasted with his son's irritating smirk. Since Vallyn had guards reporting on both men's movements, he knew neither had visited the gardens since their respective arrivals.

Roland looked from Vallyn over to Cassius, whose arm still encircled Tatiana's waist. "My son had an interesting story to tell yesterday. It seems he was mistaken."

Blaise snickered. "Or the *honorable* general was ordered to stand off to the side and watch the king put his hands all over Lady Ackroyd to remind him who she belongs to."

"She belongs to no one," Vallyn snapped without thought.

Cassius cleared his throat. "General Drake is correct. Lady Tatiana is not property. But Drake is here because he is my friend—and also because I trust him entirely with my safety."

"Surely you don't think you're at risk within your own castle walls?" Roland asked with melodramatic shock. "How concerning."

"Does your presence here have a purpose, Baron Shafer?" Vallyn asked with a tight smile.

"I'm enjoying the public gardens and satisfying my curiosity before I return home." Roland marched past Vallyn onto the bridge, trailed by his son.

As they neared the center, Stormy unleashed an earsplitting shriek and arched her back. She snapped her little beak and positioned herself between Tatiana and the Shafers.

Oh, Vallyn liked the fledgling.

"Ugh, what is that animal doing?" The baron kicked toward Stormy.

Tatiana tore away from Cassius with a gasp. Stormy screeched and reared up. Stretching out her wings, she waved her talons menacingly. It would have been a terrifying sight if Stormy had been full-grown…and one of her considerably larger cousins. Although Vallyn didn't doubt those needlelike talons and claws could draw blood if the fledgling so chose.

Tatiana crouched and swept up the lesser gryphon. "Calm, Stormy. You're all right."

"It's *yours?*" Blaise demanded. "Your…pet?"

Cradling Stormy against her chest, Tatiana went rigid. "Yes." She sounded more timid than Vallyn had ever heard her before.

"How uncivilized." Shaking his head, Roland Shafer continued past them.

At the far end of the bridge, Blaise cast another look at Cassius and Tatiana and her pet, something dark simmering in his expression. Then he turned around and left.

One day, Vallyn was going to find a reason to shove that knave onto his back.

"Are you all right?" Cassius asked Tatiana. "Has one of the Shafers threatened you?"

Vallyn missed her response, because the pounding of running footsteps and someone's labored breathing drew his attention. A servant raced down the path toward them, sweat glistening on his forehead.

"Your Majesty!" The servant skidded to a stop near Vallyn and bowed deeply. "Forgive me for interrupting, Your Majesty. An ambassador has arrived from Eynlae."

Cassius's eyes widened. The neighboring kingdom of Eynlae hadn't sent a delegate to Aedyllan in a few years, and despite Cassius sending one to Eynlae weeks ago, they hadn't heard anything from King Weston. An ambassador meant the king of Eynlae was formally recognizing Cassius's rule.

"You need to go, don't you?" Tatiana asked.

"I'm so sorry, but I should meet with him at once." Cassius lightly caressed her cheek, and that inexplicable jealousy stirred in Vallyn's blood along with the unruly edge of his fae magic. "I regret that I'll have to wait to hear you play."

Tatiana shook her head. "Your responsibility as king takes precedence, Your Majesty. Don't forget to go to your office for your crown."

"Right, yes, thank you!" Cassius hesitated, then kissed Tatiana's forehead—which for a moment had Vallyn seeing double, because Cassius was kissing the fake, shorter Tatiana. For less than the blink of an eye, Vallyn caught sight of the blonde with a fuller figure, but then she was the reedy woman with black hair again.

"I'll see you again soon," Cassius promised. He nodded at Vallyn and hurried after the servant.

Stormy squirmed in Tatiana's hold, and she set the gray fledgling down with a remonstrative sigh. The gryphon soared over the pond, and Tatiana watched her chase bugs. A breeze teased the ends of her long hair and tugged on her magenta dress.

Did she know what she really looked like? Did she know her true appearance was beautiful?

Vallyn walked up the curved bridge to stand beside her. "I'm sorry you weren't able to play for Cassius."

"There will be plenty of future opportunities." She sat down with her legs hanging over the edge.

Vallyn hesitated, then sat beside her. He had things to do—always so much to do—but he couldn't leave Tatiana alone, especially not after the Shafers' behavior. How he longed to convince her to tell him why the Shafers scared her.

The clever baron and his openly hostile son had to have more of a plan than criticizing and belittling Cassius and Tatiana at every opportunity. Roland Shafer would return home early tomorrow, but that didn't make Vallyn feel any better. If anything, it made him more suspicious. The question of taxes had to be a poorly manufactured lie so Roland could visit Highrook for a few days. To what end? To do what?

If Vallyn knew, maybe he wouldn't have awoken in the wee hours of the morning in a cold sweat from a nightmare. He'd been tangled in his bedding, which probably explained why he hadn't been able to move in the dream.

He rubbed his dry eyes.

As much as Vallyn feared he wasn't ready for whatever the Shafers would do, he wanted them to get it over with. The waiting was crushing his sanity.

"You seem stressed," Tatiana murmured.

"You…noticed?"

"Your scowl seems deeper than usual, you're tensing, well, everything, but most noticeably your shoulders."

With a deep breath, he let his shoulders relax. Oh. He hadn't realized how much he'd been holding them up.

"More nightmares?"

Vallyn jerked a nod. He opened his mouth to give the reflexive answer that it wasn't that bad, that she didn't need to worry about him, but he stopped. Was this his chance to win her trust by being vulnerably honest himself? It was worth trying.

"Have you ever had one thing, one task, that was expected of you, but you feared you wouldn't be able to do it? That you'd fail at the only thing that was important?"

As soon as Vallyn said it, he realized how stupid that was. Why would the sheltered daughter of a lord have to worry about failing?

"Yes." The single word was little more than a breath. Tatiana faced the pond, but it was like she was looking past it at something he couldn't see. "It feels like balancing on the crumbling edge of a precipice while doing a vital task. 'Don't look down,' but you can't look away from the abyss. You're doing everything you can to finish what you started, but the edge is always there, and you're one misstep away from a fall that will destroy everything you've worked for and care about. Some days you see your task coming together and you dare to hope you will at least finish before you fall. Some days you worry you've already stepped off the edge and just haven't realized it yet."

Vallyn was a man of weapons, not words. Hearing her describe the tension in his soul twisted something deep inside him. He shifted to look directly at her profile. The gray light filtering through the clouds sapped her color, and she sat so still, her face concealing all emotion.

"Yes," he murmured. "The one thing I want—I need—to do is protect Cassius. It's an oath I've kept for years. But now it isn't just my friend's life at stake, it's the future of the entire kingdom, and I wasn't made for politics. I can *feel* in my bones that something is coming, that Cassius isn't safe, but I…" His tongue caught on the words, as if voicing them aloud would make them true.

"You're terrified you won't stop it in time."

Vallyn nodded, even though she wasn't looking at him. Minutes slipped by as they sat in silence, Tatiana unmoving except for the strands of her dark hair caught in the soft breeze.

Everything in him wanted to ask what she was or had been afraid of failing. If it was in the past and if she had succeeded. Some instinct held him back, warned him she wouldn't answer.

"What do you get out of it?" she asked quietly, her gaze still locked on some point in the distance.

"Out of what?"

"Protecting the king. Helping him. Why do you do it?"

"Cas and I grew up together. He's like my brother." It wasn't the whole truth, but he couldn't admit what he was to a woman with secrets that might hold danger. "And he's a good man and a good king. He will rule Aedyllan well. Baron Shafer wouldn't."

"And he's the only other option?"

"Er…your father seems to be a good man, but I'm not convinced he has the leadership experience, charisma, or strength that Aedyllan needs in its king right now. Perhaps I'm biased, but I don't believe there is another man in Aedyllan who is more qualified." Vallyn frowned. "Who would you see on the throne?"

After a long moment, Tatiana lowered her gaze to the pond beneath her dangling boots. "Would you believe me if I said I agree with you? The Faines caused so much suffering." Her hand gripped the pouch containing her flute. "They left wounds on Aedyllan, wounds that will take time to fade to scars. Cassius is the kind of king who will help those wounds close. Is that all it is for you, then? You believe in him, so you'll fight for him? No benefit to you?"

It took him a moment to catch up to her question, because he was stuck on how personal it had sounded when she spoke of the harm done by the Faines.

"I suppose he also gives me a home and employment and status." Things that made his oath with Cassius two-sided, a bargain his fae magic could latch on to. "I get his friendship out of it, I suppose, which means far more to me. Is it difficult to believe I follow him simply because I believe he is worth following?"

At last, Tatiana turned and looked at him. Her green eyes searched his, an intensity to them that pinned him in place. "It is difficult. Yet I do believe you." She untied the pouch from her belt. "Perhaps I can't assure you that you won't fail. But maybe I can distract you from your worries for a while."

With that, Tatiana withdrew the flute and held it to her lips.

Vallyn's disappointment that he had bared his soul and learned nothing in return faded as he listened to her play. This time she played a gentle and relaxing song. He leaned back on his hands and closed his eyes. The slow, clear notes had a bright, lilting cadence that reminded him of times as a child when he would hang a blanket between two trees and lie in it and rock back and forth, unworried and content.

Too soon, the last note faded away. Slowly, he opened his eyes. A glistening line trailed down Tatiana's cheek.

Vallyn straightened. "Why are you crying?"

"I should return to my rooms. I didn't think this through." Tatiana returned the flute to its bag. "If someone sees us alone out here without His Majesty, it will hardly help matters."

Gaining a woman's trust was far harder than he'd ever imagined, and her rejection of his concern stung. She did have a point though. Vallyn clambered to his feet while she tied the pouch back to her belt.

"Do you see Stormy?" she asked.

"Hm." The lesser gryphon wasn't in the skies or along the shore or in any nearby trees. "Sorry, no."

Tatiana nibbled on her lower lip, and her shoulders drooped. "I hope she'll be safe."

She stood as well, but as she gained her feet, her boot caught on her dress, sending her off-balance. Her other foot twisted on the low barrier along the edge of the bridge, and her hands flailed as she teetered backward toward the murky water. A strangled scream tore from her.

Vallyn lunged forward, threw his arm behind her back, and caught her wrist with his other hand. Her shriek cut off, and she looped her arm behind his neck. He leaned over her as she half hung over the water, their grip on each other the only thing keeping her from falling. As she looked into his eyes, his breath hitched.

He tugged her away from the edge and spun to guide her to the center of the bridge, pulling her close on instinct to steady her on her feet. "I've got you." He raised his gaze to her face and their eyes locked.

The world went still as he lost all awareness of anything but her. Her arm behind his neck, her grip on his tunic, its fabric twisted around her hand, his arm around her middle, the mere inches separating them—

Everything snapped back into roaring clarity.

What am I doing?

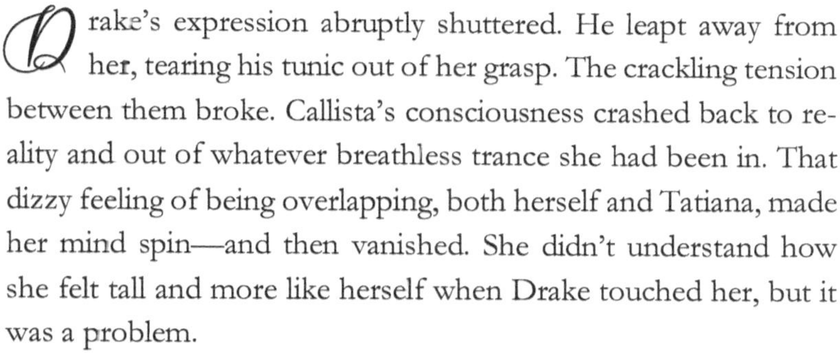

28

rake's expression abruptly shuttered. He leapt away from her, tearing his tunic out of her grasp. The crackling tension between them broke. Callista's consciousness crashed back to reality and out of whatever breathless trance she had been in. That dizzy feeling of being overlapping, both herself and Tatiana, made her mind spin—and then vanished. She didn't understand how she felt tall and more like herself when Drake touched her, but it was a problem.

Maybe not as big of a problem as whatever had just happened.

The red creeping into Drake's cheeks mirrored the heat spreading over her own body. He moved his hands behind his back, and his posture went as stiff as the palace guards when they saw the general approaching.

She didn't know whether to thank him, apologize, or ask why he'd been looking at her like that and had held her so close.

A falcon's cry pierced the air, and Stormy flew between them, sparing Callista from saying anything.

"Stormy!" She held out her hands, and the lesser gryphon flew into her arms. With excited squeaks, Stormy rubbed against her. "Where did you get off to?"

"It seems she wants to stay with you after all." Drake smiled, but there was a strained quality to it. "Let me walk you back to your rooms."

"Oh." She flinched. "I can find my way—"

"I'm not leaving you to possibly encounter the Shafers again alone," he said, his tone quiet but firm. As if he had noticed her fear. She couldn't help it, not when she'd seen the way Blaise had narrowed his eyes as he realized she had a pet.

Something she cared about that could potentially be leveraged against her. When Stormy had vanished, she'd feared Blaise had found her.

"Thank you, General Drake."

"Vallyn." He winced, almost as if he hadn't meant to say that. But then he said, "Please, you can call me Vallyn."

The proper thing would probably be to invite him to call her Tatiana, but she couldn't make herself say it. Her name wasn't Tatiana.

Instead, Callista started walking and talked to her gryphon. "You had best not beg when we get back, you feathered, furry menace. You've done plenty of hunting. Hmm. Perhaps I should bring you out here and let you hunt bugs and mice instead of having Serena bring you food all the time."

At "food," Stormy bobbed her head as she often did when excited about something.

"Oh, you're incorrigible."

Vallyn fell into step beside her, thankfully not so close that he made her feel caught between her two bodies. They didn't say a word all the way to her suite. At the door, Vallyn bowed.

"Thank you for listening and playing for me. Cassius is a lucky man. I look forward to a betrothal announcement soon." He strode away, as if he couldn't leave fast enough.

Callista was relieved to find Serena absent. She collapsed into a chair while Stormy flew to her perch. Despair clawed at her. The precipice was crumbling beneath her feet, and she didn't just fear that she would fail. She knew she would.

She couldn't kill the king.

But she couldn't—wouldn't—lose Royce.

She could never tell Cassius the truth, either. Nor could she tell Vallyn. He would choose the king over anything and anyone else.

"I've got you."

Vallyn's whispered words and dark, captivating eyes haunted her.

Maybe the truth was she didn't want to tell Vallyn because she couldn't stomach the idea of watching him lose all respect for her as the concern in his eyes turned to disgust and then hatred.

I'm so tired of being alone.

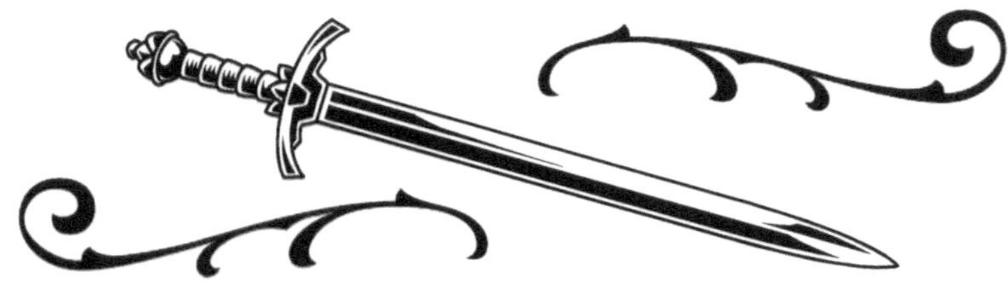

29

Vallyn retreated to his room as quickly as he could. If it wouldn't have caused a stir, he would have run.

His fingers hovered above the red gemstone. Was he really going to do this? So soon after he'd let his father walk away? What if his father honestly did want to improve their relationship but changed his mind after Vallyn selfishly called him because he needed help again?

Then he remembered the rage he'd felt at the suggestion that the Shafers were simply being unkind to Tatiana, the envy that wouldn't die every time Cassius touched her, the way his heart had pounded when he held her close on the bridge. And how every time, his fae magic had stirred alongside his emotions. This was out of control, and it had to be stopped. He didn't have anyone else to turn to.

Vallyn activated the stone. He poured a little extra magic into it, as if somehow that would convey his urgency.

It would still take time. He didn't know how Arolyin traveled between realms or how long it took. He'd never cared enough to ask.

Since he couldn't sit around waiting, Vallyn went to his office.

After several minutes of the words in a report blurring together, he shoved his chair away from the desk. It was the last thing he wanted to do, but he planted his feet firmly on the wood floor, adjusted himself to a comfortable position, and closed his eyes. Implementing the breathing technique Wilmina had shown him, he concentrated on inhaling and exhaling in a slow and steady rhythm.

Gradually, the agitation and the restless fae magic buzzing beneath his skin faded. When he felt calmer and more in control, he opened his eyes.

The clouds had thickened, blocking out more sunlight. He lit candles and returned to work.

Sometime later, Vallyn scrawled his signature at the bottom of yet another document. He rubbed his bleary eyes and leaned back in his chair. When had it gotten so dark?

He went to his window, frowning. Night had fallen, and the clouds blocked the stars. His stomach rumbled, as if his realizing how late it was had awakened his hunger. Supper would be ending in the great hall.

Ah, well. He'd go down to the kitchens and ask for any leftovers. First, though, he would go by his chambers to confirm that the stone was still activated and his father hadn't somehow materialized in his room.

Although that would be helpful. Maybe he should hurry, just in case.

30

*I*n contrast to the hopelessness clawing at Callista's soul, supper was the most pleasant meal she'd had in the great hall. Baron Shafer and his son were absent, as was Vallyn. She had no idea if the two were connected, but she didn't have to deal with the discomfort of seeing Vallyn or Blaise, and for once, no one within earshot gossiped about her.

As she walked through the halls, she returned a guard's slight bow with a nod. Cassius had been deep in conversation with a lord after the meal, so she had headed back on her own. By now, she knew the way. Anywhere other than this route, and she'd be horribly lost, but that was fine. She had little interest in roving Highrook's halls alone.

Callista turned a corner, and a figure glided out of the shadows ahead of her. Her steps faltered as Blaise entered the light of a lantern. Should she turn around? But if she avoided Blaise, Royce might pay for it.

So she continued forward. Blaise seized her upper arm and dragged her into a shadowed alcove that hosted a bronze bust on a pedestal. He shoved her against the wall.

"You're failing me."

Callista kept her tone cool and level. "How so?"

"You're not making progress fast enough."

She let her eyes droop half-closed, feigning nonchalance. "You never mentioned a deadline." Working to keep her expression cold, she pried his fingers off her arm. "I don't know what you expect me to do. His Majesty has many demands on his time. In fact, we would have had a lovely outing yesterday if not for your father. I can't woo a man I rarely see. I'm doing everything I can."

Blaise grunted. "Are you?"

"I know what's at stake." She glared. How satisfying it would be to put a dagger of magic through his throat, but that would doom Royce. "Don't doubt my resolve. I want this to be over—"

"Then explain what happened in the hallway yesterday."

Callista gulped. "I told you. There was nothing more than a commiserative embrace between two *friends*. Drake would never betray Cassius in any way."

A fact that hurt, even though it shouldn't.

"We want an announcement by the Maple Moon Festival in just over a week. If the festival passes and there is no engagement, my father will have one of your brother's fingers cut off and sent to you. Perhaps you can feed it to your pet—if it's still alive by then. I have ways of getting to your precious vermin, even in Highrook."

Her stomach churned, and she wished she hadn't eaten so much. It took a long moment to force herself to speak. "What do you expect me to do? Propose to him myself?"

"I expect you to do what you agreed to. You're a beautiful woman, *Tatiana*. Use that. Take him to your bed if that's what it requires."

A disbelieving laugh escaped her. "His Majesty is too honorable to be alone in private with me. Even if I could get him alone,

I think he'd be more insulted than excited if I attempted to seduce him."

"I don't want excuses, you irritating wench," Blaise snapped. "My patience is limited. If I don't get what I want—"

"I *know*." Callista tried to leave, but he slammed her back. She hit the wall with a pained grunt.

"I'm not done talking," he snarled.

"I'm done listening. There's nothing you can say that you haven't already said." Callista grimaced as his fingers dug into her arms. "You're hurting me. Let me go, or I'll scream."

"If you were going to, you already would have, pet."

A tremble went through her, and she turned her head away. "You've made your point. Please, let go."

Blaise chuckled. "I could do anything I wanted right now, because you're too afraid to put up a real fight."

"I'm not," a low voice rumbled, and then Blaise was dragged away from her.

Despite being shorter, Vallyn tossed Blaise to the ground like he was a rag doll. Callista sagged against the side of the alcove. Her relief at the interruption melted into terror.

Where had Vallyn come from?

And how much had he heard?

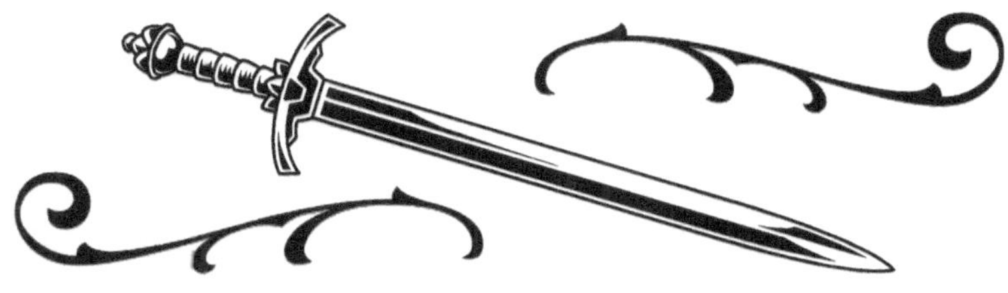

31

The fury burning through Vallyn was dangerously close to igniting. His fae magic roiled.

Blaise pushed himself up from the ground, and Vallyn drew his sword and swung. He barely stopped himself so that the sharp edge hovered next to Blaise's neck.

Blaise froze on his knees. "General. We were just having a little discussion."

"Do all young ladies find your conversation so noxious that you are required to roughly hold them against their will in dark corners?" Vallyn's grip tightened until the leather wrapping the hilt bit into his palms.

Keeping the sword steady, Vallyn looked back at Tatiana. She was pressed against the wall, the dim light from the distant lanterns reflecting in the whites of her eyes. Concern supplanted some of his fury. "Are you all right, my lady?"

"I'm all right," she mumbled. "Thank you."

"You said he was hurting you." He hadn't overheard enough to know what Blaise wanted from Tatiana, but he'd heard her pained protestations and his threats. His magic pulsed, and he shoved it back down.

Tatiana shook her head even as her right hand strayed to her left upper arm. "It was slightly painful, but I'm not injured."

That did little to smother the flames of his anger. She might even be lying since she had the ability to magically heal herself. But she wasn't bleeding, so he turned back to Blaise.

"You've assaulted the woman the king is courting. Even aside from that, you've harmed and threatened a lady."

Blaise's countenance twisted with fury. "She's uninjured and I made no threats."

"No? What was it you said?" Vallyn's voiced pitched lower, dripping with venom. "'I could do anything because you're too afraid to fight back'?"

To his satisfaction, Shafer blanched, but he recovered quickly. "It's not my fault the king's intended is a coward who is frightened by my simply pressing her into a dark corner."

"And why did you do that?"

"I'm trying to convince her to abandon Alimer and marry me."

Seriously? Vallyn glanced at Tatiana, and she nodded. No chance that was truly Blaise's aim, even if that was what he was telling Tatiana.

Vallyn sheathed his sword. "A word of advice, Shafer." He grabbed the back of Blaise's tunic and forced him to stand. "Women don't find being accosted in dark hallways attractive. You may not have done anything truly treasonous, but you've done enough. I'm going to take great pleasure in showing you to your bedchamber for the night: a cell in the dungeon."

"Tyrant," Blaise spat. He drew himself up to his full height, as if being taller than Vallyn had any impact on his situation.

"Treacherous pig." Vallyn shoved Blaise down the hall but jerked to a stop and looked back at Tatiana. "Will you be all right?

Do you need anything? A guard? The physician?"

"I'm fine, thank you."

He almost asked if she was sure, but he didn't want to pressure her, and he needed to get Shafer into a cell and then report to Cassius. "All right. Sleep well, Lady Tatiana."

Thankfully, Shafer was silent on the way to the dungeons. Vallyn's protective anger wouldn't take much prodding to roar back to life, and he was worried about what he might do.

He needed his father to hurry up.

After he locked Shafer in a cell and out of his own reach, he crossed his arms and stared the nobleman down. "What are you really plotting? And what did you threaten her with?"

"I'm plotting nothing. You can't keep me here. My father will never allow it, and we both know Alimer can't afford to quarrel with him over such flimsy accusations right now."

Vallyn took a step closer to the bars. "What if Lady Tatiana testifies against you?"

"By all means, go ask her if she would." Blaise leaned against the bars and sneered. "I'm not worried about her."

"Maybe you should be worried about me."

Blaise moved half a step back. "I don't think so. If you could do anything more to me, we wouldn't be having this conversation." He turned his back on the cell door. "No, you should be worried about how I'm going to make you pay for this, Drake."

It was laughable to think of Shafer doing anything to him. But what he was planning for Cassius and Tatiana? That did have Vallyn worried.

Vallyn stomped out of the dungeons and made his way to the king's suite. He almost turned to check in on Tatiana but decided against it. He couldn't be around her until he spoke to his father, and it was more important that he apprise Cassius of the situation.

"When a guardsman told me Blaise was skulking about near the southwest wing, I told him to go so I could cloak myself and eavesdrop," Vallyn explained.

His illusion magic could bend light around his body and muffle any sounds he made, and a little extra magic ensured people dismissed any shadowy movements or faint sounds. It had taken him countless hours of practice to be able to hold the enchantments in place while on the move, but it made him effectively invisible.

"I found Blaise and Tatiana whispering in a dark alcove." He paced in front of two curtained windows to the side of the king's sitting room, unable to sit still. Disappointment, confusion, and grim validation that he was right to suspect Tatiana tangled inside him. He briefly recounted what he had overheard and seen—that Blaise was running out of patience, wanted something from Tatiana, had pushed her around and believed she was too afraid to call for help—and how he had imprisoned Blaise.

"He claims he wants Tatiana to marry him, not you," Vallyn finished.

"That doesn't make sense." Cassius sat in a plush armchair with a high back in front of the massive fireplace. The orange light of the flames flickered over his deep frown. "He keeps saying she's an unworthy candidate!"

"He likely only wants her to break it off with you, unless he was lying, which is entirely possible. Either way, he must be threatening her in an attempt to get his way."

"An *attempt*? Does that mean she doesn't care about his threats or blackmail? Or perhaps she's stalling?"

"No idea." Vallyn spun on his heel. "I have more questions

than answers."

"Perhaps Shafer has given her two alternatives. Marry him, or…I don't know. Maybe he wants her to give him information on you." Vallyn nodded to himself. "Coercing her into spying on you in an attempt to undermine your rule would make more sense. Or forcing her to harm you herself." The thought twisted his stomach. "If only I'd heard more! What Blaise really wants, or what he's threatened her with. How long has this been going on? Why hasn't she asked for help?"

Cassius knit his fingers together and rested his chin on his hands, staring into the fire. "Fear can be a powerful motivator and impair judgment. Either the Shafers are blackmailing her with something she absolutely doesn't want us to know, or whatever they've threatened is bad enough that she won't risk them following through."

The same possibilities had occurred to Vallyn, along with one other.

"Or she isn't afraid of him. She has magic. Perhaps she sensed me and what I overheard was a ruse." He flexed his hands at his sides as he paced.

"Do you honestly think Tatiana is working with the Shafers for some nefarious scheme?"

Vallyn hesitated. The thought that Tatiana—kind, courageous, beautiful Tatiana—was being blackmailed or worse made his fae side feral. The possibility that she was a willing traitor who wished to harm Cassius was worse.

"I've watched her lie smoothly or sidestep a question more than once," he admitted. "Yet I struggle to believe she's a traitor. She sounded truthful when she said she respects you and would be a loyal queen. I detected only sincerity when she called you a kind man and worthy king. But if I'm wrong and she's planning to harm you… I can't afford to be wrong."

"She thinks I'm kind and a worthy king?"

Vallyn spun on his friend. "*That* is what you got out of this? Your intended is possibly plotting against you! Lord Ackroyd himself could be involved!"

A huff accompanied Cassius's eye roll. "Or she's being coerced, and we don't know to what end." He twisted his curls around his fingers. "If the Shafers are threatening her, we need to know how and why. However, you're right that we can't ignore the possibility that she's working with them willingly, however unlikely."

Vallyn chewed on his lower lip. "If she's a traitor, she won't tell us. If she's not, she clearly doesn't trust us. I could confront her, but she's such a good liar, and a direct accusation might drive her closer to the Shafers or make the Shafers change their plans. If I knew for certain whether she was on their side or being threatened, this would be easier." He itched to grab his sword and go to Baron Shafer, make the man confess everything.

"Has anything about her made you think she would harm me?" Cassius stood and prodded at the logs in the fireplace with a poker.

"I can hardly believe she'd wish harm on anyone." Suddenly exhausted, Vallyn dropped into the armchair next to the one Cassius had vacated. "I feel like I'm losing my mind, Cas. When monsters lurk in the shadows, how am I supposed to tell if the dark shape is a cat or a manticore without striking prematurely and hurting a cat or moving too late and giving the manticore the advantage?"

Cassius sighed. "I don't know, Vallyn. Although I know metaphors have never been your strong suit."

Vallyn sent a blank look at his friend. "Is now really the time?"

"Fine, back to the problem at hand." Cassius returned to his armchair. "I don't think we should make any sudden changes, and Blaise is right—we can't keep him locked up. I hate to treat Tatiana like bait, but perhaps it would be best if we kept a close eye on them both to see if they reveal anything. In the meantime, we can attempt to win Tatiana's trust. Thoughts?"

Vallyn tapped his hand against his thigh while he considered. "I don't like it. But I don't have a better idea right now, unless you give me permission to arrest all three of them and interrogate them until someone talks."

"Absolutely not. Imprisoning someone without evidence is what my predecessors would do." Cassius tugged on his hair. "I hope she's not working with Blaise at all. While I can't say I'm in love with Tatiana, I like her. Marriage to her would be pleasant enough."

"How romantic." The sarcastic words escaped before Vallyn realized he was speaking. Why did Cassius talking about Tatiana as his bride make his insides twist? It was ridiculous.

He *really* needed his father to hurry.

Cassius slouched in his chair. "It's about as romantic as I can hope for as king and with Aedyllan teetering on the brink of another civil war. She's already shown some vulnerability to you, so let's both work on earning her trust and learning the truth so we can stop the Shafers, and then I can marry her so the lords will stop nagging me about getting a queen and an heir."

Vallyn's fingers curled, digging into his thighs.

"I'm grateful you're in charge of military and security matters. If Tatiana is a traitor, you'll have to throw her in the dungeon. Although if her magic is as strong as your father said, you might need to kill her on the spot. I don't want a desperate, powerful enchantress breaking out of the dungeon and coming for me."

"Let's hope it won't come to that," Vallyn said.

Because if it did, he wasn't certain he could do it.

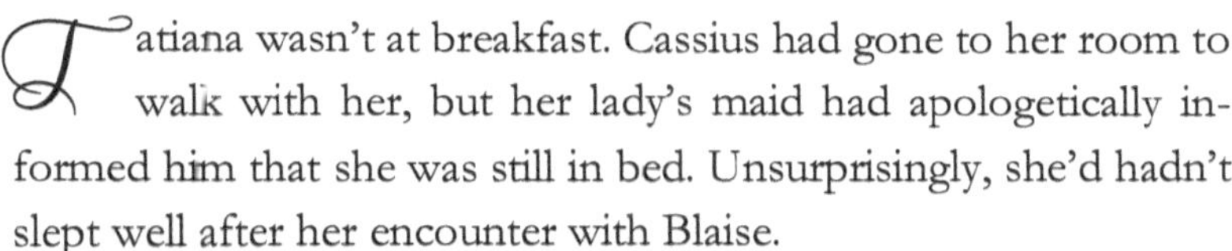

32

atiana wasn't at breakfast. Cassius had gone to her room to walk with her, but her lady's maid had apologetically informed him that she was still in bed. Unsurprisingly, she'd hadn't slept well after her encounter with Blaise.

Baron Shafer had returned home—after complaining to Cassius about his son's incarceration for a solid half an hour.

Blaise himself had been released and spent breakfast smirking at Vallyn. From what he could hear, Blaise was telling everyone that Vallyn had thrown him in a cell for the night without cause.

As Vallyn walked to his office, he mentally berated himself for not visiting Tatiana last night. He should have checked on her, assured her everything would be all right, asked again if she wanted a personal guard… He should visit her now. Strictly in the interest of winning her trust so he could stop Shafer, of course. No other reason.

He changed course, but a shout stopped him.

"Vallyn!"

Finally. He spun around and rushed to his father.

"Your men were much more helpful this time." Arolyin motioned to the guard walking at his side.

Vallyn nodded at the man. "Thank you for bringing him to me."

"Of course, General." The guardsman bowed and departed.

"Val, I'm so sorry if I'm late. I was running a military training drill and returned home to find the stone activated. I didn't think you'd call again so soon—"

"It's fine. Let's go somewhere we can talk." Vallyn took off without waiting for a response. Once they were inside his office, he made sure no one was loitering nearby, then locked the door.

Arolyin sighed. "Well. I admit to entertaining the foolish hope you simply wanted your father back, but clearly, something has you agitated. Did you lose control of your magic?"

"No. But…something is wrong."

Arolyin raised an eyebrow and crossed his arms, waiting.

"I need to know how to—to…" Now that he had his father in front of him, he didn't know how to explain. "I need to suppress my fae nature."

Arolyin's expression shuttered. "Elaborate."

"It… I don't want to be like this!" Vallyn turned away and paced until he reached the wood-paneled wall, then faced his father again. "Violent, jealous, angry, and—and I don't know."

"I don't know how to explain to you that humans experience those emotions, too."

"No, it's not the same." Vallyn pointed accusatorily at his father. "You told me yourself. Fae are more prone to violence, feel less remorse, can easily become cruel. It's why when I let my magic flow freely, I can fight more fiercely on the battlefield and not truly feel the weight of what I've done until later. Sometimes I almost enjoy it. My magic is chaotic, wild, uncivilized."

His father's shoulders drooped. "Is that how you see me?" He sat down heavily in one of the two chairs facing Vallyn's desk. "Is that why you wouldn't go home with me?"

"Partly. Mostly this is *my* home."

Sorrow reflected in Arolyin's dark eyes. "You don't quite remember what I said, but you were young. Fae magic *can be* capricious and dangerous, and yours *can* be used for battle fury. Fae *can* decide to ignore their hearts—their empathy and compassion. Such fae can become gleefully wicked. I meant it as a warning, not a condemnation of the part of you that is…me. Fae can also love fiercely, as I loved your mother. As I love my son. And if you couldn't tell from Silas Faine and his sons, humans are just as capable of malice."

"When humans love fiercely, they stay," Vallyn bit out. "They make sacrifices for the ones they love. They don't promise future sacrifice and leave."

"My court was at war! Truthfully, Vallyn, it is not merely your fae blood that drives you on the battlefield. We Drakes are warriors, and battle fury is our strength when our lord and his court are threatened. I loved your mother, but she wasn't the only person I cared about. I had family and friends who needed me. You're a general now, so you should understand I had duties, because I'm not just a warrior. I'm the Lord of the Light Court's general."

"You've never mentioned that before. Conveniently." He let all of his doubt and disdain bleed into his tone.

"I didn't want it to affect your decisions or how you viewed me." Arolyin rubbed the back of his neck. "You knew I fought a war. That isn't the same as knowing I led it. It isn't the same as knowing that in three hundred years, I have killed fae in the hundreds. You had some indication that I have status in the fae realm. That isn't the same as knowing I carry an honorary title of Prince, that I am seventeenth in line to rule the Light Court. That if you had come with me and become fully fae, you would be eighteenth.

I didn't want any of that to color your choices, and then it didn't matter."

Vallyn gaped at his father, then slammed his mouth shut. "No wonder you were slow to sacrifice your power."

"It wasn't my fault the war took longer than I'd hoped! Or that years mean less when you're immortal, or that time flows differently—"

"I know, and I don't care!" Vallyn shook his head and held up his hands. "It doesn't matter why my fae magic is bloodthirsty. I need to—to feel it less. And I need to know if my magic is making me want things I shouldn't."

Arolyin took a deep breath and released it slowly. "What happened?"

Vallyn strode up and down the length of his office, debating where to start.

"It's Tatiana," he said at last and then collapsed into his chair on the opposite side of the desk. "My magic…reacts to her, somehow. She's courting Cas. There's a chance she's working with the Shafers. But I think my fae magic, my fae nature, is forging some kind of connection with her. I get irritable when I think of her with Cassius. When someone insults her, I want to punish them. Then Blaise Shafer did nothing more than bruise her, and I wanted to kill him. I need it to stop. How do I make it stop?"

Arolyin tipped his head back and narrowed his eyes. "Hmm. I may have an idea what's happening."

Vallyn felt the blood drain from his face. "Is…it serious?"

"Potentially. When did this start?"

He'd been about to say he wasn't sure, but then it hit him. "The flute. When she played the flute. Perhaps a spell woven into the song?" That was terrifying, because she had wanted to play the flute for Cassius. "Could her spell have affected me differently because I'm half fae?"

His father made a noncommittal humming noise. "Perhaps. Tell me, in detail, about this flute-playing occurrence."

As best he could recall, Vallyn did so, including how haunting the melody had been, how she'd cried, and how beautiful she'd looked. At his father's prompting, he told him more. His conversations with Tatiana, the breakdown she'd had after seeing the door to the vault, the strange feeling in the pit of his stomach when he'd caught her when she tripped on the bridge.

Arolyin was silent for several heartbeats while sweat beaded on the back of Vallyn's neck.

Unable to take it any longer, Vallyn burst out, "Is it because I promised to keep her safe? Did I activate a fae binding?"

Another vague hum, and then Arolyin stood, moved to the edge of the desk, and held out his hand. "Let me see your hand."

Trepidation rising, Vallyn held out his right hand, palm up. His father held it between his own and closed his eyes. He felt a pulse of spirited fae magic, but he couldn't tell what it did.

"As I suspected." Arolyin opened his eyes and released Vallyn's hand.

"What is it?"

His father sat back down and casually crossed one knee over the other. "Nothing. She hasn't cast an enchantment on you. Nor have you done anything with your fae magic."

The chair squeaked as Vallyn collapsed back against it. "Then what is happening? What's wrong with me?"

The corner of Arolyin's mouth ticked upward. "You're in love, son."

After the heartbeat it took for the words to sink in, Vallyn shoved to his feet. "No. That's preposterous!"

"Why?"

"I—I wouldn't."

Arolyin gave him a long-suffering look. "Wouldn't what? Fall for a beautiful, mysterious woman you've been thinking about excessively, who you believe needs help, who is kind and brave and vulnerable, who understands you in ways you struggle to express?"

"She's courting my best friend!" Vallyn's hands were shaking, so he clasped them behind his back. "I wouldn't betray him, so my fae side—"

"No, Vallyn." Arolyin drew a deep breath and let it out in a long, heavy sigh. "Yes, your fae magic can be linked to your emotions. It wants to aid you and defend you—and those you care about. Your anger can give it strength, and it is primed for battle. Yes, fae can be tempted by possessiveness and can be particularly cunning. Your fae side might be strengthening your emotions, but it is not creating them. These emotions are as human as they are fae. Many fae do not surrender to them. I know you think I didn't truly love your mother, but fae can love. Most fae who get married magically bind themselves together and are dedicated wholly to each other. But yes, some fae choose to numb themselves to conviction and become cruel and obsessed with their own desires."

Arolyin wrinkled his nose. "The Gilded Court has been in chaos for months, ever since their lord destroyed himself first in carving out his conscience and second in attempting to exploit others for his own power. But Aedyllan is also struggling to find its path after the Faines abandoned their consciences and exploited others for their own power and pleasure.

"We fae may have a reputation for cruelty, but it is mostly because we have powerful magic and live for centuries, which allows us plenty of time to gain wisdom and hone our power. Wisdom and power can be put to good or dark uses, and humans do love to fixate on the terrible. If the cruelty of a king has more widespread and obvious effects than the cruelty of a pauper, a powerful fae indulging in wickedness can be disastrous. A fae philosopher once theorized that human tales often paint fae as dangerous because they see fae as dark reflections of themselves, their own sins magnified by wild, ancient, and powerful magic. We hate in others what we deny in ourselves. Humans most hate in fae the same traits they fear or despise in themselves."

Whether Arolyin had meant the words as indictment or not, they had the sting of unwanted truth. Vallyn's mental defenses bristled.

"You said my fae magic heightens my emotions. I don't love her; I care for her as a friend. My magic must be amplifying that beyond reason and causing the confusion, because I would *never* betray Cas like that. I can't be falling for Tatiana."

Even as he argued otherwise, he knew it was true.

He'd known since he caught her on the bridge and whispered, *I've got you.*

Because he couldn't face his own betrayal, he wanted to blame something other than himself. *Hating most in others what I fear in myself.*

"Your fae side is part of you, Vallyn." Familiar hurt colored Arolyin's tone. "It cannot create emotions or desires that are separate from you any more than my fae nature could for me or Cassius's human nature could for him. Yet you are not your thoughts or feelings. Just as any full fae or full human, you decide how and whether to act on your desires, fears, and emotions. Your choices are your own."

Vallyn flexed his hands and sat on the edge of his desk with his back toward his father. "What do I do now?"

Footsteps sounded, and then Arolyin stood beside him, leaning back against the side of the desk as well. "You have two options, son. Suppress these feelings, reminding yourself who she is, and wait for it to pass. Behave as if Tatiana and Cassius are already married and do what you would in that situation. Or tell Tatiana and let her choose. They aren't engaged yet."

Vallyn's fingernails bit into the side of his desk as he gripped the wood. "He is my friend and my king and the man I swore through a fae binding to serve. The court is already speculating that I'm trying to steal Tatiana away from him. I can't."

"Is loving her in secret and resenting him for marrying her more honorable?"

As much as Vallyn wanted to protest that he wouldn't resent Cassius, he wasn't certain that was true. His father was right. Either he had to fully accept that Tatiana was already Cassius's bride and do whatever it took to kill how he felt about her, or he needed to admit the truth to learn if she felt the same.

But what if she didn't? She'd said she would be faithful to Cassius. If she turned him down, it would put a wall between them and hurt his friendship with Cas. If she did choose him, would Cassius ever forgive him?

"Marriage to her would be pleasant enough."

Didn't Tatiana deserve better than that?

"What if it's merely a passing infatuation?" Vallyn asked quietly.

"Only you can answer that." Arolyin rested his hand on Vallyn's shoulder. "But are you confident she isn't working with the Shafers willingly?"

An important question, as all of this would be moot if the answer was yes. "I would be shocked. But it would also instantly kill any feelings I have for her. I could never love someone who is wicked."

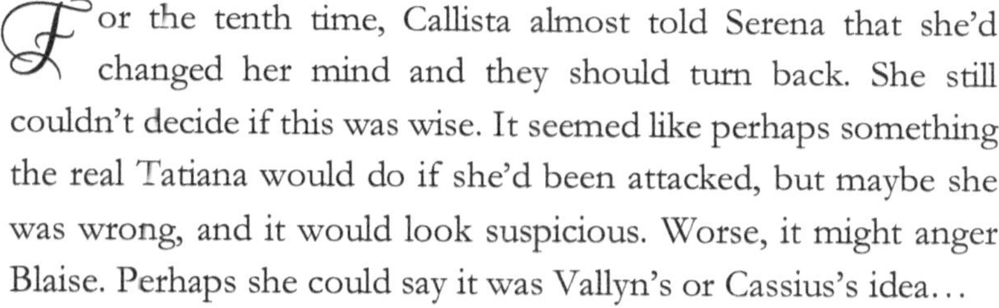

33

or the tenth time, Callista almost told Serena that she'd changed her mind and they should turn back. She still couldn't decide if this was wise. It seemed like perhaps something the real Tatiana would do if she'd been attacked, but maybe she was wrong, and it would look suspicious. Worse, it might anger Blaise. Perhaps she could say it was Vallyn's or Cassius's idea…

Oh, this was a terrible idea.

A door a short way ahead opened, and two men emerged. Callista's throat caught.

Vallyn—and his father.

What was the elder fae doing back in the palace? Another reason this was stupid. She couldn't trust Vallyn.

"I enjoyed talking to you," Vallyn's father was saying. "And appreciate the opportunity to actually give fatherly advice."

Vallyn shifted from foot to foot. "It wasn't my intention. I thought there was…more to it. I wouldn't call upon you just for that."

"I suppose you don't think me particularly qualified." The regret on the older fae's face surprised Callista.

"I meant…you're important. To your own people. Apparently."

Vallyn glanced away; his gaze briefly flicked to Callista, then his head snapped toward her as his face reddened. "Tatiana?"

His father turned toward her, his eyebrows raised. He studied her, then cast an oddly sly, sidelong glance at Vallyn. "Best of luck, son. Call for me any time."

"Unbelievable," Serena whispered. "He hardly looks old enough to be the general's father."

Callista shrugged. Of course he didn't. Fae were immortal.

"Thank you," Vallyn mumbled, but his father was already walking away. He watched his father leave, his teeth scraping over his lower lip as indecision flickered over his face. With a minute shake of his head, he turned his back on his father and faced her.

A couple strides from Vallyn, Callista stopped and curtsied. He stared at her, blinked, and then bowed, almost as if he'd temporarily forgotten court decorum.

"Is this a bad time?" Callista asked.

"Were you looking for me?" His eyes searched hers, a deeper question in them that she couldn't decipher.

"I'd like to accept that guard you offered."

Anger chiseled itself into the hard planes of his face. "Of course. Was that the first time Blaise has done something like that, Lady Tatiana?"

Was it? For Callista, no; for Tatiana, yes, but she wasn't certain what, if anything, Vallyn had overheard. If he had the impression they had spoken before and she denied it, that would look suspicious, but what in Miraveld would she say to manufacture details of some fictional prior encounter?

"Yes." She wrapped her arms over the wide leather and bronze belt around her middle. "I'm worried he'll do something again, or something worse, to prevent me from marrying the king. Until I'm queen, I would feel safer with a guard."

"Is that what you genuinely want? To be queen?" The quiet intensity of his questions made Callista uneasy, and once again, she didn't know the right answer—so she told the truth.

"I want to do what's best for the kingdom and my family."

"It doesn't *have* to be you, you know." Vallyn watched her intently. "Do you truly want to marry Cassius?"

Again with these impossible, ridiculous questions.

"As I said, he's a good king—"

"Forget the politics!" He stepped closer. "Forget everyone else. Would you still want to marry Cassius?"

"What do you want from me?" Callista exclaimed. "What answer would satisfy you? Do you want me to say I love him? Or that I put duty above my feelings? Do you want the truth? Because the truth is, I don't know. How am I supposed to separate us from our circumstances to be able to answer that question?"

Vallyn lowered his gaze to the floor and turned his head away. His throat bobbed. "I do want the truth, Tatiana. I want all of the truth."

He looked up at her, and Callista had a moment of feeling dizzy. Did it look strange to Serena? Did she notice that Vallyn was looking at Tatiana's hairline because he was looking at Callista's eyes?

"I want to know who I can trust," Vallyn said. "I want to know what the Shafers are up to, who is involved and in what ways, what I should do about it—about so many things. I want to know what makes you cry and who broke your heart and why you try to hide it. I want—" He cut off and closed his eyes, drawing in a deep breath.

"I'll assign a guard rotation to you at once." Vallyn met her eyes again, and she wished she hadn't sought him out. Wished she had never met him.

Because whatever the tightness in her chest was, whatever magic he possessed that urged her to admit to everything right then and there, it was horrible.

"I promised you would be safe. I will keep that promise if I have to accompany you everywhere myself."

Callista's heart beat faster. It should have been because the last thing she wanted was Vallyn constantly by her side.

But that wasn't it.

What she felt, she couldn't name, but it was warm and tingly and…safe. Protected.

His words and kindness aren't for you, Callista.

Serena delicately cleared her throat, alerting Callista to the fact that she had been standing in silence entirely too long.

"Thank you." She curtsied again. "I'm going to retire to my suite—"

"Do you want to visit Rincote?" Vallyn's thick eyebrows furrowed. "That is…I have to go into Rincote to check on the guard there, adjust some supply orders, and carry out other miscellaneous errands. I thought perhaps you might like to see the town? A change of scenery, and Blaise Shafer hasn't left Highrook since he arrived."

As lovely as getting out of the palace would be, she couldn't go. She didn't want to see the Royal University, and someone might recognize her—no. She looked like Tatiana. No one would see Callista, and it had been over two years, anyway. She did need to buy some iron… However, spending time with Vallyn was counterproductive to furthering her relationship with Cassius. Unless maybe something in town could give her an idea of how to save Royce and Cassius?

"Sorry, my lady." Vallyn tugged on the collar of his tunic. "It was a foolish idea."

"I'd love to go into town." Whether she'd said it because it might be her solitary chance to purchase iron or because Vallyn's disappointment saddened her, she refused to examine. "I need to get my cloak and some coin from my room first."

"I need to stop by my room as well. I'll meet you by your room, then."

They parted ways, and when Callista realized Serena was jogging at her side, she slowed to a more ladylike walking speed.

"My lady…" Serena's hands fidgeted. "Never mind."

"What is it?"

The older woman shook her head. "It is not my place, my lady. Forgive me."

Callista slowed further. "Now I'm desperately curious. Whatever it is, I assure you I won't be angry or punish you." Although she doubted Serena would say anything even close to needing punishment.

Serena glanced over her shoulder, then spoke in a low voice. "I must be wrong, because if there is anything everyone knows about General Drake, it's that first, he's terrifying, and second, he is immovably loyal to His Majesty the King. But if I didn't know better, I would think he…likes you, my lady. And that perhaps you feel similarly."

Oh. Callista had been wrong. "Is that so?" she asked, not trusting herself to say more.

"Forgive my impertinence, my lady, but…would you rather spend time with His Majesty or the general?"

Callista clenched her teeth. Yet her anger melted away to reveal the truth hiding behind the reflexive outrage.

Dragonflies had fluttered in her stomach at the suggestion that Vallyn liked her, and her heart had instantly answered, *I would rather spend time with Vallyn.*

A wiser woman might have told Vallyn she had changed her mind and no longer wished to go into town. Callista couldn't think of a good reason why she would have changed her mind, though, and going into Rincote sounded more enjoyable than spending another uneventful day in Highrook. Serena and Stormy were good company, but even the lesser gryphon could become irritating after hours alone together, and it was difficult to bond with Serena when she was Callista's servant and Callista was living a lie.

So she walked with Vallyn to the stables and rode out with him and a couple of guards. Having guards along eased her mind. The last thing she needed was another scandal.

Although maybe that would happen anyway. People rarely needed much kindling to start a gossip fire, and if Callista had learned anything at the Royal University, it was that nobles needed even less.

There were many reasons she should have declined, but as she rode at Vallyn's side down the winding road from Highrook Palace to the town of Rincote, she couldn't bring herself to regret the decision.

Falling leaves tossed on the light breeze flashed golden in the sunlight beneath a bright-blue sky. The steady sway of the horse beneath her and the clopping of hooves over packed dirt cluttered with leaves was relaxing. And it was always nice not to be boxed in. While Highrook was not as dreary or lonely as the castle ruins where she'd lived for two years, walls still felt constricting.

As they rode into Rincote, Callista tilted her head back. Above the slate, wood, and thatched roofs of multistory buildings rose a square tower of gleaming limestone, its crenelations jutting proudly into the blue sky. The tallest structure in the town, and one she remembered keenly. She'd kept the carriage shutters closed when they passed it on the way to Highrook, because she hadn't wanted to see it.

"It's the astronomy tower of the Royal University," Vallyn said. She hadn't realized she'd stopped her horse, but he'd halted his stocky piebald beside her. "It's attached to the building that houses the Enchanters College, but the other colleges have access to it as well."

Callista swallowed past the dryness in her throat. "Ah." Such an articulate, normal response.

"You mentioned you enjoy academic books. Did you ever consider applying to the university?"

She tore her gaze from the tower. "No." Before Vallyn could ask any more questions that had the power to expose her or undo her control over her emotions, she asked, "Did you? Attend or consider it?"

Vallyn started forward again, and she nudged her horse to do likewise. "Sort of. Cassius wanted to when we were young, and we did everything together, so I supposed I'd accompany him. If the university didn't accept me, I'd get a job in Rincote and be around to watch his back. But then Cas's father died, and a duke doesn't have the luxury of leaving for months to attend a university. He'd had plenty of excellent tutors and kept studying even after becoming Duke Alimer because he wanted to be a good lord, so it wasn't as if he needed the education."

"You didn't consider going without him?"

"Ha, no. Besides that I'd sworn to serve him, I wasn't overly interested in academics. My primary interest and skill were militaristic. The Royal University has colleges for studying enchantment and philosophy and mathematics and language, but I suppose they thought the knights had warfare well enough in hand on their own."

Vallyn steered his horse over to a hitching post and dismounted.

Thankfully Callista's horse understood what was expected of it. All she had to do was turn it toward the post, and it walked right up next to the general's horse and stopped. Vallyn appeared at her side and offered her his hand.

After a momentary hesitation, Callista accepted his assistance with dismounting. The full skirt and long, draping sleeves of her dress complicated things, and the distance to the ground was further than she'd expected. She stumbled forward and caught herself with her free hand against Vallyn's firm chest. His hand tightened on hers, but she didn't dare look at his face.

Instead, she withdrew with a murmured apology.

Vallyn cleared his throat and turned brusquely away, and she swore he was avoiding looking at her as he tied their horses to the hitching post.

Somewhere further down the lane, a merchant called out her wares. People talked and laughed as they walked by, and the scent of something savory drifted to them on the breeze, making Callista feel like she hadn't eaten enough breakfast.

"Right then." Vallyn walked over to her side. "Is there anything you would like to see? This is your first time in Rincote, correct? Do you want to tour the Royal University—"

"No!" Callista winced. "No, thank you."

"All right…" Vallyn offered her his arm with a puzzled expression. "Well, I'd love to show you my favorite place in Rincote. It's not far."

Relieved to move on from talk of the university, Callista smiled. "I'm intrigued."

Vallyn led her down a winding street—literally, as the road sloped downhill. Their two guards followed at a short distance. When he turned to climb a set of narrow steps, Callista realized with a start where they were going.

Her second-favorite location in Rincote, after the astronomy tower.

She didn't want to go there, either, but Tatiana wouldn't have any reason to avoid it.

The stone stairs were carved into the hill, and they curved around until they emerged into the side of an amphitheater. To their right were five short tiers of seating in front of two large pavilions surrounded by trees cloaked in orange and red leaves. As usual, young people were scattered around the amphitheater—chatting while sitting on blankets spread over the packed-down dirt, frowning as they scribbled notes in journals, pacing while practicing recitations for exams…kissing in the shadows of the pavilions. Most of them would be Royal University students.

Callista had studied and talked here often, and for the first year of her studies, her only real friend at the university had regularly joined her. Then one of the Faine princes had assaulted Aneira, and she'd left the university for good. Wherever Aneira was, if there was any healing or goodness in the world, Callista hoped she'd found it.

Vallyn tugged Callista away from the seating area, down past the large open space where performances, debates, ceremonies, and feasts were held, and past the massive columns that curved around the back of the stage area. A few feet past the colonnade, a wood railing prevented anyone from accidentally wandering too close to a drop-off that overlooked the foothills.

"Cas and I have a little disagreement," Vallyn said as he led her down the walkway. "He claims Highrook has the best views. Admittedly, if you're talking about from the walls, he's right, but unless you're on the battlements, the walls mar the view. I like how open this view is. Besides, if you come all the way to this corner here, you get a view of the mountains to one side, the foothills and forests ahead, and Highrook to the other side." He pointed to each view as he brought them to a stop.

"It's lovely," Callista said.

She removed her hand from his arm, placed it on the railing, and stared out at the rolling hills. She didn't want to look at Highrook—it brought back countless memories of standing on this walkway, watching the palace while wondering what her family was doing inside, or glaring at it and mentally cursing the Faines after her mother died, after Aneira left, and again after her father and Jacob died.

"What's bothering you?" Vallyn asked softly.

How did he know? She thought she'd perfected the art hiding her feelings. She wished she could tell him—tell anyone—the truth. A poor reflection of it would have to suffice.

"I knew living in Highrook might be difficult and stressful and at times confusing. I still wasn't prepared. Actually"—she took a deep breath—"on the subject of being prepared, I'd like to visit an armorer. I assume there's an armorer in Rincote?"

"An armorer? Why?"

"I want a dagger." Callista's gaze flitted to the sword at Vallyn's side and its leather-wrapped hilt. "For self-defense. It probably seems silly when I already asked for a guard, but…" Unable to bear the intensity of his gaze, she turned away. "It would be nice to have a way to protect myself if anything happened."

A breeze played with Callista's hair and tugged her skirts around her legs. Somewhere behind them, a group of young men broke into uproarious laughter that faded into distant conversation.

Still Vallyn was silent.

"Do you think it's a bad idea?" she asked.

"I think it's strange, given your other talents."

Her other…? Callista's hands went cold. Right. How could

she have forgotten he knew about her magic? If Tatiana were hiding that she was an enchantress, what would she do? Well, if Callista hadn't eavesdropped, she wouldn't know that Drake had discovered her secret.

"I beg your pardon?"

Vallyn stepped closer and spoke in a low voice. "I don't know why you hide what you are, Tatiana. But whatever the reason, you can trust me."

She wished that were true.

A shiver cut through her, but with the sun bathing her in blissful warmth, it wasn't cold that made her shudder.

Vallyn laid his hand on top of hers on the railing, the gentle pressure of his fingers comforting. "I can protect you from whatever it is you fear. Let me help you. Please."

Callista longed to believe him, longed to tell him everything. But even if it weren't madness to spill her deepest secrets in a public area, she couldn't tell Vallyn. He'd have to arrest her, and then what good would his reassurances be? He'd made them to Tatiana, anyway.

"I believe you." She withdrew her hand from under his. The action made her heart ache for reasons she didn't understand and didn't want to examine. "I still want a dagger."

Vallyn's hand slid off the railing and fell back to his side. "Then let's visit the armorer."

They were silent as they walked to the armorer, and Callista made sure to leave extra space between them. Not so much they might get separated, but enough it didn't look like they were *together*. He stopped outside a two-story building beneath a sign that proclaimed BEST BLADES IN RINCOTE in bright-red lettering above two crossed swords painted in white.

Vallyn motioned to the door, which was propped ajar with a

rock. "This shop buys from various blacksmiths and resells. A little pricier than going directly to an armorer, but cleaner and with a larger selection, and the owner is a respectable fellow." He pointed at another door further down the same building with a sign over it that advertised HIGH QUALITY GRAINS. "I need to adjust some supply orders there. If you're done before I am, meet me there."

Without waiting for a response, he left her alone.

Well, alone with the two guards a few paces behind her.

Callista pushed open the door and peered inside. A woman with silver braids framing a face etched with laugh lines stood behind a counter dusting weapons hung on the wall. No one else was inside. She glanced at the guards.

"You can wait out here, if you like. No one else is inside."

One of the guards nodded. "We'll be right here if you need us." They stood directly next to the door with their backs to the wall, looking incredibly conspicuous. Callista went inside, relieved they hadn't insisted on accompanying her. She didn't want her request getting back to Drake.

The woman set down her feather duster and grinned. "How can I help you, m'lady?"

"I'd like to purchase a dagger." Callista looked around. Weapons hung on every wall, racks of swords stood in two of the corners, and glass display cases held smaller weapons and—was that jewelry? "Do you happen to have any pure iron daggers? Not treated steel."

The shopkeeper frowned. "We do, but alloyed steel is a bit stronger and doesn't rust as quickly. I would recommend—"

"Pure iron, please."

"Planning on tangling with some fae?" The woman laughed,

then narrowed her eyes. "You aren't having trouble with fae, are you?"

Callista smiled while she scrambled for a lie. "Of course not. It's silly. My grandfather had a pure iron dagger that he said was passed down to him from father to son over three generations; he claimed it once saved his great-grandfather from a fae. I've been missing my grandfather and would like to have my own iron dagger to remind me of him."

When had she gotten so smooth at lying? She'd once nearly been sick all over her professor when she tried to cover up that she had forgotten to do an assignment. She hated the person the world had shaped her into.

The shopkeeper helped her pick out a little iron dagger with a thin blade and a leather sheath that she could wear in her boot. As they headed back toward the counter, Callista peered at one of the glass boxes on a pedestal.

"Why do you sell jewelry?"

The woman laughed. "Oh, that. It's all iron. Just a little side business. Occasionally we get someone paranoid about fae. Often some Enchanters College or Philosophers College student who had their first class on fae and for some reason thinks they're suddenly at greater risk of being taken. In a pinch you could use the iron bracelets or necklaces against a fae."

Callista backtracked to the box. "I know it's silly, but I'd like to buy a necklace."

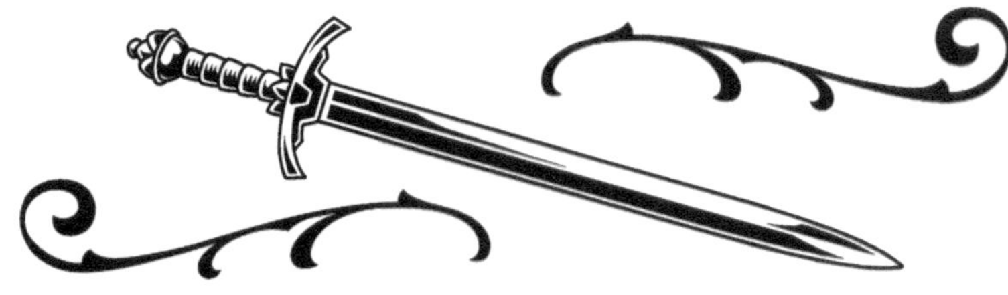

34

*J*nviting Tatiana had been a terrible idea. If it even qualified as an idea rather than a reckless impulse. As they walked around Rincote and Vallyn tried to concentrate on his errands, he kept getting distracted thinking about her.

About her hand against his chest.

About how beautiful she looked in dark green.

About the way she'd looked at the astronomy tower. It was either loss or longing, maybe both. Why?

Furthermore, why did Tatiana fear her magic so much that she kept it hidden and wouldn't use it even in self-defense? Even though she'd used magic to catch and heal Stormy, she'd done so only when she thought she was alone. Why the secrecy? The questions were driving him mad.

Not to mention that Arolyin's words had gotten under his skin.

Let her choose. They aren't engaged yet.

He shouldn't even be entertaining the idea. Cassius was his brother. It would be a terrible betrayal.

Yet as he watched Tatiana smiling and laughing with a red-faced, boisterous man selling large balls of fried dough coated in crystalline honey, he couldn't stop wondering how to get her to smile and laugh like that with him. She bought an excessive number of the man's sweet wares. If she ate all of those, she'd give herself indigestion. But then she moved a few paces away and gave some to a couple of dirt-splattered urchins. How was he supposed to watch her do things like that and convince himself he didn't like her?

Tatiana walked back over to Vallyn and held out a stick with a dough ball skewered on the end. "Thank you. For getting me out of the palace for a while."

Vallyn had the urge to bite the treat off the end of the stick in her hand, but he carefully took the stick from her instead, refusing to dwell on the momentary brush of their fingers. "Thank you. But do you not like Highrook?"

"There is some monotony, and I don't love the walls. But it isn't as lonely as I thought it would be." She bit down on one of her desserts. "Serena is wonderful, and Stormy keeps me company. And of course I enjoy when His Majesty is able to get away from his duties."

Vallyn's heart sank. He hadn't made the list.

"And you," Tatiana said quietly.

To cover his pleased surprise, he took a bite of his dessert. The glaze was incredibly sweet, but it paired nicely with the fluffy fried dough.

"Admittedly I hated you at first." Tatiana bit into another dough ball.

"I can't imagine why. Wait—it was because I accused you of attempted assassination, wasn't it?"

His awkward joke earned him a half smile. "Your thoughtfulness since has made up for it. I appreciate your kindness and protection."

Then why wouldn't she trust him?

"I'm glad we can be friends. I think my marriage to Cassius would be awkward if we didn't get along."

Vallyn shoved the rest of his dessert into his mouth. Even Tatiana knew the marriage was as good as decided. Just because their engagement wasn't formalized didn't mean Tatiana was open to other options. He took her finished sticks and dumped them into a waste bucket beside the vendor's stand, then turned back to her.

"I'm done with my duties here but have other work to attend to." He frowned at the sky, where storm clouds were gathering and turning the vibrant blue into a depressed gray. "We should return to Highrook before it rains."

Where he would hand her off to a guard and try not to think about her for the rest of the day.

Vallyn didn't help her into the saddle, and he didn't help her dismount in the courtyard, but she managed fine. If he was going to respect Tatiana's choice to be focused on her near-betrothal to Cassius and not undermine his best friend, they needed some distance. That meant no more holding her hand or embracing her or catching her. Well, he wouldn't let her *fall*, obviously, but he wouldn't steady her every time she wobbled. Definitely no putting himself in a position where she might put her hand on his chest again.

No. Touching.

Vallyn told one of the guards to accompany her and stand watch outside her suite, then promised he would set up a schedule soon so the man wouldn't be working past the end of his assigned shift. He bowed to Tatiana and bid her a good day.

He'd barely started figuring out the schedule when the door to his study opened. Cassius entered, that gaudy crown nestled amidst his curls and a smile on his face.

Shaking some of the tension from his body, Vallyn leaned back in his chair. "You seem to be in a good mood."

"I heard a rumor you took Tatiana into Rincote." Cas sat down in the chair across the desk from Vallyn. "I'm thrilled you two are getting along. Do you think you're getting any closer to convincing her to trust you? I assume she didn't tell you anything, or you'd have told me instead of coming back to your office to do whatever this paperwork is."

"Guard detail for Tatiana," Vallyn grunted. "And I don't think she could possibly be traitorous, not of her own choice. That means she'll likely end up marrying you, so shouldn't *you* be the one earning her trust? Shouldn't we want her to confide in you?"

"I suppose, but it seems like she opens up more to you than me."

"And you don't have a problem with that?"

Cassius fiddled with his curls. "I…well, I *am* busy, and we'll have plenty of time in the future. My wife and oldest friend being good friends is a good thing."

Vallyn clenched his teeth, keeping his thoughts locked inside. *I don't think I want to be her friend. Not only her friend.*

He straightened a stack of reports on his desk, avoiding looking at Cassius. "Perhaps we should send Blaise Shafer home until after the wedding. With both Shafers out of Highrook, I'd feel free to inspect the highway and town patrols myself."

"You haven't mentioned wanting to do that before. Does this have something to do with your father visiting you this morning?"

Vallyn looked up. "You heard about that?"

"Palace rumor vines are extremely efficient."

"But that would mean the guards were talking about it, as no one else knows he's my father." Vallyn scowled. Loose-lipped guards could be the downfall of Highrook's security.

"Try not to be brutal when you scold them," Cassius said with a long-suffering sigh. "And here I'd hoped you were relaxing."

"I can't afford to relax," Vallyn muttered. Relaxing opened up his heart to traitorous distractions.

"Val. Why was Arolyin here? Did you call him? How worried should I be?"

"It's…" Vallyn leaned against the back of his chair and stared at the paneling on the ceiling. "Nothing. Just my paranoia."

"Well. Perhaps something else to distract you is just what you need, then. Tomorrow, you and Tatiana and I can—"

"You take her." Vallyn waved a hand as if shooing away a fly, still staring at the ceiling. "Whatever you have in mind, I'll see you have the appropriate guard detail, but you should spend time alone with *your* future wife." Hopefully Cas hadn't caught the bitterness that bled into his words.

Cassius was quiet for so long, Vallyn wondered if he hadn't heard him leave. He straightened and found Cassius still sitting across from him, squinting with his mouth pinched.

"Something is bothering you. I might be king, but I'm still your friend. You can talk to me."

"It's nothing."

"It doesn't look like nothing to me, Val."

"It's nothing!" Vallyn shoved out of his chair and moved to the window. Water droplets covered the panes and made rivulets as they raced toward the bottom of the glass. Beyond the window, the hills at the base of the mountains were obscured by misty rain.

"Vallyn—"

"Cas, just stop." He flexed his fingers and curled them into fists.

"Are you angry with me?"

Vallyn's shoulders caved. "No, of course not."

A rustle of clothing and muffled footsteps on carpet alerted him to Cassius's approach. Cas leaned against the wall and tried to catch Vallyn's gaze, but Vallyn continued to glare out the window.

"Something is going on. If your fae magic is acting up or something is happening with your father that could affect your ability as my general, I need to know."

"No. Nothing like that." Vallyn's own wretched heart was to blame, according to Arolyin. What was worse, his father was right.

"Vallyn. If it has something to do with me, tell me."

A jolt of biting fae magic zipped through Vallyn. He clenched his fists until his fingernails bit into his skin. For the first time in his life, he hated the bond he'd accidentally created.

"Well, now I'm angry with you." He winced as that warning sensation coiled in the back of his mind. "Using the binding to command me is cheating."

"What?" Cassius gasped. "I didn't—it wasn't intentional… what do you mean? That is, you're still not actually telling me, so what—"

"My magic is warning me I'm at risk of breaking my end of the deal." Vallyn grimaced as the sensation strengthened to an ominous, painful buzz. "Take it back." He pressed a hand to his head as pressure built behind his temple. "Cas, take the command back."

"All right, but you're going to have to explain what you mean by forcing—"

"I'm in love with her!" Unable to stand the building fury of his own magic, the words burst out of him. Vallyn squeezed his eyes shut and let his head fall against the cold window with a dull thunk. "Too slow," he muttered.

The quiet pinging of small raindrops against the glass filled his ears.

At last, Cassius spoke in a barely audible murmur. "You're in love with Tatiana?"

Vallyn swallowed. "I didn't mean to… I called my father because I feared my magic was messing with my emotions. I didn't want to admit I was falling for her and was jealous every time you touched her. I didn't want it to be true that my own feelings for her were the reason I wanted to bash Blaise's head in for hurting her. I thought maybe there was something my father could tell me to do to make it stop." He shrugged, still leaning against the window, his eyes closed so he didn't have to see the betrayal on his friend's face.

"Fae magic is connected to emotions, but my father says it doesn't create them. I—I'm sorry. I didn't want to hurt you. I would never betray you. But being around her…" He worked his throat. "I can't be around her right now if I want to suffocate these feelings. That's why it would be good if I left Highrook for a while."

Cassius sighed and muttered a curse under his breath. "I need you here. Or did you forget about the Maple Moon Festival and the parade?"

Vallyn's heart twisted. "Oh. Right. I did." He forced his eyes open and lifted his head from the glass but didn't look at Cassius. "Then I will stay. But please don't ask me to accompany you and Tatiana. Other than at the parade, of course."

"Then I suppose you'll have to meet your mount for the parade by yourself."

That finally got Vallyn to look over at his friend. To his surprise, Cassius looked more tired than angry. "Mount? Why wouldn't I ride Riven?"

"Because Lord Raylor offered a unicorn for me to ride in the parade. I asked if he would loan us a second as well. I wouldn't be king without my general." Cassius smiled weakly. "They're arriving tomorrow."

A unicorn? Vallyn ignored the childish surge of excitement at the prospect. "Aren't you angry with me?"

Cassius drew in a long, slow breath. "I want to be. But if anything, it's my own fault. You're right. You've been there for her more than I have. It's not what I wanted, and I'm sorry you told me the truth because I apparently forced you to do so, but I'm also relieved you told me. I can't marry her if you love her."

"What?"

"I don't love her, Val. I believe in time I would, that we could choose to be dedicated to each other, but not now. Not knowing that it would hurt you."

Vallyn dropped his gaze to his boots. "I never meant for you to know. I'll get over it eventually—"

"And if you don't? I'm not losing my friend over a girl I'm considering marrying for political reasons."

"And my foolishness can't have negative repercussions for your rule, Cas. I can't hurt you by telling her my feelings, and even if you are fine with it, I wouldn't blame you for not wanting me to steal the woman you are courting—the nobles will gossip."

"Fae take the nobles." Cassius released a dry laugh. "Sorry. I admit it will take some adjusting, but the fact that I don't feel jealous tells me you care for her far more than I do. She deserves someone who will love her."

"I'm not sure she wants me." Vallyn returned to his chair, trying to ignore the conflicted feelings of hope and shame spreading in his chest. "Every time I ask her if she wants to marry you, she says yes."

"Really?"

"Well…I suppose more out of duty and respect than because

she's enamored with you. Still. More than she's said about me."

Cassius returned to the other chair as well. "Perhaps she thought you were trying to ascertain whether she was worthy of me, not whether she was interested in you. But it sounds like I might have to break off our courtship for her to consider you."

"You can't," Vallyn said heavily. "Not until we know what the Shafers are plotting. If I'm right that Blaise was lying about trying to convince Tatiana to marry him because he actually wants her close to you, and then you end the courtship, Blaise might blame her." He gripped the arms of his chair as his magic stirred. "I won't be the reason they follow through on whatever threats they've made against her."

"I suppose we'll have to decide what to do, then. First, though, there is something else we must address." Cassius laced his fingers together and leaned forward. "I want to know how long the fae binding has been forcing you to obey me, what exactly that means, why you've never told me, and how I can avoid it."

35

The king didn't walk with Callista to or from the great hall for meals that day or the next. When she spoke to him, he was polite but somehow…colder than previously. He found a reason to leave the conversation quickly and hadn't invited her to join him in the garden or on any excursions. At breakfast the second day after the trip into Rincote, Cassius didn't even acknowledge her, and she wasn't the only one to notice.

Vallyr wasn't in the great hall for any meals at all.

But Blaise was, and the glare he sent her way at breakfast was enough to make her blood run cold. As she left the great hall alone again, she heard the nobles whispering about what disagreement she must be having with the king.

Callista took her midday meal in her room. The king did not stop by.

Were Cassius and Vallyn avoiding her?

It didn't matter. If she didn't find a way to save Royce soon, the king's withdrawal would doom her brother. She would simply have to force Cassius to spend time with her.

Somehow.

So Callista asked her guard to take her to the king's office.

Hopefully he would be there, or she wasn't sure what she would do next.

She found Cassius in the halls before they reached his study, wearing a cloak and shadowed by a guard. She bowed and stuffed down her trepidation. "Your Majesty. Are you going somewhere?"

The king shifted his weight before meeting her eyes with a smile. "Yes. It will be a brief excursion, but you might find what I'm visiting delightful. Would you like to join me?"

It took effort to prevent her relief from showing. "I would love to, Your Majesty." She fell into step beside him, and her own guard fell back to walk beside the king's.

Cassius headed in what she believed was the direction of the stables and horse paddocks, which seemed odd if whatever he was up to was "a brief excursion." Belatedly, Callista realized she wasn't wearing a cloak herself. She glanced out a window at the sun and hoped the wispy layer of clouds hadn't blocked its warmth.

"Not going to ask where we're going?" Cassius asked with a note of amusement.

"Actually…I have a more pressing question." She gathered her willpower. "Have I offended you, Your Majesty?"

"No." But he didn't look at her as he said it.

"Then why are you avoiding me?"

"Sorry, it's nothing you did. I'm afraid some other matters have been distracting me."

This could be a terrible idea, but Tatiana was meant to be his queen, right? "Is there any way I can help? I can listen if you need to talk through a problem."

His steps slowed as he looked over at her. "Why?"

"Why…what?"

"Why do you want me to tell you?"

Callista frowned. "I want to support you. My—father," she said, nearly slipping and saying mother, but Tatiana's mother had died when Tatiana was too young for such conversations, "often told me that marriage is like a team of oxen. They work together to pull the same burdens in the same direction. Perhaps not always that literally, as sometimes it might require tackling the same problem from different angles, and sometimes when one is weak and must rest, the other is strong for both of them. A queen should not leave her king to bear the weight of the crown alone. Should she?"

Cassius stopped walking and stared at her. He said something beneath his breath that sounded like "Fae blessings. I don't blame him." He continued forward again. "Do you truly want the weight of the crown? It's remarkably heavy some days."

For herself, no. That was something she would never want. Would Tatiana? Immaterial. What mattered was finding an answer that convinced Cassius to let her get closer to him and bought Royce time.

"Perhaps sometimes we accept burdens because they are in service to something we believe in. Occasionally, we must undertake tasks we otherwise never would because it's the only way to obtain a righteous outcome we fervently desire, and any sacrifice is worth the cost."

"I might quibble with *any*," Cassius said. "A sacrifice of character, for instance, may tarnish whatever it was you hoped to achieve."

A fissure cracked through Callista's heart, opening into a vast emptiness.

"But as I trust marrying me isn't against your morals"—he chuckled awkwardly—"what do you desire to see come to fruition?"

"Justice," she said softly. "The end of power being abused to exploit others and toss them aside without thought. Protection for the innocent. Retribution for the wicked."

"And you believe marrying me will accomplish that?"

She wasn't sure if that was disbelief, skepticism, or awe in his tone. "I believe that you being king will accomplish that. If our marriage makes your rule more secure, then it is worth it."

"I feel like you just called being married to me a sacrifice you'd rather not make."

Callista flashed a genuine smile his way. "I called being a queen a sacrifice I'd rather not make. You are pleasant company."

"That's still lukewarm praise," Cassius said with a laugh.

They reached the end of the hall, and a guard standing near the door opened it for them. Cassius motioned her through first, and they continued outside. The crisp autumn air was cool against her face and fingers, but not unbearably so.

"My offer still stands," Callista said, "if you need someone to talk to."

"I appreciate it, but I don't think now's the time." The king took the path that turned toward the stables. "Mostly because I'm giddy with excitement. This will be my first time seeing a spectacular sight. Since they're so protected, I imagine it will be your first time as well. Ready to see a living unicorn?"

"Unicorn?" The world tilted around Callista. It couldn't be Tempest—could it? The unicorn had been able to see *inside* her. What if it was Tempest, and Gareth was there, and Tempest recognized her essence and told Gareth—

"Yes. Two of them!" There was an extra spring in Cassius's step as he walked faster. "Their names are Ebony and Falada."

Not Tempest. The spinning in her head steadied.

"This is the extra incredible part, though. Lord Raylor's son,

Conrad, has brought them. The poor young man was wounded terribly in the war." His voice turned sorrowful. "His father brought him home to let his son die in his own room. But one of the unicorns used her magic to *revive* him. Pulled him back from the brink of death. And now Conrad Raylor can communicate with that unicorn! They talk through some mental connection. Isn't that remarkable? I'm so curious what a unicorn has to say—and why I've never heard of this happening before."

Callista's feet rooted her in place on the cobblestone path. The king's voice sounded distorted and far away, as if he were far down a tunnel.

Then she was falling.

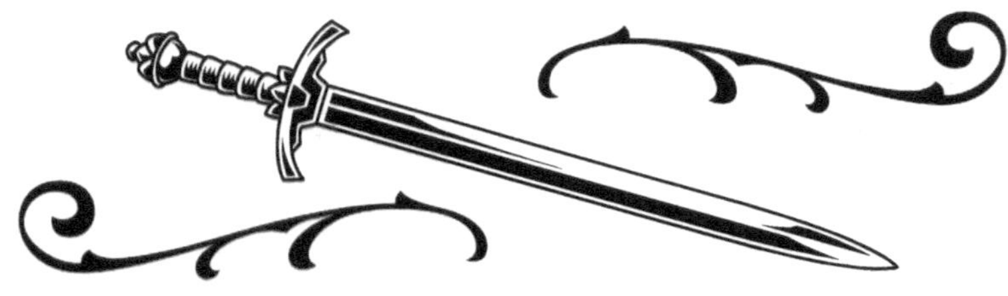

36

allyn took a moment to collect himself and calm his roiling emotions.

This was the cost of using his magical cloaking abilities to eavesdrop. He should have been more mature. His heart wouldn't feel so twisted if he had.

But no. He'd been on his way to meet the unicorns with Cassius and had been surprised to see Tatiana. That hadn't been the plan. Although Vallyn hated the plan, anyway. It was callous and dangerous—but Cassius wouldn't have changed it without telling Vallyn. Which meant Tatiana must have approached the king. She was as tenacious as she was beautiful.

But that wasn't what had his emotions in knots. No, it was that Tatiana had to be so loyally dedicated to marrying *Cassius*—and that Cassius was so fae-cursed *oblivious* to her subtle signs. Sure, Cas had caught on that she wasn't exuberant about either their marriage or the throne, but no wonder Cas hadn't earned her trust when he didn't notice her turmoil.

"Occasionally, we must undertake tasks we otherwise never would because it's the only way to obtain a righteous outcome we fervently desire, and any sacrifice is worth the cost."

The look in her eyes, the weariness with which she'd said it—Tatiana was talking about more than the marriage. Was it something in the past, or something to do with the Shafers?

Whatever it was, Vallyn could relate. Short as it had been, the war to put Cassius on the throne had required sacrifices and tasks Vallyn found distasteful. Some minor, like public speaking. Some worse, perhaps even a *sacrifice of character*, as Cassius had put it, like using his fae magic to strengthen his arm and improve his speed and suppress his conscience, all so he could kill more efficiently.

Then Tatiana's conviction and sorrow when she spoke of justice... Someone Tatiana cared about had to have been hurt by the Faines.

Vallyn would do anything to win her trust and share her burdens.

But she was carved from marble. He could plead on his knees and promise that he would understand, and she would not bend unless she wanted to.

Yet Cassius didn't even notice. He didn't understand Tatiana at all.

None of that changed that she was set on marrying Cassius. And despite saying he couldn't marry her if Vallyn loved her, Cassius still looked at Tatiana with admiration and appreciation.

Perhaps they would all have to make some sacrifices if it strengthened Cassius's reign.

For a heartbeat, Vallyn resented Cassius for being an Alimer, being heroic, being the king. He shook it off as he withdrew his masking enchantment and tucked away his fae magic.

Leaving the shadowed alcove, he followed Cassius and Tatiana outside. The sight before him brought him to an abrupt stop, and then he ran forward. Tatiana sat on the path in a puddle of skirts. Cassius knelt at her side, awkwardly holding her arm.

"What's happened?" Vallyn demanded.

"She swayed and went white as snow, then said she was feeling dizzy. I tried to steady her, but her legs gave out, and I had to lower her to the ground."

Vallyn knelt on her other side. "Lady Tatiana? Are you all right?"

"I…" She pressed her palm to her forehead. "I was all right, and then suddenly I became lightheaded. My head is pounding, and I feel rather nauseated." She squeezed her eyes closed and moved her hand to her abdomen.

"I'll send for the physician." Cassius bolted to his feet and looked to the guards hovering uncertainly nearby. "One of you! Fetch the physician."

Vallyn tamped down his rising panic. "My lady, is there any chance you've been poisoned?"

Her eyes flew open as she jerked her head toward him. "Poisoned?"

"Yes. Could anyone have tampered with your food? Or did you eat anything unusual or accept any drinks from anyone?"

Tatiana thought for a moment. "I don't think so. I—I haven't been sleeping well, though, and I didn't eat much today. Perhaps I'm merely fatigued and hungry?"

"Perhaps." He pressed his lips together. "Wilmina—His Majesty's physician—should be able to tell if there are signs of poisoning."

Tatiana nodded. "Can she see me in my room? I'd like to lie down."

"Of course." Vallyn stood and offered her his hand reflexively, then remembered he had told himself he wouldn't touch her.

Or was that moot now that Cassius was reconsidering the marriage? Before he could withdraw his hand, Tatiana clasped it.

Her fingers twining around his hand were shockingly cold, even for the slight chill in the air.

"Why are you out here without a cloak? You can take mine—"

"No, I'm all right. Thank you." Once she was back on her feet, she released his hand and turned to Cassius. "I apologize, Your Majesty."

"Whatever for? Feeling faint?" Cassius adjusted his crown, although it didn't look any different to Vallyn. "Please, allow me to accompany you back to your room."

Vallyn squinted at his friend but kept quiet.

Tatiana shook her head. "Your Majesty, I can't possibly draw you away when you were so excited to see the unicorns."

"Don't worry. Vallyn and I are to ride them in the parade, so I have time to see them."

"O-oh." Tatiana swayed, and Vallyn instinctively reached to steady her. But she seemed fine, so his fingers merely brushed her arm before he snatched his hand back. "Still. There's nothing you can do to help me, and you deserve to get away from your worries for a few minutes to enjoy seeing a unicorn. I will see them another time."

"I can escort you back," Vallyn offered.

Tatiana faced him. "Thank you, but I imagine you were also on your way to the stables, and you also are always working so hard. I'll feel worse if I make anyone else have to delay seeing actual unicorns." Her wobbly smile was entirely unconvincing, but if she didn't want him around, he wouldn't push.

Vallyn inclined his head. "Guardsman. Please help Lady Tatiana back to her suite and send the first guard or servant you see to alert the physician that she's in her rooms, no longer outside. I'll accompany His Majesty."

The guard bowed to the group. "Yes, General. My lady, do

you require any assistance?"

A bit of irrational jealousy flared in Vallyn at the idea of Tatiana leaning on the guardsman. Thankfully, she waved him off.

"I'll be all right. But I wouldn't mind if you walk close by in case I have another dizzy spell." She looked to Cassius. "Forgive me for not curtsying—"

"Already forgiven." Cassius gently pressed against the back of her shoulder, moving her toward the palace. "Please, go lie down. I'll—I hope you recover swiftly."

After the door closed behind Tatiana, Vallyn crossed his arms. "What happened to distancing yourself? Neither Tatiana nor Blaise will do something desperate or stupid if the courtship is going smoothly."

"She sought me out." Cassius continued along the cobblestone path. "I stand by what I said, but…I suspect she would make a good queen, one I could rely on. Assuming she isn't simply putting on a convincing act to get close to me."

She wasn't. She couldn't be.

Or maybe Vallyn just hoped she wasn't acting because he didn't want the woman he loved to be a fake.

They rounded the stables, and Vallyn stopped short. Beside him, Cassius did as well, his breath catching.

The unicorns were magnificent.

The nearest of the paddocks had been thoroughly cleaned and the other horses moved to leave the paddock solely to the unicorns. A blue roan unicorn with a stocky build like Riven's stood near the fence, munching on a bale of hay and alfalfa. Vallyn would swear it actually had dark blue intermingled in the white and black of its coat and the black of its mane and tail. Perhaps it was an illusion caused by the shiny sapphire horn protruding from its forehead.

A man with red hair was rubbing the nose of the other unicorn, a tall, elegant riding horse. Its white coat, tail, and mane gleamed in the faint sunlight, looking as if strands of silver ran through the white. The unicorn's forelock split around a spiraling horn of silver.

"They're spectacular," Vallyn breathed.

The silver unicorn snorted, and the man, who had to be Conrad Raylor, looked over at them with a grin. "Falada says you should come admire them closer, Your Majesty and General Drake."

"What?" Vallyn asked as he trailed after Cas.

"Oh," Cassius said. "I must have forgotten to tell you with everything else yesterday. Unicorns have an incredible amount of magic—"

"Yes, I can sense it. It's like…a warmth that borders on scorching, or a pure white light that verges on blinding."

The elegant unicorn studied Vallyn with one pale blue eye, then shook its mane. Conrad gaped at the horse, and then his gaze shot to Vallyn, his eyes wide. He glanced around at the various servants, knights, and nobles passing by or gawking. "Yes, I agree."

Cassius and Vallyn reached the gate to the paddock, and Vallyn opened it and stood aside while Cassius entered. "Agree about what? My description of their magic?"

"No." Conrad glanced around again. "She…made an observation about you in return."

"I'm sorry, what?" Vallyn trailed after Cassius toward Conrad and the unicorn.

"He can talk to Falada," Cassius supplied. "That's what I was starting to say. Because she used her magic to save his life after he was wounded in the war."

For a brief moment, the stench of blood and the screams of dying men rushed back to Vallyn.

Conrad scratched the back of his head, red blotching his cheeks. "It's, um, called being 'unicorn-touched,' I guess. We have a bond now and can communicate via thoughts. Well, she can also hear me speaking, of course. It hasn't happened in generations. Falada says that centuries ago—"

"What did she say about me?" Vallyn interrupted, not in the mood for a history lesson.

"Er…" Conrad's shoulders scrunched. He moved closer to Vallyn and Cassius and whispered so quietly Vallyn had to strain to hear, "She said your description of her magic was good, and that she sees your magic as roiling clouds hiding flashes of thunder. The power and potential chaos of warrior fae, although yours is dampened by your human blood. She said it's probably best I not repeat that too loudly, though."

"She can sense that?" Cassius marveled.

Whatever else Cas and Conrad spoke about, Vallyn was no longer listening.

He had spoken with human enchanters before. None of them had sensed his magic, let alone realized he was fae. That the unicorn could see him so clearly was both astounding and unnerving.

Wait. *Unnerving.*

"Cas," he said, interrupting whoever was speaking. "What were you talking about with Tatiana? When she started acting strange."

"You mean before she became dizzy?" Cassius squinted. "The unicorns…I think perhaps I was telling her about Conrad's connection to Falada."

Vallyn's heart cracked, and he stumbled back to lean against the fence. Somehow, Tatiana knew what unicorns were capable of and feared what the unicorn would see in her—and then relay to its human translator.

What secret could she be hiding that she'd nearly passed out at the possibility of it being discovered?

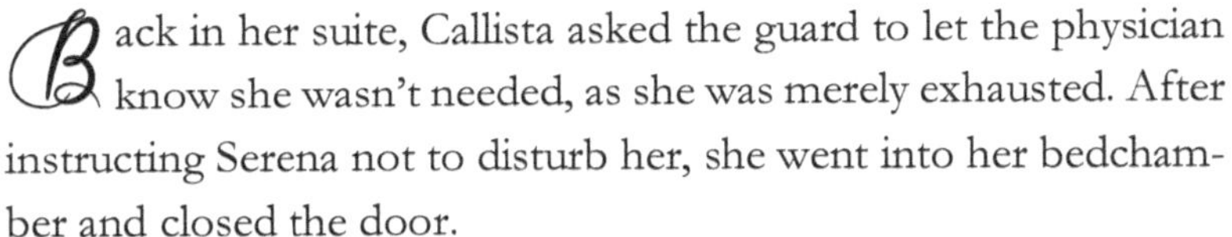

37

Back in her suite, Callista asked the guard to let the physician know she wasn't needed, as she was merely exhausted. After instructing Serena not to disturb her, she went into her bedchamber and closed the door.

Immediately a piercing cry sounded from the sitting room. Callista opened the door far enough for Stormy to dart inside, where she rubbed against Callista's legs.

"All right, it's nice to see you, too." Callista's smile faded quickly.

The unicorn-touched nobleman could be her undoing. Any unicorn and unicorn-touched would be a problem, but this was almost as bad as Tempest and Gareth appearing at Highrook. Conrad Raylor wouldn't recognize her in Tatiana's body, but he knew the name and appearance of the woman who had cursed his brother and imprisoned his sister. She didn't know if the unicorn would be able to discover her identity, but if Conrad realized who she was, he might want to see her hang regardless of the fact that his siblings had forgiven her.

A second chance had been wasted on her, and now Royce was going to die.

Even if the unicorn didn't know who she was, being exposed

as wicked would ruin everything. There would be no chance of bargaining with Cassius or convincing him to help her. But how would she explain not wanting to meet the unicorns and not attending the parade? That would still displease Blaise.

Callista flopped into the middle of her bed. Stormy clicked her beak and flew onto the bed, then curled up in a ball against her side. She ran her fingers over Stormy's feathers, through her thick, fluffy gray fur, and down to her tail.

Closing her eyes, she focused on Stormy. The lesser gryphon had grown quickly, her juvenile feathers rapidly being replaced by adult silvery-gray ones, but she was still such a small ball of warmth against Callista's side. Her steady breaths were calming, and stroking her feathers and fur eased some of the tension in Callista's muscles.

If she could steady her mind enough, surely she could think of a solution…

Callista drifted back to consciousness and opened her eyes to utter darkness. She'd fallen asleep? Despite claiming that she was going to nap, she hadn't intended to do so. How late was it?

Her stomach panged, and she had the sinking suspicion she'd slept through supper.

She stretched and then froze. There was no little lump of soft, warm feathers and fur beside her. Bolting upright, Callista called, "Stormy? Stormy!"

Something shifted at the foot of her bed, and the gryphon chirruped.

"Oh, thank the stars." She reached blindly in the direction of the movement, and a moment later, Stormy pushed her feathery head and soft cat ears against Callista's palm.

The door opened, and Callista squinted against the orange glow from the lantern in Serena's hand and the firelight behind her.

"I thought I heard you, my lady." Serena pushed the door the rest of the way open, allowing in more light. "I'm afraid you've slept through supper. It's just past the eighth bell. Are you hungry, my lady?"

"Yes, food would be most welcome." Callista eased her head to one side and then the other, stretching out her neck. "Anything will do, but something warm would be extra appreciated. Thank you."

Serena curtsied. "Of course. Before I go, though, a servant delivered a letter for you."

"For me?" Callista stopped scratching Stormy's ears. "From whom?"

"He said another servant gave it to him without specifying who it was from." Serena frowned. "That seems suspicious, if you'll forgive my saying so, my lady."

It was suspicious, so she had a good guess who it was from. "Thank you. I'll take a look in case there was a mix-up and it is important, and if it's something odd, I'll deliver it to Vallyn."

Serena raised her eyebrows. "*Vallyn*, hm?"

Heat flamed over Callista's cheeks. "He is in charge of palace security." She decided not to address using his given name. "Where is the letter? I'll take a look while you go to the kitchens. Oh—I hope you've eaten, though?"

"I didn't want to be absent if you woke and needed me."

"Then tell the kitchen I'm starved and requested two portions, and we can eat together."

Serena smiled and bowed her head. "As you wish, my lady. The letter is on the end table beside your chair in front of the fireplace; let me fetch—"

"No, that's fine. I need to move, and it will be easier to read by the fire, anyway." Stormy flew away as Callista moved to the edge of the bed.

Serena left, and Callista shuffled over to her chair, but she didn't sit down. She eyed the folded piece of unmarked paper as if it might bite her.

But standing there and refusing to read the note would not change whatever Blaise had written. Not knowing wouldn't stop him from following through on any threats. Better to know than wonder.

She pinched the paper and turned it over, eyeing the crimson wax sealing it shut. It was smooth, bearing no crest, as if someone had pressed it with a flat surface.

The wax cracked in half with a snap when she bent it. Her hands trembled as she unfolded the letter.

Current status unacceptable. Evade your shadow and meet me at the eighth bell near the royal vault—you know where. I will wait an hour. If you do not show, I will take it as your admission of failure. Consequences will be swift.

The crisp paper crinkled in her hands, and the words blurred across the page before she forcefully threw the note into the fire. As the paper curled and tongues of flame ate holes through it, she locked away her tears and took slow breaths to steady her frantic heart.

Stormy landed on her shoulder and gave a questioning chirp before rubbing her head against Callista's cheek. Her tenuous control on her emotions slipped.

"Sorry, girl. This isn't something you can help me with."

She let Stormy remain on her shoulders while she jotted down a message for Serena, claiming she'd decided to go for a walk and would be back soon, and telling her not to worry. After a gap, she wrote a note as if she'd returned to add another thought. *Poor guardsman is asleep, but I'll be fine. Let him rest.*

"Stormy, go to your perch."

Stormy's sharp cry sounded like a protest. She shifted, getting more comfortable, and draped her tail over Callista's opposite shoulder.

"Stormy." Callista flapped her hand at the gryphon. "Now. Perch."

With another cry, Stormy leapt off Callista's shoulder and swooped over to her perch, where she looked askance at Callista and flattened her ears.

Callista fetched a cloak and pulled the hood low over her face. "I'll be back soon." She hoped she would.

The lesser gryphon ruffled her wings and squawked sadly.

Now even an animal was guilting her. Great.

She readied her spell, opened the door, and finished casting the sleeping enchantment before the guard turned to face her. He slumped to the floor, leaning at an uncomfortable angle against the wall. Callista didn't dare take the time to make him more comfortable. It was already after the eighth bell, there would be many guards to dodge on her route, and she wasn't confident she remembered the way to that accursed hallway where she'd lost Royce last time.

The magic use was draining, especially when she had yet to eat supper, but Callista composed a muffling enchantment of decrescendos that would dampen her footsteps and a spell of soft vibrato notes that would make her blend in with shadows. Her stomach already gnawing, she hurried through the maze of Highrook's corridors. She avoided the patrols, and every time she approached a guard, she kept to the shadows and, when necessary, used a tiny bolt of magic to create noise as a distraction.

Perhaps her desperation sharpened her mind, because she took only one wrong turn and quickly decided it was wrong. Soon the familiar hallway loomed ahead of her, mostly dark except for the feeble moonlight coming in through a large window at the end of the hall.

Halfway down the corridor, Blaise was leaning against a wall with his arms crossed and a scowl carved into his face. She dropped the enchantments and approached him.

Blaise cursed under his breath. "Are you trying to scare me to death? You know if anything happens to me—"

"I know," she cut him off. They stood mere steps from where she'd knelt, pressing her hands over Royce's bleeding abdomen. "Can this be quick? I had to spell my guard to sleep, and my maid will return to my chambers soon with my supper."

"Yes. Supper. Where *you* were not present." Blaise's tone dripped venom.

"I—"

"And don't think I didn't notice that for the last several meals before that, Alimer didn't even look your way. The Maple Moon Festival is in four days, and you're getting further from the king, not closer. Care to explain your failure?"

"I haven't failed."

"You certainly haven't succeeded. My father is willing to have you kill Alimer before the wedding if it appears there won't be one, even though it would be harder for you to not get caught so we can pin it on Tatiana. But even that won't be possible if you aren't spending time with Alimer."

"It's not my fault," Callista ground out. "Maybe it's yours! All of your complaining and stirring up trouble—"

Blaise slapped her. The smack echoed against the stone walls and left her cheek stinging. Callista clenched her fists and rotated back to face him. How she wished she were her own height.

"Striking me doesn't make me wrong. Perhaps His Majesty is

worried that announcing the engagement would prompt more unrest. Maybe you're making so much trouble he has no time for romance."

"Don't blame me for your failure, witch," Blaise snapped. "Do you know what I think? I think you focused your attentions on the wrong man, and Cassius is too weak to do anything about it and is letting his dog have you. Did you forget which man you were meant to seduce?"

Her face burned. "It's not like that—"

"Then what exactly is the problem? I made myself clear in our last conversation. Yet I hear rumors that today, when you were finally seen at the king's side again, you collapsed and retired to your room, *alone*. That doesn't sound like you're trying very hard to woo the king, *Calli*."

"It's not my fault," she repeated weakly. "I need more time—"

"Time? How difficult is it to seduce a man who was already planning on marrying you? Instead you somehow seem to have convinced a *king* to surrender you to his subordinate. Did you bed Drake? Is that why the king is ignoring you?"

"Make an accusation like that again, and I will strike you." Callista forced strength into her words that she didn't feel.

"Do it, pet." Blaise sneered. "For every injury you cause me, I'll see to it your brother suffers ten times as much pain. I warned you before, if you aren't making progress, we will start cutting off his fingers. Do you have a preference which one we start with?"

She felt the blood drain from her face as her gaze was drawn toward the place where Royce had collapsed after being struck by an arrow. Despite her resolve to be cold and unshakeable as stone, her voice warbled. "Please. Don't hurt him. I swear I'm trying. But I—need your help."

"*My* help?"

"We…we have a problem." Callista quailed before Blaise's glare. "Have you heard about the unicorns?"

"Everyone is talking about them, and how their handler can supposedly communicate with one."

"I've met a unicorn and unicorn-touched before," she said quietly, her gaze fixed on Blaise's boots in the dim light. "Unicorns can sense magic and see the truth of people's souls. If it sees me, there's a chance it will realize I'm not who I claim to be and tell Raylor—"

"What am I meant to do about that? You're the one with magic. You stole a prized firebird out from under guards' noses. You have a far better chance of getting in and out of the stables unseen."

Frowning, she looked up at him. "The whole point was I need a reason to prevent the unicorn from seeing me."

"No." Blaise held her gaze. "You need to kill it."

"What?"

He chuckled. "Come now, don't look so horrified. You've killed before, and you've already agreed to another murder. What is the life of a unicorn against the life of your dear brother?" He turned away. "Do it tonight, pet. If I don't hear tomorrow that the unicorn is dead, I'll send that message and we will start chopping Royce's fingers off one at a time until you get better at your job."

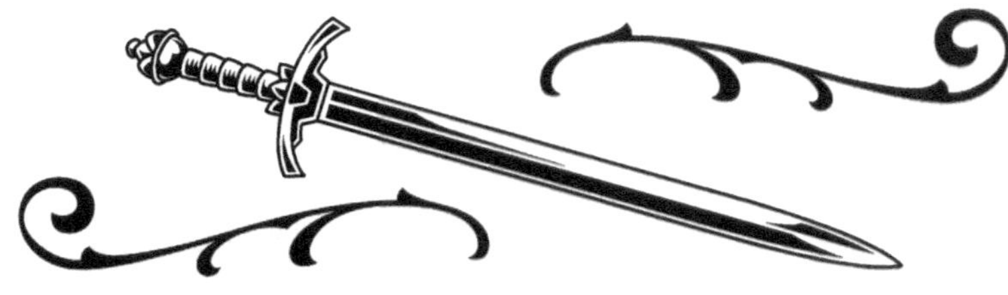

38

Vallyn knew two things.

First, he'd been right from the first moment he'd laid eyes on the enchantress. The witch.

The woman he was falling for was a fraud. She was a thief, curse-caster, and murderer. Worse, she had stolen Tatiana's identity so she could kill Cassius and frame the Ackroyds.

Second, despite all of that, even though the unwanted truth sank deep into his heart like a barbed arrowhead, he wasn't angry at her. At least not as much as he should be.

When she first arrived and started talking to Blaise, Vallyn had been furious. Hurt, angry with himself for letting her deceive him, and ready to throw her in a cell next to Shafer until her execution. For a heartbeat after Blaise said *kill Alimer*, when his fae magic roared in rage and his binding reminded him he had to protect Cassius, Vallyn considered doing as Cas had suggested and killing her right then and there.

But he'd made many rash decisions recently, so he took deep breaths and listened. And the more he heard, the more his anger cooled, at least toward the young woman.

Whatever her true identity, she *was* acting under duress. They had her brother. No wonder she often seemed sad and afraid.

Blaise strolled past Vallyn, oblivious to his presence thanks to Vallyn's magic. That same magic screamed at him to do terrible things to Blaise, monstrous things. The sharp rage that had grown as he'd eavesdropped on Blaise's mocking words—*pet, witch*—simmered under the surface, begging for release. A quieter voice stopped him, an echo of his father's.

"You decide how and whether to act on your desires, fears, and emotions."

Vallyn didn't want to surrender to his worst desires.

Besides, Blaise's punishment could wait. He needed to talk to Tatiana. No, not Tatiana. What had that accursed lordling called her? Calli?

The young woman stared after Blaise until he turned the corner and his footsteps faded away, her expression blank and eyes unfocused. In the heavy silence, Vallyn waited and watched. With a sob that shook her chest, she slid down the wall to the floor, where she wrapped her arms around her legs and buried her face in her skirt. Her muffled weeping echoed in the moonlit corridor.

The last remnants of feelings of betrayal crumbled. He'd been right, she was a fraud. But he'd also been right—she was kind-hearted and didn't *want* to cause harm.

Vallyn locked his magic away. The protective and vindictive urge to hurt Blaise Shafer dulled to a less overwhelming level. He approached Calli, and her head jerked up just before he reached her.

"Vall—General?" She hurriedly wiped her eyes. "What…what are you doing here?" Her gaze darted up and down the hall, as if she were trying to determine where he'd come from and whether he'd seen Blaise leaving.

He crouched beside her and gave her a chance to tell the truth of her own volition. "Why are you crying?"

She stared at him for several heartbeats. A single tear traced down her cheek. Then, her voice small and tight, she whispered, "Help me. I can't do it. I can't."

"Do what?" The words held more bite than he'd intended, though his anger was more for Blaise than her.

She flinched. Her dark hair slipped forward and hid her face. "I never wanted to… I'm sorry." She was crying again, her thin shoulders shaking. "You were right. I took Tatiana's place so I could kill the king. I didn't want to, but the Shafers have my brother, and I couldn't—I couldn't lose him again." Her form curled tighter as if she were bracing herself.

Vallyn removed his sword belt so he could comfortably sit with his legs crossed. He wanted to draw her into his arms, but he kept his hands to himself. "Again?"

She lifted her head and blinked away tears. "I was sent here to kill King Cassius. Aren't you going to arrest me? Kill me right now?" Her lower lip trembled. "You don't even appear surprised."

"No." He sighed. "I think, even after I gave up on the idea, I always knew. My guards have been watching you and Blaise closely. They intercepted the note. A seal without a crest is much easier to soften and open and then reseal without anyone knowing. I followed Blaise and waited in the shadows. Your real name is Calli?"

"Callista," she said absently. "My brother calls me Calli."

Callista. He savored the name. It had a strength and sharpness that fit her—better than Calli, and far better than Tatiana.

"How did you hear…" Her eyes widened. "Oh. Of course."

"Of course?"

Callista looked away. "You've known I was an imposter since that first day. I've known what you are since that first day, too, fae."

Vallyn gaped. "How?"

"I eavesdropped on you and Ca—His Majesty. He mentioned your 'fae magic.' Then I saw your ears on that outing to the waterfall."

"I knew it. That wind was your doing!"

"Mm." She rubbed her hands over her upper arms. "Is that how an Alimer survived the fae curse? Did you protect him?"

Vallyn almost laughed. "No. I don't know if any fae could have stopped that curse once it was unleashed, but I certainly don't have that kind of power. I'm half fae."

"Half…? Oh. That must be why…" She nodded slowly.

There were so many far more pressing questions, but Vallyn blurted out, "Why what?"

Was that a blush on her cheeks? Maybe the poor lighting was playing tricks on his mind.

"You didn't trust me because of my secrets. I didn't trust you because you were fae. Everything I know of them is twisted and cruel." Callista shuddered. "But you…aren't. I wanted to believe you every time you told me you would help me, protect me, that I could trust you, but I couldn't trust a fae. Yet you know I'm a traitor, and you haven't torn me apart."

How could he blame her for a belief much of Aedyllan shared? Even he had wanted to blame all of his own darkness on his fae heritage. "What do you know of the fae?"

Callista's fingers tightened around her upper arms. "I know what the fae woman said in Mortimer Faine's Blessing and Curse."

That was impossible. No one but the Faines knew what the prophecy had said. Cassius hadn't even been able to find it in the vault, as if it had been destroyed when the curse took effect. Unless…it had something to do with why she had panicked after seeing the vault?

"How?"

Instead of answering, she stood, but she didn't make a move to run. "Bring me to Cassius, and I'll tell you everything."

"Ha." Vallyn grabbed his sword belt and stood. Buckling it around his waist, he stepped in front of Callista. "You're not going anywhere near His Majesty."

Her posture deflated. "Then…then…" She turned away from him and curled in on herself. "I'll tell you," she said, so quietly he had to strain to hear.

"Can you turn around, then?"

With a nod, she shuffled back around to face him and dragged her gaze from the floor. Fast as a strike of lightning, she grabbed his wrist and raised a small dagger to his throat.

Between his surprise and heartbreak, Vallyn could only stare. Was she this desperate to save her brother? Had she lied about not wanting to kill Cassius? Or did she still think he was an untrustworthy fae?

"I'll tell you, but I want a promise from you first," she said.

Inwardly, he cringed, but he kept his expression as neutral as Callista's. "What promise?"

Her grip on his wrist tightened, and he frowned at the sensation of something thin and hard pressing into his skin beneath her hand. An uncomfortable tingling spread around his wrist.

"My brother. I'll confess everything, even testify in court or do anything else you need from me to stop the Shafers, but before you confront the Shafers, you have to rescue my brother. Alive."

The logistics of that would be difficult, especially without giving the Shafers time to protect themselves from accusations of treason and conspiracy against the crown. "I don't know if—"

"Those are my conditions." She pressed the flat of the blade against his neck. "You will swear to save my brother and that he will be allowed to go free and be left alone, and then I'll explain.

My brother must be safe before I cooperate with any trial against the Shafers or anything else you want, and then you can have me beheaded if you choose. You told me once that protecting Cassius was an oath you've kept for years. Your word means something—I fully expect Blaise to break his word the moment it's convenient, but I don't think you're like that."

"I made you promises," Vallyn said quietly. "You don't believe I'll keep those?"

Her jaw shuddered, and the pressure on his wrist eased. "I'm not a fool. You promised to protect Tatiana, not a witch who committed treason."

Understanding washed over Vallyn with icy grief. That was why she'd never accepted his offer, never told the truth and asked him or Cassius for help. She was sure the moment they realized she wasn't Tatiana, they would dive through the loophole, and all of their promises would turn to ash.

Callista tightened her grip on his wrist and straightened her shoulders. "I'm offering you the same deal Blaise Shafer offered me. My cooperation for my brother's life."

The tingling on Vallyn's wrist turned to an infuriating itch. Where the dagger touched him, his skin felt dangerously hot, and his fae magic writhed in agitation like a cornered animal.

"Iron," he gasped out.

It must be the dagger she'd bought when he took her into town. That was likely also when she'd bought whatever was irritating his wrist. This betrayal cut far deeper than the others. His anger toward her resurfaced, and with it, his frustration with himself for letting her fool him.

Callista flinched, and her gaze drifted over his shoulder. Her voice quivered when she spoke. "I'm sorry. I'm not taking chances with Royce's life. Promise me you'll help him. I don't want to have to use the edge of the dagger."

She didn't trust him, and that almost hurt worse.

The pure iron against his skin would become painful soon, but there wasn't enough of it to seriously harm a half fae, nor had it been touching him long enough to weaken him. He could grab her hand, pull it away from his neck, and yank his wrist free. He could kill her for attacking the king's general with intent to harm. Perhaps he should.

He didn't want to.

"Do you accept my terms or not? I promise I'll uphold my end." Her grip on the dagger didn't waver, but he caught the way her throat bobbed, how cold her fingers were around the iron cutting into his wrist, and how shallow her breathing had become.

What would he do to save his own brother? He'd covered himself in blood to get Cassius the throne. He'd driven himself nearly mad with worry trying to protect the newly crowned king. Even through the pain of his broken heart, protective instincts and compassion for the woman in front of him won out over logic.

Callista shoved against the dagger. The edges bit into his skin, and he sucked in a hiss of pain as the iron made two shallow cuts. Faint moonlight gleamed on the tears caught on her eyelashes.

"Please, just agree!"

"Agreed. I swear to uphold your terms. You'll remove the iron and tell me everything, I will get your brother to safety, and then you will help me prove the Shafers' guilt."

Maybe it was her desperate *please* that startled him, eroded his control. Maybe it was the iron pressing against him, sending his fae magic into a panic and distracting him with the increasing discomfort. But the moment he finished speaking, his magic leapt forward even as Callista withdrew the dagger and released his wrist. He tried to wrench the magic back, but the agreement had already been sealed.

Silver strands of light swirled around his and Callista's right hands. She gasped and raised the dagger again. "What was that? What did you do?"

"It was an accident!" Vallyn held up his hands and stepped back. "My magic—I—it's all right. It doesn't matter. At least not as long as we both keep to our fae bargain."

"Fae bargain?" Callista's face paled. "I hadn't—I didn't mean… I said *deal*, but I wasn't thinking—and you said you're *half* fae…" She lowered her weapons and slumped against the wall. "No, you're right. It's fine. Just security to ensure you keep your word. Fae cannot break a bargain without suffering terrible consequences, right?"

Grimacing, Vallyn lowered his hands. "Neither of us can."

"Right. Good." She cleared her throat. "Can we go somewhere to talk? This is going to take a while."

"Your suite," he said without hesitation. "You said your maid was bringing you supper, and I can hear your stomach rumbling."

39

Either nothing made sense, or Callista was too numb to find the logic in Vallyn's actions.

He still didn't seem furious, even after she'd used iron against him. When he'd realized what she had, his expression had conveyed more anguish than hatred. Now he was worried about her being hungry? Was he daft or playing some long game she couldn't possibly understand?

Vallyn stepped up beside her. "It will be easier if we aren't seen. Your enchantments to hide yourself were good, but not perfect, and I know that magic takes a toll on humans. My father is from a fae court that specializes in illusion, so allow me to cloak us." He looped his arm through hers and moved closer until their shoulders grazed.

Callista looked from his arm to his face. "Your magic doesn't affect you?"

"Not in the same way."

That cryptic answer was apparently all she was getting. She felt a tingle as his magic surrounded them both, invisible but tugging at the edges of her magical perception. Why should she expect a real answer from someone she had deceived? But then, she also hadn't expected any mercy from a fae. Half fae.

A confusing half fae. A half fae who, against all reason, she wished would hold her again, the way he had the last time they'd been in that hallway.

Vallyn didn't slow or stick to the shadows when they passed guards and a couple of servants, but no one noticed them. No wonder she and Blaise hadn't realized they had an eavesdropper. She'd be impressed if she weren't afraid of his power. This was why she'd wanted to talk to Cassius.

Her only consolation was, ironically, the fae binding spell Vallyn had "accidentally" cast. Granted, if using magic didn't affect him the way it did humans, maybe he could use his magic without meaning to. Another terrifying thought.

The fae bargain magic had felt reminiscent of the binding spell she'd cast on Gareth when she sent him to fetch a unicorn, but that dark magic had had a painful, vicious edge, and it hadn't been easy for her to cast. Vallyn's binding had felt…like a warm buzz tinged with eagerness. As if the magic itself had been thrilled to seal their bargain.

However it worked, it should mean that Vallyn couldn't break his word. He would have to save Royce.

Callista had held on to the fragile hope that she could save Royce and Cassius and herself, but if she had to settle for two out of three, she would happily accept their lives over her own. Perhaps she'd been living on borrowed time ever since Gareth and the Raylor twins released her, anyway.

Suddenly they were in front of her phoenix-painted door with the slumped guard still slumbering beside it. The cloaking magic retracted from around them, and Callista felt like she could take a full breath again.

Vallyn crouched beside the guard.

"Sleeping spell," Callista said, fidgeting with the iron necklace she'd reclasped around her neck. "He'll wake within the next hour and be fine, other than some confusion over how he fell asleep. I didn't hurt him, and it's not his fault, so he doesn't need to be punished."

Vallyn stood and looked at her with curiosity. "You didn't want him hurt—or in trouble. Why?"

"Because he deserves neither." She pushed the door open.

Serena spun toward them and stopped chewing on her thumbnail. "My lady! And…my lord general?" Her panicked expression faded as she narrowed her eyes.

Stormy chirped and flew off her perch to land in Callista's arms.

Callista made herself smile reassuringly. "I told you in the note not to worry."

"Respectfully, my lady, you vanished by yourself after you requested a guard, without said guard—who I tried to rouse before I saw your note, by the way, but he would not wake, which has me concerned. Not to mention that mysterious note from an unknown sender. I think I had every right to be worried!"

"The guardsman is fine," Vallyn said smoothly. "I suspect he may have gotten into some wine before his shift, and I will handle the matter."

Serena gave him a long, probing look. "Did you send her the note?"

"No," Callista said. "Now, I'm terribly sorry about this, Serena, but could you please give us some privacy for an hour or so? Not for anything improper," she hurried to add, "but we have some sensitive matters to discuss that relate to the safety of the crown."

Not entirely a lie.

"So we also ask that you tell no one I was here," Vallyn said sternly. "We need the perpetrators to think we are not on to them."

Serena didn't appear convinced, but she curtsied. "I'll take my leave, then, my lady. Your lordship." She started toward the door, but Callista's gaze fell on the two covered plates on the small table between the armchairs.

"Wait! Did you eat yet?"

Serena bowed her head. "No, my lady. I was waiting for you."

"I'm sorry," Callista said. "Please, take your food with you." Another thought occurred to her. "Do you have somewhere you can go and be comfortable? I won't have you sitting in a cold hall. We can—"

"Don't you fret, my lady." The older woman took one of the trays and turned toward Callista with a smile. "I still have my cot in the servants' dormitory, and I'll be comfortable. I'll see you later tonight." She slipped out the door and closed it behind her with a quiet click.

Slowly, Callista turned to Vallyn, but whatever she had been about to say fled her mind. Why was he staring at her with that— that soft expression in his eyes? Surely that wasn't the ghost of a smile on his lips. Perhaps the general had gone mad. "What?"

"You care about each other." He nodded toward the door.

Dread pushed up her throat, and she held Stormy tighter. "Serena's innocent. She believes I'm Tatiana. You don't have to punish her or—or threaten her to secure my compliance. I already said—"

"That wasn't what I meant at all! Is that truly what you think of me? That I'd harm someone you care about to get what I want?"

"Forgive me if I'm wary of what men might do to control me."

In two quick strides, Vallyn was standing in front of her. "I swear to you—I will never treat you the way Blaise Shafer has." He scooped Stormy out of her arms, his movements gentle and careful of her wings. "Sit. Eat. Then tell me what you have to say."

Callista could have cried, but she would not let herself. This could all still be an act. Vallyn should want her head, not to cradle her pet while she ate.

But he simply sat in one of the armchairs and rubbed Stormy's ears. The fledgling pushed out of his arms, fluffed her tail, then curled up in a ball on his lap. Why did the gryphon like him so much? Didn't she realize he was the enemy?

Except not really. Callista had been caught, and now she was trying to be on the same side as Vallyn. Whether he would want to be on her side by the time she finished her tale was another matter entirely.

She devoured her meal, hardly tasting the poultry and vegetables. Stormy tried to go after her food, but Vallyn tugged her back and quietly scolded her.

With her stomach filled and her energy restored, Callista set aside her plate and leaned back in her chair. Staring into the low fire, she said, "This is complicated, so you can ask questions when I'm done. For you to understand, I have to start at the beginning. With a gifted peasant girl whose family worked in the palace."

What felt like an eternity later, she had finished her tale. Somehow, she had made it through everything without crying. Her heart felt wrung out, and her white-knuckled hold on her emotions was dangerously close to slipping.

Vallyn had not interrupted her. At some point, Stormy had left him to bat around a ball of felt, then had fallen asleep in

Callista's lap. The popping and snapping of the fire filled the silence. When she could no longer bear waiting, she shifted to look at him.

He sat at an angle in his armchair, so he was looking right at her. Were his eyes glistening with tears?

"Sorry, I'm…looking for words," Vallyn said quietly. "Maybe 'I'm sorry' is all there is to say. I wish you'd told me sooner."

Callista rubbed one of Stormy's ears. "You…don't hate me? I wanted to tell Cassius. He's kind and just, and you're…"

Vallyn frowned. "Cruel and unjust?"

"Forceful." She shrugged. "You were transparent that you would do anything to protect Cassius, and I haven't forgotten the way you looked at me that first day. Like you wanted to lead me to the executioner yourself. You do have a fearsome reputation. You've told me repeatedly that you are the crown's sword and will punish anyone who would harm Cassius or cause trouble in the court. And…well, you're fae."

He winced. "Yes, I see why you assumed fae to be twisted and vicious. That prophecy—it was horrible. I can assure you I'd never desire something so twisted, and Cassius isn't making any unwise deals with fae." He looked down and rubbed his thumb over the back of his opposite hand. "You're wrong, though."

How could she be wrong about her own story? Or did he mean wrong about fae?

"Cassius wasn't the one to tell this story to," Vallyn said. "He will have sympathy for you, but I don't think he'll fully understand. See, Cassius participated in a few of the battles for the throne, but the actual fighting and killing he did were minimal. He was on the field as a figurehead and always surrounded by knights. He knows the weight of taking a life and understands the ugliness and tragedy of war. But I think he doesn't fully understand what it was like for me, leading his army."

He licked his lips. "I never set out to be feared. My fae magic is…volatile. My fae ancestors were warriors, their magic honed for battle. I usually keep it locked away, but for Cassius, I let it make me stronger and faster and more bloodthirsty, because I didn't *want* Cassius to take on the role of blood-soaked conqueror. Especially since he confided he feared becoming like his ancestor. They say Mortimer Faine was a harsher man after the war he fought to unite Aedyllan. Cassius's gift is being a leader in the court. Mine is getting my hands dirty. So many men fell beneath my blade, and while I felt little regret in the moment, those deaths haunt me. I wonder if I was right that swift and decisive victory was the best course of action, or if I deluded myself by thinking I was shortening the conflict and saving more lives than I took."

When he lifted his eyes back to hers, a quiet pain lurked in their dark depths. "I always knew that we were the same in some way. Trying to do the right thing for the people we care about and the things we believe in, but worrying we're not succeeding and maybe we've gone too far. I can't say I would have made all the same choices you did, but I have difficulty blaming you for them."

Callista's teeth chattered as she suppressed her tears. "You don't despise me?"

"No. But I'm half fae and just admitted my magic makes me a spirit of death on the battlefield. Do you despise me?"

"Despise?" she asked softly. "No. Trust? I don't know."

Vallyn's shoulders sagged, but he nodded. "After how you have suffered, I can't fault you for that either, Callista."

The way he said her name…she could no longer hold back her sobs. No one had said her name like that in years. Blaise said it mockingly. Royce called her Calli, and there was more sorrow and regret to it than anything. Anika and Leo had mostly said it with hatred, and even when Gareth had decided to let her go, he'd addressed her with cool detachment.

But when Vallyn said her name, it was with empathetic warmth.

She turned away and cried. Disconcerted, Stormy got up and rubbed against her torso before giving up and leaping out of her lap. Heedless of the potential dirt, Callista drew her boots up onto the chair and buried her face in her skirt to muffle her second breakdown of the evening.

Something touched her back, and she jerked up. Vallyn stood over her, one hand on her shoulder. As she watched him through watery eyes, he knelt in front of the chair and wrapped his arms around her. Her breath caught as he pulled her to his chest.

Maybe this was a trap, or maybe this moment of comfort was genuine but wouldn't last. She threw her arms around him anyway and let his strong arms hold her while she cried.

For a moment, she even dared to believe his steady embrace might mean something more.

40

allyn held Callista, determined not to let her go until she pulled away. Her story still swirled through his mind. The things she had done…she had broken many laws, hurt many people, lied to him so many times. Yet she carried a weight of regret for the innocent lives caught in the middle, a weight he felt in his own soul. Righteous rage had cracked through his sternum when she spoke in strained tones of the injustices suffered by her friends and family. A part of him wanted to go to Blaise, drag him to Shafer Castle, and threaten to cut him limb from limb if Royce wasn't released. That would be disastrous, of course, but it was still tempting.

By the time Callista eased away from him, his shoulder was damp, and his knees ached. That rug was not as plush as it appeared.

She curled into the concave back of her armchair and wiped her face. "Sorry."

"We're going to fix this together, all right?"

Callista's green eyes fixed on him. "Fix…what, exactly?"

"All of it. That is in my power, anyway." He took her hands in his, and to his relief, she let him. "I'll talk to Cassius. We will get Royce back, fix things with Tatiana, and see the Shafers punished. And no one will ever force you to use dark magic or commit any crimes or deeds against your conscience again. I promise."

"What if Tatiana wishes to see me hang?"

Vallyn shook his head fiercely. "If she does after she knows the truth, she doesn't deserve Cassius. But Cassius can pardon you, and he will. I'll see to it." Even if they had to fake her death. She had suffered enough consequences for her crimes already.

"And what do you want?" she whispered.

"Nothing." He lightly squeezed her hands. "Like you, I want justice to rule in Aedyllan again. I want to protect innocent people, like your brother. I want you to be safe and free."

And for her to love him and let him love her, but he knew better than to say that right now. Not while she was an emotional mess and still afraid of the future, and not when she might misinterpret his words as a condition. Especially not while he could tell she wasn't certain whether she believed him.

"Are you willing to help me?" he asked.

"So long as Royce is saved, I'll do anything to see my errors corrected and the Shafers punished." Callista looked away and pulled her hands out of his. "Will you retrieve Tatiana?"

Vallyn had been turning that over in the back of his mind for a while. "She and Royce are both probably safer if she stays where she is. Hopefully Blaise doesn't know her whereabouts, but it wouldn't be impossible for him to have discovered what happened to 'Lady Ackroyd's maid.' Even if Blaise doesn't know where Tatiana is, a random peasant being smuggled into Highrook and given secretive accommodations will be noticed no matter how discreet we are. I fear even checking in on Tatiana before the Shafers are dealt with risks scrutiny we're better off avoiding. We don't want Blaise to realize anything is amiss or the court to start any wild rumors. You'll also have to remain as Tatiana and be seen spending more time with Cassius."

It was even possible they'd have to announce an engagement at the festival, which made him twitchy. It wouldn't really be Cassius and Callista's engagement, though.

She combed her fingers through her dark hair, faster and faster. "What about the unicorn, though? If the unicorn is still here in the morning, Blaise will know I've betrayed him—"

"I'll take care of it. Without hurting the unicorn," Vallyn added at her dismayed expression. He placed his hands over hers, stilling their frantic movement. "Trust me."

Reluctantly, she nodded. "All right."

That might be the closest he would get to her trust for now. He stood. "I'm going to see if Cassius is awake. Will you be all right?"

Callista looked up at him with a tired expression and nodded. "Thank you."

41

The door clicked shut behind Vallyn, leaving Callista alone in the dimly lit room. Alone other than Stormy, who had curled up to sleep on her cushion by the window. How Callista wished she could fall asleep that easily.

She brushed her fingertips over the iron chain around her neck and the dagger tucked into her boot. Vallyn hadn't asked her to surrender them.

In fact, Vallyn hadn't done a single thing she'd expected him to. He hadn't hurt her or immediately thrown her in the dungeon. He'd listened patiently and betrayed no disgust or violent intent, at least not toward her. His curling lips, pulsing jaw, and clenching fists had been prompted by her stories of the cruelty of the Faines and Shafers. But for her? The worst were the betrayed look in his eyes when she'd used the iron and his sorrow that she didn't trust him, and those were harder for her to bear than his rage.

It twisted at her heart, but Callista suspected she needn't have used the iron. He would have agreed to save Royce without coercion. She'd threatened him to get what she wanted, making her no better than Blaise…and then Vallyn had demanded nothing from her when he could have used so many things against her.

His words were etched into her memory like a memorial carved into marble.

"No one will ever force you to use dark magic or commit any crimes or deeds against your conscience again. I promise."

Callista had been hurt innumerable times, lost so much, and been left with nothing too often to believe him. That was what she told herself as she stared into the fire, trying to forget how he'd looked at her with fierce protectiveness and fragile longing. Over and over, she reminded herself nothing good would come of falling for a fae. Half fae—who didn't fit the image she had formed of a fae at all. At least now she had an inkling as to why his relationship with his fae father appeared strained.

Even though she could no longer convince herself that Vallyn's nature made him untrustworthy, he was still a lord, a general, a man she had deceived and threatened, and the best friend of the king she had been sent to kill. Life was far too cruel for a man like Vallyn Drake to care about her in any lasting way.

If she'd had any tears left, she would have cried again.

She was falling in love, and it would end in heartbreak.

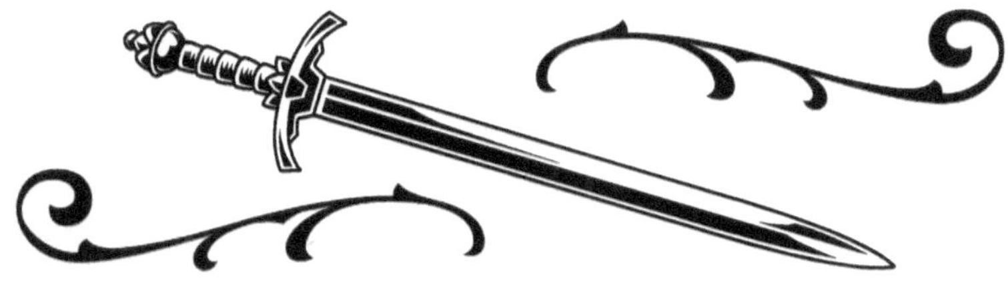

42

$\mathcal{A}$ half dozen times on the short walk to Cassius's suite, Vallyn considered delaying. He could come up with a plan on his own and tell Cassius tomorrow. Maybe he shouldn't tell Cassius at all.

In the end, his first instinct was correct. Cassius deserved to know everything, and Vallyn needed to be the one to tell him. He couldn't imagine how emotionally draining it'd been for Callista to talk about. He didn't want to watch her pretending to be fine again. Besides, it would be better if Vallyn himself explained the trouble with their accidental fae bargain to rescue Royce.

It wasn't terribly late, and Cas often stayed up to have some time to himself after a long day of official duties. So unsurprisingly, he was still awake.

Wearing a loose, thin shirt, trousers, and no crown, Cassius strode out of his bedchamber and into his sitting room. "Please tell me you're here because you want to play a game of chess and not because some new terrible thing has occurred."

Despite his emotional exhaustion, Vallyn managed an apologetic smile. "Should I come back tomorrow?"

"I should have known better than to tempt fate." Cassius took the larger of the two armchairs in front of the fireplace, half disappearing into its plush recesses. "Have a seat and tell me what's happened."

Vallyn took the other chair before the low-burning fire and launched into the tale, starting with intercepting Blaise's note and paraphrasing everything Callista had told him. After he finished, Cassius was silent for several minutes.

At last, Cas shifted in his chair and sighed. "This is…quite the tangled affair. Legally, she should be tried and punished for her crimes and curse-casting, although the only evidence other than her own testimony is her cursing of Tatiana—"

"You can't." Vallyn catapulted to his feet. "You wouldn't. Cas, I promised her she wouldn't be punished. She never wanted to hurt anyone, and she promised to help us. If it hadn't been for Blaise leveraging her brother's life against her, she would have kept her promise to the Eynlaean knight and the Raylor twins."

Cassius leaned his head against the winged back of his chair. "The coercion would obviously be taken into consideration—"

"No." Vallyn's fae magic swelled in response to his rising pulse. "She is *shattered*, Cas. You lost your parents, but you lost your father in an accident with no one to blame, and your mother's sickness was swift. She watched her mother die slowly without proper treatment that should have been given. She lost her father and brother at once to *murder* when they weren't even the intended victims, and Silas didn't care! She thought she left her brother to bleed to death for the *hope* of seeing justice done! She found a chance for a better future at the Royal University and gave it up to bring down the Faines, found people who gave her a home and had to leave them without a word, found her brother and had him torn away from her again and his wellbeing threatened, found a friend in Serena, whom I know she is dreading losing. Don't take anything else from her, Cassius. Please."

"You're still in love with her," Cas noted softly. "Possibly more than before."

"Yes." A dangerous admission with Cassius unconvinced of Callista's goodness and Vallyn uncertain she would ever accept his affection. The thought rent Vallyn's heart. "But that isn't the whole reason. She has suffered enough and just needs a chance to live an honest life."

"Throw another log on the fire, since you're standing." Cassius interlaced his fingers. "If you'd let me finish, I do agree with you. Extenuating circumstances must be considered, and I can count on her cooperation in bringing down the Shafers as her penance. Still, the Ackroyds may demand more. If I am to uphold justice, I might be able to spare her life, but I can't promise a complete pardon."

Maybe Callista had been right to question whether Vallyn could make those promises.

Vallyn threw the wood onto the fire with excessive force, causing a puff of sparks. "Fine, but anything you sentence her to, I'll take it for her. Lashing, stocks, fines, time in the dungeon, a term of indenture, banishment, I don't care. I promised Callista she would be safe, and I will *not* let you make me a liar."

"That isn't how that works, Val, but all right. If Callista upholds her end of your deal, I'll ensure she receives, at most, a light punishment."

It would have to be good enough for now. With a begrudging nod, Vallyn retook his seat. "Speaking of our deal, since I'm magically required to rescue her brother before arresting the Shafers, we need to keep the Shafers happy and unsuspecting." His fingers dug into his thigh. "I need you and Callista to convince people there's a wedding coming. If I haven't extracted Royce by then, announce an engagement at the Maple Moon Festival."

Cassius scratched his chin, his expression skeptical. "You want me to get cozy with the woman you're in love with?"

Vallyn worked his jaw. "To keep her and her brother safe? Yes."

"Very well. You know, there is an upside to all this, though."

"Oh?"

"You aren't in love with Tatiana, so there's still a chance for me with the real Tatiana. You can stop feeling like falling for Callista is stealing her from me. If anything, she tried to steal me from Tatiana. Yes, against her will," Cassius said before Vallyn could argue. He gave a wry smile. "Callista isn't a particularly good thief, though. She stole the wrong man's heart."

Vallyn hoped the firelight hid the heat in his face.

"However," Cassius continued, "what about Blaise's order to kill the unicorn?"

"I have an idea." Vallyn leaned forward, resting his elbows on his knees. "But I'm going to need your approval and then to talk to Conrad Raylor."

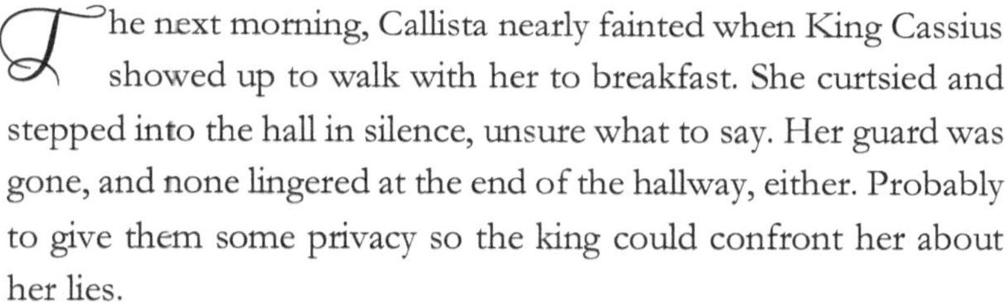

43

The next morning, Callista nearly fainted when King Cassius showed up to walk with her to breakfast. She curtsied and stepped into the hall in silence, unsure what to say. Her guard was gone, and none lingered at the end of the hallway, either. Probably to give them some privacy so the king could confront her about her lies.

Cassius offered her his arm, which she hesitated before accepting. They made it down the corridor and were turning in to another hallway when the king cleared his throat. "I'm sorry about your brother, Callista."

Her hand spasmed on his arm. "Thank you."

"You're an admirable actress." Cassius's words were neutral, an observation rather than an indictment, but shame still forced her gaze to the floor. "How do you do it?"

"Practice. First at the university. The nobles disliked me for being a commoner, so I learned to disguise any weakness. Then I was living in hiding for two years, and then I had to keep my plans secret from a…a prisoner."

Perhaps Vallyn had been right. As difficult as it had been to tell him everything she'd done, telling Cassius, a man with a righteous soul, was harder.

"It helps to keep as much truth as possible," Callista added. "I often told the truth, sometimes omitting things or switching one of my family members with Tatiana's father. Sometimes I tried to think of what Tatiana might say or what might please you, but most often I just said what I believe."

"Interesting. After Vallyn talked to me last night, I wondered whether you were skillful at guessing what I wanted to hear or genuinely meant the things I admired you for saying. It's reassuring to know that perhaps it was more often the latter." He abruptly stopped and faced her, his countenance grave. "Vallyn trusts you, so I am choosing to do the same. My general believes the two of us should be seen together to give the Shafers a false sense of security."

Some of the tension in Callista's back unknotted. Vallyn was protecting Royce like he'd promised. Even though she knew the fae binding should reassure her, hope still felt like the threads of a spiderweb, so easily broken.

"How far are you willing to go in this ruse to give Vallyn time?"

Her thoughts leapt to the cruelty of the Faine princes. But this was Cassius—surely he didn't mean anything inappropriate. "What exactly do you have in mind, Your Majesty?"

"Handholding. Sitting with me on the dais at meals. Allowing me to put my arms around you. Perhaps a kiss on the cheek or forehead."

Relief washed over her. "That I can do, Your Majesty."

"You were worried I'd ask more of you?"

Her face burned, and she ducked her head. "The King Cassius Alimer I have grown to respect would not. But my brother's life and my fate are in your hands, and your predecessors had a reputation for abusing power." She adjusted the silver chains belting her hips to avoid looking at him. "Forgive my moment of fear that your kindness might not extend to a common-born witch." She couldn't help the bitterness and self-loathing that crept into her voice.

After a moment of silence, Cassius placed a hand on her shoulder. "Vallyn is right," he said softly. "You are much more than that."

Before she could concoct a response, he offered her his arm again. She took it, and he pulled her in closer to his side.

"By the way…" The king looked down at her. "I suppose I should thank you for this crown."

"I didn't do it for you." Somehow, Callista made herself look up to meet his gaze. "But I am glad you're the one who claimed it, Your Majesty."

"You do know how to flatter a man." He quirked a smile, which she didn't return.

"If I didn't mean that, I'd have far fewer qualms about killing you."

Cassius's smile faltered, but then, to her surprise, he laughed. "Oh, I see why he likes you." He shook his head, but before Callista could ask if he was referring to Vallyn and what exactly that meant, he said, "And Cassius. Call me Cassius." He patted her hand. "Let's give your tormentor a show, yes?"

This time when they reached the great hall, Callista walked in with Cassius. All eyes were on her as she sat at the king's left hand. Cassius kissed the top of her head, and the nobles burst into frenzied whispers.

A portly man with a wan complexion beneath graying brown hair approached them. He bowed with an overwide smile. "Your Majesty! Lady Tatiana! Does this mean we can expect a wedding date soon?" He waggled his eyebrows. "That would be joyful news to counteract the tragic events of this morning."

Callista froze with her hand poised over her fork. "Tragic events?"

The lord's countenance turned morose. "Ah, have you not heard?"

"One of the unicorns was found murdered in its stall this morning," Cassius said somberly.

Her breath caught as she glanced around the room, seeking Vallyn. Taking care of the unicorn issue was *not* supposed to have included literally killing it. Instead of finding Vallyn, though, her eyes locked with Blaise's. He inclined his head and raised his cup before taking a drink. Stomach roiling, she pulled her hands into her lap and squeezed them together.

Cassius reached for his cup. "General Drake is investigating what happened. Master Raylor and the remaining unicorn have been moved to a secret location to keep them safe."

"And what of the rest of us?" demanded the lord. "If there's a murderer about—"

"Are you a unicorn, Baron Ingerton?" Cassius sipped his water. "We have no reason at this time to suspect anyone wishes to harm members of the court. General Drake is increasing guards around the stables, but without sacrificing palace security. You are perfectly safe, unless you sprout a horn."

Despite the gravity of the discussion, Callista stifled a laugh. The baron blustered something incoherent and left. Once they were alone, Callista picked up her own cup and held it in front of her lips.

"No one was supposed to die."

The king skewered a piece of ham with his fork. He stilled with the utensil in front of his mouth long enough to whisper, "Val's strength is illusion magic."

Right. Vallyn had mentioned that, but so much had been said last night. Relief settled her stomach, and she was able to make herself eat. A few more nobles approached. One of them suggested they "hold the wedding at once so you can get to work producing an heir," which made Callista choke on a mouthful of jam and bread.

"I didn't think those comments could get any more uncomfortable," Cassius said under his breath after the noblewoman departed. "I was wrong."

After breakfast, Cassius invited her to walk with him in the garden. Several times he pulled her close and pointed out a plant or statue or piece of architecture—always when someone was nearby. Nobles, servants running errands, groundskeepers, it didn't matter. People of any rank would gossip, and that was exactly what they wanted.

Except that every time Cassius held her or whispered some mundane observation in her ear to give the impression of flirting, it felt wrong. Maybe it was because she knew it was fake. Perhaps it was guilt.

Or maybe it was because a part of her wanted Cassius to be Vallyn.

That was a thought she had to eradicate. Whether she was falling in love with him or not, a future with Cassius's best friend and general was out of the question. The court and the Ackroyds might respect the king's decision not to punish her. But allow her to marry Vallyn and live among them in the palace after everything she'd done? It would never happen.

"Tatiana?" Cassius waved his free hand in front of her face, his other arm slung around her waist.

She blinked, startled, and looked at him. The sunlight behind his head cast a golden glow around the edges of his tight curls and reflected off the bright points of his crown. He even looked the part of a magnificent king.

"Are you all right? You weren't responding."

"Oh." She glanced around and released her pent-up breath when she realized they were alone. "I'm so sorry, Your Majesty. I was thinking."

"About?"

"Er…nothing important?"

Amusement pulled at the corner of Cassius's lips. "All right. You aren't required to tell me. Even though I suspect I could get it in three guesses."

"Doubtful."

"Oh, is that a challenge?"

Callista turned to fully face him, fighting a smile. "All right, sure. If you can guess what I was thinking about in three tries, I'll…" Hm. What could she even offer a king?

"Play your flute for me," the king suggested.

She would do that anyway if he asked, but she gave a firm nod. "All right. I'll play for you if you can guess correctly within three tries."

Cassius looped his other arm around her waist and laced his fingers behind her back. Her skin heated at his closeness, and she reminded herself it was just an act as she spotted the guards walking past on patrol.

"First guess," he said quietly. "Your brother."

Guilt pricked her. That should have been the right answer, but she shook her head.

"Second guess: the unicorns."

She allowed a small smirk. "No." With such obvious guesses, she knew what he would say next. Either the Shafers or what would happen when this was all over.

Cassius returned her smirk and leaned closer. "Vallyn."

She sucked in a sharp breath. "Uh…yes." She cleared her throat. How had he—no, it made sense. Vallyn had caught her and taken care of the unicorns and promised to free her brother. "I was wondering what he's planning."

"Mmm, no," Cassius said. Pressure on her back made her stumble forward until she collided with his chest. "Answer one question truthfully, would you?"

Realizing she had instinctively leaned away from him, she forced herself to relax. "Of course, Your Majesty. I promised to cooperate."

"Would you rather kiss me or Val?"

Callista's eyes widened, and her hands fisted against his chest. "Your Majesty?"

"Is that an answer or a question?"

"It—I—why—how does this help with catching the traitors?"

"It doesn't. But your answer is obvious." Cassius smiled, then abruptly released her and returned to her side. "I'm afraid I have to resume my duties now, but next time I can get away from my work, you owe me a song on that flute Vallyn picked for you."

Dazedly, Callista murmured her agreement.

What in Miraveld had that been about?

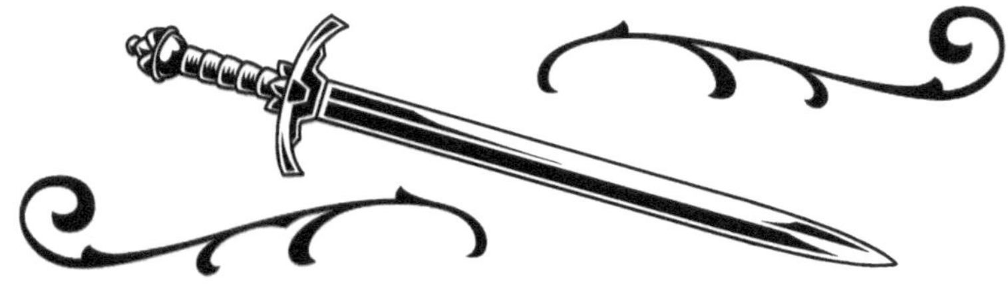

44

Five... Four... Three... Two... One...

His eyes closed, Vallyn finished releasing his breath as he counted down, then began the exercise again, counting up to five as he inhaled.

He had suggested Cassius make a show of getting closer to "Tatiana." Getting angry over his friend doing exactly what they'd discussed was ridiculous.

The act was necessary. And Vallyn had been walking a short distance behind some guards, which was probably why Cassius and Callista had been playing the part of flirting lovers. Even though he'd been looking for them, he'd immediately backtracked behind a half barren bush when he spotted Cassius holding Callista, their bodies pressed together as they looked intently into each other's eyes.

Yes, they needed to convince Shafer everything was going the way he wanted.

But did they have to be so good at it? Did Cas need to hold her that close?

On the other hand, could Vallyn complain when he hadn't told Callista how he felt? He had no right to be jealous when she didn't know he cared for her.

But Cassius did know, and that pricked at Vallyn like a thousand iron needles.

Cassius also had no interest in Callista, though. Their relationship wouldn't—couldn't—develop into anything real, and Cassius would never take advantage of anyone.

Vallyn's pulse lowered and his magic settled back down, so he opened his eyes and started forward again. He rounded the bush and spotted Cassius and Callista walking arm in arm away from him, toward the palace. He sped up, his boots crunching over the gravel.

"Your Majesty!"

Cassius and Callista stopped and looked over their shoulders between them. A frown etched itself into Cassius's expression, but Callista…was that a smile? Brief and replaced with a look of trepidation, but he didn't think he'd imagined it. She was happy to see him.

The thought sent a thrill dancing over his skin before cold logic stepped in to douse his hope. He had, after all, saved her brother by taking care of the unicorn issue. That alone might explain why she was happy with him. Just last night she'd used iron against him. That didn't exactly scream affection.

"Is everything all right?" Cassius released Callista's arm, and they turned to face him.

"So far, so good. Might I have a few minutes of both of your time, in private?"

Callista looked to Cassius, who nodded.

"I was about to return to my office," Cas said. "We can talk there."

Vallyn fell into step behind the king and Callista, ruthlessly stabbing down his jealousy when Cassius took her arm again.

Anyone passing by would see Tatiana, and they could *not* see even a hint of negative emotion on Vallyn's face. The last thing they needed was anyone to wonder if Vallyn was disloyal. Although if the Shafers could be convinced Vallyn was displeased with Cassius, perhaps they would let him into their scheming…

No, convincing them he had turned on Cassius would be arduous and take far more time than they had.

In the king's office, Cassius took the wingback chair behind the desk. When Vallyn made no move to sit down, Callista glanced at him in confusion and shifted from foot to foot.

"After you, my lady." Vallyn motioned to the two chairs in front of the desk.

Pink touched her cheeks. "There's no one here to pretend for, General."

"Vallyn," he said, and motioned at the chairs again. "Please."

She slipped into a chair, her head tilted forward so her dark hair partially hid her face. Vallyn took the other chair and ignored Cassius's teasing smirk. As he opened his mouth to discuss his plan, Callista spoke, her voice soft.

"Thank you…Vallyn. For saving me and my brother and the unicorn." She darted a look his way. "I'd like to know more about your illusions. Humans aren't proficient at that sort of magic."

Vallyn suppressed his grin. What he needed to talk about was no lighthearted matter, but internally, he rejoiced over the hint of interest and trust like a dog delighted by the smallest scrap of its master's food.

"I'd love to show you and tell you more, and I'd like to know more about your magic. We may need both if we're to rescue Royce and stop the Shafers before they start another war."

"Does that mean you have a plan?" Cassius queried.

Vallyn turned toward his friend. "I wish. I've spent most of the morning drawing up and discarding plans. I keep running into problems. Timing, to prevent raising the Shafers' suspicion. The parade is an issue, for many reasons. I have no idea what Royce looks like. If the Shafers have kept to their deal, he should be in good condition, but I also don't know for sure if I'll get to the dungeons and find a healthy man or one who requires assistance."

Out of the corner of his eye, he saw Callista twist her skirt in her fists. Vallyn hated to worry her, but he couldn't risk making a plan that didn't have a contingency for getting a weak or injured man out of Shafer Castle.

"It would be best if we rescued Royce before the festival," Vallyn continued, "but there isn't time for me to get to Shafer Castle and back before then."

"Roland Shafer will be at Highrook for the festival," Cassius said. "What about during it?"

Vallyn shook his head. "If I'm at the Shafers' estate and they realize something has gone wrong in their plans, they may take matters into their own hands with more direct violence—and your general won't be here to do anything about it. I can't leave you in potential danger.

"I'd also rather have Callista with me." At the look Cas gave him, he hurried to defend his reasoning. "She'll recognize Royce, and Royce will trust her, saving us time. If Royce is injured, Callista has some healing ability, which is not something I've ever figured out. But if Callista-as-Tatiana isn't at the parade, that will alarm the Shafers."

"So send Callista and some knights to rescue her brother. They get Royce during the festival, and you're here to arrest Baron Shafer."

A magical warning pricked at Vallyn's conscience. "Um, I can't." Before he realized what he was doing, his fingertips rubbed the pointed tip of his ear. "I said *I* would get her brother to safety.

The wording of fae deals is not lightly tampered with."

"You'd still be doing it by sending someone," Cassius argued.

"My magic says otherwise."

"Sorry, what?" Callista straightened in her chair and stared at him. "Your magic…talks to you?"

"Talks?" Vallyn chuckled. "No, thankfully. It has moods, I suppose, and sensations. Like a warning if I'm about to break a deal."

"You've made other deals?" Callista asked. Her eyebrows puckered over narrowed eyes.

Cassius was suddenly fascinated with tidying a stack of papers on his desk.

"Also an accident," Vallyn said and shifted in his seat. "I swore I would serve and protect Cassius."

She frowned, and then her eyes widened. "You accidentally made your vows of fealty magically binding."

Vallyn's surprise must have shown on his face, because she continued, "I was trying to think of why someone would promise that, which made me think of my father and brothers taking oaths as guardsmen and the young men at the university talking about oaths of fealty. That's a serious and rather dangerous vow to make magically binding."

"And I regret that most of the danger falls on Val," Cassius said. "I ensure he doesn't lack anything and granted him a title he didn't want. That feels like a poor exchange for his protection and service."

Callista fixed her cold gaze on Cassius. "I thought you were friends. Not merely bound by an exchange of assistance necessitated by a fae bargain."

"We are," Vallyn and Cassius said at the same time.

"First and foremost," Cas said.

"Fae magic reacts to strong emotions," Vallyn explained, a little alarmed by the sharp turn in Callista's attitude toward Cassius. Although he shouldn't have been surprised, not after she'd interrogated him about why he was loyal to Cassius. She might think he'd lied to her that day in the garden. "I was eleven and had little control over my magic, but we were already loyal to each other. If we hadn't both made our vows with deep sincerity, it wouldn't have been so easy for the bargain magic to take effect without my conscious effort. We'd have kept our oaths even without the binding. Just…less literally."

Callista slowly looked between them, but more of her suspicion was directed toward Cassius. With her history with the Faines and fae, he should have known she wouldn't look favorably on any hint that Cassius was the kind of person who chose friends if they were useful. At last she nodded, but she kept glancing at Vallyn out of the corner of her eye.

"Is there something else, Callista?" he asked gently.

She opened her mouth, hesitated. When she spoke, it was in that stoic, measured way that didn't betray a hint of her thoughts. "Was our bargain truly unintentional?"

"Of course. Why do you ask?"

Callista didn't meet his eyes. "Curiosity. But as interesting as your fae magic is, none of this gets us any closer to rescuing my brother."

Vallyn didn't believe that answer, but she was right. They had more pressing concerns. He slumped back into his chair. "If only I could be in two places at once."

Cassius slapped his palm on his desk. "You can! Not literally, but we can have the *appearance* of you being in two places at once. The question is, one, whether our bond will allow it, and two, how much you trust Arolyin."

"No." Vallyn shoved out of his seat and paced behind the chairs.

"Who's Arolyin?" Callista asked, but Vallyn had already started talking.

"He considered killing you! Years ago, and he seems to have let that idea go, but still."

"Perhaps for once you could make a bargain on purpose?" Cassius raised his hands in an apologetic shrug. "Your father has full control of his glamour and can change his appearance. You already look like each other, so it'd be a small change. He could take your place at the parade. Assuming your vow would allow it."

Vallyn stopped pacing and clasped his forearms behind his back. "Irritatingly, I don't think the binding would be a problem as long as you gave permission and I was confident the plan would work. But it still leaves problems. I need Callista with me, but she needs to attend the parade as Tatiana."

Cassius looked to Callista. "Are you certain you can't break the curse?"

"No enchanter can break a curse placed on themselves," she said. "Not even if they're the one who cast it. The curse wouldn't have taken if I'd tried to give myself the ability to end it. Once one of the curse-breaking conditions I built in is met, both Tatiana's and my appearance will revert, but not before then."

Vallyn ran his fingers through his hair, and the edge of his hand grazed the tip of his ear. "Unfortunately, I don't think Cas and Tatiana can fall in love before the festival, so true love's kiss is out. Obviously Cas isn't dying, and we can't execute the Shafers until Royce is safe."

"True love's kiss can break it?" There was a mischievous glint to Cassius's eyes that Vallyn didn't like. "Does Tatiana have to be the one to receive true love's kiss? Or could it be you?"

Vallyn's cheeks grew hot. Cassius was *not* about to suggest—

Callista made a choking noise. "Er, well, it's believed true love's kiss has to be reciprocal. No one knows exactly how it works or what counts as true love or even a kiss—"

"As interesting as that is, I didn't ask how it works," Cassius said. "I asked if you could be kissed to break the curse."

"I know," Callista said weakly. "I'm explaining why the answer is technically yes but truthfully no. It might work if Royce kissed my cheek. There's precedent for familial love counting. But the whole problem is getting to Royce, and…" Her voice grew small. "There's no one else."

The urge to pull her into his arms and kiss her was almost overwhelming, but Vallyn's common sense won out, followed quickly by a pain in his heart. She'd explained that it had to be reciprocal and then said there was no one.

She didn't love him.

But did that mean she never could?

Maybe it was foolish stubbornness that made him refuse to give up on loving her and hoping she might one day reciprocate. Maybe it was like the bards said, and love made fools of paupers and princes. He didn't care. Until she told him to, he wouldn't give up on her.

"Are you *sure* there's no one else?" Cassius asked.

Standing behind Callista, Vallyn emphatically shook his head. Now was not the time to spring his feelings on her.

A soft laugh came from Callista. "We would both be fooling ourselves if we claimed to be in love, Your Majesty."

The blush that darkened Cassius's cheeks made Vallyn smirk. That was what he got for meddling.

Vallyn forced his jittery body to return to his chair like a proper, in-control general. "Since we can't plan on the curse miraculously breaking before the Maple Moon—"

"How good is your father at illusions?" Callista interrupted.

He looked over at her, startled. "What?"

"You can cloak yourself entirely, so no one sees or hears you, and you extended that to me. The rumor in the great hall this morning was that Falada's head was cut off and that several groomsmen and stableboys saw the carnage. Your powers of illusion are unlike anything I studied at the Enchanters College, yet you say your father is more powerful. Could he disguise someone else to look like me? Then both of us can be in two places at once."

Vallyn opened and closed his mouth. "I…do not know."

"You could ask," Cassius noted.

"Yes, but I don't know how long it will take him to get here. We might not have much time to make a plan even if he can do it."

"Isn't it worth trying?" Callista asked. "Unless you don't trust your father?"

Vallyn shifted, adjusting the positioning of his sword against the chair. "It's not that I don't trust him, exactly. Our relationship is…complicated. Mostly nonexistent." *Which might be mostly my fault*, but he didn't say that. "If he's being honest about how badly he wants to repair our relationship, he'd probably happily do whatever I asked him, including a binding to ensure he doesn't do anything he shouldn't."

"Then isn't it worth asking?" The pleading edge to Callista's question was almost imperceptible, but for all her icy control, the slight waver spoke volumes. "It would be the ideal cover and possibly our best chance."

When Vallyn looked into her eyes, all of his excuses died on his tongue. For her, he would put himself in Arolyin's debt.

Even if he worried about what his father might want in return.

45

Callista scurried through the autumn section of the garden in pursuit of Stormy. She winced as the rapidly growing lesser gryphon crashed through a bed of frozen marigolds hunting insects that had survived the first overnight freeze of the season. She and Stormy were causing such an inconvenience to the groundskeepers, but at least her pet wasn't destroying her chambers.

She drew her thick cloak closer while her breath fogged in the pale morning sunbeams. Brown leaves with delicate patterns of frost crunched beneath her boots. She'd have chosen to stay in her warm bed, but Stormy would not be contained.

Stormy bounded around a tree, and Callista sighed and glanced back. Serena and Sir Andrew, her guardsman for the morning, stood by a small raised iron fire pit, chatting over the cups of hot tea Serena had brought along, bless her. Callista would prefer to be back by the little fire, too, both for the warmth and the companionship. Soon the truth would be known, and she would lose Serena's steadying presence. She wanted to enjoy the older woman's friendship for as long as she could, but she also had to ensure Stormy didn't do anything too mischievous.

Thanks to the cold, the gardens were deserted other than the patrolling guards, so she'd told Sir Andrew and Serena to wait by the fire while she worried about Stormy. The guardsman had reluctantly agreed after she promised she wouldn't wander further than screaming distance.

Veering off the path, Callista picked her way between half-barren bushes and wilting flowers, following the trail left by her pet. The troublesome critter had disappeared again. After a bit of searching, she opened her mouth to call for the gryphon, only to stop when she heard male voices on the other side of a thick hedge, one of which she thought she recognized. Despite the lack of leaves, the thick branches were impossible to see through. She tiptoed closer until she brushed against the sticks jutting from the hedge. The whispers were still too low for her to understand, so she composed the sharp crescendo of a listening spell.

"I'm telling you, unless they see evidence soon that his lordship's plan is working, they're going to switch their allegiance."

"Then they're the cowards I believed them to be," Blaise snapped in low tones.

Callista caught her breath and glanced back and forth. The hedge ended only a couple feet to her right. If Blaise and his co-conspirator walked that way, they could catch her eavesdropping—without her guard. Slipping away would be safer, but this was her chance to bring Vallyn useful information, to do something good. She leaned even closer, the branches poking against her shoulder.

"I'm with his lordship," the other man said hurriedly. "Even if it comes to war again. But a few of the lords have come to me with concerns about how slowly things are progressing."

"If they have a complaint, they should be man enough to bring it to me or my father. Bunch of—" Blaise spat a few colorful, descriptive insults. "Swearing they'll fight if we have to resort to a forceful coup while wringing their hands and looking for a way out. Thankfully, you can reassure them everything is well in hand. The girl won't fail us. She's easy to handle."

Her stomach soured, and it took all of her resolve to keep listening.

"Whose loyalty is wavering?" Blaise pressed. "Perhaps we will have to take steps to…secure their allegiance. If anything goes wrong, we'll need every one of them to draw swords with us."

A chirrup drew Callista's attention. Stormy flew toward her, gaining speed. Her eyes widened, and she held out her arms, hoping her pet would silently land in them.

"Ruche, unsurprisingly. Blightly—"

Stormy's high-pitched call pierced the air, and she dove into Callista's arms with surprising force. Callista rocked back a step, and a couple of longer branches rattled as she brushed against them. Silence fell on the other side of the hedge.

She clutched Stormy. *Move!* But her feet seemed to have grown roots, and her lungs wouldn't draw in air. Finally, she lurched a step away from the hedge, then another, and another—

"You!" Blaise's voice slammed into her. Heavy footsteps pounded over dirt and frigid plants. "Don't move. What are you doing?"

Swallowing her fear, Callista turned an imperious glare on Blaise. "My pet wandered off, but my guard is nearby. Touch me, and I'll scream."

"Then I'll ensure your brother has a real reason to scream." Blaise sneered. Behind him stood a scowling man with graying temples and a bushy mustache. She'd only met Lord Tolley once, but that mustache left an impression.

"There's no need for that." She tightened her grip on Stormy as the fledgling squirmed and hissed, burying her fingers in gray fur. Blaise advanced on her, and she stumbled backward, trying to keep a hold of her furry companion. "If you get any closer, she's going to attack you."

He stilled and eyed the lesser gryphon with contempt. "What did you overhear?"

"I heard a few moments of indistinct murmuring."

Blaise didn't look convinced, but before he could say anything, Lord Tolley spoke up. "Can we look forward to a royal engagement soon, Lady Tatiana?"

She lifted her chin. "I assure you I'm close to achieving our goal. Good day."

Without waiting for a reply, Callista spun on her heel and strode back to Sir Andrew and Serena as fast as she could without jogging. To her relief, the men didn't follow. She needed to talk to the general.

Callista waited outside Vallyn's office. A shame the gilded great bear on the door wasn't a drake. They should redecorate.

Stormy shifted on her shoulder, and Callista flinched as the lesser gryphon's needlelike talons pricked through her dress. Serena was optimistic that as "Little Storm" grew, her talons and claws would get thicker and duller. Callista wasn't convinced.

At last, Vallyn opened the door. His eyes widened, and he ushered her inside.

"I'm so sorry to have kept you waiting, but good timing." He closed the door behind her. "My father arrived, and I've been filling him in."

Arolyin rose from the armchair in front of the fireplace and turned toward them with a slight bow.

Callista raised her eyebrows. "He arrived faster than you anticipated."

Vallyn flushed as he hurried past her. He busied himself with placing two more chairs by the crackling fireplace, as if he thought they might be there for a while.

His father watched with an amused frown, then approached her. "Since my son is incapable of proper introductions, I'm Arolyin Drake, Military Commander and Advisor to the Lord of the Light Court."

Hm. Like father, like son in occupation, whatever their differences might be. Vallyn looked up from repositioning the armchair, his mouth pinched. Hopefully he wasn't angry with her for urging him to ask his father for help. She didn't want to hurt Vallyn by forcing him to be around a terrible father, but they didn't know anyone else with the skills they needed.

She curtsied. "Callista, your lordship."

"Oh, Arolyin is fine." He grinned. "Callista is a lovely name that suits you better than Tatiana. And it's wonderful to know the real name of the woman my son is in love with."

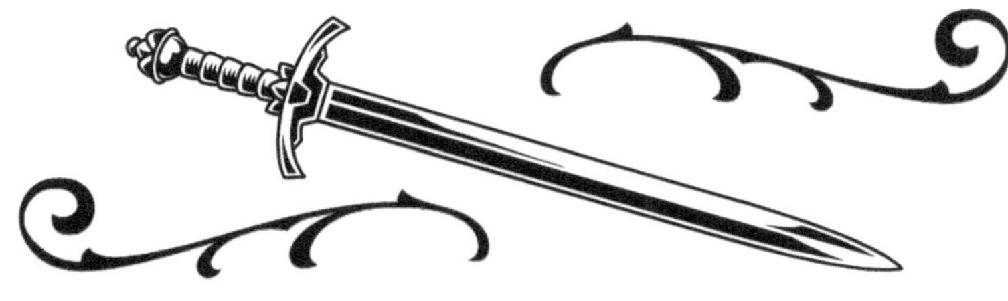

46

Vallyn gripped the back of the armchair as his knees threatened to give out. He opened his mouth, but nothing emerged. He wouldn't, couldn't, deny his father's words.

Callista's face went white. That wasn't good. A woman who was pleased to learn she held a man's affections wouldn't look afraid.

"I beg your pardon?"

Arolyin, fae take him—ugh, he despised that the strongest imprecation in Aedyllan didn't work when one was angry with a fae—glanced toward Vallyn. "You said you were relieved—"

"I haven't told *her* yet!" Yes, he'd said he was glad that Callista's true identity meant he could court her. He hadn't realized he needed to specify *after* the Shafers were executed.

His father's brows pinched. "Whyever not?"

Stormy, perched on Callista's shoulder, released an angry cry. Her fluffy tail flicked back and forth.

"Erm, Callista?" Arolyin stepped back. "Could you reassure your lesser gryphon that all is well?"

Vallyn's fingers tightened on the back of the chair. *Nothing* was well. Not when Callista appeared horrified that he was in love with her.

Callista made soothing noises and rubbed the fledgling's cat ears. The painful beat of Vallyn's heart steadied, but then she looked at him, pinning him with her gaze so he couldn't move, couldn't breathe.

"What did he mean?" A quiver cut through the end of her question.

Vallyn's tongue stuck to the roof of his mouth. He gulped and forced himself to speak. "This isn't how I wanted to tell you. You have enough tugging at your heart and mind, and I didn't want to appear to be taking advantage of your vulnerability. I don't expect anything from you."

Stormy shifted, and Callista jerked her shoulder. "Down, Stormy. Go lie down." The beastie let out a sad chirp but flew away. She landed on Vallyn's desk and curled up on a stack of expense reports.

Arolyin cleared his throat. "Well. Vallyn was just explaining the plan for me to take his place and glamour someone else to look like Tatiana for the parade."

Callista turned her attention to him, leaving Vallyn feeling hollow. "You can do it, then?"

"Easily." A shimmery silver light wove around Arolyin, and when it faded away, he was shorter, his hair shaggier, and his features altered into a flipped version of the face Vallyn saw every day in the mirror. "Glamouring a human I can also do, but not as easily." Vallyn's voice came from his father-turned-twin, and Vallyn shakily lowered himself into the armchair. "It won't hold up as well to scrutiny. But as long as your double doesn't need to fool anyone for a prolonged time at close quarters, it will work."

"Do you think Tatiana should be herself for the parade?" Callista asked.

Vallyn wasn't sure at whom that question was directed, but his father answered.

"No. The curse you cast is powerful, closer to transmogrification than an illusion, but it still shares magical energy with illusions. It will likely either repel or absorb any attempt to cast another illusion over it."

"Besides," Vallyn interrupted, "I still believe it's best if Tatiana isn't in the palace when we confront the Shafers. I'll have a guard keeping an eye on her during the parade and feast, although I won't tell him why or who he's guarding."

"I suppose that is safer for her," Callista agreed. The toe of her boot tapped against the floor, and her shoulders scrunched toward her ears. "Can you change back to yourself, please?"

"Oh, right. Sorry." After another glowing shimmer of silver, Arolyin was himself—to Vallyn's surprise, his *real* self, with his black hair cascading down his back and his pointed ears on full display.

Or at least something close to his real self. Vallyn suspected Arolyin was never without some magical enhancements. The flecks of gold in his dark eyes were too rich, his skin too smooth, and his hair too shiny to be authentic. Or maybe full-blooded fae were just that pretty.

"Serena would be a good choice, then," Callista said, openly staring at Arolyin's ears. It took Vallyn a moment to catch up and realize she meant for her maid to take her place in the parade. "She's sensible, stalwart, and kind, and she doesn't have a treasonous bone in her body. She knows me well enough to behave as my version of Tatiana, and I don't think she'd be terribly flustered by magic."

This wasn't the conversation Vallyn wanted to have, but he forced himself to focus. "Agreed. Although all she needs to know is that Arolyin is an enchanter and that you need to be elsewhere during the parade but also seen with the king."

Callista looked troubled, but she nodded. "As long as she knows His Majesty has ordered this and that it helps him, she will agree."

"I suspect all she would need to know is that it helps you," Vallyn said gently. "She cares for you, just as you care for her."

"Any sensible person would not if they knew the truth."

Vallyn paused. "Is that why you don't want to talk about my feelings for you? You think me a fool for loving you?"

A shiver went through Callista before she stiffened like a frozen branch. "I think soon you'll realize a half-fae nobleman who is also the king's trusted friend can do better than a peasant criminal, and that there is no way for a traitor and a general to be together."

Vallyn stared, unsure which part of that to address first. If only his father weren't here, but he couldn't be seen ushering his father out and then lingering alone with Lady Tatiana. Nor could he let her leave without addressing her fears.

"You're not a traitor," he said at last. "You're helping the king. Maybe you were a criminal, but not by choice, and that's not how I see you."

She shook her head and turned away, reaching for the door. At the last moment, she spun back around. Vallyn's heart leapt. He leaned toward her, waiting.

"I came to see you because I overheard Lord Tolley speaking with Blaise in the garden. Some of Shafer's supporters are wavering and hesitant to fight for him if it comes to that. The only names I heard were Ruche and Blightly, but Lord Tolley knows of others. Blaise seemed to think he knew how to ensure their loyalty. It sounded like Baron Shafer will stage a coup if I don't assassinate

His Majesty as ordered. I thought you should know, General."

Disappointment threatened to collapse Vallyn's chest as Callista left the room. The door shut with a dull thud.

Arolyin returned to the armchair by the fireplace and frowned at Vallyn. "You're not going after her?"

"Not while she's clearly not receptive," Vallyn muttered. "Thank you, by the way. That will make wooing her so *much* easier. Stellar development."

"Save your sarcasm. Your exact words were 'I'm relieved I can court her now without guilt. Overjoyed, in fact.' This is not my fault." Arolyin's mouth puckered. "Of course she's struggling to believe you love her since you weren't brave enough to ask to court her or even tell her how you feel."

"I was going to!" Vallyn clenched his teeth. "After—"

"After she has been officially pardoned and perhaps when you were certain she would accept your affection? You would tell her when the danger and uncertainty of loving her are past. I thought love was risk and sacrifice, Vallyn."

He flinched at his own words being used against him. "No, I…"

Had that been his thought, even subconsciously? Had he been avoiding the risks? The danger of tying himself to a woman who might be ruled a criminal? The threat of heartbreak if she outright refused him?

"She doesn't fully trust me," he said at last. "I want to earn her trust, and I don't want to accidentally pressure her while she feels defenseless and alone. If I were afraid of the consequences of loving her, I wouldn't have told Cassius I would take any punishment he gives her. If she is to be thrown in the stocks in front of the entire court and town, I will take her place. If she is to be flogged, I will take every stripe. If she must be banished, he can banish me. She doesn't have to love me or even trust me yet, but I will love her and protect her from any further suffering. *That* is how I sacrifice for her! So don't you dare accuse my love for her of being false."

A soft creak drew Vallyn's attention to the door; it was open a crack, but whoever had opened it was pulling it shut again. A bit of the gray-blue fabric of Callista's dress fluttered at the bottom.

"Wait!" Vallyn ran for the door. He yanked it open and looked up at Callista's pale face.

Moisture gathered along her eyelashes. "I'm sorry… I'd barely left, so… But I should have knocked. I—I forgot Stormy."

"Oh." Sure enough, the fledgling was still sleeping on his desk without a care in Miraveld. "How much did you hear?" He flicked a glance at the guard posted across the hall and then the guard assigned to "Tatiana" who lingered further back in the hallway. Surely the door hadn't been open enough for their words to carry across the hall, right?

Callista's gaze dropped to the floor. "You mentioned telling Cassius you would take…a woman's punishments if necessary."

A bit of tension eased from his muscles. If the guards had heard anything, it wasn't anything dangerous.

He moved out of the doorway. "Come in. I'm sure Stormy would be cranky if she awoke and you weren't here."

"Sorry." Callista moved past him, her thin frame curling in on itself.

Vallyn closed the door, then lightly caught her wrist, halting her. "I meant it. I promised I would protect you. Maybe I should have explained the full reason why I made that promise, but I also believe you don't deserve any more suffering, Callista."

She easily pulled out of his grasp. Before she continued toward Stormy, he caught the flash of fear in her eyes.

Why would she fear him? She didn't fully trust him, but surely she knew he wasn't a threat. Although…

He'd heard stories of men reacting with anger or even violence to a woman's refusal of their attentions. Cassius had once overseen the trial of a man who had destroyed a week's worth of a potter's work after she denied his proposal.

"If you reject my love and wish me never to speak of this again, you can tell me." Vallyn couldn't keep the note of pleading out of his voice. "It won't change how I treat you or what I have sworn to do for you. I respect that your heart may not mirror mine. You needn't fear retaliation, if that's what troubles you."

Callista cradled the sleepy gryphon against her chest. She didn't look at Vallyn as she passed him on her way back to the door, but he saw the sheen of tears on her cheeks.

She paused at the door and spoke over her shoulder. "It's not you I fear."

And then she was gone, leaving him confused and aching.

47

*C*allista would have gone to her room and wept—with shocked joy that Vallyn loved her, with self-loathing because she was terrified to admit she loved him, and with despair for what she knew would end in heartbreak one way or another. She would have spent the rest of the day pondering which would be worse: the heartache of denying her feelings now or of giving in and losing Vallyn later. Perhaps she would have asked Serena for advice, as much as she could without revealing secrets.

She would have, but as ever, the world was unkind and did not care what she wanted.

No more than ten paces from the door to Vallyn's office, Callista came to an abrupt stop and bit her tongue to keep from crying out. She tasted blood, and Stormy squawked in protest as her arms tightened around her pet.

King Cassius and Roland Shafer had turned in to the hall and were walking toward her, trailed by guardsmen and servants burdened with papers and ledgers. Deep in conversation, the king and baron hadn't noticed her yet, but she didn't care about either of them. Her gaze stuck on a tall, thin servant carrying a bag. Even with his shuffling gait and his head bowed, she recognized him.

Royce.

What was Shafer playing at, bringing her brother into High-rook as a servant? Was it a way to test her? They couldn't murder a servant within the palace, so if anything, Royce should be safer here. Shouldn't he?

Cassius noticed her then, awkwardly stupefied in the middle of the hall. "Ah, Lady Tatiana!"

Royce's head jerked up, and he stared at her, his pinched expression questioning.

"Your Majesty." Callista curtsied.

Cassius's tight smile conveyed displeasure, although with Shafer or her, she wasn't sure. "Whatever are you doing here?"

She forced herself to ignore Royce—and the gloating smirk Baron Shafer gave her—as she scrambled to think of a good explanation. "Stormy!" She held the lesser gryphon up. "My pet escaped, and we've had a rather merry chase through the halls. Thank goodness for my guard, or I wouldn't have any idea where we even are." She smiled at the man, who gave a little start as his eyes widened.

Her heart thudded, but the guardsman nodded his agreement.

Forcing a bright smile, Callista looked back to the king. "How lovely that Baron Shafer has arrived early for the festival."

The baron scoffed. "Actually, I have arrived early to lodge a complaint about how the king's new highway guard are treating my subjects. Hassling them, making baseless accusations of wrongdoing and of harboring bandits, arresting men without cause." He looked down his nose at her. "Perhaps unsurprising, given how the king's general treats honored guests like my son. His Majesty claims that incident was because my son treated you roughly, but as my son would never do such a thing, I can't help but wonder if this is a conspiracy by the three of you to punish me and my family, despite His Majesty claiming there would be a clean slate."

Callista drew a calming breath. *Be Tatiana. The guards are watching.* "Your son is an uncivilized cad who bruised my arm. If His Majesty wanted to punish you, he would hardly need to go through such a charade, and a single night in a cell isn't a worthwhile conspiracy. But as they say, those who cast terrible accusations against others are often actually looking in a mirror."

"Don't quote proverbs at me," Shafer said, and his upper lip curled in disgust.

She tilted up her chin. "Don't baselessly accuse your sovereign—people might wonder if you are untrue to your vows of fealty."

"Slander!" Shafer whirled on Cassius. "What is the meaning of this?"

The king held up a hand in a placating gesture. "Tatiana made no accusations, Roland. Only an observation and a warning that your words could be misinterpreted." He motioned down the hall. "Shall we continue to General Drake's office?"

Callista moved aside and curtsied as they passed. Royce glanced at her and quickly looked away. He seemed paler and bonier than she remembered.

In a daze, Callista returned to her rooms. She mumbled a greeting to Serena and retired to her bedchamber. After pacing for what felt like hours until her tumult of fears and fragile hopes quieted, she crawled into bed. Much tossing and turning later, the blissful unconsciousness of sleep provided a reprieve from her tangled emotions.

When she woke, it was approaching suppertime. The last thing she wanted was to go pretend to be in love with Cassius in front of the whole court, including Baron Shafer and...

Vallyn.

Vallyn, who impossibly loved her—and she wished she could let him. She longed to believe that if she accepted his heart and handed him her own, it wouldn't end with her heart so broken she'd never get it back into her chest.

But Royce was here, and while that soured her stomach, she had to put on the show the Shafers would expect. So when Cassius knocked on her door, she was ready. Stormy tried to follow her and dramatically fell to the ground with a huff when Callista told her to stay. The sight lightened her mood even though she worried again what would happen to the lesser gryphon when this was over.

"After supper, we need to talk," Cassius whispered so the guard trailing them wouldn't overhear. "You, me, Vallyn, and Arolyin. Shafer is getting bolder in antagonizing me, so we need to solidify our plan and end this soon." He strode beside her with clipped, stiff movements.

Somehow, it was darkly comforting to know Shafer had gotten under his skin as well.

To her relief, there was no sign of Royce in the great hall, but she worried her acting was unconvincing. It was difficult to keep up the role of sweet and noble Tatiana when Roland and Blaise kept looking her way. But Vallyn was perhaps worse.

Now that Callista knew how he felt, she noticed how he watched her from his spot nearby at a lower table. Before, she'd have assumed his subtle reactions were distrust of her or worry for Cassius, but not now.

Vallyn's fist tightened around his spoon when Cassius leaned over to murmur some observation about the creamy soup in a fake display of whispering like a lover. The king pushed her hair back over her shoulder, his fingers brushing against her neck, and Vallyn's jaw ticked.

He was jealous. That shouldn't have pleased her, but it did, just a little.

Callista was finishing a piece of pie topped with a copious amount of fluffy cream, paying little heed to the courtiers who stopped by the table to speak briefly to Cassius, when a nobleman turned to her.

"My lady, you're looking lovely tonight." The middle-aged man's fake courtier smile stretched his pasty cheeks. "Did I hear your father recently moved to a new location in his service to our king? I do hope your family remains alive and well and suffers no further harm."

"Thank you," Callista said, a little confused why this lord— Baron Throshe, maybe?—was bringing up Lord Ackroyd's health in such an odd fashion.

"Lord Ackroyd is very capable, and I haven't heard he's sustained any injuries," Cassius said. "Nor has he left Halleton yet, but the bandits in that area are nearly contained. He's in no danger."

"Ah, my mistake." The lord inclined his head. His intense gaze fixed on Callista. "Still, I'm sure he'll be relieved to hear about your successful courtship with the king and how polite you are toward *all* members of the court." His smile turned cold.

Callista's gaze darted past the lord to Baron Shafer, who met her eyes and nodded with a smug expression.

"Thank you," she repeated past her parched tongue. She took a drink, no longer interested in finishing her pie.

The nobleman bowed to the king and left.

"That was…graceless," Cassius said under his breath.

Callista couldn't respond because a noblewoman approached the dais. Curse these formalities. She needed to talk to Cassius and Vallyn.

When Cassius finally deemed it polite to leave, they retired to the king's suite. It was massive, with more furniture arranged around a larger fireplace than in Callista's suite. Rain clinked against the panes of the towering lattice windows in the crimson-and-gold-themed parlor. Cassius excused himself to his bedchamber to shed his crown and boots. Callista perused a wall covered in bookshelves stuffed with expensive tomes but couldn't focus on the titles. How long would they have to wait for Vallyn and Arolyin?

Thankfully, the answer was not long. A few minutes later, someone knocked, and then Vallyn and his father entered. Several expressions flickered over Vallyn's features when he looked at her, but she couldn't discern their meaning.

"Let's get started." Cassius sat in the largest, plushest armchair. Vallyn and his father sat on a couch.

Callista drifted over to another chair but couldn't sit with the nervous energy flowing through her. "I have new information." Her voice wavered, and she cleared her throat.

"Since this morning?" Vallyn frowned. "I haven't even caught Cas up on those developments yet."

"What developments?"

"Concisely," Vallyn said, "Lord Tolley is loyal to Shafer but hinted some of Shafer's followers are wavering. My father can perform the illusions necessary for Callista and me to go to Shafer Castle instead of the parade, and I trust him to fulfill this task."

"We don't need to go to the Shafers' castle." The men looked over at Callista with confusion. She gulped. "My brother is here. I saw him—you did, too. The tall, dark-haired young servant carrying a bag for Baron Shafer this morning."

Vallyn's eyes widened. "I should have noticed the resemblance. I was preoccupied with arguing with Shafer over his ridiculous complaints and…" He glanced at Cassius.

"Not a criminal paying off his debt by serving the baron," Cassius said quietly. He massaged his temple. "He was wearing manacles because he's Shafer's prisoner and leverage."

"He's wearing chains?" Her anxious energy burned up, leaving her exhausted, and she dropped into the chair.

"No, at least not earlier," Vallyn said apologetically. "Just cuffs around his wrists and ankles, with loops where chains could be attached. It's an archaic policy that is frowned on—"

"And one I plan to outlaw as soon as I can," Cassius interjected.

"—but as Shafer pointed out, it's not illegal. He is within his rights to have a freeman forced into unpaid servitude to pay off a criminal fine. Or at least he would be if Royce were truthfully a criminal and tenant of his barony."

"No wonder he seemed so smug," the king muttered. "Probably thought it humorous that he was flaunting the prisoner he used to coerce a woman into becoming my murderer right in front of me."

Callista blinked away her tears. Crying wouldn't help Royce.

"Also," she said, "that lord at dinner who said odd things about Lady Tatiana's father. He's loyal to Shafer."

"Lord Woodlan?" Cassius straightened. "That's disconcerting. He wasn't among Shafer's supporters during the battles, and his fief is in Baron Laxcombe's domain."

Callista nodded. "He was conveying a threat on Baron Shafer's behalf. Shafer brought Royce here to make sure I don't betray him." She gulped. "I think he also implied that Royce was punished for how I spoke to Baron Shafer in the hallway."

"Hmm." Arolyin leaned back on the couch. "This makes the rescue both easier and harder. Royce is also within the palace where Cassius is the ultimate authority, not Shafer. However, Shafer will have guards on your brother to kill him at once should anything go awry with his plan."

"True," Vallyn said. "And it'll be trickier to ensure Shafer doesn't know Royce is out of his reach. I bargained to rescue Royce *before* confronting the Shafers."

Callista winced. "I'm sorry—"

"Not your fault." Vallyn gave her a reassuring smile that was overwhelmingly tender.

"What if I command you to confront the Shafers?" Cassius asked. "Would that overpower the secondary bargain?"

"No," Arolyin said tightly. "Competing bargains are dangerous. He'd be forced to break his deal with Callista, yes, but that magic would rebound on him. It's hard to say what that might entail. It probably wouldn't kill him, but it would endanger him. That'd be folly. Trust me, I know quite a bit about finding loopholes in fae bargains."

His son looked over, affronted. "Excuse me?"

"I would never betray you," Arolyin said, his countenance deadly serious. "Our bargain was made carefully and purposefully. It has negligible wiggle room, and I don't want out of it, anyway. I'm more than happy with what I get from our deal, and I meant it when I said I'd do this without the bargain."

Suspicion coiled in Callista's gut, and she sat straighter. "What bargain?"

Vallyn's expression remained calm, but he didn't look at her. "Just to ensure he would behave while wearing my face and being in the palace unsupervised."

"Doesn't a fae bargain require mutuality, though?" Callista

ventured. "What did you promise him?"

"You speak as if he made a deal with the tricky and vengeful Lord of the Nightmare Court and not his own father," Arolyin groused. "He must spend at least an hour with me at least twice a year. I asked for almost nothing."

Cassius looked at him askance. "Compared to years without seeing each other, it's a lot."

Callista stared at Vallyn. She still didn't know what Arolyin had done to earn his son's dislike, but whether it was deserved or not, Vallyn wasn't close to his father. Vallyn had made this concession…for her?

"All right." Vallyn leaned forward, resting his forearms on his knees. "We amend the original plan. Arolyin and Serena will still attend the parade in disguise—"

"Does Callista really need to go with you? You know what he looks like now," Cassius pointed out.

"Yes," Callista said at the same time as Vallyn. The general nodded at her, letting her explain. "If the Shafers have hurt Royce, I can heal him. I can put the Shafers' guards to sleep if necessary. And Royce might not trust Vallyn. It'll save time if I'm there. Even if all that weren't true, I'm going. He's my brother, and it's my fault…" Her throat closed, and she dropped her gaze to her lap.

"It's not your fault," Vallyn said softly. "Shafer chose this cruelty. But I agree that you should come with me."

"What if Shafer takes Royce with him to watch the parade?" Arolyin asked.

Vallyn shifted on his chair. "I doubt he'll risk taking Royce into such a crowd where he could escape, but if the baron and his son are given a place in the parade, they'll be unable to take any of their guards or servants with them."

Cassius nodded. "I can do that."

"Then, once Royce is secure, I'll arrest the Shafers and Tolley and Woodlan. Hopefully Tolley and Woodlan will testify against Shafer and any others in a bid to save themselves. Testimony from noblemen will strengthen Callista's and her brother's testimonies. Convicting Shafer will be easy."

The idea of admitting everything she had done and suffered in front of the court terrified Callista. She'd rather go straight to the executioner, but she'd made a promise—and Vallyn had sealed it with magic. She would have no choice.

Cassius tapped his palm against the arm of his chair. "Actually… I think I have a better idea. Can you arrest Tolley and Woodlan quietly before the parade?"

"I suppose…"

"And Arolyin…might you gift us with one more use of your illusion power?"

The fae cocked his head. "I never agree to anything without knowing exactly what I'm agreeing to. Hazard of working with fae. What do you have in mind?"

A small, mischievous smile curved Cassius's lips. "The baron loves theatrics. I'd like to pay him back in kind."

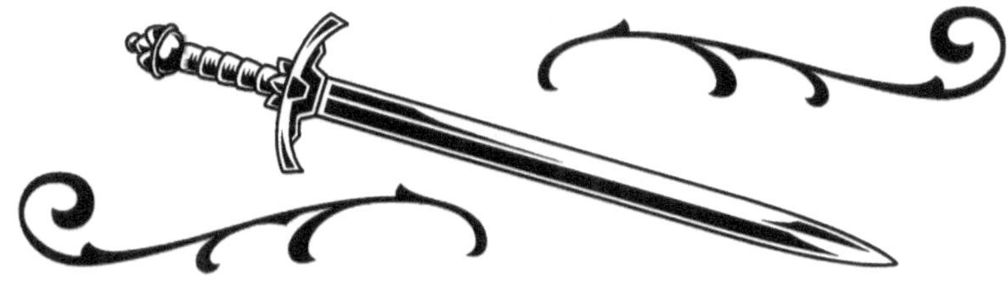

48

With a strategy in place, Cassius declared the meeting adjourned. Callista bid him good night but only glanced at Vallyn before she fled the room. Vallyn hesitated, torn between the desire to go after her and the feeling that he should respect her obvious attempt to avoid him. It hurt, though, far more than an iron dagger to the heart would, to watch her go and not know what to do or how to fix it.

"Did…something happen between you two?" Cassius asked before Vallyn made it to the door.

Tension ratcheted along Vallyn's spine, and the tips of his ears burned.

"Partially my fault," Arolyin said with a cough. "I misinterpreted something Vallyn said and told her about Vallyn's feelings before he did. I shouldn't have assumed—"

"Forgiven." Vallyn tugged down the cuffs of his sleeves. "It wasn't malicious."

It just complicated things.

"I have some work to see to before bed." Vallyn woodenly turned toward his father, who stood near the couch, uncertainty flickering in his eyes. "I'll show you to your room first."

Arolyin lifted an eyebrow. "I'm allowed to stay until the parade?"

Vallyn wasn't about to risk Arolyin missing the Maple Moon Festival because of the inconsistent passage of time in the fae world, but that felt cruel to say. "It seems most practical. Cas, try to get some sleep. I suspect Shafer's going to be a headache until the festival."

Cassius groaned. "And I have to not let on that I know the truth about Royce if he brings him along again." He pointed at Vallyn. "You get some rest, too—not an order, but a strong recommendation."

"I'll do my best." Vallyn nodded, then led his father through the meandering corridors of Highrook.

Thankfully, Arolyin let them walk in silence to the same guest suite he'd stayed in before. Vallyn didn't know what to do when his father said, "Good night, Vallyn. I love you," so he just nodded and left for his office.

He went through two reports before he admitted to himself he wasn't any better at handling declarations of affection than Callista.

The next morning at breakfast, Vallyn suffered through watching Cassius and Callista flirt. Callista's gaze darting his way repeatedly was a small consolation.

After breakfast, Cassius stole her away to the garden. Vallyn accompanied them at his own invitation as their guard. Observing their show of being an affectionate couple made him twitchy, but at least this way he knew the Shafers weren't bothering them. As they passed a group of noblewomen, Cas looped his arm around her shoulders. Vallyn's heart ached with how badly he wanted to stand in Cassius's place. Would Callista ever lean into his shoulder like that, not as part of a charade, but because she wanted to be near him?

When they parted ways, Callista once again rushed off without a word to him. The pain carved deeper into his chest. After another torturous midday meal, Vallyn struggled to concentrate on his work, so he went to her suite. Serena apologetically told him that her lady was indisposed.

Lost and confused, Vallyn found himself back in the healing rooms. He claimed he needed more lavender, but the moment Wilmina prompted him to talk, the words rushed out in a flood. Even though he knew she wouldn't tell a soul, he avoided details and names as much as possible, but he did admit he didn't know what to do with his father's renewed efforts at a relationship or what to make of "the woman's" response.

"It's difficult to advise on a situation when I'm clearly missing so many details," Wilmina said while she measured and mixed ingredients. "However, it sounds like you've decided what to do, but it scares you." She pointed a dripping stick of honey at him. "There's nothing wrong with being cautious, especially in your line of work. But don't confuse caution with a fear of discomfort. Just because it might be complicated, uncomfortable, and potentially embarrassing doesn't mean it isn't the right thing to do. A little awkwardness won't kill you or anyone you're responsible for, even if it feels like it will."

She certainly had a gift for humbling Vallyn. "I don't usually think of myself as a coward."

The physician blew an errant strand of graying hair out of her face and stirred her concoction. "Never felt afraid on the battlefield, did you?"

His fae magic did dull that fear, but... "Of course I did."

"Feeling apprehensive about an emotional battle doesn't make you a coward, either, unless you let it stop you from trying."

Vallyn stood and gathered the herbs she'd given him. "Thank you. I think I'd better talk to my father."

Arolyin wasn't in his guest suite. After talking to guards, Vallyn tracked his father to the garden, where he found Arolyin walking around a pond that reflected the gray sky. He burrowed into his black cloak and jogged to catch up.

"Father."

Arolyin spun to face him, his expression caught somewhere between excitement and surprise. "Val? Sorry, I didn't think you'd need me, or I wouldn't have wandered off—"

"No, it's fine." Vallyn looked around. The frigid breeze had driven most people inside, and no one else was in this drab section of the slumbering spring garden. He couldn't find the courage to say what he needed with his father looking at him so intently, so he asked, "Mind if I walk with you?"

White gravel clacked beneath their boots. Birds called, their whistling notes echoing in the still branches. Cold nipped at Vallyn's nose and reached under his shaggy hair to attack his ears.

"It's harder than I believed." Vallyn kept his gaze resolutely on the path. "Staying away from someone you love. Especially when they're avoiding you because they don't trust you, and you want to show them you're trustworthy and won't hurt or abandon them, but how do you do that without violating their wishes? You want to be respectful and not pressure them, but what if by leaving you're proving they can't trust you to stay?"

His father's pace slowed. "It's painful, isn't it?"

"People can have reasons," Vallyn said, a little defensive. "If Duchess Alimer hadn't taken Mother in after her parents cast her out, she might have died, and I might never have been born. Mother dealt with judgment and slander for years without knowing where you were, why you hadn't returned. I was so young, but I remember her tears when I called Duke Alimer *Father* because Cas did, and she had to explain my father was away and might never come back."

Arolyin stopped, so Vallyn did too. "I swear I never meant to—"

"I know. Maybe Mother was wrong not to trust you again, maybe I was wrong to follow her lead. But I've been there, so I understand why Callista is afraid to trust me." His shoulders caved. "Some of it is my own fault."

"How so?"

Vallyn fiddled with his hair, absently checking that his ears were hidden. "I take my duty of protecting Cas seriously and said as much many times. The only reassurance she has that my threats toward traitors won't be turned on her is my word—the word of a half fae, and she has legitimate reasons to mistrust fae."

"That doesn't mean she's right about you," Arolyin said quietly. "You're righteous and honorable and a man of your word. Don't doubt that."

"I'm not."

"Good."

"But now I know how it feels being on this side of doubt, longing to be given a chance." Vallyn took a deep breath and let it out in a rush. His boots dragged through the gravel as he turned and looked into Arolyin's dark eyes. "I'm sorry I've denied you the chance to be my father."

Arolyin's eyes misted. He coughed and glanced away. "Not being there for you and your mother is my biggest regret." He smiled sadly. "And I've had three hundred years to accumulate regrets."

Vallyn half choked on a laugh. "It makes me incredibly uncomfortable every time you mention that. Mother was twenty!"

His father chuckled. "Fae mature much slower, and time matters less."

"So you've said." Vallyn shook his head, but a hint of a smile crept in. "I'm so glad half fae aren't immortal."

In the few times they'd spoken over the years, Arolyin had made it clear half-fae were unusual and fae knew precious little about them. Most either went to the fae realm, where they became full-blooded fae, or cut off contact with their fae family entirely. The fae did know that half fae simply had longer lifespans than humans, by a decade or two at most.

"Speaking of half fae…" Arolyin rubbed the back of his neck. He continued down the path.

Vallyn followed, unease coiling in his gut.

"I've been debating saying anything, but since you're considering marrying a human, you should know. When fae marry—"

"Oh." Vallyn's feet ground to a halt, even as his thoughts raced ahead. "Fae who marry humans in our realm become human. If I marry Callista, will I lose my fae half?"

The idea was intriguing. Protecting Cas without his magic might be harder, but Vallyn was a good warrior without his fae side. Perhaps if he were human, his bargain with Cassius would no longer hold. He'd still stay and serve Cassius, of course, but without magical compulsion. Better, he'd lose the thing Callista most distrusted about him.

"Perhaps, but I doubt it."

Vallyn started. "What?"

Arolyin crossed his arms. "If I had married your mother, I wouldn't have become a literal human. Fae who reside in the human realm are cut off from the magic of the fae realm. That has consequences. We give up our immortality, our magic weakens and fades, and we start aging. To a fae, it might as well be becoming human, but in reality, we become kind of like you. Less control. Less finesse. Less power."

"That is *so* flattering, thank you."

"I'd be annoyed, but your mother's sarcastic tongue was far sharper." Arolyin smiled, his faraway look tinged with sorrowful longing. "A fae who marries a human in this realm very slowly loses his magic and can't make bargains, so you're already not like regular fae. Furthermore, if I'd given up my immortality *before* you were conceived…" He cleared his throat. "You would have been human, not half fae. Likely an enchanter with human magic."

Vallyn nearly stumbled. "Enchanters are descended from former fae?" Did Callista know that?

"No," Arolyin said. "Former fae just have an increased chance of producing enchanter offspring."

"Ah. What's your point?" Vallyn massaged his temples.

"When a fae marries *another fae*, which was what I was about to say before you interrupted"—he cast a teasingly annoyed look Vallyn's way—"it's a special, intimate type of bargain. Callista isn't fae, but she has magic. If you marry her, it's possible your magics will intertwine into something resembling a fae binding. It's also possible your magic would do its part alone, making it one-sided."

Arolyin stilled and looked out across the pond. "Your connection and loyalty to her would be magically deepened, but hers wouldn't be. It's difficult to break a marriage binding, but if it is done, it's painful, Vallyn. I've seen fae whose spouses betrayed them. They were never the same. Their magic was weakened, their ability to control glamours compromised, and their spirits broken. If a fae marriage binding affects you and not her and then she is disloyal—"

"She wouldn't," Vallyn bit out.

"All right." Arolyin turned toward him and lifted his hands in a calming gesture. "I simply don't want to see my son hurt, and I thought you should be warned."

Vallyn tugged on the edges of his cloak and drew it tighter about himself, even though embarrassment heated his face. "Thank you for the information. But first of all, Callista once told me she would not take marriage vows lightly, and I'm certain she wasn't lying. Second, human hearts don't need magic bindings to be crushed. It's a risk and sacrifice involved in loving anyone."

Certainly no magic had been involved in shattering his mother's heart.

Arolyin's shoulders caved. "Indeed it is," he murmured. "Can I offer a suggestion, as a man who has loved and lost and a father who cares deeply for his son? Forget caution. Make sure Callista knows you believe she's worth the risk and sacrifice."

49

Callista avoided Vallyn for the next two days, afraid to confront his feelings—or her own. During meals, she couldn't stop herself from glancing at him far more than was good for her cover as Tatiana. She couldn't ignore the displeasure that flickered over his countenance every time Cassius touched her or the longing in his eyes when he caught her looking. The fraying rope of resistance she clung to was close to snapping. If it did, the attraction crackling between her and Vallyn would sweep her out with the tide into unknown waters—unless she decided to trust Vallyn to catch her before she drowned, but she didn't know how to trust someone that much.

In the meantime, she saw Royce twice, shuffling after Baron Shafer with his head down. The bruise around his swollen right eye made her want to do even worse to Shafer in return.

At last, the morning of the Maple Moon arrived. Callista redid her braid for the fourth time while she waited for Vallyn and Arolyin. Stormy slept curled up on her pillow by the window. Serena scurried about the room hunting silky gray hairs like her life depended on the room being gryphon-fur free.

Callista tied off her braid and smoothed the skirt of her ruby gown. "You're going to wrinkle that dress," she said, keeping her tone teasing.

Serena straightened, and red colored her cheeks. "Sorry."

Arolyin had said it was easier for him to modify the appearance of clothing than to create entire illusory garments, so Serena wore one of Tatiana's finest gowns. Serena had readily agreed to their plan despite the minimal information.

"I was teasing." Callista tried for a reassuring smile, although she wasn't sure it was convincing. "You're going to do great."

Serena ran her fingertips over the delicate beading on her dress's bright-blue bodice. "I only have to ride in a carriage behind His Majesty and General Drake's father, then stand beside the king and smile when he announces your betrothal. It should be easy, but my stomach is in knots."

Callista went over to her. "Are you sure you're all right with doing this?"

With a deep breath, the maid nodded. "The general said I wouldn't be in any danger. I admit I don't understand how it helps you and the king, but I am honored to serve His Majesty in this way and pleased to help you, my lady."

Something twisted in Callista's gut. There were so many things she wanted to say, but she couldn't risk it. Still, this might be the last time she talked to Serena.

"I…I want you to know I consider you my friend." Callista swallowed. "I'm glad to know you and will always be so grateful for your kindness. I'm not sure how I would have gotten through acclimating to the palace without you."

"You sound like you're leaving." Serena's nervous laughter faded. "Oh… *Oh*." She bit her lower lip. "I truly am happy to help you, my lady. You've been very kind, and I know you're a good person. I want you to be happy. So I will do this and say that General Drake told me it was to help the king and claim ignorance, but…if I'm your friend, will you be honest with me?"

To Callista's surprise and mounting confusion, the older woman gathered both of Callista's hands in hers and gently squeezed them. "Where will you and Drake go after you elope?"

Callista gasped and snatched her hands out of Serena's. "What? That's not—we aren't—but even if we were, we wouldn't need subterfuge! I would simply turn down His Majesty's proposal. Why would you think that?"

Serena bowed her head. "Forgive me, your ladyship. I've noticed how you and General Drake look at each other. You don't look at His Majesty that way."

"That's not it at all!" Callista clenched her skirt. Well, it might be true, but it was unrelated to what she and Vallyn would be doing during the parade. "But after—"

A knock sounded, and Serena hurried to answer the door. Probably for the best. As much as Callista wanted to warn Serena that things would change after the parade and beg her to remember that they had been friends, it wouldn't be wise. It would be wasted breath, anyway. Serena would hate her when she knew the truth, and Callista would lose another of the few friends she'd had in her miserable life.

Vallyn and his father entered. Callista watched in a daze, not listening as Arolyin transformed himself into Vallyn and then glamoured Serena to look like Tatiana. They started to leave, but Serena stopped in the doorway.

"Lady Tatiana?"

Callista straightened. "Yes?"

"I hope things go well, whether I'm right or wrong." She glanced toward Vallyn—the real one. "And I hope you make the choice that is right for your heart."

With that, she left, closing the door behind her.

Vallyn looked from the door to Callista. "What did that mean?"

"Nothing."

"Now that's a lie," he said softly and stepped toward her. "I know now isn't an ideal time to talk, but I've let that stop me for long enough. Did what Serena said have something to do with me? With…us?"

There is no us. The words wouldn't move past her vocal cords. With a sigh, she angled away from him. "Serena thought she and your father were covering for us so we could run away together."

Vallyn tilted his head. "Why would she think that?"

"Because you're terrible at hiding your feelings," Callista scoffed. *I'm also not as good at hiding mine as I thought.*

As long as she hid her true feelings from Vallyn, she'd be all right. She'd survived many things, but if she surrendered to her feelings, she wasn't sure she'd survive the inevitable heartbreak of losing him.

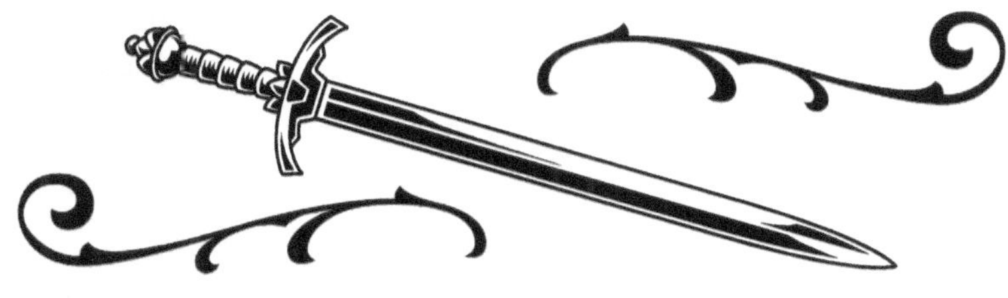

50

Vallyn didn't argue whether he'd done a poor job disguising his feelings. It wasn't important, anyway.

"That doesn't explain why Serena thought you might reciprocate, or why she implied she thinks you—well, Tatiana—choosing Cassius and not me would be a mistake."

"Please stop," Callista whispered. Her arms tightened around her middle as she stared at the door.

His heart ached. "I will if you tell me why."

"I already did. Anything between us is impossible."

Vallyn searched her face as if it held the answer to why she was pushing him away when she clearly felt something for him. "Did you love someone before who broke your heart? The person who gave you the flute you lost?"

A bitter laugh wrenched out of her. "Not in the way you mean. My father gave me my flute. Everything I have loved or valued I have lost. My family, my friends, my place at the university and hopes for my future, my peaceful second chance at life, the couple who took me in when I was alone. I'm going to lose Serena when this is over, and probably Stormy, too. Anything good that exists in my life, the world will take from me. Anything good that I desire, fate will move out of my reach."

He searched for words. "What about Royce? He came back."

"Did he?" Callista murmured. "Not the same. Royce was always the more confident and decisive of my brothers, and the stronger one physically. He's a shadow of his former self. And it's my fault."

"It's not your fault." Vallyn reached for her, but she pulled away.

"How long do we have to wait before we can leave?"

"A few more minutes."

Since he would cloak them, they could leave now. Still, it would be easier if they waited until the entire court had moved outside for the parade. He eyed the clouds through the window. Hopefully it wouldn't rain and drive everyone back inside sooner than planned.

"Callista."

She reluctantly faced him again.

"When my father was courting my mother, he made her promises." Vallyn worked his tight throat. "Then he impregnated her, left, and didn't return for years. Before I was born, my grandparents disowned my mother and tossed her out, but my mother's friend took her in—Cassius's mother. My father didn't know she was pregnant, he did have reasons, and it wasn't his choice to be gone so long, but he still left when he shouldn't have. After my father came back, my mother no longer trusted him to keep his promises. She didn't want him, so he visited infrequently. He wasn't there when my mother died. Every time he left again, it felt like confirmation my mother was right not to trust him."

Callista's defensive posture eased as she watched him with sympathy. "I'm so sorry."

"I'm telling you this because I want you to understand how

much I hate broken promises. So you'll know that when I say I never make a promise I won't do everything in my power to keep, I am deathly serious.

"Callista, I promise, I won't abandon you. I want to give you every good thing you desire, every good thing you fear you can't have." Vallyn drifted closer until his boots knocked against her shoes. "I believe Tempest was right. There's good in you, and I want to help you nourish it and grow it. I love you. Your kindness, your sense of honor and duty, the way you love so fiercely, and your courage as you keep going when so many would be crushed by the weight of everything you carry."

Looking up into her moss-green eyes, he placed his palm lightly against her jaw and stroked his thumb over her cheek. "I want to help you carry your burdens. I admire your strength, but I want to give you the safety to not be strong all the time. Let me be your shield against those who would hurt you, your sword against those who already have, your place of refuge from your worries, your home where you can rest and heal and learn to hope again."

Her lower lip trembled. "I have nothing to offer you."

Vallyn placed his other hand on her opposite cheek, cradling her head. "You have already been a retreat from the strain of my work, the one person who has been able to convince me to relax and enjoy myself since Cassius was crowned. You have understood me in a way no one else has. I see the way you love and fight for what you believe. We can make each other stronger. I don't need a title or money or status or anything else. What I desire is something only you can give: your love. I just want you."

Tears welled in her eyes. One escaped, and he brushed it away with his thumb.

A rustle of feathers interrupted the silence. Stormy flew over and wound between Vallyn's legs before rubbing against Callista's ankles. A demanding cry from the gryphon destroyed any intimacy left in the moment.

Callista's vulnerable expression shuttered, and she stepped away. "We need to get my brother."

Vallyn's hands fell to his sides. He'd been stupid to think she'd be able to consider a relationship while worrying about her brother.

"Let's go."

Wrapped in his cloak of light-bending and sound-muffling magic, they hurried through the empty halls. Most of the servants were watching the parade, while the rest prepared the feast. Even most of the guards had moved outside to keep the crowds under control.

They reached the door to Baron Shafer's suite. This was where things got tricky. Some of Shafer's personal retainers would likely still be in the rooms to ensure Royce couldn't escape. Once they opened the door, Vallyn's cloaking magic would be less effective—it wouldn't work as well if someone looked directly at them while seeking an intruder.

Vallyn let his invisibility magic fall away and withdrew a skeleton key from his belt. Callista's face was pale, but she clenched her jaw with determination.

"Ready?" he whispered.

Faint purple light swirled around her hands.

Vallyn inserted the key into the lock and turned it.

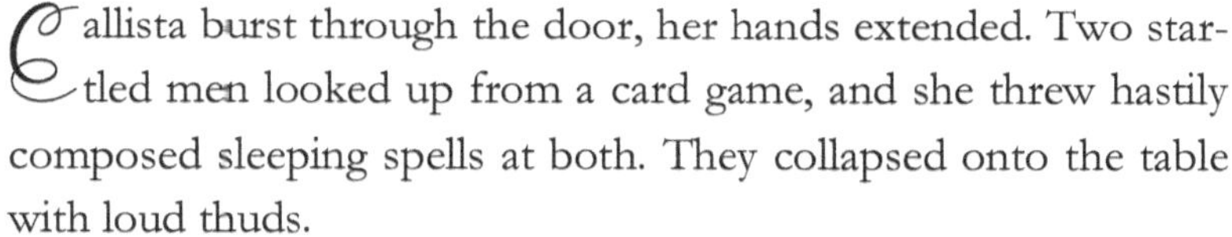

51

*C*allista burst through the door, her hands extended. Two startled men looked up from a card game, and she threw hastily composed sleeping spells at both. They collapsed onto the table with loud thuds.

No one else was in the room, but there were three closed doors, one to her right and two on her left. The leftmost opened, and a man walked out—a man she recognized. The short, brawny man who'd been at the inn with Blaise.

"What was—" His eyes widened, and she knocked him unconscious with a blast of purple before he could even reach for his weapon.

Hunger gnawed at her stomach, but she didn't release her magic as she sprinted to the room behind the brute. Empty. Muttering a curse, she turned around.

Vallyn was at the door on the opposite side of the room. He opened it, peered around, and then turned and grimly shook his head.

Her heart pounding, Callista stepped over Blaise's brute and scurried to the final door.

The room inside was devoid of windows. Faint light from the

sitting room cast weak illumination over a couple of cots and a simple wardrobe. A lump under the blanket on one of the cots shifted with a clattering of metal as the occupant threw off his blanket and staggered to his feet.

Royce bowed without looking her way. The chains connecting the shackles around his wrists and ankles to the legs of the cot clinked. Fury seared through her.

"Royce." Her voice came out strained.

Her brother jerked upright and squinted. "Calli? Is that you?"

"It's me." She blinked away tears and hurried toward him, composing a rending enchantment with the energy of a forceful scale of staccatos.

Royce's eyes widened. "Look out!" He reached for her, but the chains stopped him. "Behind you!"

Callista spun, preparing to switch spells, but relaxed when she saw Vallyn in the doorway. "He's with me." Heat flamed over her face. "That is, he's helping us."

She channeled the breaking spell into the cuffs on Royce's wrists, then those around his ankles. At breakfast she'd been too nervous to eat, and she regretted that now. Her stomach panged, and she swayed.

Concern filled Royce's eyes. He stepped forward to steady her, but before he reached her, Vallyn's arm looped around her.

Royce gaped at Vallyn's hand grasping the side of her shoulder, then tore his gaze over to Callista's face. "Did you bring food?"

"Have they been starving you?" Vallyn asked, a note of disbelief in his voice.

"No, for…" Royce snapped his mouth shut. A bit of flustered red crept into his cheeks.

"He means for me," Callista said. "Using magic makes me famished."

Vallyn's grip loosened as he withdrew enough to peer into her eyes. "But you barely ate at breakfast—"

"I'm fine, and yesterday I stashed a little food in my bedchamber." She slipped free of Vallyn and embraced her brother. "I'm so, so sorry—"

"I'm fine, Calli." Royce's returning embrace wasn't the crushing bear hug she remembered, and the strength he did put into his squeeze felt more like desperation than reassurance.

She released him, then lightly pushed him to sit on the bed. "Let me heal you—"

"I'm really all right." He waved away her prodding hands.

"Your eye—"

"Is healing on its own, without you starving yourself to speed up the process. I can handle a few minor bruises and welts. I just want to get out of here." A shudder ripped through him. "Shafer thought my presence and a black eye would be enough to ensure your continued compliance, but I'm glad he was wrong. Are we running away?" His gaze flicked to Vallyn. "With…the king's general?"

Callista shook her head. "I'll explain in my room. Shafer's men won't be asleep much longer." She turned to Vallyn. "What do we do with them?"

"Everyone attending the parade is being escorted straight to the feast, and the guards will see to it the Shafers don't detour to their rooms. We simply have to ensure these men don't escape to warn their masters." Vallyn checked the door. "Hm. No lock."

"No matter." Callista returned to the foyer. "I'll just make them sleep longer." She began to arrange the spell, but Vallyn put a hand on her forearm.

"Are you certain you can cast more magic right now?" His earnest countenance warmed her heart even while the threat of heartbreak kept her too afraid to accept his love.

"I'm certain." She composed the soothing, inaudible melody of the enchantment and spread it over the three men. Her stomach growled, and she pressed her palm against her abdomen with a wince.

"Let's get you back to your room." Vallyn took her hand, interlacing their fingers. For some reason, she let him. "Royce, hold on to me or Callista. We have to stay close for my magic to properly cloak us."

Royce took Callista's other hand. For a painful moment, a vivid memory filled her mind of her and Royce as children, holding hands and running through a field of grass as tall as they were. She squeezed his hand, a silent promise that she would do everything in her power to ensure he was never hurt again.

When they reached her quarters, Vallyn dropped the spell. Callista opened the door, and immediately a ball of gray fluff and feathers hurled into her chest.

She stumbled back a step as she caught the chittering fledgling. "Please, I wasn't gone for that long."

Royce laughed. "I'd halfway convinced myself I hallucinated you holding a lesser gryphon in the hall the other day." He reached toward the creature. "May I?"

"This is Stormy. Stormy, this is Royce. Be nice. He's my brother." When he stroked the gryphon's head, she pushed against his palm. Callista beamed. "She likes you. Let's go inside."

"Where's your food?" Royce asked the moment the door clicked shut. "I want to know what's going on, but you're pale." He frowned. "Or is Lady Tatiana just pasty? It's disconcerting to *know* it's you even though you don't look or sound like you. I don't like it. I hope your plan involves fixing this?"

"It should." Assuming the Shafers died. Or perhaps she could see if a kiss from Royce on her hand or cheek or forehead might fix it, but that seemed like too much pressure to put on him so quickly after everything he'd endured. And what if it didn't work? That would be awkward for both of them.

Vallyn stepped in front of her. Maybe she should give in and kiss him… Her face heated, and she dismissed the thought. She didn't want to deal with the disappointment of that not working—or what it might mean if it did. She would just wait for the Shafers' execution.

"Here." Vallyn took Stormy from her. "Go get your food. We don't have much time before the parade ends and Cassius fetches you. I'll fill your brother in."

Royce narrowed his eyes. "Maybe you can start with how Callista came here to court and kill the king and ended up in a romance with the king's general."

Callista choked. "That's not…" But he wasn't entirely wrong, and as much as she denied the truth, she couldn't lie to her brother. Her painfully gnawing stomach growled, and she used the excuse to scurry off to her bedchamber for food.

When she returned, Royce had taken a seat in one of the armchairs by the fireplace, and Vallyn was busy stirring up the fire. She took the other armchair and ate while Vallyn explained.

"So then, I'll bring in my father, magically disguised as Lord Ackroyd, and order the guards to seize 'Tatiana.' Cassius will ask for the court's input for their sentencing." Vallyn smirked. "Cassius's idea. We'll let the traitors unknowingly declare their own punishment, and they won't be able to argue for a weaker sentence. Then I'll have the guards remove Callista and bring in the captured lords. That way when we reveal the Shafers as the true traitors, she won't have to be present when the entire court first hears about her curse-casting."

It was a mercy Callista didn't deserve, and against her will, she loved him for it.

"It's a slightly complicated plan, but I've thoroughly evaluated it." Vallyn gave one sharp, determined nod. "I'm certain there's nothing that can go wrong."

Unless something unexpected happened. Callista knew from experience how plans could get complicated the moment you enacted them. People were unpredictable, and nothing had ever been simple for her. She was involved, so something would go wrong—just like it would go wrong if she courted Vallyn. But her only argument was an anxious feeling in her gut, so she kept her thoughts to herself.

"What do I do?" Royce asked.

"For now, you stay here and rest," Callista said.

"Eventually, His Majesty might request that you testify against the Shafers," Vallyn added. "Although it may not be necessary for either of you to ever testify in public." His savage grin held a touch of wildness, and though it reminded Callista he was half fae, it didn't make her doubt him anymore. "The lords I quietly arrested this morning were more than happy to talk to spare their own necks. Once the trial is over, you will be free to go."

Royce nodded and slumped back in the chair. He probably hadn't felt safe or truly relaxed in over two years. Her throat tightened, and tears threatened to break through her careful control.

"Both of us, right?" Royce's hands tightened around the arms of his chair. "It's not her fault, any of it. If anything, it's mine. I won't testify against the Shafers unless Calli won't be harmed and will be free to go."

Callista lowered her head. Would she be able to convince Royce to testify if he knew he might leave Highrook alone?

"She won't be harmed," Vallyn said firmly. "Even if I have to fight the entire court or let Lord Ackroyd take out his fury on me to make it happen."

How was it possible to feel both warmed and chilled by his words, both comforted and saddened? All she knew was that she loathed the idea of him suffering on her behalf.

Royce squinted at Vallyn. "And then will you marry her? Because I won't let you use my sister and then cast her aside—"

"I plan to," Vallyn interrupted. "If she'll have me. To be clear, I haven't so much as kissed your sister. Whether anything happens between us is up to her, and I…" He sorrowfully met her eyes. "I don't know if she'll trust me with her heart, even though she already has mine."

Royce frowned. "Do we have time for me to speak with her alone?"

Vallyn glanced toward the window. "His Majesty should be here any minute—"

"I *need* to talk to my sister alone." Steel underlay Royce's words, and his eyes flashed with more resolve than she'd seen in him since before she'd stolen the prophecy.

"Right." Vallyn stood and cleared his throat. "I'll knock when His Majesty arrives."

When the door closed behind him, Callista stood. "Do you need any food or—"

"Calli, sit down."

She perched on the edge of the seat. "Are you sure—"

"I'm all right. Stop changing the subject. You might not look like yourself right now, but your feelings aren't disguised. You're besotted. So what's wrong with him?"

Nothing was on the tip of her tongue, but instead she blurted out, "He's half fae."

"All…right. How do you feel about that?"

Callista spun a strand of blonde hair around her finger. "I thought I knew what to expect from a fae, but he isn't cruel or capricious or deceptive. Truthfully, Vallyn is…" She searched for the right words.

"He's everything I know I can never keep," she said at last. "Too good to be mine."

"You think he's too good for you?" A bit of anger seeped into Royce's tone. "Has he told you that?"

"No, not at all." She leaned her head against the back of the chair and stared at the wood-paneled ceiling. "Do you remember when I was accepted into the Enchanters College?"

"You babbled like a lark while hugging me so tightly I thought I'd suffocate. You had such big plans…" His tone turned mournful. "You tried to talk me out of joining the guard like Father and Jacob. You were certain you'd get hired by a wealthy lord when you finished your studies and move us all into the country, far away from the Faines, and start a farm like Mam had always wanted. And I took that from you," he added in a whisper.

Callista closed her eyes to seal away her tears. "The Faines had already stolen that dream before we broke into the vault, and I knew the consequences of my choices. My hope started dying before Father and Jacob perished, and it wasn't you who left me no alternatives. It wasn't you who tore me away from my new home, either; that was the Shafers. I don't think this world wants me to be happy. It's easier to never accept Vallyn's love than to accept it and have it torn away from me, as everything seems to be."

For several long moments, the only sound was Stormy preening her feathers. Callista straightened. "I should freshen up—"

Royce's voice stopped her, his words so quiet she had to strain to hear. "The Faines and Shafers broke my body. Broke my mind a bit, too. Somehow, it's worse to see what the last few years have done to your heart. It used to be so radiant with hope." He roughly swiped at his eyes. "Do you regret going to the university?"

She hesitated. "No. It was so much harder than I thought it would be, less academically than because of everything else. I'd finish my studies if they'd let me."

"If you could go back in time, would you not apply? Skip the dashed dreams?"

"No…"

"Because the good things were worth the pain?"

"Partly." Callista toyed with a broken thread on the hem of her sleeve. "I don't want to entirely lose that younger me who dared to hope that things could get better, even if she was a fool."

"Was she?" Royce asked. "You've lost so much, but that girl is also the girl who dreamed she could end the Faines' cruelty for everyone—and she did. You're still the girl who dared to believe she could free her brother, and you did. Can you look me in the eye and tell me nothing you've hoped for has ever happened? That all of it has turned to ash?"

Callista remained focused on the short, frayed thread. She'd wished she could end the Faines' rule without hurting anyone, and while that hadn't happened, she'd come close. Leo and Anika were all right, and Gareth had been saved. She'd hoped she would live to see what Aedyllan became without the Faines, and she had. She'd dreamed it would be better, and it was. King Cassius was even better than she'd hoped.

"After Blaise used me to threaten you, I had this guard until we came here," Royce said. "He doesn't like the Shafers, but, well…you know how difficult it is to find employment as a penniless peasant without specialized skills, and he was trying to save up enough to marry his sweetheart. Didn't take him long to notice I flinched every time someone approached."

Callista gulped down another apology, another futile wish she could have saved her brother sooner.

"He asked why I always assumed it was something terrible, why I was always anticipating pain, not my next meal or a clean blanket. I laughed and said because it was just as likely to be pain. It was easier to be pleasantly surprised than to get my hopes up and be rewarded with suffering."

A feeling Callista understood well.

"He said that was no way to live, especially when I can't actually know if the future holds pain or something good or benign. I was doing the Shafers' job for them, tormenting myself and making myself a prisoner of my own fear and hopelessness. 'You think expecting the worst protects you,' he said. 'It just makes you miserable twice over—in the present with miserable anticipation that can't change a thing, and again in the future if you end up being right. You aren't protecting yourself. You're robbing yourself of any chance of joy or peace.'"

The thread snapped off Callista's sleeve. She fought to keep her stony armor in place over her heart. She didn't want to think about a random guard being there for Royce when she hadn't been. And she certainly didn't want to listen to her brother accuse her of imprisoning her own mind in despair.

"His words replayed over and over," Royce continued. "The next time someone approached my cell, I dared to hope it was something good. He'd brought me hot soup. Being right felt better than being pleasantly surprised. So I started hoping for good things, or at least not assuming the worst. I felt less defeated. More like I had some control, if only over my own thoughts. That helped me through the times when it was something bad. And then you saved me, which was more than I dared hope."

She tossed the balled-up bit of thread toward the fire. "So

what? We're the source of our own misery? As if it isn't the Faines, the Shafers, this entire broken world?"

"Of course not," Royce said softly. "I'm just saying maybe we don't have to add to the misery the world gives us, you know? Maybe you're right, and anything good will always be taken away. But isn't it also possible you're wrong? Do you have proof that you're right? Because from what I've seen, Calli, Vallyn would never let you be taken from him. And if you are wrong…what if your belief that you can't be happy is the most formidable barrier between you and being happy? Is the chance of protecting yourself from future hurt worth the hurt you feel right now by cutting down your own hope? Is it worth hurting Vallyn now because you're afraid by action or fate he'll eventually hurt you?"

Callista stood and flicked away tears, afraid Vallyn and Cassius would walk in on her crying. She turned from her brother and watched Stormy's gentle breathing as the lesser gryphon slept by the window.

"I want my baby sister to be happy and safe," Royce said, his voice tight. "If you think there's even a chance you could be happy with Vallyn, I wish you'd take it."

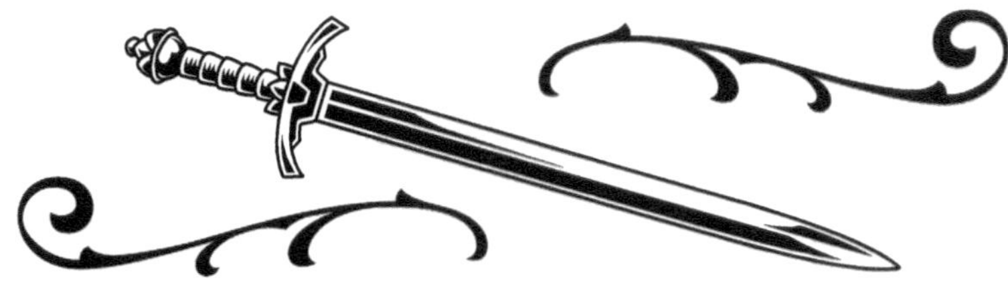

52

To escape the temptation to eavesdrop on Callista and Royce, Vallyn walked to the far end of the hall and paced. As his boots shuffled against the carpet, he wondered when he should warn Callista about the possibility of a fae marriage binding. He didn't want to scare her before she'd even accepted his interest, but he didn't want her to think he'd hidden the possibility of a magically binding marriage, either.

Footsteps down the hall captured his attention, and then Cassius, Arolyin, and Serena walked into view, the latter two still disguised. Arolyin dropped the glamours. Serena tilted her head and sent Vallyn a questioning look.

"How did it go?" Vallyn asked, ignoring Serena.

"We have a problem." Cassius pinched the bridge of his nose. "At the end of the parade, in front of everyone, Conrad Raylor demanded an immediate public audience. When I said it would have to wait, he said it was a matter of the security of the crown and the good of the kingdom. He claimed I'd be no better than my predecessors if I denied his right to a hearing before the court at once. The other nobles agreed and insisted this hearing be held before the feast. I barely convinced Raylor to allow us to change out of our riding attire first."

"What?" Vallyn choked out. "Why *now*?"

"I have no idea." Cassius tugged on his curls. "Falada has been kept in seclusion, and he can't talk to Ebony, unless he lied, so he shouldn't know anything about Callista or Tatiana or your father, but…I don't know. What could he possibly know that is so pressing?"

Something twisted in Vallyn's gut. He'd known he was tempting fate by so confidently declaring that nothing could go wrong.

"I don't like this," Arolyin said. "Regardless of what Conrad Raylor wants, this is not the plan. Just tell him you have to deal with another matter first."

"That might make the Shafers suspicious." Cassius shook his head. "Not to mention it'd start the proceedings off with every noble in the great hall questioning me and my motives."

Serena observed the rest of them with obvious confusion, but she kept quiet. Vallyn glanced toward Callista's suite. Would Royce and Callista be done talking? He didn't have much choice but to interrupt them.

"Your Majesty, you should go change. This delay means we need to hurry even more, or we risk the Shafers discovering they've lost their leverage."

"Right." Cassius nodded and took off toward his room.

Vallyn knocked on Callista's door, then ushered Serena and Arolyin inside.

The moment Callista looked at him, her face paled. "What's wrong?" Behind her, Royce stood as well, his forehead furrowing.

"Raylor requested an urgent public audience about something relating to the crown. Cassius has to listen to him before we enact our plan."

Callista's hands shook. "He knows?"

"We don't know that," Vallyn said, trying to muster an optimism he didn't feel.

"Forgive my intrusion," Serena said. "What's going on? And who's that?" She motioned toward Royce.

Callista winced. "My brother. Baron Shafer was holding him prisoner and threatening him to force me to—to curse and switch places with Lady Tatiana so I could marry the king and then kill him."

Vallyn found himself reaching for his sword, as if to stop Serena from harming Callista. He forced his hand away. Serena's bulging eyes and hanging jaw conveyed more confusion than violent anger.

After a long silence, Callista said thickly, "I'm sorry, Serena. I've been a fraud this entire time. I didn't want to do any of this, but the Shafers would have tortured and killed my brother…" Her voice cracked. "You've been wonderful, and I'm so sorry I involved you. I'm doing everything I can to right this—"

"What's your real name?" Serena interrupted, her level tone difficult to read.

"Callista." Tears pooled beneath her eyes. "Callista Marcant."

Vallyn started. She'd never even told him her surname.

Serena moved toward Callista, and Vallyn drew his sword on instinct. Callista stumbled between them, her hands raised. "You promised she wouldn't be hurt!"

"Yes, but I won't let her harm you." Still, he returned his sword to its scabbard.

Callista lowered her hands. "I don't care if she does."

Serena took a small step to close the space between herself and Callista. Vallyn prepared to drag the maidservant away, no matter what Callista said.

"Callista." Serena took Callista's hands in her own. "I'm glad you got your brother to safety. I feel like I should have realized. Many things make more sense now." She chuckled.

Callista sniffled. "Don't you hate me? I'm a fraud and a traitor."

"Oh, dear one. You weren't lying when you said we're friends, were you?"

"No. I lied as little as possible. Even most of my lies held a kernel of truth."

Vallyn's heart warmed as she affirmed that most of their conversations had been honest.

"Then I was right when I said you're a good person," Serena said. "Can I see what you really look like?"

Callista's shoulders caved. "I can't break the curse. I'm stuck like this unless…" She licked her lips, and her gaze flicked toward Vallyn so quickly he might have imagined it. "Until either the king or the Shafers die."

"You poor thing."

Someone knocked, and Cassius entered with the crackling tension of an impending thunderstorm. His crimson cape snapped around him. "I'm not sure what is about to happen. Should we have Callista remain here?"

"The Shafers will be suspicious if I'm missing." Callista extracted her trembling hands from Serena's. "I don't think we have a choice."

How was it possible for Vallyn to keep falling more in love with her? "I'll make sure you're safe. And Serena and Royce will both be safe here."

Callista looked back at Serena. "My brother is honorable. You'll be safe here, but you may prefer to return to your old room. I…won't be staying here after today."

"I'm also tired," Royce said. "Mind if I use your bed?"

"Of course not." Callista nodded.

"I'll stay here in case he needs anything, and to keep Stormy out of trouble," Serena said.

Vallyn held the door for his king, his father, and the woman he loved. He longed to pull Callista aside and reassure her that everything would be all right, perhaps try again for that kiss, but Cassius, Arolyin, and Callista strode onward. So instead, he followed the others toward the great hall to discover what Conrad Raylor wanted and put an end to Baron Shafer's plotting.

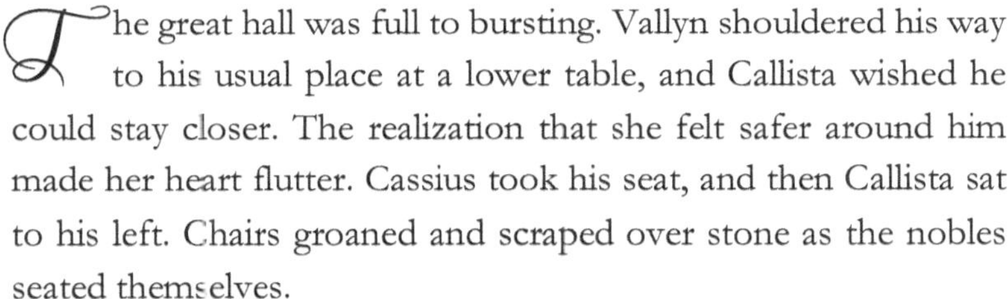

53

The great hall was full to bursting. Vallyn shouldered his way to his usual place at a lower table, and Callista wished he could stay closer. The realization that she felt safer around him made her heart flutter. Cassius took his seat, and then Callista sat to his left. Chairs groaned and scraped over stone as the nobles seated themselves.

"Before we begin this feast," Cassius said, his voice booming through the rafters, "I accept Master Conrad Raylor's petition for an immediate public audience."

A head of red hair popped up out of the crowd, and Conrad strode to the front of the hall amid excited murmurs. He bowed before the dais. "Thank you, Your Majesty. First, I would remind Your Majesty and bring to everyone's attention that I am unicorn-touched."

Callista's hands tightened around the folds of her ruby skirt.

"It's a side effect of a unicorn pouring a large amount of magic into a human," Conrad continued. "In my case, to save my life when I was near death."

Someone in the crowd harrumphed. Conrad glanced toward the audience, careful not to turn his back on the king. "Does someone doubt me?"

A lord with thick blond hair stood. "Permission to speak, Your Majesty?" At Cassius's nod, he continued. "If unicorns have the power to save lives, why have the Raylors kept this secret?"

"We didn't know!" Conrad's freckled cheeks flamed red. "Not all unicorns are equally powerful or even able to channel magic—"

"Sure," scoffed the blond lord.

Conrad raised his voice. "Not all humans are enchanters, some enchanters are far more powerful than others, and it takes time for enchanters to learn to wield their magic. Why should unicorns be different? More importantly, unicorns are intelligent and wise creatures, far more so than my family realized—well, apart from my ancestor who domesticated our original herd. He kept the knowledge to himself. Perhaps because he abused his own gift of being unicorn-touched. However, I'm not here—"

"Abused?" Cassius asked, sounding as confused as Callista.

"It's not relevant." Conrad Raylor waved impatiently. "My point is—"

"Your king requires an explanation of a claim of injustice," Cassius thundered.

Conrad paled and he bobbed a bow. "Of course, Your Majesty. Most unicorn-touched can bond only with that unicorn. But if an especially powerful unicorn pours enough magic into an enchanter, the enchanter can communicate with all unicorns and has limited control over them. The first Lord Raylor exploited that ability to domesticate unicorns over one hundred years ago. The captured unicorns swore never to save a human again—but now the unicorns in our herd believe their magic is waning because they've neglected it. They fear losing it entirely, so one of the unicorns saved my life after I nearly died fighting to see Your Majesty wear that crown."

The king nodded regally as the line of his shoulders eased, and he leaned back in his chair. "Thank you for your service and sacrifice, Master Raylor. What you have shared troubles me. We should free the unicorns if what you say is true."

Some nobles nodded their agreement, while others looked like they wanted to argue. Callista relaxed. Why freeing the unicorns was so pressing, she didn't know, but at least it had nothing to do with her.

Then Conrad shook his head. "The unicorns can't survive in the wild after so long in captivity. They do request more freedom, but that's not why I asked for this audience."

Her stomach dropped. Beside her, Cassius's fingers curled on the arm of his chair, his nails scraping the wood.

Conrad squared his shoulders. "The court was told someone murdered the unicorn I am bonded with. In actuality, General Drake"—Conrad motioned toward Vallyn—"heard of a plot to kill the unicorn. We faked Falada's beheading with the help of an enchanter."

No. No, no, no. Callista gulped and wished the goblet in front of her weren't empty. Gasps and a flurry of whispers echoed through the great hall. Now the Shafers knew Falada wasn't dead, which meant she hadn't killed the unicorn as ordered, which could only mean she'd betrayed them. It took all her willpower not to look toward Baron Shafer.

"You were strictly ordered to keep that in confidence, Master Raylor," Cassius said, his tone cutting.

"Yes, until the culprit was discovered," Conrad said. "I wondered why someone would want to kill Falada. The murderer had to know about the wisdom, intelligence, and magical acuity of the unicorns and didn't want Falada to talk to me. I have discovered why! Because someone told Falada a tale, not knowing that Falada was capable of speaking to me—"

"Falada was to be hidden from all," the king shouted over the low mumble of shocked exclamations from the court.

"I apologize, Your Majesty." Conrad turned his palms skyward in a gesture of powerlessness. "Falada sensed a curse and escaped to investigate without my knowledge. She met a young woman working as a goose girl close to the cabin where we were hiding."

The blood drained from Callista's face. Beside her, Cassius sucked in a sharp breath. Roland's crimson face contorted in a snarl, and Blaise clutched the hilt of a steak knife with murderous intent. Vallyn pushed up from his seat, but there was nothing he could do as Conrad pointed at Callista and declared, "This woman is a witch!"

Gasps rippled through the hall.

"She cast a dark curse that switched her appearance with that of Tatiana Ackroyd," Conrad continued. "Her curse prevented Lady Ackroyd from telling any human the truth in speech or writing, but she was able to tell animals. Tatiana told Falada, and Falada told me. Lady Ackroyd fears Your Majesty's life may be in danger. I agree."

As his hand dropped to his sword, Conrad's voice rose. "After Falada repeated this story of treachery, she led me to the real Tatiana!"

Callista's hands went cold.

Vallyn's eyes widened, and he reached forward. "Raylor, stop—"

"Let him speak!" a lord shouted.

"I recognized her," Conrad thundered. "Tatiana is cursed to wear this fraud's appearance, and I know who you are and what you've done, *Callista*."

Her pounding heart battered her ribs. *Please, no. Not like this.*

"Months ago," Conrad said, every word vibrating with fury, "this witch kidnapped my brother and cursed him to become a fox, kidnapped my sister, used dark magic to force a man to steal a unicorn from my father, and murdered an Eynlaean knight. My siblings escaped and captured Callista. They are currently in Eynlae, but in a letter, they told our father that Callista had reasons for her actions. After she swore to never use dark magic or harm anyone again, they granted her mercy and released her. Yet here I find her, having cursed Tatiana Ackroyd! She's a wicked, dangerous trickster and might as well be a fae!"

Deathly stillness hung over the great hall, the nobles momentarily stunned into silence. Callista couldn't move or speak as dozens of faces stared at her with an array of shock, disgust, anger, suspicion…and fear.

Conrad drew his sword. "You're going to pay—"

"Stand down!" Vallyn leapt forward and grabbed Conrad's sword arm. For a moment they were entangled, and when they separated, Vallyn held Conrad's sword. "You have no authority to draw your weapon here, Raylor!"

With an echoing clatter, Baron Shafer knocked his seat over as he jumped to his feet. "Your Majesty! You must have this witch arrested at once." He looked to Vallyn. "And it pains me to say it, but your general as well."

Even Callista gasped along with the rest of the crowd.

"Look at him." Roland motioned exaggeratedly toward Vallyn. "He stood even before Master Raylor made his accusation. He *knew* what Raylor would say and tried to stop it. Now, when Raylor rightfully wishes to enact vengeance upon this evil woman, does Drake race to protect Your Majesty? No, he disarms the valiant man who exposed her treachery. There have been rumors about the woman we thought was Tatiana Ackroyd being close with Vallyn Drake. Can't you see, Your Majesty? Your own general is working with this woman to trick you, probably to kill you once she has the title of queen so she can then marry Drake and seize the throne with him." The outraged clamors of the nobles almost drowned out Shafer's next words. "They deserve to be publicly executed! In fact, have them drawn and quartered at once!"

Cassius rose and held up his hands. "Enough!" The chatter quieted. "Guards. Seize this witch and"—his jaw tensed—"Vallyn Drake."

No one moved. Not Vallyn, who stared at his best friend in shock. Not Callista, who struggled to understand Cassius's new plan. And not a single one of the many guards scattered around the room, whom Vallyn had put in place to arrest the Shafers and their co-conspirators.

"It seems your guards have already shifted their allegiance," Roland said with a judgmental lift of his eyebrow.

"Drake and this witch are traitors to the throne and Aedyllan," Cassius declared. "Any guards who do not follow my commands will hang with them!"

Guards burst into action. Swords glinted in candlelight. Boots thunked against stone. Two sets of hands seized Callista's arms and dragged her out of her seat.

"Have them kneel before me," the king commanded. His icy calm made Callista's heart nearly stop.

Dazed, Callista let the guards manhandle her down the couple of steps from the dais to the floor. Two guards hauled Vallyn forward, while others surrounded them with their weapons ready. Her captors shoved her to the ground, and she bit her tongue as her knees slammed into the stone. Beside her, a guardsman kicked the back of Vallyn's knees. Vallyn grunted and collapsed to kneel beside her. Two guards held their shoulders, and two more placed the naked blades of their swords against their prisoners' throats.

"Careful, Cas," Vallyn said, just loud enough for the king to hear. "Our *connection* is at stake."

A bit of concern, perhaps even fear, broke through Cassius's control, but he shuttered it away.

"Can your bond tell if he's faking?" Callista whispered.

The guard holding her tightened his grasp on her shoulders. "No whispering! You'll cast no curses here, witch."

That wasn't how curses worked, but the epithet still cut into her heart.

Vallyn shrugged, but worry creased his forehead.

"Is this true?" Cassius demanded. "Have you both plotted against me?"

"Your Majesty!" some noblewoman exclaimed. "General Drake has served you—"

"Silence!" The king glared over the assembly. "Callista, if that is your real name, if you confess now to your plan and Drake's and anyone else's part in it, you will save yourself torture to extract the secrets from you."

Her vision swam. Surely this was an act, right? Cassius didn't mean that.

"She's a powerful witch!" Roland shouted. "Every moment she's allowed to draw breath, everyone in Highrook is in terrible danger. She should be killed this moment, before she can cause further harm!"

"What proof do you have, Shafer?" Vallyn challenged, although he kept looking straight ahead. "For all we know, you bribed Master Raylor to make these baseless accusations so you could get rid of me and Lady Tatiana, weakening Cassius and leaving him vulnerable."

Several nobles shouted their assent.

"Slit Drake's throat while you're at it." Bootsteps echoed in the hall, and Roland approached the dais, trailed by his son. "To have deceived you so thoroughly, Drake must have a silver tongue. Perhaps some hidden magic of his own that he used to control Your Majesty. Such cold-hearted betrayal and conniving prove both he and the witch are too dangerous and wicked to live. Traitors should be dispatched without hesitation or mercy."

Callista lifted her eyebrows. The plan might not be going correctly, but Roland Shafer had still neatly ordered his own execution.

"That is your judgment, Baron Shafer?" Cassius's calm façade slipped into surprise. "What if they conspired with others? You would have me kill them without uncovering their supporters?"

"As it is said, without the head, the monster dies," Blaise interjected. "If anyone does support them, their immediate and merciless execution will be a dire warning to abandon thoughts of insurrection."

Vallyn snorted.

Roland stopped a couple steps from Callista. He stared her down and gripped the sword at his side. "Besides, who knows what lies a user of dark magic might manufacture to save herself."

Cassius hummed his agreement. "Indeed. What might a guilty person say to save their own life? Guards. Check the main entrance to the great hall. You'll find guardsmen waiting with two persons of interest to these proceedings."

Some of the fear pounding through Callista's veins subsided. Good. Cassius would get them back on track.

Courtiers whispered. The massive double doors groaned on their hinges. Shuffling footsteps and rattling chains mingled with shocked and outraged exclamations, the cacophony moving toward the front of the hall. Callista knew the moment Roland recognized Tolley and Woodlan because his face drained of color. The guards pushed the new prisoners to their knees on Vallyn's other side.

King Cassius splayed his hands against the tabletop and leaned forward with a menacing air. "These men have a very different story to tell of treason and planned regicide, Baron Shafer. Guards, release General Drake and Maid Callista."

"What?" Conrad gasped above the chattering of the nobles.

The swords left Callista's and Vallyn's throats, and the guards released them.

Vallyn rose and helped Callista to her feet. He brushed hair out of her face, his eyes earnest. "Are you all right? I—"

"Look!" Blaise shouted. "They're conspiring right in front of our eyes! They must be stopped before they act!"

"Stop him!" Cassius roared.

Callista spun around, out of Vallyn's grasp. Her lungs froze. Blaise charged at her, his sword drawn. Guards fumbled with their weapons and moved to intercept him, and she reached for her magic. They were all too slow.

The blade arced toward her neck.

And then a blinding silvery light burst around her.

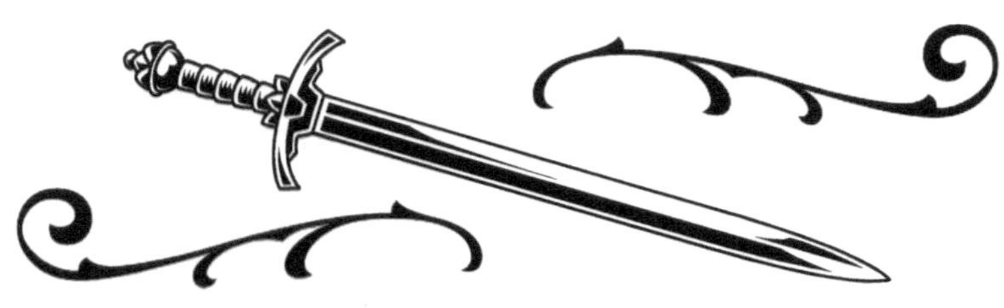

54

$\mathscr{U}$nbridled fae magic rushed through Vallyn's veins, wild, eager—and furious.

The light from his palms slammed into Blaise and threw him back until he collided with the wall. A quick glance at Callista confirmed she was unharmed, just shocked. As he passed her, he was distantly aware of screaming and shouting, but he ignored everything and stalked his prey.

Blaise groaned. Vallyn seized the miscreant's doublet, and Blaise weakly tried to evade him. He could end Callista's tormentor right then and there. He could put his sword through Blaise's chest and blame it on his fae warrior instincts—but he remembered Arolyin saying that his choices were his own. Blaise deserved to die, but Vallyn wasn't a murderer. He was a general serving an honorable king.

He dragged Blaise to his feet. "Time to tell the truth, Shafer."

"See, Your Majesty?" Roland shrieked. "Drake is a witch himself, and he's attacked my son for defending you!"

Vallyn swung around, Blaise stumbling after him, to find Roland cowering on the dais behind the corner of the table. With a sneer, Vallyn shoved Blaise toward the dais. He needed to put some space between himself and the human bit of refuse while he got his magic under control—magic that the whole court had witnessed. It wouldn't be long before they realized he wasn't an enchanter, but it'd been worth it to protect Callista.

"I attacked your son because he attacked a woman under my protection in the middle of the king's court." Vallyn crossed his arms and stared down the treacherous baron.

"Of course she's under your protection. She's a witch like you!"

Cassius flicked a disdainful look at Roland. "Do you honestly believe I don't know my oldest friend's secrets? You are right about one thing, though. Vallyn and Callista have been working together—with me. To stop *you*, Shafer."

"I told them everything," Callista said, and Vallyn doubted anyone else noticed how she hid her shaking hands in the folds of her skirt. He'd hoped to spare her this public scrutiny and pain. "How you threatened me and my brother and the granddaughter of the Ackroyds' steward to force me to curse Tatiana, how you wanted me to kill King Cassius. I also told them about your co-conspirators." She waved toward Tolley and Woodlan.

"They, in turn, told us everything." Vallyn crossed his arms.

"I gave you a chance, Roland." Cassius's authoritative voice rang over the gaping crowd. "I was merciful in my victory at Althre Fields. This is how you repay me?"

Roland looked from Vallyn and Blaise to the king and then to Callista. He grabbed the corner of the table and pulled himself up. "When word of this reaches my men, they will kill your brother—"

"No." Callista's smile was sharp with fury. "We already rescued my brother. And the king knows everything I've done." She straightened her thin shoulders. "You have no power over me anymore."

Roland's jaw clenched. "Did you, all of you"—he waved between Cassius and Vallyn—"think I had only one plan, contingent on one woman? Sure, her killing Alimer would have made things much easier. I'd have looked like a hero, coming in and claiming the throne after Alimer's ghastly murder at the hands of his wife, Ackroyd's daughter."

Horrified exclamations flooded the great hall, crashing up to the rafters before hushing again into tense quiet. Vallyn smirked. This conviction would be easy.

"Now I'll simply do this the classic way: with an outright coup."

Vallyn grasped his sword, but Cassius slightly lifted his hand in a staying motion. Though the command was unspoken, the magic of the bond held him back. Everything in Vallyn wanted to take the Shafers down before this went any further, but if Cassius wanted to see how it played out, he didn't have any choice but to go along with it. He supposed Cassius had a point. Roland would doubtless call on his fellow conspirators. A battle might erupt in the great hall, but at least they'd know who was loyal.

Roland scowled at the king, then turned back to Callista. "Help us, and I swear I'll still let you and Royce go free. That's a more generous offer than you'll receive from Alimer. He's too purehearted and concerned with following the law to let you go unpunished."

Callista's lower lip trembled.

Blaise chuckled. "Last chance, pet."

She whipped her head to the side and met Vallyn's gaze with desperation in her green eyes. He hoped she saw the promise in his own—he would never let Cassius hurt her. Even if he had to defy his fae bargain with Cassius and die to protect her.

Her chest rose and fell with a slow breath, and she looked back to Baron Shafer. "You're not the only one who has sworn oaths to me, and you aren't the one I trust."

Vallyn's heart soared. Her trust was the most precious gift he'd ever been given.

"Suit yourself." Roland looked to Blaise. "Kill the witch. Down with Alimer!"

As Vallyn raised his sword, the hall erupted in chaos, and several things happened at once. A few guards turned on their fellow guardsmen. Some noblemen leapt up with shouts and bared their blades. Blaise retrieved a long dagger from his boot, and Roland drew his sword. Violet light gathered over Callista's palms as she faced Blaise. Cassius drew his sword while Roland raced toward him.

Vallyn started to turn toward Cassius, but another movement caught his eye. Two traitor lords, one wielding a short sword and the other a long, curved hunting knife, charged Callista's unguarded back.

"Callista! Behind you!" Vallyn turned from the dais and rushed toward Blaise, letting his fae magic lend extra strength and speed to his limbs and fill him with the fire of battle.

Blaise glanced over his shoulder, and his eyes bulged. He started to turn too late. Vallyn rammed his sword through Blaise's back until the crimson tip emerged from the villain's chest. Without pause, Vallyn yanked the sword free. He jumped over Blaise's falling corpse.

One of Callista's attackers screamed and batted at purple flames burning the front of his jerkin. The other narrowly parried a fireball. A guardsman knocked down an opposing guard and spun toward Callista, aiming his sword toward her middle.

Vallyn knocked the man's blade off course with enough force to rip the hilt out of the guard's grasp. The sword crashed against the stone floor and slid away. Vallyn drew his sword back.

"Traitor!"

The guard raised his hands and dropped to his knees. "They have my son!"

It took a moment for the words and the tears in the man's eyes to break through the rage pulsing through Vallyn. The guardsman flinched as Vallyn stopped his sword a hairsbreadth from the top of his skull.

"That will be taken into consideration at your hearing," Vallyn growled. "As will whether you pick up your sword and join the *right* side of this fight."

"Yes, General!"

A stab of magical warning and fear tore through Vallyn a heartbeat before Cassius screamed, "Val!"

At the same moment, Callista cried out in pain.

Vallyn spun away from the guardsman.

Up on the dais, Cassius was backed into a corner, surrounded by Roland, a traitor guardsman, and Lord Tolley, who wielded a dagger with remarkable agility considering his wrists were still shackled.

In front of the dais and just as far from Vallyn in the opposite direction, Callista stumbled backward, grasping her upper right arm. Blood trickled between her fingers. Conrad Raylor pursued her, a faint sheen of red along one edge of his sword.

Steel crashed against steel, and Cassius shouted for Vallyn again. The fae binding tugged deep in his chest, warning him to keep his vow to protect Cassius. He turned his feet toward the dais, but his attention was pulled toward Callista like iron toward a magnet.

"I can't fight you." A tear raced down Callista's cheek. "I won't hurt your family again."

"No, you won't." Conrad hefted his sword. "I'll make sure of it."

"Vallyn!" Pressed into the corner, Cassius strained to push back on his sword against both Roland and the guardsman. Tolley darted back and forth, looking for an opening.

Time slowed, stretching between two beats of Vallyn's racing heart. If either Cassius or Callista died, Vallyn would never forgive himself—assuming *he* survived. A painful force squeezed his heart, warning him to get to Cassius with haste. If Cassius died, Vallyn might, too, and his hesitation was about to cost him *both* of the people he loved most.

Unless…

Vallyn shifted his sword to his left hand and ran toward his king, but he held out his right hand and looked toward his beloved. An illusion of himself popped into existence between Callista and Conrad, his sword raised menacingly.

"Touch her and die," Vallyn snarled, and his illusion spoke synchronously—for the first time. He'd never managed to get an illusion to speak before. His father would be proud.

But despite his fae magic rejoicing in his chest, he couldn't appreciate the achievement. He gripped his sword in both hands and swung, removing Tolley's head. The traitor guardsman swiveled around and parried Vallyn's thrust.

"Stand down!"

The guard sneered. "And let Alimer rule? He wouldn't even be king without you. He doesn't deserve it."

Vallyn cut toward the man's neck but couldn't get up enough speed in the confined space. The guardsman blocked, and Vallyn pushed against the man's sword. Threads of twining silver light raced down Vallyn's blade. The guard's weapon shattered, and a piece of shrapnel buried itself in the traitor's throat.

Vallyn kicked the man's falling body out of his way. Roland pinned Cassius's blade against the wall with his own sword. Leaning his weight against their weapons, Roland slammed his left elbow down against Cassius's wrist.

"Augh!" Cassius's grip weakened.

Stepping to the side for a better angle, Vallyn drew his sword back.

Cassius's eyes flicked toward Vallyn. "Alive!"

With a muttered curse, Vallyn changed trajectory and stabbed his sword into Baron Shafer's thigh.

Roland screamed and dropped his sword. Vallyn yanked his weapon free, and Roland slid down the wall, clutching his bleeding leg.

With Cassius safe, Vallyn lurched back in Callista's direction. If Conrad had tested the illusion, it would have vanished like smoke—

Vallyn skidded to a halt. Conrad stood scowling with his arms crossed and his sword at his feet in front of…a rather smug Arolyin. Callista stood behind his father, but she was facing Vallyn, and she smiled as he met her gaze.

Then Vallyn noticed the illusions.

Scattered around the great hall, a dozen identical palace guards waved their swords at the rebels as they corralled them toward the front of the hall. Cassius came to stand at Vallyn's side. A captured lord spotted the unharmed king and stumbled. The illusion guard reached forward and…shoved him?

"Are you doing this?" Cassius asked in wonder.

"No." Vallyn descended from the dais and approached his father and Callista. "Yours have physicality? Mine are just…mirages."

"In a manner of speaking. I can trick more senses than sight alone. Your power is weaker and, more importantly, less honed by both time and practice." Arolyin turned toward Vallyn with a frown. "So *why* did you use an illusion as a shield for your beloved? You may as well have protected her with gossamer!"

Vallyn flushed. "I had to help Cas, but I couldn't leave her—"

"It made him hesitate long enough for me to retreat and for Arolyin to intervene." Callista stepped closer, her expression soft. Her eyes misted. "You split your focus for me. You revealed your magic to save me—twice." She dropped her voice to a whisper. "You saved me with magic enchanters don't have."

Awareness of his surroundings filtered in. Many of the people in the great hall stared at him. His magic-enhanced hearing picked up whispers of "Fae?" "I studied at the Enchanters College. Drake's magic is unlike anything I've seen." "Do his ears look pointed to you?"

Involuntarily, his left hand released his sword to fumble with his hair. He usually fought and trained while wearing a helm and fabric cap. In the fighting, his hair had parted around the pointed tips of his ears.

Vallyn swallowed back his nerves. "Keeping my identity secret or protecting you is an easy choice. Let them despise me. I don't care, as long as you don't hate or fear me."

Gently, Callista ran her fingertips over the ends of his ears. Vallyn shivered.

"I don't hate you," she whispered. "I don't fear you."

He angled his face up toward hers and leaned closer…

"So that's your secret, Alimer." Roland's acerbic voice was brittle, on the verge of breaking. "Your ancestor took Aedyllan through a fae deal, and you took Aedyllan by the power of your pet fae general."

Vallyn pivoted to face Roland. Two guards supported the

limping baron between them. Roland stared at his son's corpse, silent tears staining his cheeks. The Shafers were no longer a threat, but the rest of the court were watching and listening closely.

"I'm half fae," Vallyn said. He faced the court, hoping he didn't look as uncomfortable as he felt. "Half Aedyllanian human. I have as much right to fight for the man I believe should be king as any other Aedyllanian. King Cassius made no fae deals for the throne. Nor did he resort to kidnapping, blackmail, bribery, murder, and whatever other sins Roland and Blaise Shafer have committed."

"Don't you dare say my son's name," Shafer rasped. "You killed him!"

Vallyn whirled back toward Shafer. "Your treasonous lust for power killed him!"

"Wasn't that your recommendation for traitors, Shafer?" Cassius crossed his arms. "Immediate execution, without mercy or hesitation?"

Roland hung his head, but several prisoners protested.

"Your Majesty," Vallyn said. "Some of these men may have been coerced. We need to interrogate them to determine who was treasonous and who has family that is still in danger."

"I know where to find them," a captured noble said. He shoved to the front of the prisoners. "In exchange for a pardon, I'll tell you!"

Cassius turned a stony glare on the noble. "You will tell us. Whether you receive any mercy is another matter. I will review all the evidence and the law to determine punishments, but there *will* be executions. This court, this kingdom, is to be a place of peace, justice, and righteousness—and that means the wickedness exhibited by Roland Shafer and those who aided him must be eradicated. General, see to it that these men are escorted to the dungeons and interrogated, and have the gallows prepared for a public execution in a few days. And send guards you trust to retrieve Lady Tatiana."

Vallyn bowed again. "Yes, Your Majesty." He faced Callista. "Go to your brother, and I'll see you as soon as I'm able." He looked to his father. "Please stay with her and ensure she's safe?"

"Gladly."

The first thing Vallyn did after seeing all the prisoners locked in cells was speak to Sir Ultram, the noble who knew about the people Roland and Blaise Shafer had threatened. The man was reluctant to give up any information without promises of his own safety, but when Vallyn made it clear his options were to talk or to have his wife and children join him in the dungeon, Ultram complied. Blaise had pressured him into using his secondary house to hold five captives to blackmail three guardsmen, a servant, and a nobleman.

Which meant the next thing Vallyn did was raid Ultram's townhome in Rincote. The captives were all healthy and unharmed, but terrified. Two of them were young children. Vallyn narrowly arrested every guard in Ultram's townhome. Narrowly only because of the amount of self-control it took him not to execute them on the spot for enabling such wickedness.

He'd known that decades of the Faines' cruelty and power-hoarding had poisoned much of Aedyllan. He hadn't realized getting rid of that taint would be more complicated than putting a good king on the throne. Cassius had his work cut out for him. The thought tempted Vallyn toward discouragement, but he had hope. If anyone could manage it, Cassius could. Vallyn would help him. And another person gave him hope as well.

Someone who so badly wanted to see a better Aedyllan that she had risked everything to take down the Faines, who so believed in the good that Cassius could do as king that she'd been willing to sacrifice herself. Callista had seen the worst the Faine court had to offer and still had kept her love for others and her dream of a healed Aedyllan where good prevailed—even if she struggled to have hope for herself.

And now she trusted him.

Vallyn was dying to return to Callista, but first he had work to do. He returned the captives to their families, incarcerated new prisoners, conducted interrogations, and gave orders for the gallows. Wilmina was right. He needed to delegate more.

Considering two guardsmen had been genuine traitors, his faith in his men was shaken. Still, he had some lieutenants he trusted…or perhaps he should summon the man who had replaced him as captain at Alimer Barony. He'd make a good second-in-command. Either way, he planned to find someone to take some of his duties so he could spend more time with the woman he loved.

Once finished with everything else, he tracked down Cassius in the king's office and reported his findings—including his impressions of which men had been unwilling accomplices.

Cassius rubbed his eyes. "Noted, thank you."

"Are you all right?"

"Drained is all. I've had hysterical friends and family pleading on behalf of the prisoners and cranky nobles claiming the violence today was my fault. They can't say what exactly I should be doing differently, but I'm certainly doing it all wrong. That's to say nothing of the paranoid idiots concerned about me having a half fae leading my military and advising me."

Vallyn tensed. "I'm sorry."

"Don't be. They'll get over it."

"Fae take me if I believe that," Vallyn muttered.

Cassius chuckled. "Many are halfway there. I reminded them that they've been around you for months without danger." He leaned into the recesses of his wingback chair. "I've sent for Lord Ackroyd and Lord Raylor."

Vallyn jerked a nod.

"Many of the nobles want to know why Callista wasn't arrested, and I suspect Ackroyd and Raylor will voice similar concerns."

"What did you tell the nobles?" Vallyn asked through tight vocal cords.

"That Callista has proven her loyalty and that extenuating circumstances led to her crimes. However, I promised to take their concerns under advisement."

"Under advisement?" Vallyn clutched the arms of his chair and leaned forward. "Tell them she helped us willingly! That she came to us—"

"That wouldn't be true," Cassius said softly. "She was caught."

"Maybe, but you didn't see her crying, hear the brokenness in her voice when she asked me to help her and said she couldn't go through with it, and…" Shame made his skin cold. "She didn't trust me. I'm fae, and I'd made it obvious I'd do anything to protect you. She wanted to tell her full story to you. If she hadn't been afraid of me, she might have told you the truth a long time ago."

Cassius sighed. "But she didn't. I can judge her only on what she did do—and she's done terrible things, Val."

"To get justice for her family and to protect her brother." Vallyn dragged his hand down the side of his face. "Do you know how many men I've killed to protect my brother?"

Cassius's bronze skin flushed. "That's not the same."

"Perhaps not. But she did the right thing in the end. She loves justice and peace and protecting people and puts those things above herself. She may not have always pursued them in the right way, but she was alone, with no one she trusted to ask for help. Remember that orphan boy? You'd been duke for a couple years, and he was breaking into homes and businesses to steal provisions. He caused a lot of property damage and got into a fistfight when he was caught."

"I remember." Cassius rubbed his temple. "You're going to throw my own words back at me, aren't you?"

Vallyn steepled his fingers. "You said, 'How much harder must it be for a person untethered from any relationships, who has not felt any love or community affection, who has no one to lean on in times of trouble, to do right by others? Why would we be surprised when someone wandering alone in the cold acts from a cold heart?' You said he deserved a chance to show who he could be when not left to fend for himself."

"Sir Daveth has grown into an exemplary young man."

"He has." A triumphant smile tugged at Vallyn's lips. "Callista deserves another chance and a proper home, not punishment."

"But it's not the same, is it?" Cassius asked. "Daveth was twelve. He took necessities and gave a tanner a black eye. Callista kidnapped and cursed people—nobles, Vallyn—and colluded to commit regicide."

"Since when do you value nobles over commoners?"

"That's not…" Cassius groaned. "The nobles are demanding. More importantly, what would it take for her to go back to dark magic and misdeeds? Should someone threaten anyone she cares about—"

"No," Vallyn said. "That's my point! If someone threatened Royce again, she has people she trusts who have the power to help.

You, me, even my father. And again, she'd already decided she wouldn't kill you and the unicorn. She simply hadn't resigned herself to losing her brother. Look, I'm sure once you've had a chance to rest, you'll agree. But I also meant it when I said I'd take any punishment for her."

"Your father spoke to me about that." Cassius's mouth pinched like he'd tasted something sour. "If I order you harmed when you haven't broken our deal, then *I* will have defied our bargain, and Arolyin wasn't sure what that might do to me."

An idea occurred to Vallyn then—an underhanded, terrible, fae trickster–level idea. An idea that was going to anger Cas, but he didn't care.

"Is that so?" he asked, feigning innocence. "Interesting. Because Callista is under my protection. I claim her as my own, and I'm going to ask her to marry me. She'll be of my household, of my family, of my own flesh in Aedyllanian tradition." He blamed his feral grin on using so much fae magic recently. "If you order any harm done to Callista, I will consider our deal broken—and so will the magic."

Cassius's jaw went slack. "You conniving…" Shaking his head, he laughed. "Well played, Val. Very well played."

"You're…not furious?"

"Mm, perhaps I should be, but honestly, I'm relieved to have my hands tied. Explaining my reasoning will be more complicated, so I am annoyed with you about that, but…" Cassius shrugged. "It's good practice for not letting the nobles bully me."

"Happy to help you grow your leadership skills, Your Majesty." Vallyn winked.

Cassius huffed. "Get out of here. You have a woman to propose to."

55

Although Callista was disappointed to leave Vallyn when she'd finally found the courage to talk to him about her feelings, she gratefully returned to her suite. There, she and Arolyin relayed everything to Royce and Serena.

"His illusions appeared to have substance—it was incredible," Callista gushed.

"It's only incredibly tiring." Arolyin lounged on the floor against a wall, his legs stuck out in front of him and his hands folded over his stomach. "Fae magic doesn't have side effects the way human magic does, but using a lot does drain us physically and emotionally, and our store of magic does empty, so to speak. I'll slowly refill here, but the fae realm is overflowing with magical energy that replenishes us." He yawned and closed his eyes. "I need to return home soon, but not until Vallyn arrives to take charge of you himself."

Royce scowled. "Take charge? Is she a prisoner?"

Arolyin snorted a laugh. "More like treasure. Not that she's an object, mind, but Vallyn wants her protected because she's precious, not guarded because she's dangerous."

Serena sighed dreamily. "I knew he was greaves over helm for you. And you for him." She winked, and Callista's face warmed. "It was the flute, wasn't it? That made you fall in love with him?"

"Flute?" Royce perked up. "You still play? I worried you'd given it up. It always brought you such joy."

"I did give it up," Callista murmured. She slouched against the back of her desk chair and buried her fingers in Stormy's gray fur. The lesser gryphon shifted in her lap, getting more comfortable. "I had to trade away the one Father gave me. I mentioned I used to play but had lost my flute, and Vallyn bought me a new one."

Warmth filled her as she recalled the awkward way he'd taken credit for the gift when he'd thought she didn't like it. Perhaps Vallyn had been trying to help Cassius court her at first, but it felt like he'd been the one courting her all along.

"But no, I don't think that's when I fell in love with him. I'm not sure when it happened."

"I like him," Royce declared. "Although, if he proves false, I don't care if he's half fae. I'll kill him."

Callista laughed. "I don't think you'll have to—" Emotion choked her, and she swiped tears from her eyes.

Royce straightened in his armchair, looking like he was ready to spring to her side. "Calli? What's wrong?"

She smiled through her tears, for once not trying to bury her feelings. "I'd thought I'd never see one of my brothers being all blustery and overprotective of me because of a suitor." Her words came out choked. "I'm glad you're here, Royce."

"Me too," he whispered. "Thanks to you."

Suppertime came and went. Serena saw that food was brought in for all four of them and cleared away the dishes. The autumn sky went from gray to pink to star-studded black. At Callista's insistence, Arolyin went to sleep in her bed, where Stormy curled up at his feet—the fluffy little traitor.

Still Vallyn did not appear.

Serena took it upon herself to place Royce in the suite of rooms next door. Callista helped her clear out the cloths covering the furniture and get a fire going. Royce sheepishly requested a bath. Serena gladly fetched the water, reluctantly allowing Royce to help her. She proclaimed he looked too worn down to be put to work. Callista was tempted to agree, but she saw how badly he wanted some control over his own life. After they filled the tub, Callista magically heated the water and left Royce's suite.

No one was in the hall. Disappointment pressed on her. Was Vallyn all right? Why was it taking so long? Tiredly, she pushed open her door, but then stumbled to a stop on the threshold.

Vallyn stood in the middle of the room. She was certain his dark-blue tunic with silver stitching and a matching cape were not what he'd been wearing earlier. The points of his ears peeked out of damp hair. She'd been worrying about him while he'd been…bathing and changing clothes?

She glanced down at her own attire, the same ruby dress she'd worn to the banquet. It was rumpled, and although she'd healed her arm, the left sleeve had a blood-crusted hole where Conrad had nicked her arm. Perhaps she should have bathed and changed as well instead of sitting about fretting.

As Callista looked back at Vallyn, she realized no one else was present. The door to her room was open, and Arolyin was gone. Serena was nowhere to be seen, and for that matter, neither was Stormy.

"Where—"

"I asked for some privacy." Vallyn crossed and uncrossed his arms, clasped his hands in front of himself, then moved them behind his back. "Can you come inside?"

His odd behavior tempered her eagerness to speak with him, but she stepped inside and eased the door shut. "Is everything...all right?"

"Yes. Everything is going to be fine." Vallyn's lips curved in the softest of smiles, and it melted something inside her. "I have something I'd like to discuss with you. Preferably not from halfway across the room."

Callista blushed and crossed the short distance between them, her heart beating faster with every step. Everything she'd wanted to say fled her mind as she looked into his intense, dark eyes.

"Callista—"

"Wait!" Her voice squeaked, and she cleared her throat. "I need to say something first. And give you something. Sorry, just—one moment." She hurried into her bedchamber and fetched a cloth pouch from her bedside table.

When she returned, Vallyn was watching her with bemusement. She stood in front of him and held out the long blue pouch, balancing it flat on her palms. "I—"

Vallyn's expression sagged. "Why are you returning that?"

"Returning?"

"It's...not the flute?"

Callista looked between him and the pouch before laughing. "Goodness, no. You couldn't force me to give up the flute." She raised her eyebrows. "This isn't even long enough to be a flute."

"Oh. Right." He half chuckled, half cleared his throat. "Erm...continue, please."

Callista drew in a deep breath, then spoke in rushed words. "I'm sorry. I'm sorry I ever bought these, and sorrier I used them. I know that doesn't make it all right, but just...here." She shoved the pouch toward him. "I'm giving them to you, because I never want to use them or anything like them again, and I don't know how else to apologize."

Tilting his head, Vallyn took the pouch and eased the top open. He peered inside, and his lips parted before he looked back at her, something she couldn't decipher shining in his eyes. "You really don't fear me anymore."

Her thick throat refused to work, so she shook her head.

To her shock, Vallyn withdrew the iron dagger and balanced it on his unprotected palm.

"Stop!" She stole the weapon back. "What are you *thinking?*"

"That you should know that since I'm half fae, iron has to touch me for a while to do any real damage. You didn't hurt me or capture me with this blade and chain. It would have burned me eventually, yes, but it was merely unpleasant and made my magic grumpy."

"Oh." Callista scrunched her shoulders and lowered her head, but then a thought occurred to her. "You stood there and let me feel like I was threatening you, and you could have easily escaped?"

She didn't need to ask why. The answer was written all over his face. Tears threatened her eyes.

"I'm so sorry," she said again.

"I understand why you did it," Vallyn said softly. "And even as you held that blade to my neck, I could see how much you hated doing it. I promise you'll never again feel alone and afraid and like you're stuck fighting to survive. Callista, I want us to be there for each other for the rest of our lives. That is…if you want the same thing."

General Vallyn Drake had a reputation for being hard and intimidating. He had a glare that could cow the toughest soldiers, broad shoulders that were often thrown back in confidence, and a stride that declared he would not be stopped. Yet as he held her gaze, his expression was vulnerable and uncertain, his heart laid bare before her with a hint of fear that she would break it.

"Earlier, Serena asked me if I fell in love with you when you gave me the flute." Callista took the pouch back, slipped the dagger inside, and tossed it away. "I told her I wasn't sure when it happened. I've been pondering it. Maybe that was the start, but I hadn't realized yet. Perhaps I fell in love with you when you held me without judgment while I cried, even though you didn't know why I was falling apart. Maybe it was when you caught me on the bridge in the garden, when you swore to me in Rincote that you would protect me, when you accepted me after I told you every-thing I'd done, when you told your father you'd take my punish-ment, or when you said you loved me. Maybe it was all of those moments and more chipping away at the granite I'd wrapped around my heart. I don't know when it happened, but I love you. I trust you to keep me and my heart safe."

Vallyn's face brightened. "You love me?"

"More than I thought I could ever love anyone. Vallyn—"

Before she could say another word, Vallyn grabbed her waist and the back of her head and pulled her close. Callista didn't have to think, and for what felt like the first time in forever, she didn't hesitate. She wrapped one arm around his back, held the side of his face, closed her eyes, and kissed him.

Tingling heat raced through her, from the top of her head down to her curling toes as Vallyn deepened their kiss. She leaned into him, her mind hazy, and focused on the man she loved. The scent of lavender and pine that clung to his shaggy hair, the hint of mint in his kiss, his muscled shoulders as he shifted his grasp to draw her even closer.

A rending pain tore through Callista's limbs. She gasped

against Vallyn's lips. Her knees buckled, and she caught herself on his shoulders as white spots danced behind her eyelids. She opened her eyes to Vallyn's panicked face.

"What's wrong?"

She bit back a groan. "I need to sit down," she ground out.

Vallyn lowered them both to the carpeted floor, drawing her into his lap with a tenderness that made her heart sing. "Did—did I hurt you somehow?"

The horror in his voice almost made her laugh. "No…well, sort of, but it's not your fault." Every muscle in her body tensed, and she whimpered.

Vallyn looked like he was about to either cry or scream.

At last the pain and prickling sensation faded away as quickly as they had started. She relaxed into his arms and rested her head on his shoulder.

"Do you believe in true love?" Callista asked softly.

Vallyn gulped. "Cassius's mother used to say true love isn't some magical, fated thing. It's what happens when two people choose to fully give each other their hearts and their lives, without reservation. So I suppose I do. Do you?"

"I attended the Enchanters College, Vallyn. I read enough about true love's kiss breaking curses to know it's real, whatever people choose to believe about what exactly that means. I like Cassius's mother's definition, though. I thought it would scare me if you truly loved me. I was afraid of loving you that much and being loved that much, because I was afraid of experiencing that and then losing it. But right now, I'm not afraid."

She nestled closer against him. "I can't express how good it feels to be loved enough to break a curse."

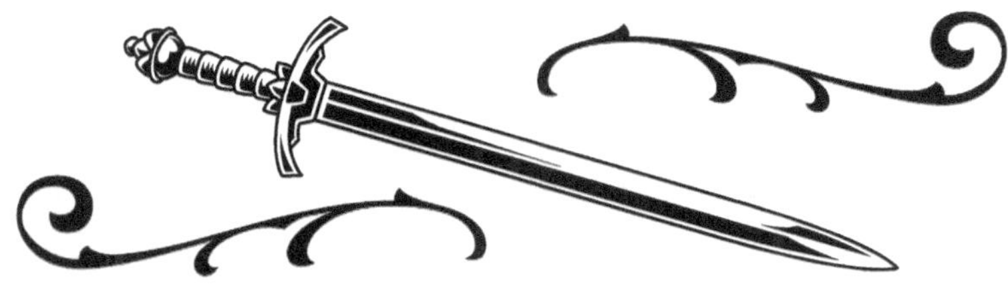

56

allyn's heart still raced from the shock of Callista collapsing in his arms. One moment, he'd been in otherworldly bliss, the next, he'd feared his world was falling apart in front of him. But understanding wormed into his scattered, panicked thoughts, and a sense of wonder replaced his fears.

"The appearance-switching curse? It's broken? By my kiss?"

She nodded against his shoulder.

"I love you so much." Vallyn tenderly kissed her temple. If he'd had any doubt that she loved him back, he had none now. "Did you not try with Royce? Or did it not work?"

Callista fell silent for several long moments. "I didn't think about it. Maybe part of me was afraid of it not working. Maybe because it's only a matter of time until Roland Shafer dies. But ever since the banquet, I've been waiting for you. Not to kiss me, but I couldn't think about much else other than talking to you and apologizing and thanking you again for saving me. Not just at the banquet, but over and over, in so many ways. I can't ever thank you—"

"You've given me your heart. That's all I could ever ask for. Can you stand?"

"Oh." Callista practically leapt to her feet. "I'm sorry, I didn't realize—"

"No, I'd gladly have stayed like that until my legs went numb." Vallyn grinned. "However, I want to do this properly." He knelt before her on one knee and took her right hand between both of his.

"Callista Marcant, I love you. I have a question I want to ask you, but—"

"Yes!" The smile she bestowed on him was shining with joy that he had dreamed of seeing on her beautiful face.

"*But*," he repeated, "before you agree, my father told me—"

"Yes, yes." Callista waved her free hand. "Arolyin told me earlier about the potential side effects. I don't care. I don't love you for your magic, but neither do I fear it. I don't mind a magical marriage binding, but if it doesn't affect me, I swear to live as if it does. I told you once I wouldn't take vows of marriage unless I had every intention of keeping them, and that wasn't a lie."

She hesitated, her mouth pinching. "Are you all right with all of that? If a fae binding affects only you, will you…resent me?"

"Never," he said. "So, officially—I love you and want to be by your side for the rest of my days. Will you marry me, Callista?"

"Yes!" She laughed. "Now stand up and kiss me again."

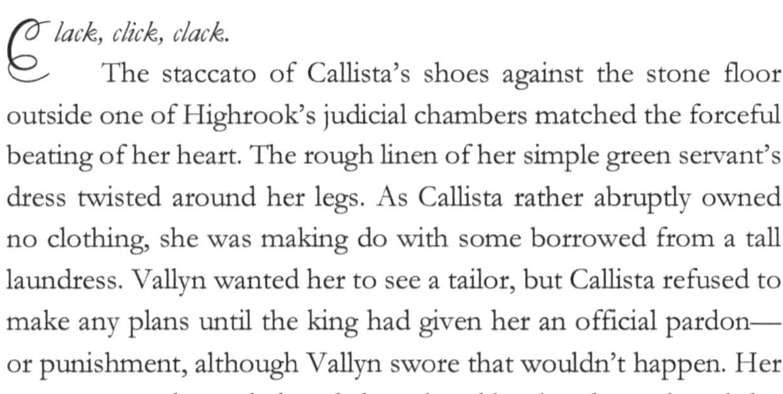

57

lack, click, clack.

The staccato of Callista's shoes against the stone floor outside one of Highrook's judicial chambers matched the forceful beating of her heart. The rough linen of her simple green servant's dress twisted around her legs. As Callista rather abruptly owned no clothing, she was making do with some borrowed from a tall laundress. Vallyn wanted her to see a tailor, but Callista refused to make any plans until the king had given her an official pardon—or punishment, although Vallyn swore that wouldn't happen. Her empty stomach gurgled, and she splayed her hand over her abdomen. She'd been too stressed to eat breakfast.

Inside, Cassius, Vallyn, Lord Ackroyd and his son and Tatiana, and Lord and Conrad Raylor were gathered to discuss her fate. They'd read her written testimony, which she'd rewritten several times, and her transcription of Royce's testimony. Royce's writing had never progressed beyond the minimum needed by a guardsman. Vallyn told her they also had testimonies from Steward Anders, Serena, and Roland and his former supporters.

Yesterday Callista had met with the unicorn Falada, answering questions and letting the unicorn use her magical perception to evaluate her. After she left, Falada spoke to Conrad. Whether the unicorn's impression had been favorable, and whether Conrad would accurately relay the unicorn's testimony, Callista didn't know.

A creak behind her announced the opening of the door, and she spun around. Vallyn slipped out, and the door clicked shut behind him. Her stomach twisted in on itself, and she was glad she'd skipped breakfast.

"They've reached an agreement, but you can say anything else you'd like to add to your testimony now." Vallyn's smile was encouraging, but Callista's feet still itched to run away.

Instead, she took a deep breath and followed him into the chamber.

The room was small and simple, with moderate adornments in comparison to most of Highrook. Cassius sat on a wood throne on a miniature dais, his regal expression inscrutable. The Ackroyds and Raylors sat in the first of three rows of benches facing the king. A single guard stood in the far corner.

Vallyn led Callista to a small side podium between the dais and the benches, then slipped back to sit in the second row. The gazes of those she had hurt bored into her, tunneling into her soul.

Callista stepped to the side and curtsied as low as she could. When she straightened, she kept her head bowed. "Lady Tatiana, Lord Ackroyd, Master Ackroyd, Lord Raylor, Master Raylor. I have hurt you and those you love. While I cannot regret my reasons, I do regret the suffering my actions caused you. I apologize, although I won't claim to deserve your forgiveness."

"Forgiveness is never deserved," Tatiana said, her voice soft. "I admit, I find it easier to forgive you knowing how you also have suffered and that you didn't wish for any of this to happen. But you still made your choices and still caused harm, and that cannot be undone."

Callista slumped. She had accepted this, but it still hurt to hear.

"And…" Tatiana paused. "I forgive you, Callista."

She jerked her head up.

"I forgive you," Tatiana's brother said. "I'd have done the same if someone threatened Tati."

"I forgive you, for I see no benefit to me in harboring anger over the suffering you caused my daughter." Lord Ackroyd cleared his throat. "Forgiveness may be extended, but the law must also be considered."

"Indeed." Lord Raylor nodded gravely. "We have considered this at length. I admit this was easier for me, as I trust the judgment of my twins. I'd already forgiven you. If anything, I begrudgingly admire you for having the nerve to fulfill that prophecy despite the cost, even if I still wish you'd used someone else's children."

"Are they…all right?" Callista asked. "I have no right to ask, but—"

"Safe and sound in the Eynlaean palace." Raylor smiled. "I'm relieved I can now let them know it is safe to return. Although between winter approaching and my daughter courting that prince, I regret that I probably won't see them until spring."

Anika and Prince Gareth were courting? Callista allowed a small smile. Of course they were. Even with her mind otherwise occupied, she hadn't missed how painfully, obviously enamored they'd been with each other.

"I almost feel *I* owe you an apology for publicly accusing you, trying to kill you, and cutting your arm," Conrad said. "But I still think none of your good intentions excuse your crimes."

She bowed her head. "I know."

Conrad sighed. "However, even though I am struggling to forgive, I understand and respect why my siblings released you. Perhaps I will simply consider us even."

Some embarrassment and a minor cut hardly seemed evenly matched with the weeks of fear and sorrow Conrad and his parents had experienced, but she wasn't about to argue. Maybe before she'd arrived at Highrook, she would have. But not now—not when she had so much to live for.

Vallyn stood. "His Majesty will now deliver his judgment."

Gripping her skirt in sweaty hands, Callista faced the king. He nodded, a small movement so as not to dislodge his glittering crown.

"After consultation, the aggrieved parties have reached an agreement. The downfall of the Faines was needed and merits some clemency as regards your actions toward Anika and Leo Raylor and the Eynlaean knight. As for the cursing of Tatiana Ackroyd, Blaise Shafer's death and Roland's execution have met the demands of justice. Your own suffering and your cooperation in building our case against the Shafers are considered penance enough. To decree further punishment would be more akin to revenge than justice. Furthermore, I don't believe you are a threat. I am satisfied.

"I, Cassius Alimer, sovereign ruler of Aedyllan, hereby grant an official pardon to Callista Marcant. May she be considered guiltless in the eyes of the law. This hearing is concluded. All are dismissed."

The words washed over Callista, warmer than the summer sun. She would not squander this chance to use her life and her magic for good. Vallyn would love her anyway, and Cassius wouldn't take back his pardon, but she was determined to be the kind of person they believed she could be—not to earn her pardon or prove she deserved this chance, but to express her gratitude for the love and freedom she'd been granted.

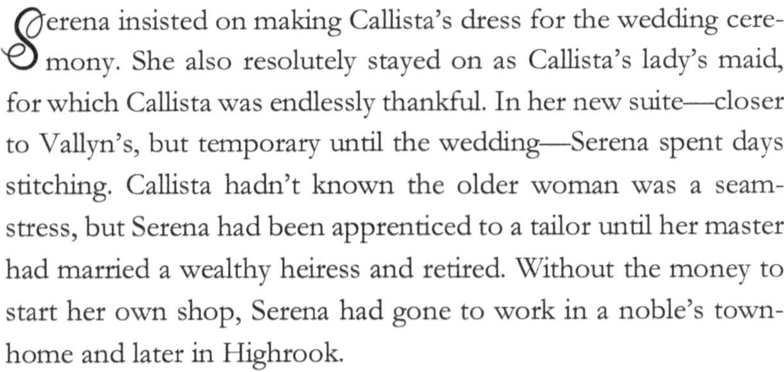

58

Serena insisted on making Callista's dress for the wedding ceremony. She also resolutely stayed on as Callista's lady's maid, for which Callista was endlessly thankful. In her new suite—closer to Vallyn's, but temporary until the wedding—Serena spent days stitching. Callista hadn't known the older woman was a seamstress, but Serena had been apprenticed to a tailor until her master had married a wealthy heiress and retired. Without the money to start her own shop, Serena had gone to work in a noble's townhome and later in Highrook.

Even after the dress was done, they didn't pick a date, they simply waited for the weather to improve.

Autumn weather was fickle, especially in the mountains, but every day brought rain and bitter cold. Callista was torn between giving up on her chosen location and giving up on the wedding itself for fear that the weather was a bad omen. When she confided those fears to Royce, he sternly reassured her that storms could be survived and that they always ended. He encouraged her not to surrender her dream location, because he didn't want to see her settling for less than she deserved ever again.

"Practice having some hope, Calli," Royce said. He stood by

the window, petting Stormy—who was growing at a shocking rate and had shown no interest in returning to the wild—and watching the rain tracing down the glass. "Besides, I'm having such fun watching that man of yours come up with ridiculous excuses for why he had to leave his office and come see you. Like bringing you those books on magic and music. I think he keeps buying more half to make you happy and half to give himself an excuse to visit you. He knows he can just say 'I wanted to see you,' right?"

Callista laughed. "Ending his stress-fueled addiction to work is going to take time. I'll accept his excuses for now and eventually convince him he doesn't have to feel guilty about taking a break."

"Fair enough." Her brother chuckled, and the sound soothed her. "I suppose I won't give him too hard of a time about it next time we train."

Royce was working toward rejoining the Highrook guard. While Callista was glad her brother wanted to be a guardsman again, she'd also been relieved when Vallyn had told Royce he was required to recover physically and mentally first. "If you don't visit the physician, then I won't accept you into the guard." Royce had argued that he didn't need a physician, but Wilmina quickly won him over. The old physician met with him daily to help him figure out the best ways to feed, care for, and exercise his body to recover from years of malnutrition and torture; she also helped him work through his mental and emotional pain. As she'd recently decided his healing regimen should include training, Vallyn and Royce had private training sessions most days. Her brother was alive, and while he wasn't the same, Callista had hope that they both would thrive.

Another week of poor weather passed. Callista debated writing to Ian and Marie, but she wasn't certain how well they could read, and the story was far too long and personal—and the information too sensitive in some cases—to put in a letter. Vallyn promised he and Callista could visit them after the wedding. Facing them and admitting everything she had done would be hard, but Marie and Ian deserved to know why she'd vanished on them. And selfishly, Callista hoped they could still be friends.

Nearly three weeks after her pardon, the weather finally cleared. As Serena helped Callista don her gown, someone knocked on the door.

"Come in," Callista called. "I'm behind the screen, so no chance of seeing anything."

"Good," Vallyn said from the other side of the dressing screen. "I don't want to spoil seeing this dress on you for the first time." He cleared his throat. "My father's here. He just happened to choose today to visit, but he's excited this means he can attend the wedding."

Callista froze, and she wished she could see her betrothed's face. Although Arolyin had looked forward to getting to know his son and his daughter-in-law better and even hinted that he would stay in Aedyllan forever if asked, Vallyn was still struggling to believe his father wouldn't abandon him. Nor was Vallyn comfortable asking his father to sacrifice his immortality and magic to stay. It would take both men a while to navigate their new relationship. And since she and Vallyn hadn't set a wedding date and couldn't predict how long it would take for Arolyin to arrive after Vallyn activated the calling stone, Vallyn hadn't invited his father to their wedding.

"How do you feel about that?" she asked.

Vallyn let out a long, slow breath. "I'm relieved. I think I didn't want to admit to myself how much I *do* want my father here. And, well…we have so little family left, you and I. It'll be nice to have them all present."

Callista relaxed her shoulders. "I'm glad, Vallyn, and happy to have him. I'm grateful all our family members who can be there, will be." A tear slipped down her cheek, and she flicked it away. Serena paused in lacing up the dress to rub her back comfortingly.

"I may not have known your parents," Vallyn said, "but from everything you and Royce have told me, they'd be so proud of you and happy for you."

"Thank you," she murmured. "I know your mother would be incredibly proud of the kind and loyal man you've become."

"I try to be who she raised me to be," Vallyn said, his voice thick with emotion.

Callista wished she could go to him. "I'm blessed to marry the man she raised. I'll see you soon?"

"Yes, but there's another reason I stopped by. A wedding present of sorts."

Since Serena had finished lacing up the dress, Callista went up on her tiptoes to peek over the dressing screen. "A secret wedding present? But I didn't get you anything."

Vallyn chuckled. "You're marrying me, and that's all the gift I desire. I've been working on something since you were pardoned, and this morning, I got the answer I wanted. I meant to surprise you after the ceremony, but I can't stand to wait a moment more."

She'd never seen such a wide, giddy smile on his face. "You don't look like you're hiding anything."

"It's not a *thing*, exactly. With your written testimony, and with me, Cas, and Falada as character witnesses, the dean of the En-chanters College has agreed to let you re-enroll and finish your course of study."

Callista clapped her hands over her mouth and dropped back onto her heels. Tears welled in her eyes, and she leaned against the wall to prevent herself from collapsing and wrinkling her gown. A sob wracked her chest as her vision blurred.

"Callista?" Vallyn called. "Are you all right?"

She couldn't make herself speak. Serena looked at her with concern and placed a hand on her upper arm.

"Is this like the flute?" A nervous chuckle undercut his words. "Are you so happy you're overcome? Or did I muck this up? I'm sorry; I should have asked you—"

"Turn around," Callista gasped out.

"What?"

She pushed off the wall, smiling through her tears. "Turn around and face the door. Are you facing the door?"

"Um, yes, but why?"

Callista picked up her skirt and ran out from behind the screen. She collided with Vallyn's back and threw her arms around him in a fierce embrace.

"Thank you," she choked out. "They never let in anyone who has cast dark magic…they can test for signs that you have, and I thought… I never…" She squeezed him harder as he wrapped his arms over hers. "I don't know how you convinced them, but thank you. I love you so much."

"I love you, Callista."

She closed her eyes, soaking in the way he said her name. He made it sound so decadent and cherished.

"We should both finish getting ready." He patted her hand over his chest. "I'll see you soon, my bride."

Reluctantly, Callista released him. She'd have the rest of her life to hold him and show him just how much she loved him. A life that would hold challenges, yes. She would always miss her parents and Jacob, and some of the things she'd done would always haunt her. She'd seen enough married couples to know marriage could be difficult. Being Lady Drake, wife of the king's half-fae general, would come with unique complications.

But there would be good and beautiful things, too. Perhaps there would even be more good than bad. Whatever came, she and Vallyn would face it together. And that was enough.

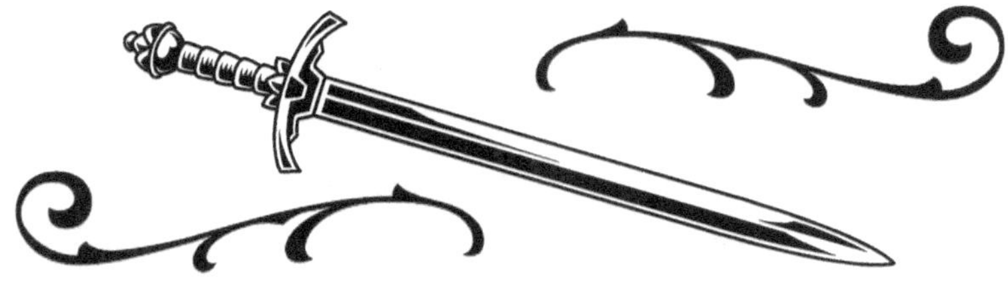

59

The sky brought out her brightest blues, and the sun mustered enough warmth even in the partial shade of the pergola in Highrook's autumn garden that Vallyn pushed his cloak behind his shoulders. He'd laughed when Callista told him where she wanted to have their wedding ceremony, but he'd agreed reclaiming the place where they'd first met was perfect.

By this late in the season, the vines covering the structure had lost their leaves. With Cassius's permission, Serena had taken crimson flowers from the greenhouse and tied them around the front posts. A long, narrow burgundy carpet scattered with white petals stretched down the garden path, ending where Vallyn stood. Three wooden chairs had been placed for the tiny audience; two were already occupied.

Vallyn started to check his ears and stopped himself. It didn't matter whether the pointed tips were hidden. Everyone knew the truth, and more importantly, everyone present accepted him for what he was.

Cassius stood under the pergola to Vallyn's right and a little behind him, waiting to officiate.

His father sat on the single chair on Vallyn's side of the carpet.

On its opposite side sat Royce, his soon-to-be brother-in-law.

Serena emerged from behind a large bush still bearing a few dark-red leaves. She made her way to the remaining seat beside Royce.

And, hidden out of sight behind that same large shrub, was Callista. The love of his life.

Of course, not far away there were also guardsmen, ensuring their ceremony was undisturbed. Still, it was a small, intimate ceremony with the people they loved. Just as he and Callista had wanted.

Serena held up Callista's flute and murmured something. The enchantment Callista had put into the flute took effect, and a light, soaring melody poured from the instrument.

Vallyn straightened his shoulders and wiped his palms on his calf-length traditional formal tunic—black with silver stitching, of course. He'd never cared for stuffy traditions with no real usefulness, but Callista had fond memories of her parents dancing in their wedding clothes every year on their anniversary. She'd always hoped that if she married, her husband would wear a traditional tunic like her father had, and Vallyn was more than happy to honor this tradition for her.

The flute music swelled, and Callista emerged from behind the hibernating shrub. A smile lit her angular face, and her green eyes glistened. Creamy white brocade with intricate flower patterns clung to her torso, flaring out into a full skirt that swished around her legs. A narrow white-and-gold cloth with long gold tassels belted her waist. Gold beading sparkled in the sunshine along the hem of the skirt and around the neckline just below her collarbones. The sleeves puffed a little above a band of gold embroidery on her upper arms, then draped into long, flowing sleeves that skimmed the ground. Her black hair cascaded down her back and over her shoulders.

His bride was breathtaking.

Callista stopped in front of him, and he took her right hand in his left as the flute music faded away.

"Can you walk down the aisle again?" Vallyn murmured. "That wasn't long enough for me to properly appreciate how indescribably beautiful you are."

She laughed. "And delay marrying you? You can admire me later." Her cheeks tinged pink as she looked him up and down. "And then I can appreciate how attractive you look."

Cassius coughed. "Save it for your chambers."

Snickering, Vallyn turned toward his friend and king.

"We are gathered here today to bear witness to the joining of Vallyn Salvius Drake and Callista Amelie Marcant as husband and wife." Cassius grinned. "It is my honor and my pleasure to officiate their union. Please face each other and take each other's hands."

They did so. Vallyn looked up into Callista's eyes and almost forgot to listen to what Cassius was saying.

"Do you, Vallyn, enter into this marriage to Callista freely and honestly, without reservation, without deceit, with your whole heart, for the rest of your life?"

"I do." He poured all of his dedication into the short words.

"Do you promise to cherish and love her and only her, honor and protect her, be her safety and support, and share her life through the good and the bad, through the easy and the challenging, through times of joy and times of sorrow, until death parts you?"

"I do."

"So may it be. Do you, Callista, enter into this marriage to Vallyn freely and honestly, without reservation, without deceit, with your whole heart, for the rest of your life?"

"I do." She squeezed his hands. Tears glimmered along her eyelashes. Vallyn swallowed, suddenly fighting tears himself.

"Do you promise to cherish and love him and only him, honor and care for him, be his home and support, and share his life through the good and the bad, through the easy and the challenging, through times of joy and times of sorrow, until death parts you?"

"I do."

"So may it be," Cassius intoned. "Please exchange your vows."

"My—" Vallyn's voice cracked, and he couldn't make the words emerge. He coughed, thankful they hadn't done this in front of a large crowd. "My dear Callista, I vow that I will be faithful to you. I will always be there and will not abandon you. No matter what may come or what you may face, I will be by your side. I will be your shield, your sword, and your fortress, to protect you and your heart, that you may never face another battle or challenge on your own."

Callista pulled one hand free to dry her eyes, then reclasped his hand. "Vallyn, my true love, I vow that I will be faithful to you. I will not hide from you, lie to you, or abandon you. I will love you when you're stressed and when you're joyful—even when you're paranoid." She giggled, blushing, and Vallyn's joy burst out in a loud laugh. Even Cassius chuckled. "Whether you're filling the role of husband, friend, royal advisor, or general, I will be your bolster and your reinforcements, and I will face every challenge and battle at your side."

Cassius extended his hands to both sides. "By the power vested in me as king of Aedyllan and Vallyn's liege, by my right as Vallyn's friend and brother, and in the presence of these witnesses to your binding vows of fidelity, I declare you husband and wife.

You may kiss the bride."

Vallyn released Callista's hands so he could grab her hips and pull her against him. Her hands found the sides of his neck as he brought his lips up to hers. Maybe it was the symphony of emotion rushing through him, maybe it was the thrill of knowing that now he was kissing his wife. He swore it was the sweetest, most intoxicating kiss—a kiss that made every delectable prior kiss they'd shared pale in comparison. A kiss he never wanted to end, even though he heard his father, brother-in-law, and best friend applauding and laughing.

A zing rushed through his veins, and the familiar pull of magic prompted him to open his eyes. Callista broke away at the same moment, her eyes fluttering open. Twisting strands of silver and lavender light wove around them, then burst in a shower of ephemeral sparks.

"Was that on purpose?" Royce asked.

Arolyin hummed. "Congratulations, you two. You're officially wed by Aedyllanian custom and fae binding magic."

Callista's thumb brushed against Vallyn's cheekbone. "I wouldn't have my heart bound to anyone else."

Vallyn wrapped his arms around her and kissed her again, and from the way she held him close and deepened their kiss, he knew she understood.

Magic binding or not, his enchantress had his heart, and he had hers.

Acknowledgments

This book would not exist were it not for the grace of God renewing my strength day by day. While writing and revising this book I often felt like I didn't know what I was doing and like I'd forgotten how to write or edit a book. I had many existential crises and generally felt insufficient, weak, and often foolish. How fortunate am I, then, that my "sufficiency is of God," (2 Corinthians 3:5b, KJV), that God's "grace is sufficient for [me]: for [His] strength is made perfect in weakness" (2 Corinthians 12:9a, KJV), and that "God hath chosen the foolish things of the world" (1 Corinthians 1:27, KJV). Thank you to my sustainer, life-giver, shelter, home, merciful savior, and source of identity and hope—my God who pursues me with unfailing lovingkindness.

And thank you to everyone who prayed for me while I was working on this book.

Thank you to the ladies of the Virtual Coffee group for your support, encouragement, and sympathy.

Thank you to everyone who encouraged me while I worked on this book, whether directly or indirectly, through messages, comments about being excited about it, resharing my posts, lovely reviews or fan art of past books, or otherwise. Your words mean more than you can possibly know.

Thank you to my therapist for listening and understanding and helping me through not just my life mental & emotional struggles but also my many writing, publishing, feedback dread, reviews, and marketing related crises, even though you don't have direct experience with writing and publishing.

Thank you to my parents for supporting me in so, so many ways. This book also wouldn't be possible without you.

Thank you, Jenni, for repeatedly nudging me to write a *Goose Girl* retelling until the idea wormed its way into my brain. XD

Thank you to my alpha readers: Mom, Alexis, and Becky, and to my beta readers: Charis, Elisabeth, Fay, Janice, Katelyn, Kelly, and Mom again (and again), for your encouraging feedback and your critiques and suggestions to make this book stronger.

Thank you to Becky for convincing me to watch *Love Like the Galaxy* and thank you to *Love Like the Galaxy* for partially inspiring Vallyn and thus this book.

Thank you, Tatum, for another beautiful cover illustration (and for putting up with all of my tweaks and feedback with grace).

Thank you to Kate for bestowing your copy-editing wisdom upon this book, straightening me out every time I think I've figured out grammar and in fact have not, and for helping me smooth out some funky sentences and bring the final word count down. You deserve all the chocolate and quiet campgrounds.

And finally, thank *you*, dear reader, whether you're new to my books or have been a fan for a while, for taking a chance on this book. Thank you for reading and for making this dream of mine a possibility and a reality.

About the Author

Selina R. Gonzalez is a Colorado native with mountains in her blood and dreams that top 14,000 feet. She loves chocolate, fantasy, costumes, bread, history, superheroes, faux leather, things that sparkle, medieval Britain, snark, dogs, and Jesus—not in that order.

She loves to travel and has driven coast-to-coast in the US, visited Britain three times, and has a list of places to go as long as Pikes Peak is tall, but always comes back home to Colorado.

You can find Selina raving about books she's enjoying (or adding to her bottomless pit of a to-be-read pile) on Facebook at Selina R. Gonzalez, Author and on Instagram at @NightTooIsBeautiful, and being generally goofy and snarky as well as talking about writing, life, and the antics of her family's dogs in her IG stories. Make sure you don't miss any of Selina's future books, plus get bonus short stories, playlists, and more, by subscribing to her newsletter at:

SelinaRGonzalez.com/newsletter-subscription